Table of Contents

CHAPTER ONE: March 20, 3748
CHAPTER TWO: April 20, 3748
CHAPTER THREE: May 20, 3748
CHAPTER FOUR: June 20, 3748

One Sunny Night

Dedication:
For all the kids who have ever had a difficult
time getting from one place to another

CHAPTER ONE: March 20, 3748

It was a bright and sunny day. Leroy stood in the slowest concession line in the world, drenched in sweat, fierce solar rays assaulting his hatless head, bouncing impatiently on his toes in an attempt to see past the shoulders of guys bioengineered for excessive size.

They all had arms thicker than his legs, except for the guy in front of him, who had a prosthetic arm that was so creepy Leroy couldn't stop sneaking glances at it; slender and black, with a few extra joints and a vise grip for a hand, protruding from a stump covered with scar tissue and regenerated skin dappled in contrasting shades of sunscorched brown. A veteran.

The stadium was full of veterans, celebrating the seventh anniversary of Vanram's victory in the War, as depicted in many films, such as *Fists of Fire*, which had a musical number where waves of robot spiders had attacked this very stadium. Leroy had watched it just last week in his comfortable living room, with his best friends Lenny and Dan, who were currently sitting in the very top row, while Leroy stood in line to get his little sister Marilyn some more fried peppers.

He was missing the best part of the clashball championship. The first half had been painfully boring and full of time-outs. Then there had been a long halftime show with a band playing unamplified horns and drums, sweating heavily into red and gold uniforms while rearranging themselves into intricate patterns. Shortly after that, Leroy's hat had accidentally wound up in Marilyn's fried peppers, ruining both.

If this had been the stadium back home, there would have been coolers blowing chilled air on the crowd, and cleanbeams whisking away their sweaty odors. Everyone would be looking at their delds, or at big video screens explaining what was happening on the field. None of that stuff worked in Vanram. Leroy had learned this the hard way by forgetting to stow his deld in the locker on board the *Principessa Larisse*. He found it in his suitcase when they got to the Hotel Argalia, all dry and crackly, with the screen peeling away in flakes. Marilyn had made fun of him for forgetting about the instructional cartoon that they'd seen in the orientation, about circuitry-eating microorganisms left over from the War.

The crowd let out a deafening cheer and began to chant "Rufe Rules!" until Leroy felt like he was surrounded by barking dogs. Rufus Marshall had finally scored, and he'd missed it. He fidgeted and bounced and exhaled noisily through his nose, and counted the number of people ahead of him over and over. He was dripping with perspiration and impatience. He had never been this uncomfortable in his whole life.

He was here mostly by accident. During a junior varsity clashball game last fall, he had unintentionally blocked a kick with his face. Someone filming the game had caught the kick, along with Leroy's stunned reaction, a stripe of mud slashing from his eyebrow to his cheekbone that was remarkably similar to the stripe of reconstructed skin across Rufus Marshall's reconstructed left eye.

The video clip had made its way to the Nothing But Sports Network, where the announcers had joked about Rufe's scar having the power to win games by itself. NBS had licensed the clip, playing it whenever Rufe scored a goal, and Rufe had gone on to score a record number of goals. Enough to vault the Rams into the championship, even though their country had barely recovered enough to sponsor a team or host a game.

His parents had a long discussion when Leroy had been invited to the game, and he had overheard part of it. Especially the part where Mom had said, "this could be our only chance to applaud for our son in public."

It still stung. Of his two best friends, Lenny Reyes was a visual artist who specialized in fantastic creatures and regularly won applause at art shows. Dan Kral was a musician who got his fill of applause every time he played live. Mom was a union gaffer who worked with lighting rigs for live action motion pictures, and she got applause whenever the credits rolled. Dad had just been applauded while receiving a Teachy award from the Institute of Academic Popularity just last month, for his lecture series on film history. Even Marilyn got applause at her dance recitals.

Leroy, in contrast, rarely did anything worth celebrating. His grades were always average and his performance never peaked. He had a typical, forgettable face, distinguished only by a pair of sleepy-looking eyes, which were a non-descript brown, just like his skin and hair. He wasn't even distinguished as a fan, as he gravitated toward movies nobody else liked, and unpopular bands, and fringe sports like clashball.

He considered himself to be a person without talent. It didn't really bother him, but he could tell his parents worried about it, going out of their way to reassure him they loved him no matter what. It made him popular in a disconnected sense -- he was on everyone's mailing list as someone who would show up to watch them show off, and applaud when they were done, without ever asking them to reciprocate.

Truthfully, Leroy hadn't been interested in going to Vanram at all, but his family had been so enthusiastically supportive of his one shot at applause that he didn't want to let them down. This was a prestige event, according to the media, and tickets were expensive. The single camera covering the game was big and bulky, heavily shielded, and connected to a roaring generator. Mom had laughed her horsey laugh when she saw it, explaining that the output would look as jerky and muted as an old silent movie. That was part of the reason the stadium was packed. This wasn't a game you could watch from your cool and comfortable couch. You had to be here.

Leroy's fingertips gently probed his scalp, which was frying in the oil from his sweaty hair. He longed for a cleanbeam. The hotel only had water showers, with water that always seemed to be a few degrees hotter than the ambient air, so that you worked up a fresh layer of sweat while rinsing the last one off.

They did have cars and motorcycles, with noisy combustion engines that spewed dark smoke. They had unreliable phones that were connected to the walls, and slowly turning ceiling fans. And they had plenty of guns. The hotel security guards had rifles strapped to their backs, backed up with pistols at their sides. Leroy had heard one explain to a nervous guest that while most everyone who fought in the war had no difficulty whatsoever adjusting to peacetime, it took a lot of firepower to stop the few that did.

Leroy's brief, two-block exploration of Argalia had confirmed this. Everybody was packing.

Especially the cops. Leroy counted seventeen separate weapons on the first cop he saw. The cops had been too much for Lenny to handle, and he had argued eloquently for returning to the hotel before they all got shot for breaking some law they didn't know existed.

Leroy's parents had refused to leave the hotel at all, camping out at the semi-comfortable swimming pool with Marilyn, but they had given the teenagers permission to explore. Leroy, Lenny and Dan had started at the War Memorial across the street, full of stern statues carved out of local reddish stone and decorated for the anniversary with fresh flowers and ribbons. Then they cruised through a marketplace full of aggressive vendors approaching them with red and gold Rams merchandise and cinnamon jalapeno slushies.

They checked out the local teenagers from a careful distance, since most of them were packing too, with throwing stars and brass knuckles doing double duty as jewelry and compact, teen-sized guns holstered on their thighs and breasts and bellies. Both girls and boys had intricate hairstyles involving lots of precision shaving and tight braids. They had thick slabs of muscle, and sometimes fat, spilling out of the ripped-up distressed fatigues that were fashionable here, and even the smallest of the girls looked capable of throwing Leroy several meters, and seemed mean enough to do it.

Dan dragged them into a club, interested in the local version of live music. Here, that mostly consisted of a guy bellowing a rhythmic speech while other people laid down a counterpoint rhythm track by banging whatever they had in their hands against whatever was near. A fistfight had broken out within minutes of their arrival, followed by a squad of riot police that were decked out with even more weapons than the regular police. That had been Lenny's breaking point, and they had retreated to the hotel to lie around the heavily fortified pool.

Everyone had been up for the adventure at first. On the ship they'd all called Leroy things like "Your Grandiosity" and "Exalted One" while pointing out all the luxuries they were enjoying on his account. By the morning of the game it was starting to sound sarcastic. Everyone was ragged from trying to sleep through the heat, and the nearby noise from their fellow hotel guests, and the slightly farther away noise from the locals, including occasional bursts of gunfire.

Marilyn, who was only nine, had dropped the charade entirely and had moved on to sulking and complaining. Leroy was starting to wonder if all the rest shared her opinions, and he felt responsible for bringing them on such a miserable trip, for such a stupid reason, that he hadn't really wanted to take, because his parents thought he needed applause.

A commotion arose up ahead and the stench of fresh vomit drifted back. Leroy gagged and clapped his hand over his nose. The crowd reorganized around him, clearing a space for the vomit and in the process he found himself in the outside row, squashed against the railing, gasping with the influx of slightly fresher air as the metal flaked under the pressure from his ribs, drawing dark reddish stripes across his shirt.

Somebody slipped and cursed, somebody else laughed, and Leroy heard the sound of flesh smacking into flesh. The crowd undulated around him as people retreated from the fight while others surged in to join it. Leroy's hands tightened on the crumbling rail as he looked down. The game was paused for some reason, and the players were clustered around in the end zone. He could barely make out the numbers on their shirts.

He was up high, in the nosebleed section. Probably even higher than the top of the first drop on the Raging Dragon roller coaster at the Royal Beach Boardwalk. He felt a wave of dizziness and he raised his head, looking off in the distance. To the south, towards his right, were reddish mountains and very few trees. He couldn't see the hotel as it was behind him, but he could see the east side of Argalia, full of warehouses and foundries. And smoke. It looked like something was on fire at that end of town.

The sea was on his left, coming right up to the edge of the stadium. He could see a flock of iridescent domes floating on top of the waves, like massive jellyfish, and he wondered about them, until he noticed the *Principessa Larisse* heading slowly out of her slip. That was odd. She wasn't supposed to leave until later tonight, after the gala celebratory dinner, and Leroy was looking forward to being aboard. He stood on his toes, straining to see, and as he was doing that, the railing cracked and collapsed.

He was falling. Someone grabbed a handful of his shirt but it ripped free as his arms pinwheeled, grabbing for anything they could find. He turned a somersault in midair and slammed sideways against one of the banners hanging there to remind everyone that seven years ago, Vanram had won a War.

He caught hold of the banner, three of his desperate fingernails peeling back painfully as he clawed at it. His feet were hanging free and he kicked them as he clung to the banner, gathering the rough fabric in his hands. Just as he got a good grip the banner came loose and he was falling again.

He landed with a crash on something that splintered and collapsed. He couldn't move, and he couldn't breathe. A vision appeared, of a snarling animal with impossibly wide jaws, ready to devour him. A slender white hand reached out and grabbed his shoulder just as his nerve fibers all announced simultaneously to his brain that extreme pain was happening, right now. Everything went dark.

●

He climbed to his feet. His heart was pounding, and his mouth was dry. Someone was helping him stumble through wreckage, into a dark and shady area where he stood blinking and dazed. The field was directly ahead of him, and he watched a pack of Rams snatch the ball from an unfortunate Tiger.

Something bumped against his knee. He looked down and saw a dog. He gave it a friendly pat and it nosed his hand. As he stroked its pointed ears, someone grabbed his shoulder. He let out a startled yell. The dog darted away as a waterpod glittering with beads of cool condensation appeared, offered by a slight man with pale skin and blond hair, wearing a red-and-white doctor's shirt, his mouth moving as though he were talking.

He accepted the water and drank it greedily as he watched the players gather for another time out. Gradually, his brain reassembled the doctor's vocal sounds into words. "Can you hear anything I'm saying? Do you know what day it is? Hello? Sonny?"

"I'm – yes." That must be his name, Sonny. He had more names but he couldn't seem to think of what they might be.

"I'm Doctor Quicksilver, and you've just had a full restore. Tell me what you remember."

He noticed his clothes were in shreds, and he was covered in faint scratches, freshly scabbed over. Then he noticed he was covered in blood, and streaks of it were decorating the doctor's clothes too, and in fact he was standing in a trail of it leading to a large red puddle coating the wreckage he had just climbed from. A cage. Nearby was an intact cage containing the Rams' mascot, an ill-tempered specimen of the sheep they raised here, bioengineered for tasty meat, bulletproof wool and the ability to thrive in scorching temperatures. He had landed on the cage for the Tigers' mascot, a dog with tiger stripes on its back end. The one whose ears he had been stroking.

"You're really very lucky. I was standing right nearby, got both of you stabilized before you bled out, and then the nanobots went to work. You'll be excreting them over the next several days. Absolutely a textbook presentation, multiple fractures, impaled through the liver, probably some brain trauma. You don't remember any of it? Did someone push you? Perhaps we should fill out a police report. Sonny? Can you tell me your name? Do you know where you are?"

His mouth felt thick and clumsy. He blinked. He was bursting with energy, and he began to pace back and forth in tight little circles, trying to come up with answers to the doctor's difficult questions.

A woman screamed.

His ears picked it out of the surrounding roar, reverberating from the old reddish masonry. Down at the end of a hall. An impending-danger kind of scream. He charged toward it, down a dark hallway and around a corner.

As he turned he saw the open door of a private box. It was somehow cool inside, with a huge window overlooking the Rams' dugout. It was furnished with puffy red chairs, and a little table bearing a silver ice bucket stuffed with a sweating bottle of champagne. It contained an old man dressed in a red uniform jacket dripping with gold braid, and he was slapping a beautiful woman.

Rage flooded through him. The stadium rocked, the crowd screamed, and Sonny took it as a natural consequence of his rage.

The woman turned to face him. She had a mane of complicated curls spilling over her shoulders and down her back, a thousand subtly different shades of cinnamon and raven and chestnut and mahogany flowing over velvety amber skin. Her brief blue dress clung to a compact assortment of breathtaking curves. Her face was round and sweet, with big hazel eyes and round cheeks, and a perfect little mouth that was open in a perfect circle of astonishment as she touched her slapped cheek with her red-and-gold fingernailed hand.

The old man growled and raised his hand, preparing to smack the woman again, and Sonny charged, driving his forehead straight into the old man's nose. It crunched wetly. The old man staggered back.

The woman screamed again as the doctor burst into the room, shoving Sonny to the side. Directly into the woman's arms. He gaped at her, dazzled. "Hi," he said. "I love you. Will you marry me?"

"Sure." She let out a laugh that was self-conscious and horrified at the same time. He nodded at her in sympathy, just to show her he was sensitive as well as protective. She embraced him, burying her face in his shoulder as the stadium rocked again. His rage melted away at her touch. He buried his face in his new fiancee's hair, which smelled faintly of oranges.

He looked over her shoulder, through the window. All of the players were clumped together outside, both teams together, pointing and having a heated discussion. As they argued, far above them, a bright projectile flew through the air, landing somewhere in the top rows. It detonated in a big cloud of greenish smoke.

Another projectile landed right in the middle of the field, filling their view with green gas.

"Get your hands off me!" The old man dealt the doctor a punch that sent him flying. The effort of punching didn't seem to agree with the old man and he clutched at his chest, his blood-smeared face contorted.

Green gas crept into the private box, even though it was well sealed to keep the coolness in. The gas had a sweet, fruity smell and it seemed to be clearing Sonny's head. The crazy sense of energy was subsiding, and his heartbeat was slowing to normal. Beyond the beautiful woman's orange-scented hair he could see the old man, bent over in pain, scrabbling inside his jacket. His hand emerged holding a big ornate, ceremonial-looking revolver.

Sonny had temporarily inconvenienced people by killing them with digital guns in multigames, plenty of times, but he had never had one pointed at him in real life. He stared at the bobbing barrel as the old man tried to aim. Blood ran from the old man's squashed nose, sweat poured from his forehead, and he seemed like he was having trouble staying on his feet.

The stadium rocked again, hard, and the window exploded inwards, showering the room in shards of glass as Sonny dived sideways to the floor. He caught a surge of red and gold as a player burst through the broken window. The gun discharged into the floor where Sonny had been, filling the room with smoke.

The woman was beside him on the floor, half underneath him, in fact, with her boobs squashed against his chest and her orange-scented hair against his cheek. Sonny closed his eyes in bliss until he realized she was trying to get away. He braced his palm on the floor, cutting his hand on a shard of broken glass and raised his weight so the woman could wiggle free, which she did, sustaining a few slices of her own.

The doctor grabbed her hand, hauling her to her feet. Sonny got his knees beneath him. There was an enraged bellow from behind and then something heavy fell against his back, knocking him back down with a startled "oof."

A warm, cozy sense of relaxation passed through him. He wanted to lie there among the glass shards and take a nap. He was in pain, though, from several fresh cuts and also from something poking into his ribs. He reached down, exploring, and found his hand wrapped around the barrel of the gun. He shoved the gun barrel off to the side and it fell right out of the old man's limp, unprotesting fingers, into his own.

He squirmed around and found himself face-to-face with the old man, who was dead. One of his eyes was staring straight ahead and the other had been smashed to jelly by the blow that had caved in his forehead, leaving a scattering of protruding bone splinters. A clashball player loomed behind him, looking large enough to bench press a mountain. A familiar slash of scar across his eye. Something fell from his hand and shattered.

Running footsteps echoed in the stone tunnel as Sonny stared at the dead man. He finally summoned the strength to shove at the corpse, wincing as it dribbled blood and brain matter down his arm. As he did that two shots went off at practically the same time, both hitting the corpse and throwing it back.

Two men stood in the doorway, beyond the smoke cloud. Not terribly big nor very memorable men, other than the fact they looked exactly alike. Identical twins, sharing a face with sharp cheekbones and a pointy nose. Dressed as sports fans, one for each team. Their smoking guns were square and businesslike and not ornate at all. They seemed perplexed, and they were both pointing their guns at Sonny as he lay there dazed. He realized he still had the old man's gun in his hand.

"Don't shoot!" The woman screamed, at the top of her voice, cutting through to their overwhelmed ears. The first twin turned toward her, his gun hand sweeping along with his eyes. The second twin kept his focus on Sonny.

"Drop that," he ordered. Sonny lowered his ornate revolver, moving slowly and carefully, staring into the second twin's intense dark eyes.

Rufe took full advantage of the fact nobody was looking at him. There was a brief flurry of movement, and then the first twin was howling over his gruesomely broken elbow, gun dangling in his useless hand as Rufe held him in a chokehold, pointing him toward his brother like a shield.

They froze in a standoff for a few seconds, listening to the first twin's agonized shrieks as his stubborn brother waved his pistol in tight arcs. Sonny finished slowly and carefully placing the ornate pistol on the floor, and as he slid it away, he saw a dark streak dart around the corner of the hallway.

The tiger-striped dog snarled and charged, and leaped. Rufe lifted the first twin and threw him, dodging to the side as the second twin fired, opening up a large exit wound in his brother's back. The dog landed on the second twin and brought him down, tearing at his throat with an impressive assortment of teeth. Once the second twin was dead, the tiger-striped dog released him, and yipped proudly at them all before darting back down the hall.

"Go!" Rufe bellowed, gesturing at the hallway as he relieved the dead men of their weapons and headed after the dog. The doctor darted toward Sonny, grabbing his arm and hauling him to his feet. Sonny felt a sharp stab from the doctor's fingertips, and a second later his head began to clear enough to step carefully around the dead bodies and run after the beautiful woman, who had gone after Rufe. He caught up to Rufe at the end of the hall, killing a third twin, and a fourth, with his new guns.

They emerged into a chaotic scene of unconscious bodies and green fog. Robotic load lifters were unfolding from a staging area, and some of them were already arranging limp, uncomplaining people in rows and sliding them into people-sized cylinders, and loading the cylinders into racks standing near waiting boats. All the people running the load lifters were identical to the twins, all of them dressed in sloppy sports fan attire. Some of them had backpack rigs that fired more of the greenish gas. Sonny didn't have much time to look around because Rufe grabbed him and threw him right through the window, into the sea.

Soon after, the woman and the doctor splashed down, followed by the dog. After another burst of gunfire, Rufe cannonballed into the water beside them. They swam toward the docks, submerging to avoid gunfire and the foul debris floating on the surface. Bullets whizzed past them as part of the stadium collapsed into the water, making a wave that pushed them away. They got to a pier and swam underneath as the boards above them pounded with panicking feet.

They made their way to a wooden platform at the end of the pier and clambered on top of it, where they sat to catch their breath. The air smelled of harsh smoke from the burning warehouse district, which added a new layer of sweltering heat to an already scorching day. Every alarm and siren in the city was going off, making one big angry chord. The tiger-striped dog pressed tight against Sonny's leg and he hugged her for reassurance.

They sat and stared, watching boats headed to and from the *Principessa Larisse*, delivering racks of people and returning empty to collect more.

●

Rufe finally moved, peeling his jersey off and draping it around the woman's shoulders. She thanked him graciously and introduced herself as Risha. Her makeup was smudged all over her face and her hair was one big tangle, and Sonny didn't think this detracted from her beauty at all.

"I'd be willing to exchange large sums of cash to get out of this country immediately if anyone has any connections whatsoever." She removed the jersey from her shoulders and stepped into the neckhole, then tied the sleeves around her waist, transforming it into a skirt of conservative length. "Train, ship, dirigible, pack mule, I don't care."

An explosion caught their attention, out toward the sea. A flock of the jellyfish-like domes were clustered around the last remnants of the Vanram Navy, sinking it. Slender cannons protruded from them like antennae. Sonny could see people scrambling around on top of some of them. A cruise ship that had been anchored in the harbor was slowly trundling past them, heading toward the *Principessa Larisse*. All the rest of the biggest ships were sinking, leaving the smaller ones bottled up behind the harbor gate.

"They've got my family," he said. His knees went weak, and he sat down. "And my friends."

"Over there." Rufe stood up and pointed, and began striding down the pier. Sonny couldn't tell where he was headed but he got up and followed, as did Risha and the doctor, the dog trotting along behind. Rufe's destination turned out to be a saloon that had escaped the flames by virtue of being built directly over the water. It was overflowing with agitated people. Rufe parked himself out front and shouted about how he was willing to pay an extremely high price for passage, which set off a mocking chorus of other voices asking the same thing.

The dog whined uneasily and Sonny stepped back from the crowd to reassure her. He tried not to think about her teeth. She had a lot of them, packed into an unusually long snout. Sonny had grown up with a dog named Oscar, a spaniel with long silky ears and a gentle disposition, who had passed away last year. He missed having a dog. The family had talked about getting a new dog, but since Sonny was headed directly toward college and adulthood Marilyn's wishes came first, and she was more inclined toward a pair of cats, or perhaps rabbits. He sat down and wrapped his arms around the tiger-striped dog, and she licked at his forehead.

"Hey."

A raggedy, smelly guy with sun-weathered skin beckoned. Sonny blinked, feeling the dog shift against him. "Hi."

"Is that guy with you a doctor?" He pointed toward Quicksilver, standing near Rufe with Risha sandwiched between them. "I know a guy needs a doctor. He's got a boat."

Sonny got the doctor's attention, and a moment later they were headed down a dark hallway in a building adjacent to the saloon, Rufe bringing up the rear and grumbling they were probably headed into some kind of trap. A door at the end of the hall led to a darkened room, and as they piled in behind the raggedy man someone struck a light, illuminating a scowling face covered in swirling black tattooed lines.

"Got your doctor," said the raggedy man, holding out his palm.

The tattooed man filled it with folded paper, hanging his lamp from a ceiling hook and settling back down into a chair. His hair was in jet black braids, with small carved ornaments hanging from the tips. He had a pot belly that strained at his buttoned waistcoat, purple velvet with gold dragons chasing each other up the sleeves. The thick-fingered hands emerging from his sleeves were also tattooed, Sonny focused on a laughing pig decorating the base of his thumb as he looked them over, still scowling, his gaze lingering on Risha before finally settling on Quicksilver.

"I am prepared to leave this nation immediately once a medical emergency among my crew has been alleviated," he said, in a deep melodious voice. "I should, however, advise that the situation is not entirely without controversy as to matters of international law. I should further advise that the patient is anatomically complex."

The doctor sighed and gave him a brief uncomfortable nod.

Risha stepped forward, sliding a bracelet from her wrist and offering it for inspection. "We're willing to pay for passage."

The tattooed man accepted the bracelet and looked it over, twirling it around on his big finger. A big white smile interrupted the tattoos on his lower face. "I am very pleased to make your acquaintance, madame. You may call me Kai. I am captain of the *Lono*, a modern recreation of a ship from the past."

"Charmed." Risha showed dimples.

Rufe peered through the window. "Can't break the law if it ain't there. Let's get going."

They followed the captain out the door and pushed their way through a crowd. Gunshots crackled nearby, and embers from the blazing warehouse district peppered them with flying cinders. The tiger-striped dog pressed close to Sonny's leg, snarling whenever a stranger got too close. They walked fast toward the slips, which were guarded by a lone cannon-bearing jellyfish, methodically sinking a couple of yachts that were trying to escape. Sailors in white uniforms were gathered atop the jellyfish, aiming the cannons. Beneath them was a dark undulating shape easily bigger than both yachts put together.

Most of the slips held ships made of pitted, weathered composite, the type that hauled miscellaneous freight up and down the coast. The last slip held a two-masted schooner made entirely of wood. *Lono* was painted on the bow in fancy letters, beneath a voluptuous mermaid figurehead.

"A ship like this could sail in deepwater, all around the world," Rufe commented as they hurried up the gangplank.

"It does," the captain replied.

The captain and the doctor headed rapidly belowdecks as sailors gathered around, pulling the gangplank up behind them. A few of them seemed interested in the tiger-striped dog, who was still pressed against Sonny's leg. Sonny noticed the sailors all had Asian features and it occurred to him they might actually have sailed from Asia. He also couldn't help but notice that some of them were removing the covers from a pair of cannons mounted near the bow.

The captain emerged from below, carrying an unconscious Quicksilver slung over his shoulder. The ship shuddered. Rufe looked pointedly at the sails, which were still wrapped tight around the masts and Kai handed him the limp doctor, barking orders to the crew. A couple of sailors appeared to escort them down two flights of stairs, into a dark, stuffy cargo hold sparsely furnished with empty pallets and barrels and coils of rope.

Rufe propped the doctor in a corner and Risha fussed over him, making sure he was wedged into a comfortable position. There were three tiny windows, not too far above the waterline, and Sonny stationed himself beside one as the ship moved through the harbor much faster than one would expect from a motorless ship with its sails tied down.

They reached the mouth of the harbor, where they stopped short at a barricade made of several logs encrusted with rusty spikes, strung across the exit and threatening to puncture the hull of any ship drawing near. Beyond it, the cannon-bearing jellyfish was sinking a tugboat.

On a pier beside the lock was a wooden shack, next to the capstan that raised and lowered the spiked logs. A battle had recently taken place outside the shack, and bodies were lying around the platform. People with strong opinions were clustered around, expressing them. A dark-skinned woman in a soot-streaked uniform was waving a pistol in the air and yelling at the mob. She seemed to be more in charge than anyone else and the captain hailed her.

"Madame! The *Lono* formally requests that you remove the obstacle impeding our egress."

"Shit on toast," Rufe said. He dashed toward the stairs.

Hina barked excitedly and took off after Rufe. Sonny followed. He emerged onto the deck in time to see the woman fire her pistol into the air, which made the mob recede a couple of meters. "I regret that I cannot comply with your request, captain. They're destroying everything that moves. If they get in here there won't be anything left afloat."

"I am willing to assume that risk. Please open the lock."

"Do you see that man?" She turned to face them and Sonny noticed that she had a pronounced limp. Her close-cropped hair was shot through with gray. An oversized key hung around her neck on a thick chain. She was gesturing at one of the corpses. "He was all set to retire next week. Now he's dead. Because somebody took issue regarding opening the lock."

"Dee!" Rufe bellowed. He stepped up to the bow, making himself visible.

The harbormaster startled at the sight of him, taking a lopsided step back. "Aren't you supposed to be winning a game?"

"Game was called."

"In ten seconds I shall fire upon your lock, destroying it," Kai announced. "I urge you to stand clear."

"You folks heard him!" The harbormaster turned her attention to the mob, firing into the air again and shooing them back.

"Don't do it," Rufe said. He reached out to grab the captain by one of his embroidered sleeves.

The captain turned to face him and they exchanged a brief glare, for only a few seconds, and then the captain yelled something in a foreign language which apparently translated to "Fire!"

The ship bucked as both cannons fired. The shack and the capstan collapsed into the water along with the end of the pier. The harbormaster limped rapidly away, but she was too slow to avoid being pegged by a chunk of flying debris and she fell onto the pier, then she fell again as the pier collapsed, splashing into the water.

"I told you --" Rufe did his best to loom over the captain, but the captain was well versed in occupying space.

"Mutiny carries harsh penalties," he said.

Rufe lowered his head and backed away. He glanced over the side, and suddenly he was moving fast, grabbing a rope and leaning over the gunwale to throw it. Sonny patted Hina, who was very anxious from all the artillery, and went to the side to see what was going on.

The harbormaster was swimming, and the ship was moving swiftly past her. Rufe's aim was perfect and his rope landed on top of her head. She grabbed it and hauled herself hand over hand, her teeth bared in pain. As she got closer Rufe began to lift from above. Sonny and a few of the sailors pitched in to help, which wasn't particularly necessary as she wasn't heavy at all.

When they laid her on the deck it was apparent her leg was broken. Sonny winced and got out of the way as people attended to her. He headed up to the bow, cautiously. Risha was right there, arms wrapped around Hina, watching the ship advance on the cannon-bearing jellyfish.

The cannons dutifully fired. The jellyfish also fired, and since it didn't correct for the ship's recoil, its waterline shot hit the water instead.

"He's going to ram it," Rufe yelled, grabbing a harpoon from a rack.

"I do have a ramming bow specifically for occasions such as this," the captain replied. He gave another shout, and he also stamped his boot heel on the deck three times, hard.

The *Lono* seemed to gather like a pouncing tiger. She shot forward, almost catching air, revealing the blunt spike of a ramming bow protruding from the tip of her bow. Rufe let out a crazy laugh and brandished his harpoon, ready for battle. The jellyfish shot long, shimmery tentacles at them, groping for the bow of the ship as the impact happened. It was a soft, fleshy, yielding sort of impact. The jellyfish tore open, revealing the wall of some kind of container inside it. When that ruptured, sailors spilled out into the sea. They were all the same size, slender and dark-haired, very much like the ones who had taken over the stadium.

One of them jumped. Holding something shiny which stabbed into the side of the *Lono*. Sonny's first inclination was to throw something to knock the sailor back into the sea, and he groped around for something to throw. His hands found a rope, the same one Rufe had used to rescue the harbormaster.

He could throw the rope instead. Then they would have a prisoner, who would know where his family was being taken.

Sonny threw the rope. His aim was bad, but the rope eventually drifted to the sailor's free hand. A few seconds after that, the sailor climbed onto the deck and produced the shiny thing, tucked into a belt holster for the climb. A utility knife, made of coated obsidian. After throwing down the weapon, the sailor stood with raised hands and said, "I surrender."

"What's your name?" Rufe stepped forward.

"Kayliss."

Sonny stared at the enemy sailor, who was much younger than the twins from the stadium. About Sonny's age, with smooth cheeks, and the same pointy nose and intense eyes as all the rest. Short, dark, neat, straight hair, with a smear of something white stuck to it on one side.

"Where are you taking my family?" he blurted. Hina barked for emphasis.

"I can't submit to interrogations outside protocol. Sorry."

"You were taking people out to the ship. My family was with them." Rage surged through him and some of it came out in his voice.

"A lot of my family just drowned. Life can be harsh. I'm still not going to be interrogated outside protocol."

Rufe suddenly backhanded Kayliss, who went flying. "Here's some protocol for you."

Risha shrieked. "Stop it! He surrendered."

"They all surrender." Rufe spat for emphasis. "Primary directive: preserve your hide, and that of your fellow clones. Am I right?"

"I demand that you conduct this circus somewhere other than my deck," the captain said. "Back to the hold, if you would be so kind. I shall send carpenters to turn it into luxurious passenger accommodations forthwith. Please restrain that prisoner. Supper will take place at sunset."

The ship was still moving rapidly as they made their way downstairs, putting the land far behind them.

The harbormaster was in the hold, along with the doctor and a couple of sailors who had laid them on makeshift cots. The doctor's pale hand lay against the harbormaster's dark arm, and her leg was in a heavy dressing. Both of them were sound asleep.

Rufe grabbed a coil of rope and used it to tie Kayliss' hands together, and once that was accomplished he bent over the harbormaster, concerned. "We go way back."

"Excuse. Hello." A new sailor appeared, and the hold was starting to feel crowded. "Captain said to build some racks. How many?"

"We need two rooms, actually." Risha stepped forward. "One for the men, and one for the women. With a latch on the door, that works from the inside."

"We need three rooms," Rufe said. "We'll need a cell for the prisoner, with a latch on the door that works from the outside."

"You can put me in the room with the other women," said Kayliss. "I'll latch myself in."

Rufe grabbed a handful of her shirt and pulled it tight across her chest. Sonny stared. They weren't very large, but she definitely had boobs. A girl twin.

"You don't need to tie her up," Risha said." I don't think a teenage girl is going to singlehandedly take over the ship. She surrendered, and we can turn her over to the authorities when we get to shore."

"Captain's orders," Rufe snarled.

"I'll be on my very best behavior," Kayliss said. "I'm an officer. And I do have a stunrod on my belt, but I think the seawater killed it."

Rufe made a big show of unfastening her belt, and whipping it rapidly through her beltloops, and uncranking a window, and tossing it outside. While he was doing that, Risha smiled at the translator, showing dimples, and clasped his hand in hers. "Two rooms. And a washroom."

"Two. Yes." The translator grinned, stuttering slightly. Then he turned and spoke with the sailors, and soon after that hammers were pounding and saws were flashing. Pallets and barrels and other scrap lumber were turned into walls and doors, and latches, and sturdy bunks.

All the sailors liked the tiger-striped dog, and they built Sonny an extra-wide bunk to share with her, adjacent to the window. After it was constructed he huddled there, stroking her bristly fur and staring into space as everyone else got settled. Rufe lifted the unconscious people into their own bunks, then he left the women to their own room as the latch noisily fell into place behind him.

There was something approximating a bathroom between the mens' and womens' rooms, with buckets standing in for toilets and basins, and a window for convenient disposal of whatever wound up in the buckets.

The sailors brought thin mattresses, and blankets and pillows, and armfuls of clean dry clothes in various sizes. Sonny watched Rufe paw through the shirts in search of a fit.

He sat up, feeling dazed, and peeled away the remnants of his shoes and socks. He emptied the pockets of his ripped-up pants. He had some soggy pieces of paper, and some ruined cinnamon candies, and a key to room 314 at the Hotel Argalia. His ticket to the game. And his wad of cash for the concession stand, which he smoothed out on his knee. Forty-seven dollars all together, printed in bold red ink. Staring from the center of each bill was an old guy in a uniform, scowling over a watermark of crossed swords. Probably wouldn't be enough to buy a slice of pizza back home.

He shoved it in his pocket. Then he pulled one of the bills back out and stared at it. Old guy in a uniform.

The blood rushed out of his head and he sank into his bunk, where the tiger-striped dog was already curled up sleeping. "Rufe?"

Rufe was busy ripping the sleeves off of one of the donated shirts. "Yeah?"

Sonny held out the money without saying a word. Rufe glanced at it. "Hey, kid, don't worry about money, I've got enough to get you home as soon as I get the captain to drop us off down the coast."

Sonny shook his head and pointed at the portrait in the center of the bills. "No. Him."

"Him." Rufe slid his modified shirt over his head and sat back against the wall, studying Sonny with his artificial eye. "No longer among the living, from what I've heard."

"I hardly remember anything," Sonny babbled.

"No," Rufe agreed. "You probably don't."

Sonny stuffed the cash into his pocket and curled himself around the tiger-striped dog, soothed by the regular rise and fall of her chest. There was nothing to see outside the window except for blue sky and blue sea.

Rufe went out to the staircase, braced his feet and did a long series of sit-ups. Sonny wondered if this was his way of handling anxiety. He wasn't exactly sure how he should handle his own anxiety since he'd never had this much before. He stared at the undulating blue water as his thoughts leapfrogged from one worry to the next. His body ached, and he was pretty sure he could feel the exact lines where the nanobots had hauled his tissue back into alignment and glued it into place.

●

Just before sundown the ship slowed down, and the anchor splashed over the side. A sailor rapped on both doors and told them "the captain requests the pleasure of your company at dinner," in one big hastily-memorized rush. He brought bowlfuls of fish and water for the tiger-striped dog, which she nosed with interest. The doctor climbed out of his berth looking frail and tired. The harbormaster was awake, and Rufe carried her upstairs to the top deck.

A festive sunset painted the sky as they filed into the cabin at the rear of the main deck. In front was a windowed room containing the huge wooden-spindled wheel. Behind that was a salon, compact and opulent. There was a bookcase full of leatherbound books, a writing desk with jeweled bottles of ink, a table for eight, several mirrors and paintings, a guitar, a globe in a fancy wooden stand, some hanging plants, a brass telescope, a brass longitudometer, a bar, a harpsichord, a little red bird in a cage hanging from a ceiling beam. Toward the back and behind a carved-wood screen was the captain's bed, covered with a paisley quilt and tasseled pillows. On the floor were thick Oriental rugs.

The table was set for dinner, with the captain already seated in the largest chair. Sonny squeezed into a seat near him, not sure if he had an appetite. Kai was pouring from a decanter, showing them his tattooed hands. He had letters on his knuckles, spelling out "hold" and "fast." The pig at the base of his thumb was joined by stylized chickens and rabbits and fish that danced across the backs of his wrists, and he even had spirals going across his palms, although parts of those were obliterated by ridges of callus.

"I apologize for the impromptu nature of the refreshments, as I was not expecting passengers," he said as he handed cups all around. "Neither was I expecting terrorists to attack Argalia."

Kayliss muttered something below her breath. Rufe snorted.

The captain took a deep sip of whatever was in his cup and went on. "The cargo that formerly occupied the hold in which you are currently staying was in a warehouse adjacent to the wharf, where it was consumed by flame. Fortunately, it was heavily insured, and I have no doubt that the insurance company's report will mention the words 'terrorism' and 'attack.'"

"It's quite a lovely hold," Risha said. "Thank you for accommodating us on such short notice."

"You can drop us off anywhere along the coast," Rufe said. "A town would be nice."

"Our destination is a complicated subject and discussion must wait until the table is clear enough to accommodate maps." Kai tossed back the rest of his drink as sailors playing waiters brought in food. There was a tureen of soup, and platters of fish prepared several different ways, and steaming bowls of rice and noodles and vegetables. It all fit into cleverly designed wooden racks built into the table in anticipation of rough sea. The sea wasn't rough at all at the moment. It was flat, the setting sun glittering on its surface, a waxing crescent moon ready to take its place.

Sonny most definitely did have an appetite, and everything he tasted was delicious. Risha shared his opinion and kept up a running conversation with the captain about food, and about his chef, who came from Osakobyoto. Her face was scrubbed clean and her hair tied back in a loose braid, and she looked beautiful in a natural and effortless way. Kayliss sat in stark contrast beside her, looking awkward and plain. Her unflatteringly short hair had been brushed, and the light streak was still there, bleached into the side in what Sonny assumed was a failed attempt at decoration.

The harbormaster's name was Leah Dean Blocker, Dee to her friends, and she was stretched sideways with her splinted leg propped up on another chair. The spaciness in her eyes hinted she was still feeling Quicksilver's anesthesia, and the lines in her face indicated some of the pain was still getting through. Rufe sat beside her, guarding her bad leg and occasionally crowding Sonny with his hamlike elbow. The doctor sat on her other side, arranging shrimp tails in neat rows on his plate and staring into space.

After a rich, heavy dessert, the sailors replaced the last of the dishes with a steaming silver coffee service as the captain brought out a portfolio of nautical charts printed on waterproof paper, which he spread out for their perusal. Sonny blinked sleepily at the looping squiggles. He suddenly felt tired and overwhelmed. He wanted to collapse in a fit of tears until some wise, soothing adult appeared to whisk him off to a cool safe place where he could sleep for a month, and then wake up back home, in his bed, to the scent of pancakes.

He was wrestling with the idea that wasn't going to happen. A cold stony ache had developed in his chest. He kept telling himself he could get emotional later, when he was alone, and wasn't surrounded by strangers likely to treat him like a baby if he acted like one.

Since the charts confused everyone, which made Sonny feel slightly justified, the captain grabbed an old wooden globe from a decorative brass stand, palming it like a basketball and spinning it on the table for them before stabbing his spiralled finger into the Caribbean Sea.

It was an antique globe, coated with layers of preservative. The current configuration of the Mericas had been painted on top of the carved lines depicting what had once been there, before the meteors, and the dome generations, and all the rest of it. The western cluster of volcanoes, which had opened up after the meteor strike, were painted in red over the landbridge that formerly connected Namerica with Samerica, currently an archipelago of thousands of islands.

Sonny's eyes immediately went to Royal Beach, smack in the middle of the north coast of Samerica. On the old map this was right in the middle of the Amazon rainforest, but now it was the country of Braganza, a popular vacation destination and the middle of the three Samerican countries. Vanram was the one on the west, a jagged shape separated from Braganza by ridges of mountain.

Kai's finger was in the Caribbean, which was much larger in the current configuration, right above Argalia and only a pinky width away from Royal Beach. Three days on the *Principessa Larisse*, which was much slower than the *Lono*.

The captain dragged his finger across to Zentaro, the country east of Braganza. "We'll be landing here in approximately two weeks."

Sonny cleared his throat. "I live right on the way. In Royal Beach. Maybe you could drop me off?"

"Out of the question. My navigator is a Siren, and Braganza forbids them."

Sonny swallowed hard at this confirmation. Of course the captain had a Siren working with him. There weren't too many other explanations for a sailing ship moving over the water fast enough to tow water skiers without even using its sails.

"They're not legal in Vanram either," said Blocker.

"That's why they needed a doctor," Quicksilver sighed. "I'm still thrashed. Try manufacturing several million highly specialized microscopic robots in a factory implanted below your spleen sometime and see how you like it. And I'd just done a full restore on Sonny."

"Nepenthe encountered a projectile trap. In Braganza they have toxic coral planted all around the perimeter and I am therefore forced to give it a wide berth."

"I'm not hearing any of this," Blocker muttered, sinking her nose into her coffee cup.

"Two weeks." Rufe drummed his fingers on the table. "How much money would convince you to shift course?"

"That's funny." Risha smiled. "I was about to ask the same thing. For example, what if we were to sail north?"

"North?" Rufe screwed up his face in outrage. "To Namerica?"

The continent of Namerica had receded considerably since the globemakers practiced their art, with a south coast that sliced west from Raleigh and a northern border encroached by frost, similar to the south end of Samerica. Hogging most of the continent was a country called Bonterra, which encompassed everything west of the Virginialina sprawl and the United States of Scose. Risha's fingernail, her red-and-gold polish beginning to chip, was pointing at a spot toward the northwest. "It's a town called Chianina," she explained.

The captain drummed his tattooed fingers and stared at her. "You are proposing I navigate through some network of freshwater rivers?"

"There's a train, from Austin. That's on the south coast. We can take it all the way to Chianina.

Once we get there, I'll give you a lot of gold, and then you can be on your way."

"Out of the question." Rufe folded his arms and leaned back, doing a good job of looking large. "I need to get back to Vanram as soon as possible."

"Why aren't you there now?" Blocker asked him. Rufe deflated somewhat. "If you hadn't thrown me a rope I'd still be there, trying to restore some order. Presuming I managed to survive having a cannon fired at me."

The table erupted in an argument between Kai and Blocker and Rufe. Sonny found himself eye-to-eye with Kayliss, which reminded him of the last time he'd been held at gunpoint. "What are your people doing with my family?"

She stared down at her own plain fingernails. "Protocols."

"There's no engagement," Rufe bellowed, smacking the table. "Therefore, there are no rules of engagement. No protocols. Unless my country has declared war on yours since we left, which is doubtful, although it would probably be a good idea."

"They're safe!" She held up her arm to ward off an imaginary blow. "Nobody's going to hurt them. There's a town already built for them. In Chelisary. There's room for fifty thousand people, with shops and restaurants, and a park."

When she realized everyone was staring at her, Kayliss blushed bright red and focused even more intently on her nails.

Sonny's fingers were digging into the arms of his chair. Rufe leaned over and gave him a shoulder hug that was probably meant to be reassuring. "They're hostages, right? That's why they took everyone alive. Some high rollers in that crowd. Lots of ransom money, am I correct?"

"I don't know about any ransom, and I wasn't involved in the planning, but I've seen the houses." Kayliss bit her lip.

"We don't have a lot of money to pay a ransom." Sonny's voice changed pitch again. He had hoped it had finally stabilized somewhere in a low tenor range as the uncertainty of never really knowing whether a boy voice or a man voice would come out of his throat was annoying.

"How old are you, Sonny?" Risha laid a gentle hand on his wrist.

"Fifteen." A moment after he said it he wondered if he should have lied, in case maybe she might be interested in, perhaps, an eighteen year old. Not that she would. She was in a league he hadn't even realized existed until recently. Not only that, she was actually touching his wrist.

"And you're from Royal Beach?" She gave his wrist one last comforting squeeze and withdrew her hand, leaving tingling imprints where her fingers had been.

"Yeah."

"I've always wanted to go there. I've heard it's really nice." She smiled, showing several dimples, and and Sonny sat there, transfixed by how beautiful she looked. The fact that she was being nice to him had nearly reduced him to tears. "I don't want you to worry, Sonny. If there should turn out to be a ransom, I'll pay it. In gold. You may have to help me get to Chianina, which is where I keep my gold."

"We should go there," Sonny said in a scratchy voice.

Kai burst out laughing. "Do you have your own gold mine out there, full of dwarves with pickaxes and pointed hats?"

"More of a trust fund. In Bonterra we do business in gold. No bank fees, no nosy tax collectors."

"I do business over the internet, like normal people." Rufe was on his feet pacing, careful to avoid the décor. "I can live with Zentaro in two weeks, although if you can expedite me to the coast any faster I will authorize a fund transfer to your shipping company or whatever other private drop you'd like."

"Are we voting?" Blocker shifted in her seat and grimaced with pain. Quicksilver leaned over and touched his fingers to her wrist, then squeezed her bicep. When he took his hand away Sonny could see the indentations in his fingertips from his retractible syringes. "If we're having an election, I vote for a nice clean hospital. I believe Zentaro has those, whereas I believe in Bonterra they still use leeches."

"We have medicine," Risha snapped, her sweetness melting away just enough to give a glimpse of anxiety bubbling beneath.

"Are you stable enough to travel?" Kai offered Blocker a cup of something, which she accepted with a trembling hand.

"Here I am, traveling," she replied.

"She's stable enough," Quicksilver said. "I daresay she'd be a tad happier in nice clean sheets with a painkiller feed and a couple hundred hours of soap operas. I know I would."

"It's a two day train ride from my house to Midsea. Another few hours on the dirigible and you're back home in Deuce."

Deuce was an aircity. There were three of them in the Mericas, although only two contained people. On the globe they were represented by spots of silver. The one in the Atlantic had a long name full of words like "Administration" and everyone just called it Justice for short. The one in the Pacific had an equally long name, and since it consisted of two identical towers, everyone called it Deuce.

"Deuce is just as good as Zentaro as far as I'm concerned," Rufe said. "Which one is fastest?"

"Primarily, one cannot accurately adjudge how long it will take to navigate from one point to the next in deepwater. Secondarily, I direct your attention to the orange section, which is infested with pliosaurs."

"A certain country that I won't mention made them during the war," Rufe said, while glaring at Kayliss. "Trying to shut off our shipping traffic. There's a bunch of them off our west coast. Megalodons as well. The scientists assure us they'll die out in a generation or two, but so far that hasn't happened."

"The Sirens have managed to contain them with coral barricades." The captain threw Kayliss a fierce expression. "If you inform your overlords of that fact I'll rip your tongue out of your skull with my bare hands."

"There are ways to get past them," she replied, unrattled by the threat.

"They don't often venture outside the barricades. Encroaching into their territory is unwise. In order to reach Namerica we'd have to pass right next to it. I can't tell you whether that's feasible until I've looked at all the information and until I have discussed with the crew whether they choose to take unnecessary risks because a beautiful woman claims there is gold waiting on the other side." Kai sighed and rubbed his forehead.

"She has the gold." The doctor poured himself a cup of the same thing Blocker was drinking and tasted it, making a face. "Mizz Risha Petrichor has plenty of gold."

"Among other things." Risha wrestled the bottle away from Quicksilver and poured a slug into her coffee cup. "I have to be home to get my hands on it, and that's in Chianina. And I have to be there by May first."

"I shall bid all of you goodnight," Kai said. "I will let you know what is decided."

He began extinguishing lamps. A sailor lit their way back to the hold, where Sonny was enthusiastically greeted by the tiger-striped dog.

"She's bonded to you," Quicksilver said fuzzily as he climbed into his bunk. "An animal like that carries a chip inside her head, sort of similar to the apparatus I've got. Makes her bond very strongly to a particular owner. I think during the restore she fixated herself on you. Her name is Hina, by the way. She's a reconstructed thylacine, which was a marsupial wolf that lived in the South Pacific hundreds and hundreds of years ago."

Seconds after words stopped pouring out of him, the doctor began to snore.

"Hina," Sonny said, experimentally. The tiger-striped thylacine yipped ecstatically, licking his face. He crawled into his own bed and wrapped his arms around her, and fell asleep holding her tight.

●

The sun woke him by shining an uncomfortable patch of heat onto his forehead. Hina stirred and licked his face. She climbed out of bed and went into the bathroom, where she relieved herself neatly and precisely into a bucket. Sonny got out of bed and opened the window, tossing out the contents of the bucket. Then he used it himself, and tossed that, and sloshed it out with seawater from another bucket. He sponged himself off, staring at his reflection in a little mirror hanging on the wall. His eyes were still sleepy looking, and there were dark spots beneath them, even though he'd slept soundly. There was a fringe of scraggly beard creeping around his jawbone that made his face look dirty.

There was a fresh pimple on his cheek, and it made a satisfying pop when he squeezed it.

The mens' room was silent. Rufe and the doctor were gone, and aside from Hina, he was alone for the first time since he'd left Braganza. For a few scary moments his mind ran to dismal places, reminding him about all the things that had recently gone wrong in his life. He fumbled to fasten his disintegrated shoes to his feet and thought of Marilyn, unconscious inside a tube, and he wanted to cry, and to punch things.

He thought about the pink stucco house with black ironwork where his family lived. His bedroom, with its comfortable foam bed, and the floor to ceiling wallscreen, and the window looking downhill toward the water. Royal Beach curved like a big lazy grin, faced by rows of glittering houses looking down on the sea, and the beach, and the amusement park, and the casinos and hotels, and the world's tallest waterslide, and the harbor full of brightly colored sails. Where everything was clean and comfortable, and all the people gave you friendly smiles.

At least he still had a friendly smile. It occurred to him he should keep it on his face. He hugged Hina, tossed the remains of his shoes in the corner and padded barefoot to the stairs.

Rufe was working out with several sailors on the bow, sun glinting off his layers of muscle. Everyone else was gathered in the parlor, eating pastries and drinking coffee. The captain was wearing a peacock blue jacket today, and he was discussing nautical charts with a couple of sailors in a language Sonny didn't know. Risha was sitting at the harpsichord, playing soft arpeggios.

The doctor was painting a coating of plaster onto Blocker's leg. Kayliss was assisting, holding the leg steady with grim concentration. The patient was casually sipping at her coffee. Sonny wished them all a good morning and helped himself to a sweet roll.

"Good morning, sleepyhead." Blocker studied him with bright eyes as he munched. "I believe I failed to get your name."

"Sonny." He poured syrup and lightener ionto his coffee, trying to make it resemble the sweet frothy lattes people drank back home.

"That's not the name your mother gave you."

He ate a big bite of pastry so he could have extra time to figure out to say while chewing. "I don't remember." He said it with a scared little quiver in his voice, and then he smiled bravely through the pain.

"He had a full restore," the doctor chimed in. "Fell from the top deck, many fractures, brain injury. Fortunately, I was standing right there. Does a number on your system. You slept for nearly twelve hours. Any nightmares?"

"Falling." There had been a few more, but he didn't feel like going into detail. He composed his face in a friendly expression and let it set, like plaster.

"I hear that." Blocker let out a bitter laugh as Quicksilver patted the last of the plaster against her ankle, admiring its neat edge against the dark brown skin of her foot. "Suffered quite a fall myself recently. Probably the worst one I've ever had."

"I gave you ample and sufficient time to retreat from that pier," Kai said, gathering up his charts as the sailors departed.

"Yes, you did. It was my hip that slowed me down." She wriggled as Kayliss gently lowered her foot. "It was one of your people that did it, right after he surrendered. Back in the War. Half my pelvis is fabbed, and it doesn't fit quite right. Gives me occasional pains, I walk with a limp."

She stopped short and took a deep breath. Quicksilver leaned forward. "Pain?"

"None at all. Completely numb." She looked back at Sonny in a way that made him feel like she was about to reprimand him for missing school. "Bad memories make their way back to your mind much faster than the good ones."

Sonny studied the last pastry, deciding whether he wanted to eat it. Just as he began to reach for it Rufe burst in, grabbed it, and wolfed it down. He was dripping with seawater. Beyond him Sonny could see his workout buddies sloshing each other down with buckets, simultaneously rinsing off the deck. "You finally woke up! Tomorrow you'll have to join us. Don't want to get all deconditioned from lounging around on this luxurious cruise ship, do you?"

"I will if the doctor says it's okay."

"The day after tomorrow." Quicksilver moved behind him and massaged at his shoulders. Sonny felt the quick sting of his fingertip needles. "Make sure everything's solidly cemented in place, cognitive function's intact. Talk to us, Sonny. Tell us what you remember about yourself."

He slurped down the rest of his syrupy coffee and turned to Rufe. "You remember the kid who got kicked in the face?"

"From the viral video." Rufe snapped his fingers. "I thought you looked familiar."

"That was me. I'm from Royal Beach, and I'm terrible at sports. I was at the game with my friends

Lenny and Dan, and my parents, and my sister. I'll be sixteen in August. I've never been out of my country before."

"Congratulations," Kai said. It was hard to tell whether he was being sarcastic beneath the tattoos. "The crew is discussing it and my navigator has indicated it may be feasible to head for Austin, unless Carmelita will suffice."

Risha played a dissonant chord and took her hands away from the keyboard. "Not Carmelita. There's no train, we'd have to take a stagecoach."

"Carmelita would be far simpler," the captain groused. "If we do elect to head north to Austin, my navigator will take an alternate route and rejoin us at a later time, which will slow us considerably."

"I don't like that word, 'slow,'" Rufe pointed out.

"They fixate on Sirens," Kayliss said softly. "That's why they were made."

"You made the Sirens to kill us, but they started killing you instead. Then you made pliosaurs to kill them," Rufe reminded her.

"I'm sixteen," Kayliss said, struggling with her temper. "I didn't do any of that stuff. I'm sorry about your pelvis, Mizz Blocker, and I'm sorry about your family, Mister Sonny, and I'm sorry about all the stuff in the ocean, and I wish I could fix all these problems but I just can't. I'm sorry about the hostages too. That was not my idea. My job is sailing submarines. I've been doing that since I graduated last month."

Blocker massaged her temples and sighed. "As a law enforcement officer, I'll be blamed if anything happens to any minors before we return to civilization. That is one of the reasons it would be helpful to know your name, Sonny."

"I'm not a minor," Kayliss said. "Not by our laws."

"Anyone over thirteen is an adult in Vanram," said Rufe. "And you're out of your jurisdiction, Dee. Or are you?"

She closed her eyes and concentrated on breathing. Then she opened them and stared at the captain. "I'm with Ambit. Special agent."

From his last civics module, Sonny knew that Ambit was an international organization that had formed after people came out of the domes and built new cities and countries. All the different Merican nations were members. Ambit would send food and medics and engineers if a disaster happened, and they also collected data, to make sure countries weren't mistreating their land or people. They had a building downtown near the casinos where tourists could go if they accidentally spent so much money they couldn't afford to get back home. According to the movies, they also had special agents who spent all their time drinking champagne, parkouring off buildings and catching crafty villains. Usually these special agents looked more like young actors beginning their careers with physical roles than salt-and-pepper-haired ladies who walked with a limp.

"I should throw you over the side," Kai said. "You've seen enough to send me to prison."

"There will be no throwing anybody over the side," Risha scolded.

"Exorbitant fines, forfeiture of my ship." Kai drummed his bananalike fingers angrily on the table. "My crew took on the chance they could die at sea, not the chance of lengthy incarceration."

"Captain, you have my word that if I survive this, I will never speak a word against you or your crew." Blocker repositioned her leg, grimacing.

"You have *my* word, Captain," said Rufe, "that any of us causing you needless stress and potential delay by fighting, or arguing, or threatening your freedom or your livelihood, will have to answer to me."

With arguing forbidden they fell silent, each of them lost in their own thoughts. Sonny sat back in his chair, wearing his friendliness like armor. He ran his fingers over the polished wood of his chair's arm, studying the grain. Most things back home were made of composite, some of which looked like wood. Fake wood grain was predictable and regular, but the real thing was more random.

He missed having digital amusement constantly available in the palm of his hand. Normally he'd have fifty or sixty hours of video available for instant watching and rewatching depending on his mood, plus a few books and comics and several hundred songs. Plus his school work, plus his regular infotainment feeds, plus the constant flow of messages from his friends. Without it he felt strangely lonely, even though he was surrounded by people. He was pretty sure they weren't up to speed on the latest pop songs and movies from Royal Beach, and he wasn't sure he knew enough about anything else to carry on a conversation.

If only he had a talent. Talented people always had something to talk about.

He glanced at Risha, playing something he thought he recognized as Mozart, although he only knew it from a dance version that had been popular a couple years ago. She had musical talent, in addition to her beauty, which was sort of like a talent all by itself. Back home she'd have made a zillion movies by now. If he'd had a deld it would have been full of pictures of her.

He watched her until he wondered whether he was approaching the threshhold of creepiness, and then he turned around to look at the captain, standing at the wheel while having an animated conversation in some foreign language with a couple of sailors. Talent on top of talent, and if Risha's beauty counted as a talent, then Kai's artwork stood for an unusual ability to hold still, not to mention dedication. The swirling spirals tattooed on his face gave him a permanent pondering expression, making it extremely hard to guess what he might really be thinking.

Rufe sat listening to the music with his head tilted toward the side, staring out at the horizon. He occupied number one on Sonny's personal list of most talented athletes. In fact, he had been secretly hoping he'd get to meet Rufe at the celebratory dinner. Shake his hand, listen to him say some perfunctory things about sports before moving on to the thousands of other people who wanted his attention.

Rufe came from a country where everyone was tall and strong and muscular, and even there he stood out as being in extraordinarily good physical shape. He had the kind of face built for howls and roars and grimaces. In repose, it was plain looking, possibly even a little bit ugly, with dark stubble peppering his scalp and his chin, lighting up red when the sun caught it.

The champagne bottle. That's what Rufe had used to kill that old man. Sonny blinked and the ruined face of the corpse appeared on his inner eyelids. The champagne bottle had been sitting in the ice bucket and Rufe had just hopped through the window and whacked the old man in the head with it, killing him. Saving Sonny and Risha, because the old man had been ready to shoot them both.

He got up and bolted downstairs. A few minutes later he was huddled on the floor, cradling a bucket of vomit while Hina licked his ear. He managed to stagger to his feet and dump the bucket into the sea. And rinse it, and dump the rinse water, and slide back into his bunk thinking how nice it would be to feel his mother's hand stroking his forehead.

Instead he had Hina, and he curled his body around her and sobbed, as quietly as he could. The ship groaned sympathetically around him, rocking him in a comforting way. When he heard footsteps on the stairs he wiped his face with his sleeve. The doctor came in, fanning his nose at the smell. "A little bout of seasickness?"

"I was thinking about what happened right after I met you." Sonny sat up, sniffling. "That guy who died."

"Sometimes people feel a little anxiety after having a parade of nanobots trampling through their veins. They might have hallucinations, or fever. Sometimes nausea." He sat down on the floor next to Sonny's bunk. "Nobody would fault you for having a fuzzy memory. By the same reckoning, if you were to start talking about your memories, other people might accuse you of having nothing more than a fever dream. I can keep you sedated throughout this entire voyage if you can't manage to hold yourself together any other way, but I certainly hope it won't be necessary, since it may cloud your memories even further, or possibly cause them to evaporate entirely."

"I can hold it together," Sonny said curtly. He took a deep breath. Friendliness. "Thanks, doc. It really is kind of fuzzy. About all I remember is how you heroically saved my life."

"Seeing your first dead body is always harsh. Think you can eat? Dinner's happening up top." Quicksilver bustled around opening windows.

Sonny brought Hina with him and she was welcomed, and given her own versions of each course. Several of the sailors came in to meet her. Rufe joked about being glad Sonny had saved the opposing team's mascot, since the ram wasn't nearly as well behaved at dinner parties, and Kai complained about the bet he'd placed on the Tigers. The doctor confessed he had bet on both sides, but wouldn't name the amounts.

As food began to arrive Kai officially announced that they would be heading north to Austin. Risha clapped her hands to her face, and then she got up and wiggled around the table, planting a big kiss on his tattooed forehead before returning to her seat. Kai sat there in a daze as Sonny found himself sitting up straight in his seat, mildly irritated.

"I can't wait to see where you live." Rufe beamed rakishly.

"It's a little old house on a hill." Risha pushed her plate back. "Been in my family for generations."

"I'll bet it's got a horse stable out back," Blocker said. "And chickens running through the kitchen."

"Those chickens fry up real nice in grandma's seasoned pan. Yes, we have horses. We even have a terminal so you can interface with the outside world. It's in the middle of town, heavily shielded."

"I'm not looking forward to any kind of train rides." Blocker said. "Or camping out on the prairie."

"There is a long train ride," Risha agreed. "The seats are nice and springy, and once you get to my place you can rest up on a soft featherbed. And I know it's inconvenient, and even dangerous, and I want to thank all of you."

"There are only about fifty pliosaurs," Kayliss said. "They can't make new ones. Eventually they'll be gone forever. The last one will eat all the rest."

"I hope I live to see that day." Kai drank a toast to the very idea. "My crew, in addition to being highly skilled sailors, are mostly students and scientists. Once I explained we'd be passing briefly through pliosaur territory they were beside themselves with excitement. The cash bonus seemed to bring joy to their hearts as well."

"Most expensive trip I've ever taken. I'll have something to brag about." Risha sighed as a single tear worked its way down the soft slope of her cheek."Even though it's entirely to my detriment. Once I'm back in that house I'm going to be stuck there for a while."

"I thought you *wanted* to go to Bonterra." Rufe pointed out. "We could go straight to Zentaro without encountering a single sea monster."

"I do want to go to Bonterra." More tears appeared. "Or rather, I have to."

"Are you chipped for several Asian languages, captain?" Quicksilver leaned forward. "I've looked into that."

"It's not instantaneous," Kai said. "You have to configure it to your individual idiom. I'm chipped for Korean, Thai, Hindi and Japanese, and I'm sufficiently intelligible in a few others."

"It would be nice if we could just plug them right into our brains and start talking."

Sonny peeked at Risha, who was blotting her tears. "Why do they have so many languages?"

"Lack of meteors." Quicksilver pushed his plate back. "People in the Mericas used to speak several different languages, but by the time they came out of the domes everybody spoke Merican, which is a creole made up of English, French, Spanish and Portuguese. It has regional dialects but it's been remarkably stable over the last thousand and whatever years."

"The ancient Polynesians shared a language from one side of the Pacific to the other," Kai contributed to the history lesson. "Whereas on larger land masses people living less than a day's travel apart developed distinctly different tongues."

"I guess it all depends on how much you hate your neighbors." Rufe plopped another helping of fish onto his plate.

After they were full of fine seafood, as the sunset painted the sky in loud equatorial colors, the captain took over the harpsichord and played something grand and thoughtful, until the only light left came from the stars and the waxing moon. "Lamp oil is tremendously expensive," he said softly after covering the keys. "I shall see you in the morning."

After the excruciatingly embarrassing business of peeing noisily in a bucket in close proximity to several other people, Sonny hid under his blanket, which was made of some kind of material that kept itself clean and soft, the same stuff that covered his mattress and pillow. He hardly needed a blanket at all in the heat, especially with Hina's hairy bulk pressed against his side. Rufe and Quicksilver were breathing slow and regular. The women were chattering softly in their cabin, but Sonny couldn't tell what they were saying.

In the dark, without the necessity of keeping a friendly expression on his face, worries flooded his mind. There were so many of them he had trouble picking out the ones that were just plain silly. His memories were no refuge, as they were full of people he missed.

He wasn't worried in the slightest about the fact his arms were wrapped around an animal that had recently killed someone. In fact, he felt a lot safer with her beside him. Hina's tail slapped against his leg and he stroked her coarse fur until he was relaxed enough to surrender to sleep.

●

He woke up early. Usually he woke up little by little, paddling around in the shallow end of sleep until his music went off. On this particular day, waking up was sudden and rude. There he was, wide awake, staring at the grayish morning. He couldn't remember his dreams but he assumed they'd been horrible. He felt hollow, and he held very still as he prepared himself for another day of fake friendliness.

Rufe woke up next, suddenly rising and heading to the bathroom while Quicksilver stirred in the top bunk, complaining faintly in his sleep. By the time Rufe Sonny was sitting up expectantly, and in the spirit of friendliness he followed Rufe to the top deck, where they met with several of the sailors. They did warmup stretches until Sonny was sore and wobbly. Then he sat down off to the side and watched. He assisted with the part where they threw buckets of water at each other, and then the crew thanked each other and attended to the actual business of sailing the ship.

The passengers gathered in the salon for breakfast. The captain bragged about his ship while they ate, with occasional digressions into nautical history and maritime geology. Everyone else smiled and said only small polite words, Sonny among them.

When breakfast was done, he asked the captain, in a friendly way, if he could do anything useful.

Kai tossed him a length of rope. "Tie a knot."

The only knot Sonny knew was the bow he used to keep his sneakers from falling off, so he tied a nice one with big balanced loops. Kai stared at him balefully from beneath his tattoos and Rufe snickered.

"If you are offering to work as crew aboard this ship, you are required to have basic nautical skills."

Sonny was introduced to Nguyen, who was older than the other sailors and spoke the most Merican. He took Sonny and Hina to the crew's salon on the second deck, and before long Sonny had mastered the anchor hitch and the bowline.

Most of the other sailors were working and the ship was flying along at a good speed, but a few took breaks in order to stop by and scratch Hina's ears. Sonny had clumsy conversations with them, Nguyen serving as interpreter. They talked about dogs, and Sanjit's dissertation on oceanic oxygenation, and a movie called *Rhubarb Chrysanthemum*, an adaptation based on a Chinese film which had won several awards in Braganza last year.

They taught him to tie a total of seven different knots, and gave him a length of rope for practice, as well as a pair of soft-soled shoes. Then they pronounced him proficient and sent him back to the other passengers.

He spotted a blue glow along the way, the glow of screens and electricity, and he was drawn to it. He found himself standing at the top of a narrow stairway. The glow issued from a partly-open door at the bottom. Sonny pushed the door open and found another set of stairs leading down, and soft orchestral music. He descended, Hina padding silently behind him.

Most of the floor was taken up by a convex window in the hull that was probably a couple of meters across. Something dark was moving against the dark blue of the sea and Sonny couldn't see it very clearly. He could see a mermaid, floating in the air above the window. With long hair braided down her back, and a smooth, dolphin-like tail, and a bra made of starfish and seaweed. She looked up at Sonny and gave a little wave. She was ghostly; he could see right through her.

The captain also looked up. Sonny hadn't noticed him despite the bright pink velvet jacket he was wearing today. He was holding a map lit by a glowing orb floating over his shoulder.

"Um, I'm sorry to bother you." Sonny headed back up the stairs but Kai beckoned him back. The mermaid flipped her tail and an array of displays appeared behind her. Some had numbers and bars, others were more abstract.

"Try not to step in the water." Kai motioned him toward a stack of cushions and Sonny collapsed there, pulling Hina next to him. Now that he was up close, he could see that it wasn't a window at all. Something was keeping the water's surface tension intact without letting it spill through this large hole in the bottom of the ship, and he suspected it might have something to do with the colorful blobs arranged around the rim of the underwater side. An aquatic creature swam below them, hovering.

"Is that a thylacine?" The mermaid inquired. She had an unusual voice that sounded like three women singing in harmony. One high, one low, one in the middle.

"That's what the doctor told me."

"The lad can't remember his name, so everyone consequently refers to him as Sonny," Kai said. "Sonny, this is Nepenthe."

"Pleased to meet you." The mermaid did a little animated flip. "The captain said you were from Royal Beach."

"Yes." He nodded and the music suddenly changed, to a pop song that had been playing on their way to the *Principessa Larisse*, all of them squashed into a taxivan with their luggage. Squealing girls, singing about the queen of the party scene, turning sweet sixteen in a limousine. Marilyn singing along, sitting on mom's lap and bouncing to the beat. The sky as bright and blue as it always was as they cruised along the highway, heading to an adventure. It was a bright brassy song with an infectious beat, and it felt like a hammer slamming against his chest. Tears ran from his eyes. "Yeah, that's from Royal Beach. Could you please play something else?"

The music immediately shifted to something light and inoffensive as the animated mermaid apologized profusely. "I probably should have explained to you in advance that communication between our species is fraught with misunderstandings and I have absolutely no malicious intentions."

"Just a sad memory." Sonny wiped his eyes with Hina's ear. "It wasn't sad at the time, but it is now."

"Maybe it will be happier in the future."

Sonny smiled. "I hope so. Are you on the internet? Can you call people?"

"Not precisely." The mermaid went through a brief animation where she grew legs and stepped onto the shore to find a beach littered with cutlery and broken glass. "We're locked out of yours, but we have our own. If I were in the Pacific, I could do something, but not out here."

"Her system is the only one that provides useful information on subjects such as topography at the bottom of the ocean," Kai added. "Information we shall lack once Nepenthe parts company with us."

"I will find you once you make your way back to the Pacific."

"You're a Siren," Sonny said out loud, and both the captain and the mermaid snickered at him.

"I look more like this up close," said the mermaid, morphing into something halfway between a whale and a seal. The lines of her animation melted into an ancient ink drawing, with a label beneath that read "Stellar's Sea Cow." "Sirens and thylacines were both extrapolated from creatures that extincted in approximately the same historical period and geographical region, so you might say we're cousins, although we aren't precisely the same as we were back then."

"I don't think thylacines are equally adept with navigation systems. Are you?" Kai asked Hina, and she opened her mouth in a doggy smile and wagged her tail, but didn't add anything further.

"I thought you looked more like sharks," Sonny said hesitantly. He peered down at the creature in the water. It was bigger than the largest sea creature he had ever seen, a marlin caught by an ecstatic tourist.

"Propaganda and lies."

"I shall see you again soon," Kai said firmly, and the drawing turned back into the mermaid, smiling prettily. She waved at them as her whole display dissolved and the music faded out. Kai fitted a cover over the hole in the floor and stamped it in place with his boot. Enough seawater sloshed in to dampen Sonny's new shoes but the seal held, watertight.

●

Time passed, and Sonny felt like he was gradually losing the ability to keep track of it. There was dawn, when everybody woke up and got to work, and there was night, when they anchored if possible. When anchoring wasn't possible, sailors had to work through the night keeping their drift controlled so they didn't slide back to where they'd already been.

During the daytime the captain and crew ignored the passengers, working around them as they sprawled in the parlor or paced in circles on the deck. Sonny worked out with Rufe every morning. He played cards and dice and backgammon, and he learned how to tie a monkey's paw, which was a big heavy knot that you could use as a stopper or a weight. He occasionally asked Kai if he could help, and sometimes he was given a mop or a polishing cloth, but usually the answer was no, leaving him with absolutely nothing to do.

The lack of structured time was just one of the things that made him wonder if he might be going crazy. He had grown up with an appointment calendar that appeared on the wall, helpfully directing you to the next segment of your life, whether it was school or some activity or the release date for something new. He had never realized that nebulous stretches of unplanned days even existed.

His emotions were on random shuffle. Sometimes his belly felt hollow and he wanted to curl up in a corner and cry. Sometimes he was full of energy and anger. Sometimes it was a dead, scary emptiness that didn't really care if he never saw his family again because he'd probably die before that happened and there was really no point. There was also plenty of anxiety about letting these emotions contaminate his outward display of friendliness.

He didn't seem to be able to focus on anything. He was easily capable of staring out the window at nothing for long periods of time. Sometimes he spent entire mornings reading the same sentence in one of Kai's books, which mainly seemed to be compilations of other books, printed in a small font on slippery waterproof paper and rebound in ancient-looking leather. There were plenty of books in Sonny's family's library and usually he liked reading them as they scrolled across his palm. In the morning, to help start his brain, or at bedtime, to help quiet it down. He had never actually read from a paper book before, with static letters that weren't backlit at all, and couldn't be resized, and the effort of decoding them was large. Staring at the horizon was much easier.

Maintaining friendliness wasn't too difficult. Everyone else seemed absorbed in their thoughts, and conversation was light and inoffensive. Kayliss seemed to be serving as Blocker's personal nurse and assistant, even to the point of emptying her bedpan, and was never far away from her, and Risha stuck close to them, sewing pieces of slightly water-damaged silk into new clothes.

Rufe was fascinated with how the ship worked and spent a lot of his time reading the gauges or climbing around in the rigging. He and Kayliss seemed to be in denial over each others' existence, although both of them were friendly with Blocker, and would studiously ignore it whenever she spoke with the other one. Blocker was growing on Sonny. She had a gloomy sense of humor that was perfect for their circumstances.

The water got rougher, Rufe's beard filled in, and one day the captain told them they were all confined to quarters. "You can expect some moderate waves as we are on course to bypass the storm. It might take us half a day with the wind at our backs and it might take us half a week if conditions are suboptimal."

They took the dice and cards and retreated below. Sailors brought them mesh wraps that hooked around their bunks to keep them from flying out while they slept. There were also necklaces with fat orange pendants for everybody. Once you broke the seal on the pendant the necklace would inflate, hopefully enough to keep your head afloat, assuming you weren't trapped inside a room. Everyone had to wear a neck float at all times, even Hina.

True to the captain's warning, the sea became violent. The doctor sedated Blocker, which prompted an argument with Risha about whether she'd be able to activate her neck float.

"It doesn't really matter out here," Quicksilver said. "It's not like another ship is going to come along and pick you up.

"It could happen," Kayliss retorted.

"Are you wearing some kind of communicator?" Rufe stood up, jamming his hand against the ceiling to stay upright. "Calling your friends to pick you up?"

"I believe there was an agreement not to argue." Quicksilver squeezed past Rufe's encroaching bulk and climbed into his own bunk, cinching himself in. "As her physician, I report she is not sending or receiving any external signal, although further medical disclosures are confidential in nature and can only be released following a full inquiry and investigation."

"I'll watch out for her," Kayliss said.

"I will blame you if anything happens to her." Rufe glared down at Kayliss for a while and she stared right back at him, not even slightly intimidated.

They retreated to their corners. Rufe and the doctor resumed their dice game. Sonny could hear Kayliss and Risha having some kind of discussion behind their door, with occasional raised voices. He couldn't imagine what they might be saying to each other as they didn't seem to have anything in common other than the fact they were both female, and they had completely different ways of being female. The fact that Risha preferred to spend her time talking to a terrorist instead of Sonny was so unfair it made his arm hairs stand up.

He tied more knots, and untied them, and retied them again as the ship bounced from one extreme angle to the next. Twenty-four hours later, he was still doing the same thing. There had been occasional acrobatic visits to the bucket room, which was even more challenging in rough sea. Food now consisted of noodle soup in bland broth flavored heavily with ginger, delivered in containers with lids. It was designed to be as inoffensive as possible should it come back up, but so far nobody had puked, and that was all to the doctor's credit. He gave everyone regular jabs of something that cut the nausea, and something else that kept them calm. The dice score climbed into the hundreds of thousands. Sonny added five new knots to his repertoire.

At some point during what was probably the second day of rough sea, they heard an extremely loud thunderclap. Rufe overreacted, springing from his bunk and spilling dice all over the floor. Sonny caught one as it bounced off the wall. The bathroom door banged open and Risha stood there, hair partially undone and eyes wide. "What just happened?"

"Maybe the mast broke off," Quicksilver said, gathering the rest of the dice.

"I'll be right back," Rufe said, slamming the door behind him.

"If the captain is going to have anyone flogged for getting in his way, it might as well be him." The doctor scrabbled at the wall as the ship tilted sharply, dropping the dice again. They clattered into Sonny's bunk when the ship tilted back the other way. Hina grabbed at one but apparently didn't like the taste and spat it back out. She was tucked beside Sonny, strapped down with webbing. Occasionally she struggled until he released her so she could stretch and use the bucket but she spent most of her time plastered against his side.

"There's a cloud." Kayliss appeared behind Risha, looking grubby and rumpled. "In the sky."

Sonny pressed his face to his window. The doctor and Risha leaned over him, and Risha's proximity made his heart beat faster even though she smelled sour and sweaty. All of them did.

There was a large dark cloud, way off to the west. It was shaped like a mushroom, and took up a large portion of sky. They stared at it until it lost its shape, and Rufe came stumbling back in, soaked to the skin. "Captain says he'll keelhaul the next one of us that goes up top before things are clear. I'm not quite sure that that is but it sounds harsh."

"What is that?" Risha pointed.

"Western cluster." He peeled off his wet shirt and wrung it into the nearest bucket. "Something's erupting. Either that or your people are setting off big explosions."

"We wouldn't do that." Kayliss didn't seem absolutely certain. "Do you think your people are attacking?"

"Should we?" He leaned over her to look through the window, dripping water on Hina, who squirmed and complained. He aimed his artificial eye at the cloud and stared at it for a while. Then he got up and climbed back into his bunk and strapped himself in. "It looks like the western cluster but I couldn't tell for certain because of the wave, but the fact there is a wave would tend to confirm my theory about seismic activity."

"I don't see any wave." Risha leaned closer. A tangle of her hair brushed against Sonny's arm as a wave nearly knocked her on top of him, but she managed to steady herself against the windowframe.

"It's about eight minutes away. You might want to strap yourself down."

Sonny unhooked his bedbelt and sat up, clutching his knees to his chest, to make room for Risha to sit beside him but instead she headed back to her room, moaning, Kayliss behind her. "I just want this boat ride to be over."

Quicksilver took advantage of the space instead, staring into the endless series of waves. Sonny looked at them too, but he couldn't see any that particularly stood out. He watched the cloud unravel across the sky until he heard the doctor inhale sharply. "Oh for the – I knew we should have headed straight to Zentaro, in fact we'd be there right now."

"Shut it and assume crash position, doc." Rufe was almost serene, trussed in his web like a huge caterpillar. "You too, Sonny."

Then Sonny saw it. A mountain of water, heading toward them. The doctor's presence vanished from his side and Sonny could hear him fumbling with his straps as he stared through the window, hypnotized by the sight. Hina whined and started to get up.

"Fasten the strap. Now." Rufe raised his voice. Sonny broke out of his trance and pulled the webbing around himself and Hina, cinching it tight and clicking the buckles home. He could hear the wave approaching but he didn't dare look at it. He had one arm around Hina and the other on his neckfloat, ready to trigger it.

In case he found himself floating. Out here, where there were no ships. Just pliosaurs.

The ship plowed up the wave at an angle. It was nearly over the top when it heeled over hard to the side. Water poured down the open stairway as the *Lono* leaned over, lying on its side to cross the crest of the wave. Sonny and Hina hung from their webbing, looking down at the wall, the window showing nothing but a deceptively cheerful slice of blue sky. The ship screamed and complained, its timbers and ropes straining against each other, and then they were sliding downhill fast.

The ship gave a tremendous shudder and popped upright. Sonny slammed his elbow against the wall moments before all the water from the staircase forced the door open and rushed in, landing mostly in his bunk before spilling to the floor. The ship sped down the back side of the wave at high speed, gracefully rejoining with the ordinary choppy waves while the tsunami continued on its way east.

"That's the word, tsunami," Quicksilver was babbling. "Japanese word, although they certainly weren't the first people to ever see them, and you're absolutely right, Rufe, they do generally come about through seismic activity and volcanoes erupting and things like that, and if we had communications I'd be on the phone right now warning someone, although I don't suppose there's much in its way until Europe. Is anyone injured? Sonny?"

"I'm all right," he wheezed. He unhooked his harness and sat up, water streaming from his clothes.

Hina bounced up and headed to the bathroom to use the bucket.

Sonny wrung out his damp bedding, adding to the water already on the floor. There was a drain back by the stairs but it was clogged up with debris, and he went out to clear it while Rufe peered through the window at the volcano. It had just occurred to him that a volcano was yet another thing to add to his list of worries when Blocker let out an unearthly howl. Rufe nearly trampled him as he rushed in, prompting outraged cries from Risha, and the doctor.

"Stay there," Sonny ordered Hina, and she did, climbing into their bedding-less bunk and sinking her nose onto her paws.

He climbed the stairs very carefully, gripping some solid part of the ship with every step. He dragged himself to the wheelhouse, where Kai was standing at the wheel. His velvet jacket was gone and he was dressed mostly in tattoos, along with a pair of cargo shorts. He had a harness strapped around his chest that connected him to the floor, and he was talking to Nguyen and another guy Sonny didn't know. The crew seemed very busy at the moment, with several men up in the rigging putting their knot-tying skills to practical use.

Sonny braced himself in the doorway as the ship took a wave and the captain turned in his direction. "Have you sustained any casualties below?"

"I think Blocker's hurt. The doctor's with her."

"I have a crewman with some kind of fracture. Please be so kind as to ask the doctor to attend once he is finished with his patient."

Sonny nodded, wondering if he should say something like "Yes sir!" or "Aye aye, captain!" He couldn't help but notice Kai's torso was as heavily tattooed as his face, all in thick black lines. "They think it's a volcano erupting in the western cluster."

"It appears so." He pointed ahead of them and to the side. "We were on course to avoid that storm entirely, but due to our new trajectory, we may intersect."

Sonny could barely see the storm but he could smell a metallic tang on the breeze. "I'll go back down. Thank you. For doing whatever you did. That was crazy."

Kai shrugged a decorated shoulder. "A pity we have no cameras."

He made his careful way back to the damp and smelly hold. All the doors were open in the name of ventilation, and Quicksilver was tending to Blocker, who was breathing through clenched teeth. Sodden chunks of her cast were lying on the floor and the doctor had replaced it with a splint, which he was tying in place.

"The captain said to tell you there's an injured sailor. Also, we might be heading into a storm."

"I'm going to die out here. I am certain of it." Blocker's skin was grayish, and she was clutching the headboard so tight that her fingernails were leaving dents in the wood.

"You can't say that!" Kayliss surged to her feet, jostling Risha, who was sitting cross-legged on her bunk with her lap full of colorful cloth.

"The only thing we can state about the future with absolute certainty is that we don't know what it will bring." The doctor tied the last knot with a flourish and headed upstairs, leaving his patient with her leg swaddled in bandages, pillows and rolled up blankets tucked around her for extra cushioning.

Rufe had seized the opportunity of having the room to himself to take up most of the floor doing pushups. Sonny stepped carefully around him and joined Hina in his bunk. He could look right into the womens' room with all the doors open but the only visible portion of Risha was her knee. Rufe yelled toward the next room, "You're not going to die, Dee. You're gonna stick around and watch me kick the ass of whoever's fault this turns out to be."

"It's not *my* fault," Kayliss interjected.

"If I thought it was your fault, you'd already be dead." He switched to one-armed pushups.

"If I die, I am charging you with my vengeance." Blocker pointed her bony finger at Kayliss. She sputtered, and Rufe let out a sarcastic laugh.

"I am serious." Blocker grabbed something hanging around her neck and pulled it up over her head. The key, to the harbor lock capstan. Flakes of metal came off on her hand as she thrust it toward Kayliss. "Take it as a reminder and promise me you'll set things right."

"I can't do that." Kayliss' hair stuck out in fifty directions and her face was red and blotchy, like she'd been spending a lot of time crying. As she should be. Sonny decided she was the ugliest girl he had ever seen.

"Tell me who else can." Blocker extended the key again and this time Kayliss took it, slipping it around her own neck. It left a stain on her shirt, but she already had several others.

The doctor returned with their supper of gingered noodles and a slab of fish for Hina, reporting that the cook's assistant had dislocated his shoulder and broken a couple of ribs. He gave everyone a round of antinausea medication after they ate. The sun departed and Sonny noticed that the moon was all the way full, and partially covered by smoke from the volcano.

The ship kept moving all through the night, and when they woke up there was a pile of damp gray volcanic ash at the bottom of the stairs. Nguyen tracked it all over when he delivered their daily ration of fresh water, and breakfast, which consisted of a loaf of bread and a bunch of blackening bananas. He looked exhausted beneath his own layer of ash and he didn't stay long.

The first raindrops began to fall shortly after Ngyuen left. Not long after that, Sonny found himself clearing the drain again as the ship seesawed back and forth. The rainwater cleaned him up while simultaneously painting him with new streaks of ash and when he came back in Rufe laughed and accused him of getting tattooed like the captain.

Sonny stalked back into his bunk without saying a word, suddenly furious at Rufe, as well as Kayliss, and the whole situation, and the fact that his clothes and bedding were neither wet nor dry, and the volcano, and the rain, and being at sea. Hina sensed it and got up to stretch, her claws sliding on the wooden floor. Sonny grabbed his latest monkey's paw knot and thumped it rhythmically against the wall.

"I just want to say I'm sorry." Risha suddenly appeared in the doorway. Her face was streaked with tears.

"We could have been in Zentaro by now. Eating dinner at one of those little restaurants outside the university, where they have live music all night long." Rufe flopped to the floor and did some situps, oblivious to the filth.

"Cleanbeams and climate control," Quicksilver said dreamily.

"If we die and it's my fault, I just wanted to be sure I apologized first."

"I'll bet the captain will charge you extra." Rufe reached out his arm to steady her as the ship swayed but she had a pretty good grip on the doorframe.

"I'll gladly pay it." She shoved her hair back with her forearm in a gesture that made Sonny recall Kai's comment about the lack of cameras. "I'll pay all of you as well." She lowered her voice. "And I'll pay you even more if you'll say I was never in that particular room on that particular day."

Rufe stood up and flexed various muscles. "I think I'm getting deconditioned. And by the way, what were you doing in that particular room on that particular day?"

"That's private," she snapped. Rufe laughed.

"Sure," Sonny said. Risha was probably the least irritating person on the ship. Everyone else looked grubby and miserable, but Risha looked like she was ready to step in front of a camera. Always. Even when she had dirt smeared across her cheek, as she did now, it only drew attention to the perfection of her cheekbones. Sonny blinked mistily, feeling his negative emotions bubble away. "You were never there. Some girl was there, I think she had blonde hair, but she ran away."

"Your memory is unreliable," Quicksilver reminded him.

"How long does yours last?" Risha glared at the doctor and something passed between them. Sonny wasn't sure if it was a flirt or a threat.

"Three months," he said brightly. "I've timed it down to the second."

"I'm the one who killed him," Rufe said. "You all saw that."

"With a champagne bottle," Sonny said as the image of the old man's dead face flashed through his mind.

"Good boy," Rufe said. Sonny looked up, studying them, infuriated by their undercurrents of grownup secrecy.

"What I remember happening," he said, "is mostly about missing my family, and I'll remember whatever I have to remember to get them back."

"That's the spirit. Do you require anything further, madame? A sedative?" Quicksilver flexed his fingers. She shook her head.

"You'll remember the truth," Rufe said to Sonny as Risha stumbled back to her room. Sonny watched her knee appear in the frame of the doorway as she sat down on her bunk. Blocker and Kayliss were both sleeping, from the rhythmic sound of their breath.

His hands were becoming callused from constantly retying knots, but that was all his brain seemed to be able to handle. Loop around this way, pull through that way, tighten, admire, undo and repeat. Rufe and Quicksilver returned to their ongoing dice battle as he knotted, and unknotted, and stared through the window at gray sky and waves taller than he was. The ship creaked and groaned around them and the wind replied with eerie moans.

At some point in what was probably the afternoon, he saw a pliosaur.

He thought it was a wave at first, irregular and out of synch. Then he thought it was a whale. Then he remembered there weren't any whales in the Caribbean, they lived much farther away. For a moment he hoped it was a Siren, such as Nepenthe, coming to bless them with superfast speed.

It was a shiny bluish-grayish curve, surfacing parallel to them. Pacing them. Sometimes it dipped down beneath the waves but it always came back up. The sailors must have seen it too, as a cannon fired, directly above them, followed by several gunshots. Everyone let out a yell of some kind, and Quicksilver jumped to his feet, only to fall on his butt as the ship recoiled from the blast.

Sonny was glued to his window, hugging Hina to his chest. More of the curve surfaced, rain pouring down on it in sheets. Sonny could see tinges of red in the froth surrounding it. He thought he saw a wound; then a moan involuntarily escaped his lips once he realized it was an eye. The size of a large pizza. Staring directly at him.

Rufe swore and pounded up the stairs. Kayliss made the kind of sound most girls would make upon seeing a kitten. Hina was emitting ear-piercing yowls, just to let everyone know there was a pliosaur outside. The pliosaur's head slowly rose, mottled blue gray, with a long crocodilian snout, packed with teeth. Something about the set of its eye and the curve of its mouth gave it a sullen expression, as though it personally resented the world and everything in it.

The cannon went off again. Sonny let go of Hina and grabbed the window frame as the ship bucked and lurched. Hina streaked across the room, retreating to the stairs. When the ship recovered, they were much, much closer to the pliosaur. Sonny was close enough to count its teeth. He could see darker-blue tissue inside the monster's mouth, and a scar along the gumline towards the snout where it looked like a couple of teeth had broken off. He could see several holes in its flesh made by bullets and cannonballs, some of them oozing a dark purplish blood.

The creature suddenly convulsed, as if someone had run a massive amount of electrical current through it. It uttered a loud toneless sound and rolled sideways. A thick, fleshy dorsal flipper surfaced, convulsing madly, slapping against the side of the ship, momentarily blocking the window as Sonny bolted from his close-up view and headed for the stairs, making it up to the next deck before he collapsed, heart pounding, a small whimpering sound leaking from his throat. He didn't want to be here. He wanted to be safe in a bed that wasn't moving, in a place where nothing was trying to kill him. He was full of rage at all the grownups who had let everything happen. He had peed on himself, just a little but enough to make him deeply embarrassed. Overlaying all of that was a thick helping of sheer terror.

Hina yipped at him but refused to climb any higher. The ship protested even more than usual, and everyone else on board was screaming right along with it. Sonny turned his face to the sky, letting the rain wash it. He watched the sails churn as the sailors struggled to get them facing in the right direction.

He saw the head of a pliosaur casting a shadow down on the ship. Taller than the sails, taller than the mainmast. This one didn't have any cannonball holes in it yet, and the cannon fired to rectify that, sending the boat rocking wildly back as Sonny twined his limbs around the staircase railing, clutching it tight.

A spear of lighting arced out of the sky, aiming for the mainmast. The pliosaur was also aiming for the mainmast, with gaping jaws, and it met with lightning instead. The lightning slowed the pliosaur's approach a little, so that it only crunched down on the very tip of the mast, splintering it with a force that vibrated all through the ship. The pliosaur screamed briefly in agony during its fatal electrocution. An indescribably foul smell erupted from its burned flesh as its sullen pizza-sized eye went glassy and it slid down into the sea. The tip of the mast thunked to the deck, landing at the top of the stairs. Sonny could see a broken tooth protruding from it that was as long as his hand.

"You're soaked," Rufe said, quite some time later. He was soaked too, with rivulets running from his beard.

He grabbed Sonny's shoulder. Sonny let go of the railing, discovering he was numb and cramped. Afraid to move, afraid to talk, afraid of letting anyone see how scared he was, just generally and essentially afraid. He had been there when a team of sailors dragged the mast tip away, and at some point night had fallen and he was still there. The *Lono* was still surging its way north, but there had been no further cannons, and no new pliosaurs.

Hina barked below, encouraging Rufe as he got a shoulder under Sonny and dragged him back down to his bunk. Once he got there he checked the window anxiously and saw no pliosaurs outside, but there was a smear of something dark on the glass that might have been pliosaur blood.

A small lantern was lit. Risha and Blocker were sound asleep, and Kayliss was curled up in her bunk sobbing. The doctor was so pale he looked translucent in the feeble light. "Shall I knock you out too?"

"I'm fine," Sonny said in a hoarse and scratchy voice.

●

Cessation of movement woke him up. He slept surprisingly well, possibly because he had taken care of his nightmares while he was still awake. Bright sunshine poured through the window, and the sky was deep blue. And not only that, he could smell something that smelled suspiciously of land.

The doctor was snoring fitfully in his bunk. Sonny headed up to the top deck, where he found Rufe working out on the deck. A few of the sailors were slouching around in slow motion, tidying things up. The ship was anchored near a big field of seaweed, giving off the landlike smell Sonny had noticed.

The captain was asleep with one tattooed bare foot hanging out of the covers. His red bird was grumbling in its cage and grooming itself. Sonny's stomach growled but there was no food in the parlor. He knew where the galley was located, behind the crew's quarters, and he walked past a chorus of snores to get there.

Inside the galley was a slender guy with his hair tied up in a knot on top of his head, and villainous cheekbones. When he saw Sonny he said something, gesturing at his hand. He had a can of bandage spray that required two hands to activate, and one of his had sprouted a scattering of blisters, some of which had already burst. Sonny carefully sprayed a new bandage on for him. They exchanged names, and he learned he was dealing with the cook himself, Hideo Watanabe from Osakobyoto.

The galley was full of nifty gadgets. It had pop-up shelves and slide-out cutting boards, spice racks and hanging strings of peppers and onions. Everything was carefully designed in keeping with the archaic atmosphere, and modern touches like coldboxes were hidden in wooden cabinets.

Hideo talked Sonny through breakfast, which involved a lot of gesturing with his good hand, as they had no words in common. That day's menu consisted of rice porridge, garnished with little bits of meat that hadn't gone bad and the good parts of the remaining fresh vegetables. When it was finished it tasted like comfort food, even though Sonny had never had it before. He packed up servings for the crew and passengers and delivered them.

Breakfast revived the ship, and soon people were moving around doing things. A crew led by Rufe was sent out in a smaller boat to fetch wood, which was needed to patch the mainmast as well as a gouge below the waterline that had nearly punctured the hull.

"And it won't be the *right* wood," the captain grouched. He had forsaken his finery and was wearing his cargo shorts, as it was humid and hot and lacking in breeze. "The *Lono* is made out of wood that has been specially bioengineered to resist suboptimal oceanic and atmospheric chemistry."

"It mostly has to do with oxygen levels shifting after the meteor, when the poles refroze and the oceanic acidification changed," Kayliss interrupted. "My people have been inventing all kinds of ways to gradually reverse that, so people can travel around the world again like they did in the old days. Transmit radio waves through the air, launch satellites. That kind of thing."

"Creating new sentient races." Kai nodded his head toward the field of seaweed and for the first time Sonny noticed it was full of Sirens, their big dark bodies obscured by the greenery. "And dangerous creatures." He pulled a pliosaur tooth out of his pocket and dropped it on the table in front of her with a thunk.

"I wish you hadn't killed them. If you have repellant you can sail right alongside them. They're oxygen makers too. It converts in their intestines, and then they fart." Kayliss was looking unusually alert and interested. Sonny thought she smelled especially bad today, speaking of farts. The metal key was rusting away against her flat and boring chest, her lower legs were covered with dark hair and she was getting pimples. He had a pimple himself in fact, right in the center of his forehead, not quite ready for squeezing. "It's already bad out here," Kayliss went on. "It's not like we're making it that much worse, and nobody ever comes this way."

Risha's leg hair was fine and silky, and when humidity clung to it her legs looked like they were coated in magic pixie dust. Today the hair on her head was in several little braids twisted into a big braid. "You've only been this way once yourself, isn't that right?"

"Last month, I think. I'm not sure what day it is."

"April fool's day," said the doctor.

"January twenty-eighth." Kayliss frowned. "It seems so long ago. Anyway, I lost my mother, and they told me I was assigned to submarine duty. I went to Chelisary with a bunch of the others, spent a couple of weeks there, then they sent us on a mission."

"My sincere condolences on the loss of your mother," the captain said.

Sonny closed his eyes for a moment. A truly friendly person would say something kind at this point. He was only pretending to be a friendly person, and deep inside him there was a warm spark of satisfaction at her suffering, and the beginnings of rage over the fact she would proceed to inflict pain on other people a couple of months later despite knowing how it felt. He focused his eyes on the deteriorating key she was wearing, sitting at the center of a big rusty stain on her chest. "Yeah, I'm sorry. That's tragic."

"I would hate to lose my mother," Risha said. "Even though we don't really get along."

Kayliss glanced around at them. "Your mothers are all still alive?"

"Mine worries about me." Kai smiled. "She helped build the *Lono* so she could make it as safe as possible. Most of my family are shipwrights, out in Carquinez."

"We all lose our mothers at sixteen." Kayliss shrugged. "Then it's time to be an adult."

The doctor cleared his throat and scratched at his pale, bony chest. He was pink with sunburn at the moment but that would clear up overnight. "The country organized under the name of Dysphoric Szystems, Incorporated, known familiarily as Dysz, with its principal headquarters in Chelisary, has been in deep water with Ambit ever since the end of the War over its lack of genetic diversity," he said. "The last several generations include individuals who are taller, shorter, darker, lighter, even female, but they are all basically clones derived from the DNA of one particular man, Adrian Qoro." He rolled his eyes and added, "with a Q."

"Interrogations go much more smoothly when nobody is stomping around being intimidating." Risha bit the end off her thread and held a silky blue garment up to the sun. Apparently it pleased her, and she puddled it up in her lap. "We can even argue if we want to."

"Ambit has been concerned about the lack of diversity in Dysz," Blocker said. "We have a member nation whose population is entirely digital, and one composed of people sealed up in vats. Some are opposed to admitting a nation made up of endless copies of a single person. Dysz came up with a creative solution."

"You grabbed my family and all those other people to force them to be citizens of your country."

Sonny folded his arms. Part of his brain kept repeating the word "friendly," but the rest of his brain wasn't listening. "So you wouldn't get kicked out of Ambit."

"If they get kicked out of Ambit nobody will spring to their defense," Blocker said. "Open season."

"It's pretty much guaranteed your people will be well cared for," Quicksilver interrupted, reaching for Sonny's arm. "They're needed. Essential. Precious. Perhaps you could use a nap."

Sonny pulled his arm away and used great mental effort to force his face into a smile. Kayliss actually looked ashamed, with flaming cheeks, and that made him a little happier. "It wasn't my idea," she said. "I'll do whatever I can to help get them back. I'm sorry, Sonny."

Her fist clutched around the key, causing several grimy flakes to work loose and drift over her grubby clothes. Sonny started to say something to the effect that she'd better do just that when he noticed Watanabe had entered the room and was carrying on a hushed conversation with Kai. They mentioned his name, and pointed at him, so he stood up, glad for an excuse to turn his back on Kayliss.

"Watanabe-san would like me to tell you that we have a lovely catch of fish for tonight's dinner, and your assistance is required in the kitchen. Assuming, of course, you are still interested in offsetting your passage by performing labor."

"Absolutely," Sonny said in a positive, friendly sort of way as he followed Watanabe to the galley.

●

He had never killed a fish before. He had seen plenty of tourists parading their catches at the wharf but locals didn't fish very often. They seeded the waters several times a year with hatchlings raised in a lab so the tourists would have something to catch. Sonny had done this himself on school field trips. Most of the seafood his family ate was vatgrown tissue that came in smooth regular oblongs in various flavors, similar to meat.

Watanabe flipped open the lid of a locker full of seawater and mostly living fish, some of them as long as Sonny's forearm. He gestured at a rack of knives mounted on the wall. When Sonny hesitated, Watanabe beckoned over another sailor for a demonstration. Grab the fish just so, pin it down on the chopping board, aim it so it bleeds into the basin. Slash its throat and don't let it wriggle away during its death throes.

By the time he returned to eat dinner with the passengers, Sonny had murdered and eviscerated over thirty fish. The first one had been the hardest. He had also boiled a net bag full of live shrimp, and he had cut one of his knuckles beheading them and peeling off their shells. He had grated ginger, pressed garlic and chopped onions until the tears ran down his cheeks. He had prepared Hina's seared filet, with a side order of choice fish bits chosen by Watanabe, which she devoured eagerly. Everyone praised his efforts, and even more important, they ate every bite.

Rufe's crew came back after a couple of days, floating a chain of several logs behind their boat. The *Lono* then limped to an island off the shore where everyone made camp while the logs were turned into spare parts and Watanabe turned the lumber scraps into a fragrant barbecue. Sonny learned a basic kitchen vocabulary in Japanese, and slew many more fish.

Their island vacation lasted several days, and Sonny spent most of it cooking. He chased Hina up and down the beach and swam in the gentle surf during his breaks. He met Watanabe's wounded assistant Saito, who was bored and wanted his job back, and helped to the extent he was able.

Risha had made the ruined silk into colorful sundresses for all the women, and Blocker looked slightly healthier in rainbow colors. Her skin had lost its grayish cast and she seemed to move easier despite her bulky splint, stained with seawater and ash. Her thin, muscular limbs were bare and her splinted leg was splayed to the side, showing a patch of regenerated skin streaking across her thigh, reddish tan in contrast to her default dark brown.

"Can't land in Bonterra dressed like vagabonds," Risha said as Sonny delivered a pitcher of chilled desalinized seawater with a couple of drops of lemon extract to the area where everyone was lounging, under a canopy made out of the mainsail. "Not women, anyway."

"Held to a higher standard?" Rufe scratched his beard, which had come in dark and full. Quicksilver had a layer of rakish stubble, and Sonny felt something vaguely fuzzy on his cheeks. He realized it had been a while since he looked at a mirror.

"We're generally the ones holding the money." Risha sighed and that gloomy expression started to creep across her features. Usually once it took hold she'd be silent and withdrawn for a couple of days, according to the information Sonny had compiled from constantly sneaking glances at her.

"That's hardly fair." Rufe grabbed the pitcher and filled her glass with an exaggeratedly long pour, handing it to her with a flourish.

"I heard women can't own money in Vanram, and that's not fair at all." The cloud lifted from her face a little and she smiled at him.

"There's a good reason for it. Back in the early years of the War our women began having difficulty getting pregnant."

"All those mods your great-grandparents got to make yourselves huge and musclebound had nothing to do with it." Kayliss said, softly. Rufe threw her a brief irritated glance.

"I believe your people provided the mods, and told us they were safe. Women who can't have babies, or who choose not to have them, are the same as anyone else. They get jobs, get married, have their own money, whatever. The women who can have babies are special. We don't want them leaving. Therefore, they own nothing, and it's all in their current husband's hands."

"Does he keep her chained up in the basement?" Risha wrinkled her nose.

"Do you think you could keep a female version of me chained up in the basement?" He did something flirtatious with his eyebrows that made her giggle. Sonny felt vaguely irritated by this. "They're not as big as us, but you still don't want to cross them. They've all got rich men lined up to give them a life of leisure if the current one disappoints them, even the repeat widows. One of my sisters went through seven husbands in as many years. A fertile woman would have to have a body count in the triple digits before anyone would even think of asking her to please calm down."

"Do you have a big family?" She wiggled her eyebrows back. Sonny didn't like that at all.

"Fourth wife, fifth son." A similar cloud worked its way across Rufe's face. "My dad was a general. They get more action than everybody except pro athletes. Lost him on the very last day of the war."

He stood up and dashed toward the water, diving in with a splash and swimming out to sea. Risha's own cloud returned and she sighed, and Sonny took the empty pitcher back to Watanabe's camp, where it was time to stir the marinade.

●

They all cheered when the *Lono* popped upright after they hauled it back into the sea. They sailed along for the rest of the day and anchored for the night, and in the morning the wind went away.

The sails hung limp from the masts. The deck turned into a griddle that would blister your feet if you stood on it too long, and the hold was as hot as a sauna. Hina took to sleeping on top of the drain by the stairwell during the daytime, and you had to step over her if you wanted to escape. They spent an entire day sitting still. They spent the next day doing the same thing, and the day after that.

"When ancient mariners spoke of the doldrums, this is what they meant," the captain informed them over a supper of cold noodles with shrimp.

"Probably has to do with the volcano," Kayliss said. "Inversion layers."

"Can't those other Sirens do their ..." Risha looked up at him with big eyes, but the captain shook his head.

"Nepenthe's the only one with any interest in interacting with humans that I've ever met. They're off in their own world. I gather she told them we were non-hostile."

"They pointed us toward the nearest island with trees," Rufe said. "With arrows floating on the water. Then they guided us right back."

"And I suspect you may be correct with regard to the volcano," Kai said, nodding in acknowledgment toward Kayliss.

The volcano hadn't spit ash toward them in a while but it was still shooting a column of smoke into the sky. Kai brought out the globe to show them. "There are three ways by which one can exit the Caribbean and enter the Pacific. You can hug the south coast of Namerica and pray for wind, as we are now doing, which nobody else ever does, and perhaps we now know the reason. You can head south of the cluster, along with all the ships carrying freight." His finger sliced across what once was Baja California. "Or you can head along the coast of Samerica. That route is not advised."

"Mangancla," Rufc said. Kai nodded. Blocker moaned, and the doctor reached over and squeezed her hand.

"We're approximately north of it. I wouldn't sail near it."

"That's where your people live," Rufe said to Kayliss in an accusatory way.

"We're south of the cluster. And intelligent enough to evacuate if it's dangerous." Kayliss folded her arms defensively.

"The danger isn't necessarily from volcanoes," Blocker said. "It has to do with all the poisons you've put into the water, and all the monsters you made to swim in it, and mostly from the city of Manganela itself. Most poisonous place on the planet. Probably catch a dose of something fatal if you get closer than a couple hundred meters."

"You got out right before it happened." Rufe pointed his accusatory finger at Quicksilver. "And you owe me a motorcycle."

"I left it with an enlisted man."

"You bailed out the day before I got in." Blocker said. She flashed a big toothy grin. Quicksilver and Rufe clasped hands with her.

"All three of you were there?" Risha looked incredulous. "I remember when it happened. I was in college. We had a candlelight vigil."

"I was with Ambit then." Blocker took a deep sip from her mug of tea, tasting it thoroughly. "I went deep cover so I could stay in Argalia because it's such a beautiful city. Got a nice low-impact government job with occasional latitude to supplement my income with bribery. Reported to Ambit the whole time. Kept an eye on things. Didn't do such a good job."

"Bribery. You admit it." Kai made a disgusted sound. "Occasionally I regret my decision not to throw you over the side."

Rufe stretched his arms out above his head, displaying his musculature. "I would probably get a little bit emotional if such a thing were to happen."

"If anyone were to get too emotional I might have to sedate them for a while," Quicksilver contributed, studying his fingernails.

The parlor was tense and silent for several minutes. Kai's red bird clucked softly in its cage, mimicking a ticking clock. Sonny mentally tracked the progression of a droplet of sweat as it sprung from his forehead, worked its way over his collarbone and trickled down his belly.

Kayliss shoved her chair back. "Do you pus-oozing assholes have any clue how many times I've fantasized murdering every last one of you? I could probably sail this ship myself. You especially, Rufus Hotshot Marshall. Crush your skull while you're sound asleep. You all have to sleep at some point. But I haven't. Do you want to know why? Because I promised."

She pointed to the disintegrating key hanging against her chest. Blocker reached over to take her arm in a calming sort of way. Kayliss stiffened against her touch but didn't reject it. "We cut a deal," Blocker said. "She's under my protection. I'll see she gets treated fairly until she is officially taken into custody. In return, she has agreed to take care of me so I can survive long enough to do that, follow orders and mind her manners."

"Piss on your manners," Kayliss grumbled, bringing back the uncomfortable silence.

Sonny broke it. "What exactly happened in Manganela?"

"They don't teach it in school?" Blocker asked, after a long pause.

"Not in my school. I've seen a few movies. You know, scorpion tanks."

Rufe laughed a small echo of his prior laugh. "Scorpion tanks. It figures."

"I know they don't teach it in your school," Blocker said to Kayliss, and she shook her head.

"It happened seven years ago," Quicksilver said. "And a handful of days."

"There hasn't been anything as bad since." Blocker stared into her tea mug. "A third of a million people dying all at the same time. Tell me what you children know of history before the domes."

"Dinosaurs, Romans, castles, trains, movies, computers." Sonny shrugged.

"Aeroplanes and rocket ships," Kayliss added in a wistful voice indicating she clearly felt left out by missing them. "We had enough time to make the domes before the meteor landed, and there was room for everyone who wanted in, but some people didn't want in, and they all died. We stayed in the domes for a hundred years, then we came back out and went our separate ways."

"Some of the other domes wanted to go off and form their own faction, and everyone from the countries that later formed Ambit fought them," Blocker said. "All the soldiers and all the scientists headed to the west coast of Samerica to duke it out with the rebels, and after they won they split into two countries: Vanram and Dysphoric Szystems, Incorporated. Not long after that, they started mixing it up with each other, and we refer to that as the War, with a capital W, since it's the only one that has occurred in the Mericas in the centuries since we left the domes. Everyone else manages to get along. Except for you."

She pointed a couple of bony fingers at Rufe and Kayliss for emphasis.

"We barely get along with each other," Rufe said. "At first we went through a period that lasted a couple decades where we couldn't hold an election because both candidates would turn up mysteriously dead before the votes were counted. We'd just been through some gruesome fighting with the rebels and Dysz was turning on us, and people were crazy. Finally this one guy, Premier Verra, managed to live long enough to be sworn in, even though he'd been poisoned with something that must have been eating away at his brain. He passed a law stating that if you managed to kill the incumbent on the spring equinox, you could have his job, but if you assassinated a politician at any other time, all the opposing parties had to cough up a huge fine regardless of whether they had anything to do with it. Kind of like making the whole squad do pushups if one guy screws up. Then he added some flowery language about the glory of battle, and ordered a statue of his dog to be erected in the capitol square, and gave half the treasury to disabled veterans, and decriminalized gambling. He died shortly after midnight, and the thing is still law. It's framed in the capitol building with a big bloody handprint on the side, preserved for centuries. He gave it a title, in his mother tongue, which translates as the decree of the midnight sunshine, or the bright evening, or the sunny night. Everyone just calls it the Equinox Decree, and kids put on school plays every year to commemorate it. I got to be Verra once. Usually I played one of the assassinated politicians."

"That would make a good movie," Sonny mused.

"It would," Rufe nodded. "The Equinox is a big deal in Vanram. It's the day the War ended, the day Manganela died. No doubt that's the reason our friends dropped by to help us celebrate."

"There was a siege." Blocker cleared her throat and took over. "The city's name was Maricela, but everyone started calling it Manganela. A joke, because a manganela is something they used back in the days of castles, to fling rocks and dead animals and shit at the enemy. The siege had been going on for years. Big old army camp right outside of this glowing, streamlined, enclosed city, sitting up high on a cliff with its back to the sea. Vanram couldn't get in, and Dysz wouldn't come out. At some point Captain Rufus there got himself placed in charge of it, despite being a young boy with peach fuzz on his cheeks barely older than yourself."

"I was twenty-one," Rufe objected. "My dad put me there because I was drinking too much and he thought it would dry me out. The only combat I ever saw was with the drones they'd send out of Manganela sometimes to mangle and demoralize us. A drone did this." He pointed to his eye as Blocker resumed.

"Ambit agreed they both had grievances, and nobody could figure out who started it. They agreed to let two of its members fight it out if they stuck to a set of rules of engagement. No biological weapons with aftereffects lasting more than ninety days. No butchering civilians and displaying their mutilated corpses on billboards. The fact those rules had to exist might indicate how dirty the fighting was before we stepped in. Now, I'm originally from Scose, and my background has always been in search and rescue, and I trained in the deep snow. Naturally they sent me out to a hot slab of desert to travel around collecting monitor readings and complaint forms. That's what I was doing at Manganela."

The captain produced a small flask and held it toward Blocker in a querying gesture. She nodded and extended her teacup, and he poured in the last of the flask's contents. The final rays of sunset flared bright around her.

"I was in the infirmary when she arrived," Rufe filled in while she sipped. "Recovering from this. You've never had a headache until you've had to break in an artificial eye, believe me. A drone shot me in the face while I was fighting with Aiello Qoro."

"Aiello." Kayliss pawed at her sweat-spiky hair.

"On paper, Manganela had no soldiers, but we caught Aiello prowling around with a gun. An anonymous informant produced a video of him operating drones. We decided he qualified as a soldier and took him prisoner. He surrendered, and cooperated." Rufe nodded toward Kayliss.

"Then the war ended. Manganela was the last Dysz outpost on the mainland. They had moved their government to the island of Chelisary." Blocker's hand trembled as she set her teacup into its notch on the table. "Half the army showed up so they could dress up in their finest dress uniforms and march into Manganela and have themselves a great big photo op. Everyone wanted to see these people who had been locked up for years in their shiny self-sustaining city. You could call them up and talk to them, they were doing business in the real world all this time. They just couldn't go outside, and the army made certain nobody took anything inside. They were growing their own food in there, reclaiming seawater, running around in simulated environments. They didn't need the outside world at all.

"The doors opened and everyone went in. I didn't go in. I was a neutral observer, it wasn't my day. Rufe's daddy went in, and a bunch of his brothers. A few minutes went by and we realized we hadn't heard anything, and nobody had come out to stand in the sunshine. The commander selected someone to go look inside and that person was me. So I went inside. And everybody was dead." Blocker bent her head. A tear ran down over her cheekbone. "Too late to restore them, and too many."

"Over three hundred thousand civilians," Rufe said. "Nearly eight thousand soldiers. My father, my brothers." He snapped his fingers. "Every single citizen of Dysz, in fact, who is not a Qoro."

"Aiello said he could cancel the self-destruction, and that it was going to spread all manner of plagues and contagions if he didn't. Dysz had made it known that various containers of deadly bacteria were implanted in their walls so that breaching them could result in the devastation of humanity, but they weren't particularly concerned. So I went with him. And he lied. Ran inside, shut the door, killed some more people in the process and gave me a blast of something noxious right in my left hip, which is why my pelvis had to be reconstructed, which is why I walk with a limp, which is why I fell off the damn dock."

Kayliss had gone nearly as pale as Quicksilver. "I never ... they didn't tell me any of this stuff. I didn't know."

"I had him on camera, though." Rufe ran his fingers through his beard, making it look even more barbaric. "An enemy soldier, accepting full responsibility for Manganela. After the surrender had already been officially announced. And I made sure the rest of the world knew about it. Not that they did much, aside from register shock and disgust, but it did get Ambit to start an investigation."

Sonny was gasping. He was nauseous, and thought he might even pass out. The air was a thick, wet blanket occasionally studded with fat flakes of ash, demon butterflies that left smudges on their faces and clothes, and he didn't think he could sit upright under its weight for much longer. He stared through the window. The full moon had come and gone, and it was too hazy to see the stars, so he fixed his gaze on haze until he got a handle on himself.

"I could talk about it all night," Blocker said. "But I've already got enough nightmares lined up."

Kayliss, the ugliest, smelliest and most repulsive girl in the universe, was in tears. She looked even uglier crying. Sonny wished his eyes were laser beams that could burn holes in her. He wished he could magically transform her into a fish, and filet her for dinner.

●

They all had nightmares. Rufe woke up sobbing like a baby more than once. Sonny dreamed of cities full of zombies and woke to Hina urgently licking his face. The sails still hung limp. In the afternoon, they

lowered a longboat, tied a line to the *Lono* and began
to row.

Rufe provided most of the power. The captain
and crew did their share, and Sonny sat amidst them,
struggling with the unfamiliar motion. Quicksilver
declined, which meant he was in shape to repair their
sunburns and blistered hands when they climbed back
aboard at sundown. Kayliss declined the first day of
rowing but she was there for the second, hauling on
her oar without complaint and bearing her blisters
stoically.

They rowed for four days, towing the ship
behind them. There was a mild current running
against them, and sometimes they had to fight the
Lono as it tried to drag them backwards. They rowed
for six hour stretches, in two alternating crews, and
they napped when they could. Sonny's arms became
accustomed to rowing. Rufe would sometimes
entertain them with jackhammer-beat poetry, which
typically told the story of some feud or showdown. He
explained that was the kind of music you made when
you couldn't get a signal because the enemy was
messing with your power source, and they'd already
blown up all the musical instruments, and all you had
left was angry voices. The sailors enjoyed listening to
him, although it was hard to tell whether they could
comprehend his lyrics or just admired his spirit.

On the fifth day they were rewarded with a puff
of breeze that fluttered the sails. They celebrated by
sailing through the night, and then they sailed for two
days more. Finally the town of Austin appeared to the
north, a cluster of white buildings hugging the coast.
Tiny, compared to Sonny's expectations. A steep cliff
rose behind it and he could see a black line of train
tracks climbing to the north.

Risha, sitting beside him as the longboat splashed into the sea, burst into tears.

Sonny wanted to embrace her and comfort her. Instead he patted the back of her hand. She squeezed his fingers. She had insisted on dressing the women in new silk outfits she had made, ankle length dresses with low necklines that revealed cleavage, or in the case of Kayliss, where cleavage would be if she had any. Her short shaggy hair looked incongruous with her flowing silk.

Sonny was dressed in sailors' rejects, the same as Rufe and the doctor, but at least they were clean. Kai was dressed more formally, in his purple jacket. His braids were tied back in a carved leather clasp, and he was wearing plenty of bone and wooden jewelry in his ears and around his neck. Beside him was a large steamer trunk. Nguyen would be taking the *Lono* to Carmelita for more repairs, rejoining the captain in Deuce.

Austin was a shallow water port which mostly did business with flat-bottomed barges that sailed up and down the Colorado River to hook up with the railroad. They did have fishing boats, and the *Lono* was anchored near a cluster of them. The buildings were whitewashed stucco with roofs made of colorful tile, and flowers growing everywhere. Sonny could see a few families playing on the beach. It was a small and bucolic place, a sharp contrast to Royal Beach with its mobs of tourists. He could see horse-drawn wagons moving along the streets, but he couldn't spot a single car. The air was cooler, with a chilly refreshing breeze from the north.

As Rufe and Sonny and a handful of sailors rowed to shore, a group of people gathered to receive them. Sonny counted eleven of them, dressed in blue double-breasted uniform jackets with gold epaulets.

As their keel crunched sand, the uniformed people, who all had beards except for two women, drew their weapons in one coordinated fluid motion. Guns. Big, heavy ones with decorated grips.

"Step away from the boat," boomed the voice of the one who was apparently their leader, a graybeard with extremely broad shoulders and double-layered epaulets. "And keep your hands where we can see them!"

CHAPTER TWO: April 20, 3748

Sonny didn't see exactly who fired as he was getting out of the boat, slowly, with his back turned and his hands in plain sight. He startled at the sound of it and froze. Then the shallow waves dragged him backwards, and he fell on his butt. He struggled to the surface and crawled out of the surf. When his hearing came back he heard Hina barking, and was suddenly terrified they'd try to shoot her, but then he saw Risha had her arms around Hina's neck, and nobody was dead, and one of the cops was yelling at another cop who had apparently gotten excited and fired a shot out into the water. Several people were yelling, in fact. Blocker was advising all present that she was a peace officer, and Quicksilver was holding his hands in the air and letting everyone know he was a medic.

The cops would have made Sonny laugh if they hadn't been pointing guns in his direction. Their long-sleeved tunics were covered with gold braid to complement their epaulets, and "Austin Municipal Police Department" was embroidered over their sleeves. Their badges were embroidered right onto their shirts. They all had long hair flowing past their shoulders, and they wore lots of jewelry – wristbands and necklaces and earrings and headbands and cuffs for enclosing locks of hair and rings, all made out of wood and leather and feathers and seashells. They smelled of various perfumes and colognes.

And they were large. Some were even fat. Two of them had their guns aimed directly at Kai, who was standing silently with his hands extended at his sides, next to Rufe, who was in a similar position.

A male cop with a silver beard and impressively shaggy eyebrows finally got everyone calmed down. According to the embroidery on his chest, his name was Sergeant Marlon Stone. He began explaining that everyone was under arrest, brushing off several attempted interruptions from Risha, until she said something halfway under her breath that Sonny didn't quite catch. It caught the other cops' attention, and they began to discuss it.

Stone stepped forward, glaring sternly at Risha, ready to yell at her, and he had just opened his mouth to do that when he stopped, and looked at her again, his head cocked at a slight angle, like a curious dog.

"You heard me." Her jaw was set, and she stepped forward. "Bring my cousin. Nathaniel Petrichor. You'll find him at the railway office."

"With all due respect, ma'am,"one of the younger cops spoke up. "Old Nat's having himself an eight-and-forty, doing some bass fishing."

"Is he off with those boys from Ripple Creek?" Risha looked disgusted. "Fat Billy and them? Didn't know they were still friends after that business with Charley's boat."

The younger cop laughed. According to his chest, his name was Brandon Grove. "So you know about that? Charley's finally got his boat running."

"I – I am so sorry, Mizz Petrichor." Stone looked like he had swallowed something jagged. "I guess I was so busy looking at these strangers I didn't get a good look at you. Looks like you've been through some hardship. Can I get you folks a ... doctor, or a cold drink?"

"These men from the ship want to get provisions. The others are my guests, and they'll be heading on to Deuce after we stop by the house.

They're just passing through. You're not really going to arrest them, are you?"

"Oh, no ma'am. It's just that … we had a report of some terrorism. Something about a sports game. Then we lost connectivity during that storm, and haven't been able to get an outside line ever since, and then the mountain went and lost its top, covered the whole place in ash. We had an earthquake not too long ago, fortunately there wasn't much damage. Forgive us, but everyone's on edge."

A wagon was fetched, drawn by a large and patient horse. Rufe lifted Blocker into it, and they rode a short distance to the Austin Hotel, which had all of three stories. The desk clerk flattered Risha, and laughed as though she had said something outrageously funny when she mentioned they didn't have much luggage.

Sonny sat down on a bench in the lobby, trying to ignore various locals that were trying to sneak a look at him. He watched Kayliss gawk at everything like a provincial simpleton, peering at each of the paintings cluttering the walls, inspecting the little restaurant off the lobby, which was currently closed yet still exuded the fragrance of slow-cooking meat. Something caught her attention and she dived for it. A little shelf hung on the wall with a sign saying "take a book, or leave one." She selected one and did a double take at the cover.

Sonny stood up and headed over. The shelf was crammed with little books the size of his hand, printed on heavy paper. Each one had a brightly printed cover showing people engaged in adventurous, outdoorsy things. Riding horses, twirling lassos, loading a young maiden who had apparently lost her shirt onto a stretcher. In fact, most of the covers featured women with gigantic boobs, and some also had men with well-defined abdominal muscles. He grabbed one called *Trouble On The Trail* by C.G. Hill that had a cover showing people fleeing an approaching forest fire that had already consumed their shirts.

Risha appeared with a handful of carved wooden keys, each with the room number sculpted into the handle. Sonny received 329, which was a private room with a full bath. His face burst into a grin when he heard about the bath, and Risha laughed at him and said something about sending up some clothes, and that she'd call him for dinner. A bellman appeared with a wheelchair for Blocker and loaded them into a gigantic elevator that had a couch in the back, and an elevator operator in a uniform even gaudier than the ones worn by the police.

Once inside his room, Sonny locked the door, just because he could. He placed the old-fashioned key-shaped key on top of a solid wooden bureau. The windows were wide open, and there was a refreshing icy chill underneath the salty shore breeze. His room had a small fireplace, and a big soft bed covered with patchwork quilts and fat pillows, several of which Hina had already claimed. From the window, he could see the ocean, and lots of flowery yards and streets and houses, and a place across the street called the Café Yeehaw. Live music was playing there, guitars and dulcimers.

In the bathroom was a gleaming white porcelain bathtub. Sonny smiled at it for at least a minute before turning the faucets to fill it with warm water. There were accompanying bottles of bubble bath and shampoo and soap, and an old fashioned manual toothbrush, which he immediately used. He found an ice bucket and filled it with water for Hina, and she roused herself from the bed and took a good long drink.

Once the tub was full he sank into a cloud of bubbles scented with pine and sage and washed his hair three times. Cleanliness and privacy washed over him in blissful waves, and he vowed he would never take either one for granted again. He stayed in the water until the dulcimer band changed to a piano and saxophone, and his fingertips shriveled.

There was a plush bathrobe hanging on the back of the door and he slipped into it and spent several minutes staring at his face in the mirror, trying to decide if he wanted to try to shave with the straight-edge razor sitting in its rack next to a mug and a brush and a neatly labeled chunk of shaving soap. Back home shaving was done with a little gadget you held in your hand and rubbed over your face, and it took about two minutes. He wasn't sure he had enough beard to risk cutting his own throat over it. He had the start of some decent sideburns, and the seeds of a mustache. All of his hair was lighter from sun and sea exposure, even his arm hairs, and his skin had darkened to the exact shade of a perfectly cooked grilled cheese sandwich.

His stomach growled at the thought of grilled cheese sandwiches. There was a knock at the door and he answered it, hoping it was somebody with food. Instead he found a guy slightly older than himself, overdressed in the local way with a burgundy paisley duster and leather boots that went up to his thighs. He produced, with a flourish, a hand-lettered business card identifying him as Malcolm Berger, Apprentice Tailor. Then he took Sonny's measurements, and had him stand on a special piece of footprint-trapping paper with damp feet. Shortly after Berger left there was another knock from a man in a hotel uniform, delivering a bowl of dog food for Hina, and a brush, and some freshly baked apricot muffins, and a pitcher of lemonade.

Hina's short coat didn't require a lot of brushing, but grooming her was soothing, especially with live music to listen to while they sat on a comfortable couch overlooking a nice view. Sonny's ears were starved for music. It was strange not to be able to just hit a button and fill the room with sound.

He watched through the window as the *Lono* sailed off to the west. Hina went to sleep with her head on his thigh, and he opened *Trouble on the Trail* and started reading.

The knock at the door startled Hina awake. Sonny dropped his book and stood up, rubbing at the numb spot on his leg where Hina's head had cut off circulation. The room was full of late afternoon shadows. The band had changed to three ukuleles with a stand-up bass. And at the door was Malcolm Berger, carrying boxes and string-wrapped packages and a garment bag on a hanger. Sonny thanked him. He was a little chilly in his bathrobe but he had been so caught up in his book that he hadn't noticed.

Trouble on the Trail was about outriders. These were people who rode around outside, on horseback, in little packs, camping and collecting scientific data and living off the land. All of these things were very important to them, and they constantly gave each other little lectures about the virtues of sleeping on mountainsides and the freedom of not having ceilings. When they weren't moralizing, outriders had incredible adventures. They rescued people from all types of disasters including forest fires, and they explored isolated, rugged terrain. They dug up artifacts from pre-dome cultures, and they monitored the spread of re-introduced plants and wildlife. The author, C.G. Hill, had been an outrider for over fifty years, and the book was a series of anecdotes about all his experiences, accompanied by painstakingly detailed woodcut illustrations. Sonny was already halfway through it.

He unpacked his parcels and discovered three new pairs of pants, and five new shirts, a long duster-type coat, and a pair of soft leather boots that went up to his knees. Underwear and socks were included, and a pair of golden brown pajamas, and a nice leather suitcase to carry it all. Everything was of high quality, with thick cloth and distinctive buttons. Quite different from the clothes he'd grown up wearing, colorful creations spat from fab printers that would usually start to fall apart in three or four months, right when the fashions changed, reminding you to toss them in a recycler and buy something new. In Bonterra, it apparently took much longer for the fashions to change. Assuming they ever did. These clothes seemed sturdy enough to last for a hundred years.

He was dressed and adjusting his boot cuffs when he heard a commotion in the hall. He opened his door and saw Kayliss struggling with a fancy wheelchair, with a woven wicker seat and wheels that had a flower design worked into the spokes. Blocker was sitting in it, wearing a new green dress. Kayliss was also wearing a new dress, in lavender, and had managed to run the wheelchair over her skirts, and was swearing under her breath as she disentangled herself.

"Allow me." Rufe popped out of a door down the hall. He was dressed much the same as Sonny, in different proportions. His hair was trimmed and his beard was sculpted on the sides. His generously cut jacket allowed for flexion of his biceps as he lifted the rear of the chair. Kayliss snatched her skirt away.

Quicksilver came out looking dapper, his jacket reframing his skinny torso as a slender one. The captain already had his own finery, and he also had a new hand-tooled leather belt illustrated with scenes of Bonterran natural beauty, which he needed to hold his pants up as their recent hard labor had deflated the roundness of his belly.

As they concluded admiring each other, Risha appeared to make them more humble. Her blue dress hugged her curves. Her hair was a waterfall of honey and molasses and cola and lager and stout. Her sweet round face was dusted lightly with makeup and she smelled of flowers.

They all stared at her, unable to drag their eyes away, until she made an embarrassed little cough and brushed away a few muffin crumbs clinging to her cleavage. Kai stepped forward with a little bow. "Madam, I am most grateful to you for ensuring that I attract a few less stares at dinner this evening. Your hospitality knows no bounds."

"I was about to thank you for the same thing." She took his arm and led them to the elevator. "Time for some home cooking."

They all attracted plenty of stares, seated around the largest table in the hotel's restaurant. Risha waved away the menus and ordered for everyone, signalling the beginning of a parade of rich, heavy, delicious foods. Tart and crunchy salads, steaming fresh bread, chunks of slow-cooked meat. Half the population of Austin watched them eat it. Fortunately, most were discreet, eyeballing them from behind the walls of foliage decorating the patio, or side-eyeing them on the way to the restrooms. Sonny understood why Risha had been firm about making sure they were appropriately costumed. These people seemed to spend most of their time watching each other, probably because they lacked wallscreens.

Sonny sat at the opposite end of the table from Risha. That end, which included Rufe and Kai, got several visitors, some of whom seemed to be old friends. Sonny's end of the table included Kayliss, who thought you were supposed to eat biscuits with a spoon. The only locals who approached him were two teenage girls, both displaying wide expanses of tanned and freckled cleavage, who demanded to know if he was related to somebody he'd never heard of. When he shrugged and said he didn't know they took their discussion elsewhere, apparently having decided he was irrelevant.

"It's a trade-off," Blocker was saying. "Either I can sort of walk, and be in pain, or I can not walk at all, and not be in pain. On the ship you'd never know when you might need to get the hell out of something's way."

"We've got a problem," Quicksilver interrupted her. "They want to take the party across the street." He pointed to the Café Yeehaw. They serve all manner of adult intoxicants, and the drinking age in these parts is sixteen."

"Everyone but me." Sonny didn't really mind. Lying in bed reading *Trouble on the Trail* was more in line with his idea of a pleasant evening.

"All of us. There's a good chance they'll ask for paper identification, and they might even go so far as to check the internet. If Ambit has to verify you at a nightclub when you're supposed to be convalescing it might not look good. As for Sonny and Kayliss, either they'd get arrested for not having papers or we'd get arrested for trafficking minors without papers, and either way it wouldn't be any fun for anyone involved. We're all technically in the country illegally."

"We can stay in the hotel," Kayliss said. "I don't mind."

"I have to be able to swear you were with me at all times," Blocker said. "That part's important."

"Have fun," Sonny said in his best friendly voice.

He pushed Blocker's chair to the elevator. Kayliss made him stop at the free book shelf on the way, where she grabbed two more books. Sonny grabbed a couple more for himself. He said goodnight to Blocker, but not to Kayliss, as he manhandled the wheelchair into their room.

In his own room, Hina thumped her tail on the bed to welcome him back. Someone had been in to turn back his covers, and leave a chocolate truffle on his pillow, and light the little fireplace in the corner. It was needed. After sundown Austin was decidedly cold. A mob of acoustic instruments had assembled at the Café Yeehaw to jam away, occasionally interjecting an accordion or banjo solo, and the place was all lit up with candles and lanterns. Sonny curled up happily in bed with Hina and *Trouble on the Trail*, and when he finished it he started on *Stampeding Havoc* by Jez K. Meadows.

●

After dreaming an interesting dream where he had to give cardio massage to a girl with big boobs while fleeing from both a tornado and a gunslinging desperado, he woke up to a bright blue morning. He lay still for several minutes, enjoying his ability to stretch his legs all the way out.

Five hundred years. According to the plaque on the wall, that was how long this hotel had been sitting here. Sonny appreciated the fact that it hadn't moved at all during that time, and wasn't likely to move now.

He also appreciated the fact there was no particular reason to wake up yet, and fell back asleep. He woke up again a few more times until the last one stuck, and he finally decided to get out of bed.

The Café Yeehaw was still partying in a quiet, early morning sort of way, with an earnestly-singing girl with a jangling guitar. Sonny washed his face and sank into a chair to read *Stampeding Havoc*. He was halfway through it when a room service tray arrived bearing pancakes and bacon, and dog food. And a note from Risha, written in loopy letters and informing him that the train was leaving the station tomorrow. Sunday the twenty-first, at seven in the morning. And that she would make sure he had a ticket, and that he should charge whatever he wanted to eat to the room.

There was a grassy park across the street. He took Hina there after breakfast for a game of fetch the stick, and then they walked through the town, touristing. The locals seemed to approve of him now that he was dressed like them, and he thought Hina's company also helped. People smiled and said good morning, and asked his opinion of Austin, and admired his taste in animals. He stopped inside a little museum, crowded with hundreds of years of arts and crafts, run by a pleasant little old lady who showed him pictures of the old city of Austin that used to be sort of near here, within a few kilometers, before the domes, and before whatever had happened to bring about the cliffs behind them.

He stopped in a bakery, where he and Hina were each given a fist-sized sweet roll fresh from the oven, no charge, nice to see visitors in town, enjoy your stay. He admired the gardens, and the horses. There were big horses, like the one that pulled the hotel's wagon, and there were horses smaller than

Hina that trotted beside their humans like dogs, occasionally carrying things in saddlebags. There were dogs everywhere too, and cats, and he was relieved that Hina pretended not to notice most of them.

He stopped outside a school to listen to a chorus of kids singing a song with several interlacing parts. He looked at the Café Yeehaw from the front, a dark cave of raucous laughter and mysterious scents. Right next to it was a bookstore with a shady tree outside. Hina was fascinated by the tree, and couldn't resist peeing beneath it. While she was doing that, Sonny headed into the bookstore.

It had a comforting musty smell. Paperbooks were stuffed into ceiling-high racks, several rows of them, with even more stacked on top in piles that would have been precarious if they hadn't all been leaning on each other. Fat squishy chairs were placed amidst the book piles, and one had a big gray cat curled up on it. There was a lady behind the counter in her own cushy chair, reading a book while keeping one eye on the store. At the moment Sonny was the only customer.

"I don't have any money," he explained. "I'm just looking."

"Are you from that crowd that came in on the *Lono*?" Her eyes twinkled. She was a little older than Risha, with lots of carved jewelry and hair decorations, and her deep cleavage was surrounded by a bodice with books embroidered on it.

"With Risha, yes ma'am." He smiled back. Friendly time.

"This shelf over here is usually for trade. But it's getting kinda full, and you can't really trade if your hands are empty. So why don't you take a few of those, and if you're still in town after you've read them, you can trade them for more."

"I'm leaving town tomorrow," he said. "I could use something to read on the train. Which ones are good?"

"As a general rule of thumb, look for the ones with lots of wear and tear. Sometimes they fall right open to the good parts." She watched, amused, as he selected a stack of ten. She got up and reached past him and added a dozen more, packing them up in a cloth shopping bag. He thanked her profusely and carried them back to the hotel, where he dumped his new books all over the bed, admiring the way they took up physical space. Then he stacked them neatly on the desk and selected a couple that were nice and well-thumbed and took them back downstairs. The hotel had a wide porch full of wooden lounge chairs and he settled himself in one. Hina curled up beneath it.

He was absorbed in the tale of a band of outriders doing battle with a cult that kept a bunch of naked people locked up in a barn when he heard the bump and squeak of Blocker's wheelchair. He looked up from his book and watched Kayliss maneuver it toward the other end of the porch, parking it at the end of the row of lounge chairs and carefully setting the brake. She looked like she'd been practicing walking around while wearing a skirt. Today she even had a hat, with a trail of feathers down her neck that made it look like she had long hair. She was still ugly, and he still hated her.

Even though he was holding his book high and pretending he hadn't seen them, Blocker called and waved. He moved to a lounge chair beside them, stacking his books possessively between his knees. Kayliss had her own book stack, and she glanced at his.

"We needed some fresh air," Blocker informed him.

"Did you have some of those pancakes? They were delicious." They had also been eaten hours ago, and his stomach was letting him know it was nearly time for a refill.

"Very tasty," Blocker agreed. "My appetite is a bit off. Last night's dinner was more than I usually eat in a week."

"They eat a lot here," Kayliss commented. "That's probably why so many of them are fat."

Some of the Austinites were definitely plump. They also had startlingly irregular features. In Braganza you could head into a makeover clinic and pay the bot to swap your looks around, melt away any excess fat, even out your skin tone. As a result, there was a certain sameness to everyone's faces and bodies. Nobody was unusually short or tall, or skinny or fat. Most everyone's skin was a warm golden brown.

In the rest of the world, or so he was learning, faces came in a much wider variety of configurations. Some of them were so ugly he couldn't understand why they hadn't fixed it. Possibly some of them had no idea they were ugly, or didn't even care. There was also a strong possibility that too much exposure to Risha had raised his standards to an impossibly high level. Or that Bonterrans paid so much attention to boobs that they didn't even notice faces.

"I wouldn't mind having something to drink," Blocker said. "Kayliss, would you step inside and order me a lemonade?"

"Inside?" She glanced toward the lobby. Her rusted key bobbed against her sternum, making the stain on the front of her dress bigger.

"I'll do it," Sonny said with a friendly smile. Kayliss had no idea how much he hated her, he realized. He could be nice to her all day long while imagining her burning to death in a big fire, and she wouldn't have a clue.

It occurred to him while he was sitting at the restaurant counter watching a grandmotherly woman wring juice from a fresh lemon that he could probably fool Kayliss into thinking they were friends.

Even thinking about it made him feel dishonest and wrong. Friends were supposed to be people you truly had a heart connection with, or a business connection, or because they threw a lot of parties and needed lists of people that would respond to invitations. Not evil clone terrorists, although Kayliss probably wouldn't know much about friendship at all, given that most of the people she knew were evil clone terrorists like herself.

She was his only solid connection to his family, though. And since he didn't have his own submarine fleet to storm her evil clone island, his only real weapon was friendliness. This was certainly more than a fake business friendship. Lives were at stake. At least some of her people had no problem with killing entire cities in the time it took to blink, and the sooner he could get his family out of their clutches, the better.

He blinked. Tears were clogging up his eyes. The grandmotherly lady patted his arm, concerned. "I'm sorry, hon? Did you want something else?"

"A chocolate milkshake," he said. "Two."

He placed the milkshake in front of Kayliss, serving Blocker her lemonade. He settled down in his lounge chair and began slurping at his own milkshake. It was a work of art as far as milkshakes went. Served in a fluted glass cup jeweled with droplets of condensation, crowned by a halo of whipped cream and topped with a single fresh cherry, sliced open to show it was pitless. The actual chocolate part was dense and rich. Quite possibly the finest chocolate milkshake he had ever had.

"I've never had this before!" Kayliss sat back and smiled, hands clasped over her belly. "What's it called?"

"Chocolate milkshake," Sonny told her.

"You drink too many of those and you'll look like that lady over yonder," Blocker said.

"I don't care. And I don't blame her."

Sonny settled back in his lounge chair with his book, slowly consuming his milkshake. From the corner of his eye he watched Kayliss spoon every last drop of chocolate from her glass. She wasn't stupid, although her mind seemed to be narrowly focused. There was a possibility she would see right through him. It would be sort of like acting, except he couldn't break character. Not even once.

"Sonny?" Blocker nudged his elbow with her knuckles. "I hate to bother you. Could I ask you to run in there and fetch the doctor?"

"Sure." He got to his feet right away and jokingly told Hina to guard the ladies. She answered him with a lazy tail thump. He strode across the street, right into the Café.

He stepped into a cavernous, crowded room with exposed beams and rough wooden tables, decorated with a hodgepodge of wall art. The band at the moment featured a dirty-sounding guitar played by a man who looked like a pirate, right down to the eyepatch. He was backed by a piano and an upright bass. Once his eyes adjusted to the dark Sonny noticed the actual stage was pretty small, in a little alcove set off to the side. The rest of the café was huge, cluttered with booths and tables. There was a big fireplace filling the room with fragrant smoke.

He ran his eyes over the crowd, searching for Quicksilver. The two burly women playing pool were not Quicksilver. Neither was the rangy looking guy with the long beard and the dusty boots. It dawned on Sonny that he was looking at an actual outrider. His pants had their seams on top of the thighs, not up the inseam – an important outrider fashion choice, according to the books he'd read, since it wouldn't chafe during long stretches of riding.

Strapped to his hips were a set of revolvers. Both of these were Red Tagged For Town, with neat red bandannas tied around their barrels. He had read about this too. Outriders all had guns, most often with interchangeable composite barrels and firing mechanisms and elaborate handcarved grips. Outside town, most everyone carried live weapons at all times. Outriders' adventures typically had to do with rescuing people and gathering scientific data, but occasionally they ran into a villain who had to be put down, which they usually did in dramatic shootouts full of witty quips that went on for pages. That all happened outside town.

Inside town was a whole other world. One where guns could only be carried only by law enforcement, unless they were guarded, which mean they were unloaded and had all their safeties engaged, and were wrapped in red bandannas. Outrider stories indicated townies were absolutely the worst thing one could be. Lazy, soft, cowardly, lacking in intelligence. Cowering under their ceilings. To spare their delicate townie feelings, outriders guarded their firearms because it was part of the outrider code to be protective and chivalrous and law abiding and all of that, especially towards weaker folks, such as townies.

"Sonnnaaayy!" Rufe bellowed from a card table across the room. Sonny made his way over.

Quicksilver was dealing, his long fingers flashing their way through a fancy shuffle. Kai was evidently winning, from the stacks of gold in front of him. They were playing against two townies and an outrider with a walrus mustache. Risha was in a nearby booth, chattering with a middle aged couple. Surrounding them were lots of curious locals, as well as a great many pitchers and glasses and plates of sausage and cheese.

As he waited for the doctor to finish the hand, Sonny's eyes bounced around the cavernous room. He noted that there were some flat-chested women in Bonterra, and they wore their necklines even lower; past the navel in one case. He spotted a couple in a corner that might have actually been having sex. He stepped back as someone threw a double handful of herbs onto the fire, filling the room with a dank and heady fragrance.

Kai let out a bass chuckle as he collected the winnings. "I owe you some back pay, sailor." He plucked two of the gold coins from his shortest stack and handed them to Sonny. "Don't get drunk and spend it all."

"Thanks." Sonny glanced at the rearing bull decorating the coins. They felt solid and heavy in his hand. He remembered hearing somewhere that gold held up longer than all other metals, even in the ocean. He tucked the coins in his pocket, immediately thinking of the bookstore. He followed the doctor outside and across the street, his lungs grateful for the clean afternoon breeze. He noticed that Kayliss had finished his milkshake. She had also thumbed through his recently acquired books, and left them in a slightly different position.

Quicksilver squeezed Blocker's arm, making her sleepy, and after that he reached into his jacket and pulled out an envelope made of heavy paper. Inside it was a stack of tickets. He peeled off three and dealt them out. Woodcarvings of locomotives decorated them, and the date of departure had been filled in by someone with splendid handwriting. Friday, April 21st, at 07:00.

"I'm headed back. I've been curing hangovers as fast as people can earn them." The doctor tipped an imaginary hat at them and vanished back into the Café just as the pirate went into an extended guitar solo.

"I'd best go back to bed," Blocker said faintly.

"Need any help?" Sonny looked at Kayliss, who was already releasing the wheelchair brake.

"No. I mean. Weren't we going to have lunch?" She wheeled Blocker carefully toward the elevator and he collected his pile of books and followed, Hina rising from her nap spot to tag along. "Do they deliver it, like breakfast? Or does a milkshake count as lunch?"

"I was just going to eat in the restaurant," Sonny said. "Risha said to room charge it."

Kayliss pondered this all the way to the third floor. Sonny stood back as she helped Blocker transfer out of the chair into her bed, which had several extra pillows. The other bed had books piled all over it.

"I'll be fine," Blocker murmured as Kayliss adjusted the pillows around her. "You can go out and look at the town if you want. You have my permission as long as you don't get into any trouble. If you do, you're a renegade desperado and I was in fear for my life."

Kayliss laughed. She bent over and kissed Blocker on the forehead. Sonny blinked, not really having thought of her as having emotional connections like a regular human before. He backed away into his room, leaving the door open. He put his railroad ticket safely away in his suitcase. The hotel maid had tidied up the room and left fresh dogfood for Hina, who squeezed past him to devour it.

Kayliss appeared in his doorway. "So. How exactly does this restaurant thing work? Is it like last night, with the big crowd of people? Can I have a second milkshake after lunch? Are those your books? Where did you get them all?"

"They're awesome, aren't they?"

"I can't stop reading them."

"It wouldn't be a crowd of people," he said. "Just the two of us."

"I don't like crowds."

Fortunately the restaurant wasn't crowded. In fact, they were the only two people there. The grayhaired waitress giggled at them, and Sonny realized she thought they were on a date, and this annoyed him. He had always assumed that his first actual date would happen with someone he actually wanted to go on a date with, and Kayliss was not in that category. She had her very own category all to herself, as he had no other enemies that he was pretending to like. All of her clones fell into another category, of crazy scary dangerous people that he hated with furious intensity, and the minute his family was safely away from them he intended to proclaim it as loud as possible. Therefore, if he wanted that day to happen, he'd better do a good job at faking friendliness.

Sonny smiled charmingly and lowered his menu. "Everything looks so delicious."

"I can't eat all of this," Kayliss said, putting her own menu down and rubbing at her temples.

"You don't have to eat them all." He gave her a kind, warm expression instead of the mocking laughter that he stifled. "Pick the ones that you want the most. An appetizer, an entrée, and a dessert. I'm feeling a little hungry, so maybe we should get three desserts. And share them."

"Are milkshakes desserts? I don't see them listed. What's apple pandowdy?"

"You know what we should get? Chili and cornbread." According to the books, these were two foods outriders always seemed to be cooking in cauldrons and skillets, over open flames and underneath stars.

Her face lit up. "Yes! Chili and cornbread!"

Sonny ordered for both of them. The waitress seemed pleased by his order, mentioning that their particular recipe went back almost two thousand years, adding more than he really wanted to know about the heritage herb garden out back where they grew all the spices. Kayliss seemed interested.

"I was reading in one of those books about a pollen curtain they have in the central region, where they have all kinds of heritage plants grown from the seed bank," she said after the waitress left.

Who cares, Sonny thought. You probably just want to find a way to turn them into weapons. It figures that you'd waste all your time reading the science parts instead of skipping ahead to the exciting parts like a normal person. "Wow, that sounds fascinating."

"I've never read books like these before. They're not like textbooks."

"No fiction?" Sonny raised an eyebrow. "No novels? Comics? Stories? No movies?"

"Lots of movies."

"Movies with actors?"

"Movies that teach you how to do things, like calculus."

Sonny groaned. "You're missing out on a lot. These books aren't even *good* stories. The kind where the plot kind of makes sense, and the characters seem like people who might actually exist, sort of, and they're all about deeper themes, not just people running around avoiding danger, and boobs."

She gave him a blank look. "Boobs."

His cheeks flamed red, just as their heritage-spice-flavored chili and authentic prairie cornbread served in a miniature cast iron skillet arrived. He dug in. Kayliss carefully watched his silverware method, and cornbread buttering technique, and copied him. The chili was as delicious as promised, and just spicy enough. Conversation gave way to chewing sounds, all the way to the three desserts, but they could only finish two, and the apple pandowdy sat forlorn and neglected as they patted their rounded bellies.

"So basically you would come in here knowing what all the desserts are, and then you would just pick the one you wanted." Kayliss looked at him as though expecting a passing grade.

"Yup. And then you have to pay for it." He awkwardly printed "Sonny" on the room charge slip, using the sharpened quill and pot of dark green ink provided. The waitress uttered a tsking sound at his penmanship. "In some restaurants you have to pay before they'll bring you the food."

"How can you tell the difference?"

"You ask." He stood up and stretched.

"That's what I'm doing, dumbass." She stood up, staggering a little as she adjusted to her new center of gravity.

"Is that how you talk to each other back home? Dumbass and all that? Exotic foreign cultural tradition or something?"

She snickered. "Risha and Blocker have been trying to get me to stop. I would have just lost ten points if they had heard me. That's how we talk to our friends. Apparently it's a threat display to you people, and a sign of disrespect."

"Go sniff a fart, shitlicker." He smiled angelically.

Kayliss let out a loud whoop of laughter. She fell back down in her chair, cackling hysterically until tears ran from her eyes. Sonny stood by idly pleased, having never reduced a human being to this stage of amusement before. The waitress shot him a dirty look. Kayliss dried her eyes on her napkin and rose a second time, wobbling only slightly. She was slightly taller than he was. "Ten points," she announced.

"Bring them on, assface." He beckoned her toward the door. "Let's go look at the town."

She cast a worried eye toward the elevator, then she looked back at Sonny, appraising him. "She won't stand by me if there's trouble."

"There won't be any trouble. I was walking all over town this morning. It's nice. You'd like it."

"You're being nice to me." It was a statement, rather than a question.

He was very close to turning his back on her and heading back upstairs to read his books until it was time to catch the train. He either had to step up his acting or face the fact he couldn't even convince someone who had never seen a single actor in her life that he was friendly.

"I want someone to hang out with," he said. "I'm used to spending time with other people, not being a party of one."

"Even if I'm your enemy. And you could get me sent to jail, or maybe just walk me into some dark alley and hit me over the head with some kind of weapon, which men sometimes do, I am told."

Sonny frowned. "I'm the guy who threw you a rope."

He turned his back on her and took a few steps toward the town. He heard the floorboards creak as she followed him. "Wait. Why did you do that?"

"If you saw a stranger who was about to die, but they were struggling and you could see they wanted to live, and you could make a difference, what would you do?" He turned around. She was right behind him and she stopped short.

"I've never been in that situation. I don't think you'd know until it happened."

"That's why you should come outside and look at Austin. Have you ever been in a city full of people that weren't clones of yourself before?"

She shook her head. "Nope." Then she squinted, pointing at something across the street. "What's that?"

It was a horse, and it had ribbons and bows threaded all through its mane and tail. It was a little smaller than Hina, and upon its back was strapped a load consisting mostly of bananas. It was heading up the street in a determined way and Sonny headed after it, keeping a distance so as not to startle it. Kayliss followed him, and together they trailed the small horse three blocks. It trotted up to the front door of a cozy bungalow beneath a shady tree and kicked the door three times, until someone appeared to let it in.

Kayliss was lost in sensory overload. She goggled at people and plants, buildings and animals. Sonny steered her gently by the elbow, taking her to a quiet parklet with a couple of benches and a burbling fountain so she could catch her breath. He spotted the train station where they would be reporting in a few more hours. It was covered in brightly painted decorative trim, and there was an equally decorated train nestled against the platform, plucked out of a cowboy movie. The cars were painted emerald green, with blue and brown accents, and plenty of scrollwork. The engine had a big smokestack with a red band painted around it. Several railroad workers were bustling around, wearing uniforms even grander than those of the Austin Bay Municipal Police.

"The parts that would have been steel are made out of weather-treated composite," Kayliss said excitedly as they checked out the train from behind the station fence. "Sculpted to look like steel. I read that in one of my books."

Sonny jingled his two gold coins in his pocket, intending to win her soul forever. "Let's check out this little store I found."

But when they reached it, they found a "closed" sign hanging on the doorknob. The big gray cat glanced at them smugly from its chair as they peered through the window. Kayliss was impressed and devastated at the same time, ruining Sonny's big finale, and he looked around desperately for a replacement as Kayliss poked around the back wall of the Café, listening to the latest band, which had several people singing in harmony.

He spotted a little shop with an open door. He pointed it out to Kayliss and they headed over and discovered it sold the little carved wooden ornaments everybody was wearing in their hair and hanging from their ears and sewn to their clothes. The store was filled with racks of them. Feathers, bones, gems and rocks. Sometimes carved or set, sometimes not. The carvings covered hundreds of different animal and plant species, although pliosaurs were not included.

Tiny sunsets and mountains and lakes peeked from carefully arranged layers of different colored wood.

Sonny spotted one in particular, and closed his hand around it. A key, of the type he would have thought old-fashioned aside from the fact he happened to have a functioning one in his pocket. A round handle, a long barrel, a couple of stems sticking out. Covered with swirly carving and about as long as his pinky.

He turned to Kayliss, who was pawing through the racks. "You know, that thing you're wearing on your chest isn't going to last much longer."

She gave him a dirty look. "It's symbolic."

"If it's symbolic, then you could replace it with another symbol." He opened his hand to reveal the little key. Kayliss poked her fingernail at it admiringly.

The shopkeeper also apparently thought they were on a date. He gave Sonny several coins worth of change in exchange for one of his gold coins, and threw in a delicate carved wooden chain. Sonny made sure the key was firmly attached to it with knots of ultrafine thread. Kayliss removed the rusty key, which crumbled in her hand, and looped the wooden one around her neck.

When they came out they found a lamplighter, going around with a long torch illuminating lanterns around the Café Yeehaw. They followed him, listening to an energetic boogie woogie piano solo, and when they got to the back door Sonny noticed it was Risha playing. He grabbed Kayliss by the elbow and pointed. Risha had plenty of other spectators; the club was even more crowded than it had been when Sonny ventured inside. Couples were dancing. Rufe was among them, twirling a curly-haired girl with a big smile plastered across her face.

Risha spotted them and waved her arm, playing the bass with one hand. She stepped up the progression of her chords and Sonny tapped his foot, unable to hold still, fascinated by the way her shoulders moved to the beat.

"Everyone's moving around," Kayliss commented.

"They're dancing." He turned around and faced her, taking her hands and moving in a simple two-step. "Try it."

She copied him, moving smoothly without stepping on her skirt. He threw in a third step and Kayliss figured it out right away. Sonny didn't consider himself a great dancer, but he knew lots of moves from dance class at school. There were dance clubs all over Royal Beach, and people went out dancing all the time. He flashed to a memory of one he'd visited a couple months ago, with Lenny and Dan and about a dozen other assorted acquaintances. Sipping neon-colored candydrinks, checking out everyone's new clothes. Flirting and dancing, not necessarily with the same people. It didn't really matter if you danced with the same gender you were flirting with, and there was a particular kind of dance that amounted to an argument, and losing one would cost you status. That was how one did battle in Royal Beach, with subtlety and style. Sonny was having a mild version of one of these with Kayliss, and she was too thick to realize it, and that amused him enough to keep a big smile on his face. He lunged, she ducked back. He snuck in a few half steps for her to copy, she returned them. He twirled her and she kept her balance as her skirt flew out, patterned with rusty hand prints.

Risha did a showy little fill and a band kicked in, fiddles and a steel guitar and a trap drum and some acoustic guitars and a goofy looking twangy blue bass. And a singer who must have been in his eighties, wrinkled and energetic and missing several teeth.

"*When-a I get home,*" the singer sang in a nasal twang, "*Imona sit in the shade! When-a I get home, s'gonna be a holiday parade! We're gonna drink some wine, we're gonna have a reeee-al good time!*"

Homesickness slammed Sonny in the chest like a sledgehammer. He missed a step, losing the argument. He would have been mocked mercilessly for at least a week if any of his people had been watching. Fortunately they hadn't, and he retreated back into the simple two-step as the fiddles and the steel guitar wailed out an ethereal solo.

"*I'm coming fast as my horse can take me, I hope my townie girl don't forsake me, everybody's finally gonna 'preciate me when-a I get home!*"

Risha brought it home with a big flourish and stepped back from the keyboard, laughing and shoving her hair back with a sweaty forearm as the crowd applauded. Sonny stopped the dance and bowed to his partner. She bowed back. Her cheeks were flushed and her eyes were bright. And she had a pimple beside her pointy, unattractive nose, and a smudge of rust on her too-narrow chin, and the same dark beady eyes as those rotten assholes who had pointed guns at him and stolen his home, and he wanted to grab her by the shoulders and rattle her until she put everything back where it belonged.

Nobody took the stage after Risha. Sonny wasn't in the mood for any more dancing anyway. "I'm kind of tired," he said. "We have to wake up early."

She was in agreement. "Let's go back to our rooms and read."

As his final act of friendliness for the night, he stopped her before they opened their doors and clasped her hand. "It was fun hanging out with you."

She squeezed his hand back. "Thanks."

Hina greeted him with a joyous chorus of yips and he rolled around on the floor with her, and told her all about his evening while she sympathetically licked his ear. Then he had a hot bath, scrubbing the rust stains from his hands, and climbed into bed with a book until sleep found him.

He woke up early, just before dawn. It was chilly in the room and he shivered as he dressed and packed up his stuff in his new suitcase. It was a tight fit due to all the books. He made sure his ticket was in his shirt pocket and got back in bed with most of his clothes on, where he cuddled with Hina until the sun finished rising. Once he heard movement in the hallway he opened his door and found Kai lugging his steamer trunk.

They assembled in the lobby and the bellman loaded their luggage into the horse cart, which took them the three blocks to the train station. Blocker's wheelchair wouldn't fit through the door so it was loaded with the cargo, and Rufe carried her into their compartment. There were two long velvet couches, extra springy and facing each other, with tables you could slide between them if you wanted. It converted into four bunkbeds at night, split in half by a sliding partition. The bathroom was next door. The wallpaper was blue and brown stripes, and the lamps on the wall were covered with stained glass flowers.

"We'll arrive in Chianina on Sunday," Risha said, once they were settled in. The engine began chuffing faster, in agreement. "One week ahead of schedule. I can't thank you enough, even though I am devastated."

"Four days of sitting." Rufe let out an irritable growl.

The train slid out of the station, and once it was a reasonable distance from Austin Bay, it blew its whistle. Sonny and Kayliss faced each other in the window seats, both twisted sideways to gape at the view and examine the expanse for traces of outrider activity as the train chugged steadily up the cliff. Once they reached the top and leveled out, breakfast was delivered. Waffles and bacon, coffee and berry juice, butter and jam and three kinds of syrup. Sonny was still full from last night's dinner and Hina was kind enough to help him finish his bacon.

"If I lived here, I'd be fat," Rufe said. "The food is too good."

"It's real food," Risha replied. "None of that nasty processed stuff they eat in other countries. Everything is grown right here. See those farms?"

The farms were far away, but they did see a scattering of clouds way off to the west, and Rufe said he could see some horses, plowing fields. Sonny was amazed by all the unoccupied land. Braganza had lots of lakes and parks and natural areas, but you could still see the city lights from most of them, and you were never more than a couple of hours from all the civilized conveniences he had taken for granted until recently. Toilets that flushed, temperature controls, knowing what day it was, being able to talk to people that weren't standing next to you.

"Granted, it's not heritage," Risha went on.

"They keep the heritage crops separate, behind pollen curtains," Kayliss interrupted. "It's actually a triple-redundant curtain, and they patrol it to make sure it hasn't been breached by wild animals. Most of the plants out here are modified so they have a high nutritional yield, thanks to scientists from Dysz."

"Apples for everyone," Risha agreed. Sonny noticed she had barely touched her food.

"Some of the islands in Carquinez are like that," Kai said. "A few high yield plants, a fishing net and you're fine. As for myself, I like to keep moving around. I tried staying home once but I was so bored I started getting tattoos. Then I ran out of skin."

"That's a possible option," Risha said thoughtfully. Then she began to cry, tears pouring down her cheeks as her expression collapsed into an expression of such sadness that they all reached out their hands to touch her sympathetically. She ignored them all and sobbed for a couple of minutes. Then she blotted her tears with her napkin, pushing her plate away. She went around in a circle, squeezing everyone's hand in thanks for their concern. She blew her nose.

"When I get home," she took a long, shuddering breath and started again. "When I get home, I will be staying there. I was on my last trip out of the country until someone else takes my position. My little sister was filling in for me, and we negotiated a deal where I could spend five months a year out of the country as long as she was in school, but now she wants to leave. And be an outrider. With our father. The trust requires a female heir on the maternal line to be resident in the family house at all imes, and I'm the oldest. So I won't be leaving until my daughter becomes of age, presuming I have one. Hopefully several, to increase the odds one of them will actually want the job."

"Your dad is an outrider?" Sonny and Kayliss were fascinated by this news and she smiled at them.

"He's hardcore. Hasn't slept under a ceiling since he was five. He'd visit all the time, but he'd always go off to his camp at night, and take mama with him."

Rufe started to argue, then he took a deep breath and sighed. "What happens if you just tell them all you're not interested, and leave?"

"My little sister would be stuck in the house instead, and I'd be broke and penniless and disinherited, probably facing a bunch of lawsuits. Thousands of peoples' livelihoods would be affected while the paperwork changed over and all the contracts got renegotiated. My mom's heart would break. My father would be destroyed. My sister Dioni would hate me every morning when she woke up under a ceiling and every night when she fell asleep under one. Someday she'd have children, and they would hate me for turning their mother into a bitter and resentful shell. Shall I go on? I've thought about this very carefully. Fortunately I made it back before Mayday."

"By one week," Quicksilver said quietly. She shot him a stern look.

"My house, the Petrichor house, was built by some of the first people to leave the domes. Most of the town is flat but my house is right on the border of one of the national forests because it was a Petrichor who decided where the border was going to be, so it's uphill from the rest of the town. It's a beautiful house. It's owned by an eternal trust that's been in place ever since, and thanks to good decisions made by my great-grandmothers, and thanks to several generations putting up with this family tradition, I'm very rich. But only when I'm at home." She sniffled. "Indulge me by making my last journey a pleasant one."

The train rolled out of the forest and onto a plain that was flat as far as the eye could see. No roads, no buildings, nothing but green grass fading to yellow under a bright, hot sun that lit up the west.

A woman wearing a vest with trains embroidered all over it brought them sandwiches and potato salad at lunchtime. By then Sonny was engrossed in another book, although he couldn't quite reconcile the vast expanse of nothingness outside his window with the glorious descriptions of nature he was reading. He was vaguely conscious of the card game that broke out, and that Kayliss also had her nose buried in a book, and that Risha only stared sadly through the window without saying anything.

Night fell, and with it came chicken and dumplings, and apple turnovers. They converted their compartment to two cramped bedrooms. It took Sonny a while to fall asleep given his bellyful of rich food, and the train noise, and his stiffness from sitting all day.

The scenery improved somewhat the next day. They climbed uphill into a forest, where they stopped for a couple of hours to clear some tree branches that had fallen on the track, giving everyone a chance to stretch. They crossed a rickety bridge across a river, and slowed to walking speed to navigate a twisted section of track that ran alongside a steep drop. Then there was another long, flat stretch. Far ahead was a cloud, hovering like a parked tornado. As they approached the cloud, they began to smell it. Lots of dust, and lots of animals.

"They're moving the herds," Kayliss informed everyone. "Their droppings help remediate the soil, so they get moved around to areas that need nutrients such as potassium."

"Herds of what?" Rufe asked.

Sonny knew the answer to that question, and he pounced on it. "Arotars. They are a medley of bovine genetics played across thousands of years. Their sources include Buffalo, Texas Longhorn, Silesian, Wagyu, Holstein, Aurochs and Yak."

"Made by Dysz," Kayliss said quietly.

Risha pulled a coin out of her purse and slapped it on the table, pointing to the rearing bull with his proud set of horns. "These. They can stampede and knock a train right off the tracks. You don't want to make any loud noises when we go past."

A few minutes later, the train slowed to a less threatening pace. An attendant came by to warn them not to do anything loud, or hang things outside the window, or make sudden movements. They chugged along at a stumbling speed for over an hour before spotting their first arotars. They came in various shades of brown, although here and there you could see one that was darker, or lighter, or spotted. They had thick, shaggy coats, and although their horns weren't as perfectly stylized as the coin depicted, they looked capable of punching large holes in things. Or people. Sonny thought of the hapless rider in *Nighttime On The Trail* who had gotten gored through the leg, and dragged. The largest of them were even bigger than the cart horse in Austin. Occasionally they bellowed, loud enough to rattle the train's windows.

Outriders on horseback came into view, nudging the arotars away from the tracks. The horses weren't quite as big as the arotars, but the arotars yielded, while complaining loudly. Sonny and Kayliss pressed their faces against the glass.

It took the train most of the day to inch past the herd. More outriders showed up to form a line alongside the train. Risha explained they would try to break up a stampede, in the event one started.

"Outriders do everything," Kayliss said. "Gather scientific data, catch bad guys, deliver mail, take care of medical emergencies."

"Ride around having adventures and then write breathless stories about them." Risha smiled. "My dad should write books. That's what most of them do when they get too old and feeble to ride. Sit around and reminisce. I wouldn't like it myself. I hate sleeping outdoors in the rain. I can ride horses, but I don't really get along with them. I like soap too much. And shampoo."

"This country could use some cleanbeams," Quicksilver said.

"My neighbors will just love you if you start lecturing them about how they need more high powered technology," Risha said. "Go ahead and try. You should be able to heal all the injuries they'd inflict on you."

"You have coldboxes," Kayliss noted. "Even the outriders use those. Dysz invented those too."

"Food is important," Risha said. "We make sure to collect the spent ones, and we remediate more damage than they put out. When it's cold you wear more clothes, and when it snows, you light a fire. If you're interested in news from the outside world, you read a newspaper, and then you recycle it so they can make it into tomorrow's newspapers."

As they moved upwind of the herd, the smell of arotars was nudged away by the smell of the outriders' cook tent. The train came to a full stop and a couple of people got out, apparently to haggle over dinner. They brought back several large, covered containers. A few minutes later, the train was picking up speed as the sun set, and they were all eating chili, and cornbread, and grilled meat, and cactus salsa, and fried cherry pies.

There was a delay the next day when they encountered a rockslide on the tracks, and more delays as they stopped at a series of small towns to drop off freight and exchange bags of mail. The towns were very small. The people in them ranged over a wide spectrum of skin and hair color, but they were all large. Barrel chests, wide shoulders, cavernous cleavage, bushy beards. They were also cluttered with jewelry and embroidery, although the style was a little different than it had been on the coast.

Chianina was the largest town yet. Twenty thousand people, Risha informed them as they rolled in at 15:45 in the afternoon of Wednesday the 24th, a day behind schedule due to the arotars. She left them stretching and rubbing their backs beside the luggage pile while she went to find a taxi.

The Chianina station made Sonny long for a camera. It had polished wooden floors with a loopy inlaid pattern, and paintings of animals and nature scenes on all the walls. Planters were everywhere, overflowing with leaves and vines.

He helped heave luggage into the taxi, which was pulled by an elegant looking matched pair of black and white horses, and then he was sitting again, riding through a town made of wood and tan brick, and decorated with flowering plants, in hundreds of different shades. Spilling out of containers and marching along in orderly rows. Swarming over garden statues, and bursting out of windowboxes. In between the gaps in the flowers you could see wooden scrollwork, and stone statues. Trees arched over the wide roads, keeping everything dappled in patterned shade.

Risha's house was, as promised, uphill from the rest and visible from a good distance away. Sonny thought it looked more like a ridiculously expensive hotel, or a movie set. Not a place where people actually lived. It had columns, and wide panels of stained glass that sparkled in the setting sun, and even a couple of pointy towers. There were a bunch of outbuildings behind it, and he thought he saw the blue of a swimming pool.

Risha hopped down from the taxi and went to open the gate, with Rufe following to help. A woman in a blue dress who bore a strong resemblance to Risha came out of the house, and Risha excitedly waved at her. "Hi Mom! I need some money!"

Risha's mom turned and went back inside the house as people gathered on the front porch. All of them had the same lips as Risha, and all those lips were frowning.

"Come inside, before people see," Risha's mom said as she paid the taxi driver. "You look terrible."

"I just rode through town." She scrubbed her fingers through her hair. "It'll be on the front page of the paper tomorrow, no doubt."

As the relatives swarmed forward to criticize her for being late, and failing to advise she was bringing guests, Risha singled out a teenage girl wearing pants. "Dioni, could you help find everyone rooms so they can get cleaned up for dinner?"

Dioni looked very similar to Risha. Her hair was lighter and not quite as curly, and she had a different shape to her nose. She was not earth-shatteringly beautiful in the same way as Risha, despite the resemblance, and Sonny was puzzled by this. She was a perfectly ordinary looking girl, the kind you might run into anywhere. She also seemed to be in pretty good shape, given the way she helped Kai maneuver his steamer trunk down the hall.

The bedrooms were located in a wing off the main house, and were all stuffed with furniture and decorations which Dioni said had mostly been in place for the last few hundred years, although every now and again somebody got motivated and contributed something new. She gave the closest room to Blocker and saved Sonny for last, showing him to a musty smelling bedroom that overlooked the back of the house, where there was an even bigger lawn, and a corral where several horses were grazing on green grass.

"Are those your horses?" He interrupted her from explaining the fireplace yet again. "It's okay, I remember about the flue switch."

"Most of them belong to the house," she said. "The one with the white splash on his withers is mine. Do you ride?"

"I've always wanted to." He opened his suitcase and showed her his book collection, and she grinned. "We don't get a chance to read about this kind of stuff where I come from."

"Look." She grabbed him by the upper arms and stared into his face. "Is my sister really going to stay home this time? If she's going to sneak away again, I need to know."

He wasn't hypnotized by her eyes in the slightest, even though they were the same shade as Risha's. "She said she was coming home, and she promised people lots of money if they would bring her home as fast as possible."

Dioni digested this information. "All right. If you're still here in the morning, townie boy, I'll show you how to ride a horse. And I'm afraid I'm going to have to ask you to keep your dog back there, with the other big dogs. Mom doesn't let the big dogs in the house because it makes the cats and the little dogs nervous."

She stared pointedly at Hina, who was being extremely well behaved even though Sonny could tell she wanted to run. "Okay," he said, and Dioni led him through a back door, past the corral to a barn, which had stalls for horses and a row of kennels where several large dogs were napping.

There was a separate enclosure with an extra large doghouse painted in bright colors. "Risha used to keep her wildcat in here. Mama made her pen it up because it was killing the chickens."

"Your lodgings, oh exalted one," Sonny told Hina as he untied her makeshift leash. She ran off to sniff the grass. Dioni brought dishes of food and water before leading Sonny back to his room, promising to fetch him later for dinner.

He figured out how to open the window, which replaced some of the mustiness with flower scented breeze from the garden. The bathroom had a floor of mossy flagstones, and a pump for water, and a toilet hidden inside a wooden cabinet. There was a complicated shower involving a charcoal burner and a series of clay pipes, and a large bathtub made of carved stone, and since both of them looked time consuming Sonny washed up in the sink, combing his hair with a carved wooden comb.

He squeezed a pimple on the end of his nose while studying himself in the mirror to see whether he had visibly aged over the last month. He couldn't quite tell, but he was dismayed to learn that his beard looked much more scraggly than it felt. Then he bounced on the overstuffed mattress with its layers of quilts, looking at a series of small paintings showing outriders building a bridge, and cooking meat over a fire.

Dioni returned at sundown, dressed in a dress. She lit his way to the dining room with a candle, which, she explained, was easier than lighting all the individual lamps in the hallways. He found everyone seated around a big table that had room for several more, where he was formally introduced to Risha's mom, Arabella, and her aunt Auralee, and her grandmother Celeste, and her cousin Jerod and her cousin-in-law Davin. All of them wore plenty of embroidered fabric, and jewelry, and accessories. Jerod and Davin both had high maintenance facial hair that made Sonny feel self conscious about his scruffy fringe. Risha looked like a princess, her slightly damp hair piled on top of her head. Sonny passed behind her to get to an empty seat and caught a whiff of soap and herbs.

"... so she planted a bunch of daisies in with his marigolds. He wasn't upset at all. Just said he'd sort it out when they're all in bloom." Davin grinned at them all and Jarod laughed at his joke as though it was the funniest thing he'd ever heard and popped the cork out of a bottle of wine. Sonny slid into his seat as Aunt Auralee brought in the last item -- a steaming pyramid of biscuits – and set it down near a platter of sliced meat and some serving dishes of vegetables and gravy.

"Everyone's here," Risha said quietly, and the table fell silent. She cleared her throat. "Welcome, visitors, to our home, where you will be enjoying our hospitality, until it's time to continue your journey. Family, it's wonderful to be back. I am home to stay. And we appreciate the labors of those who provide us food. May peace and happiness follow us."

Her family murmured about peace and happiness, and raised a toast after Jarod poured wine all around, with very small servings for Sonny and Dioni and Kayliss. Risha settled back into her seat and the food began orbiting the table. "What's everybody been up to?"

"We were going to cut down that fig tree," Aunt Auralee replied. "Out by the porch?"

"I wouldn't let them do it," Dioni said. "I love that tree."

"Hasn't had figs on it for years," Aunt Auralee said. "Just drops leaves on whoever's sitting there."

"I'll put some fertilizer on it and if it doesn't fruit next year, chop it up for firewood." Dioni speared a biscuit with her fork. "Because I'll be gone, gone, gone."

"Did you find anyone to take care of the horses yet?" Risha opened a second bottle of wine.

"A very nice young couple," Arabella replied. "He was an outrider until he got injured, and she's expecting their first child."

"See? You're losing me but at the same time, you're getting three other people." Dioni held out her glass for more wine. Risha pretended she didn't see it.

"It will be so nice to have a baby in the house again." Arabella grabbed the bottle and helped herself.

Sonny ladled a little bit of everything onto his heavy china plate and dug in. The food was as fresh and delicious as everything else he had eaten in Bonterra, and it distracted everyone from conversation for several minutes, until they paused while Arabella went to find dessert, and Grandma Celeste fixed Risha with a disapproving stare. "Where were you this time? And who are these people?"

Risha poured out cups of tea from a pot decorated with a row of rabbits chasing each other in a neverending circle. "I was at a party in Deuce, and some of us decided to go to the big game. In Vanram. So I did that, and terrorists attacked the stadium. It was all chaotic, and I don't remember much. These people rescued me, and brought me back."

"Oh, my." Grandma Celeste fanned herself with her napkin. "Terrorists."

Jarod got up and went into an adjacent room and a few moments later piano music began, light and rippling. Arabella brought in a cake with chocolate icing. She sliced it up and passed a large slice of cake to Risha, along with an irritable look. "What do you think you would have accomplished if you had been killed?"

"I wasn't killed. I'm back before Mayday. I'm early."

"I'll be leaving as soon as the paperwork is done," Dioni said, accepting her own slice.

"I'll get it started tomorrow," Risha promised. "Everyone needs to connect with the outside world, so we'll be heading into town, if you would be so good as to drive us."

"About eleven, then," Dioni said.

"What time do they open?" Rufe smiled charmingly at Arabella in response to a question whether he wanted a second piece of cake.

"It's the same terminal," Risha explained. "The bank has access through a slow line, so you can get approval on outside credit, but sometimes it takes a day or five. The newspaper has a slightly faster connect, and they can get you into the mill where you can get the best access."

"The mill," Quicksilver waved away cake, patting his belly. "It sounds so quaint. Is there a reason we can't get access tonight?"

"Several of them." Risha sighed. "None of them make any sense."

"Using electronicals after dark is just plain wrong," Grandma Celeste said in a stern voice.

Sonny opened his eyes and savored the mountain of warm bedding on top of his non-moving bed. Dioni knocked a few minutes later. She was carrying a pile of clothes, and she explained they'd probably had someone of every conceivable size living there at one point or another, so she'd grabbed things that seemed like they were in his range. He wound up with an outfit that fit reasonably well and included a long brown leather duster-style coat.

One of his outrider novels had discussed these coats in detail. The outside was arotar leather, but the lining was woven from a special kind of wool which would keep you warmer as the temperature got colder, and could even keep you afloat if you fell in the water. Back home he would have looked like he was headed for an audition, but here it felt sort of grand, especially combined with his new pants with seams on top of the thighs. His new boots had already been broken in by someone with similarly sized feet, and he found his own version of Dioni's confident stride as they went down the back stairs and across the grass, leaving trails in the dew.

"Hina can come along if you want," Dioni said. "I was going to bring a couple of dogs anyway. I should probably tell you that I carry a pistol when I'm out on the trail. It's tagged now, but once we're out there I will not hesitate to use it on anything that threatens us or the horses, including Hina. If you don't think she'll behave herself, we can leave her here."

Sonny unlatched the dog pen to let Hina out. "She'll probably attack you if you point a gun at me. Other than that, I think she'll be all right."

"You know that for a fact?" Dioni stepped back as Hina opened her impossibly wide jaws and yawned.

"It's a fact." Sonny nodded.

"If you need hurting, I'll remember to shoot her first." She grabbed his shoulder and dragged him toward his horse, Raspberry, a gelding with a white face and three white feet who stood patiently through Sonny's clumsy approach to mounting. Dioni helpfully called out directions from the back of her horse with the white-splashed withers.

They rode along a narrow dirt road along the back of the house, with Dioni holding Raspberry's reins while lecturing Sonny about how to sit, and where to put his elbows and butt. She listed several things he could potentially do wrong that would result in massive pain, and added she'd give him more pain if he did them. They went through a gate, and found themselves at a trailhead. Dioni dropped Raspberry's reins and glanced back, then she kicked her horse and Raspberry took off behind her.

The horses charged up a narrow forest trail they apparently knew quite well. Hina raced along behind them, yipping excitedly as Sonny's initial terror melted into exhiliration.

The forest felt old. Tall gnarly trees made a canopy over their heads, the rising sun slowly lighting it up and throwing leafy green shadows. Birds sang, butterflies fluttered. The horses slowed as they reached a stream, splashing across and climbing a steep spiraling path that finally broke through the trees onto a ledge the size of a clashball field, mountains ascending into clouds behind them, forest stretching out below them. Behind them were a couple of small waterfalls feeding back down to the creek, flanked by patches of colorful flowers. They could see the house in all its sprawling grandeur, and the rest of the town beyond it.

"This is amazing," Sonny said. And it was. He was familiar with a carefully cultivated version of nature, landscaped for maximum dramatic effect. This meadow achieved the same thing with no intent whatsoever.

"You're a semi competent rider," Dioni complemented.

He thanked her. "We don't have a lot of horses where I'm from. Only people who know what they're doing are allowed to go near them."

"I wouldn't say you know what you're doing yet, but you're on the road." She flopped down on her belly. "That tree has pears, in case you're hungry."

Sonny climbed up and picked one. It was full of flavor and very juicy, and he rinsed his hands off in the stream after he finished it. Dioni was flopped onto her stomach, staring down at the house, and she rolled over and looked at him. "How well do you know my sister?"

"She …" Sonny shook his head. He looked down at the house. It was even bigger than it looked from the inside. The swimming pool was disguised as a natural pond, or maybe it was a natural pond doing service as a swimming pool. Several gardens, and an orchard of fruit trees. He had to admit to himself that his first assumption was that Risha had been one of those pretty girls you always saw hanging around with successful men, like Premier Lance. Not the kind of a girl who owned a house like this. "She was at the game. Clashball world championship."

"Risha hates sports." Dioni kicked a rock downhill.

"It was a big game. Lots of important people were there."

"Did she say anything about getting married?"

"Married?" He flashed on his embarrassing memory of proposing to Risha at first sight of her. "No, she didn't."

Dioni made a long, exasperated noise. "I've wanted to be an outrider ever since I was little. I'd be one now if it weren't for that stupid house."

"It's quite a house," Sonny admitted.

"Full of hundreds of years of history," she said in a sarcastic voice. "If she gets married, I'm the trustee, so I have to live in it until one of us has a daughter."

"You can't be an outrider and still own it?"

She pointed. "Do you see that middle hill? Where the forest breaks up, right at the bottom? That's where I'm headed. I'll never have to sleep under a ceiling again."

"It's a nice view," Sonny agreed, even as he detected her deep loathing for ceilings. He could tell she was about to get all mystical on him but he wasn't feeling it, so he decided to complain. "I'm preoccupied. My family are in trouble and I might get some news today."

"I am sorry to hear that. In Bonterra?" She sat up straight, ready to spring to action in case it was a problem that could be fixed by outriders.

"Nope. Somewhere out in the ocean."

"Breakfast's cooking." Dioni pointed back at the house. Sonny could see a thin plume of smoke rising from the kitchen. "Time for the sleepyhead townies to get up, and time for us to head back down."

Either he did a better job of riding on the trip downhill, or Raspberry had grown accustomed to his mistakes, as the return trip was much faster and easier and far less exciting. Sonny put Hina back in her kennel, and helped Dioni unsaddle the horses, and then he helped her hitch four different horses to a wagon, and bring it out to the front of the house. He found everyone in the dining room finishing up breakfast. Arabella placed a stack of pancakes in front of him, and he wolfed them down. Then, after changing back into townie clothes at Risha's request, he joined the rest of them in the wagon, and Dioni drove them to town.

Sonny mistook the bank for a medieval cathedral at first. It even had stained glass windows depicting trees with gold coins instead of leaves. It was full of dark solid furniture and a handful of serious-looking bankers who were tending to a line of customers. A man in the back spotted Risha as she came through the door and called to her.

The lined-up customers grumbled as he waved her toward a door, and she beckoned the rest of them to follow her into a swank office, full of paintings and bookcases, and enough solid leathery chairs for everybody. Behind a massive desk was a middle aged woman, grinning like a happy crocodile. A little wooden sign on her desk read "President."

She and Risha pretended to be delighted to see each other, and then they exchanged smalltalk before the president went to the vault. She came back with an assortment of leather pouches, heavy with coins, and plopped them in front of Risha.

"For the captain," Risha said, handing the fattest one to Kai. Then she handed pouches around to everyone else. "For medical services, entertainment, sundry acts of heroism and letting me have my way."

Sonny pulled out a coin from his pouch. It was the size of his ear, with an engraved arotar bull on one side, a smiling woman holding an overflowing cornucopia on the other, and "50g" centered at the bottom. His fortune consisted of ten of them. He tried to thank her, but she dismissed everyone's thanks and herded them back into the wagon.

The offices of the Chianina Gazette looked very Roman, with columns and statues painstakingly carved from sand-colored stone. The inside was chaotic and inkstained. There was a gigantic press for printing paper newspapers, surrounded by stacks of paper and barrels of ink. Some people were setting type, inserting inky letters in a big wooden frame. One of them was a woman with short blonde hair who got up and squealed when she spotted Risha. She wiped her inky hands on a rag as the two exchanged various pleasant-sounding words.

"This is Meggy Boggs," Risha introduced. "Publisher of the Chianina Gazette."

"I'm so happy to meet you all! Unfortunately, I was just telling Risha that the terminal isn't available for a couple of days." Meggy clasped her slightly-less-blotchy hands and rocked forward on her toes, giving them a bright smile.

Rufe stepped forward before anyone else could react, standing extremely close to her. "What's the obstacle?"

Meggy stepped back, appraising him. "It's downloading a story."

Quicksilver approached from her other side. "It's a pleasure to meet you, and might I inquire as to the particulars of your download protocol?"

Kai approached her head on. "Madame, you are disappointing people in several different countries."

Meggy focused on Risha, and her expression of goodwill faded. "I don't know why you think you can get away with bringing all these foreigners in here, to threaten me."

They all took several steps back, giving Meggy plenty of space as she turned a dark shade of red.

"Let me see your stupid download," Kayliss blurted. "You're probably doing it wrong if it's taking two days."

"I could make this official business," Blocker said quietly from her wheelchair.

Risha approached Sonny and slipped her flower-scented arm across his shoulders. "This young man suffered a tragedy and was separated from his entire family. Are you going to delay his efforts to contact them even further?"

"Your whole family?" Meggy gasped. "That's terrible! I'm so sorry! What exactly happened? You know, if you need to talk about it, I'm here for you."

"One big sympathetic ear," Risha agreed. She brought out one of the big coins and slapped it down on a counter near Meggy. "Rental fees in advance."

Meggy pounced on the coin. "Jack! Could you come out here and help these folks get online?"

Jack Brooke was the communications technician. He was slender by Chianina standards, with intense blue eyes and ginger-colored muttonchop sideburns doing battle with his braided mustache. He led them out the back of the building and along a haphazard stone path alongside a swiftly moving stream. There was a waterwheel up ahead on the stream bank, under a lazy tree trailing its branches in the water, and a small stone building covered with red warning signs. Jack explained that the wheel provided power as long as the stream was running. When the stream ran dry, they had to power it via bicycle, or mule.

More warning signs glistened on the triple-locked door. Jack opened each lock from a separate keyring and opened the door on a dusty chamber containing an old wooden desk, along with a leather chair that had seen better days. There was a keyboard carved into the desk, tiny leather pads for each key bearing fancy engraved letters. Inside an elaborately carved box mounted beyond the keyboard was what looked to Sonny like a crappy reconditioned deld. It was about the size of one, big enough to stretch across the average person's palm, and the display was flickery, with washed out colors. Quicksilver and Kayliss were both staring at it with their mouths hanging open.

"See, we have modern technology." Risha giggled.

There was a printer in the corner rattling away, extruding a roll of thin, crackly, yellowish paper. Jack lifted the output and studied it. "The story has finished printing. It has to do with an earthquake. Oh my, and a riot."

"Did you feel the earthquake up here?" Risha leaned over his shoulder. "We were at sea. Oh, this is about Vanram!"

Jack sliced the story away from the extruding roll and cut it into pieces, distributing sections randomly. "Sonny, why don't you go first?" Rufe said as he accepted his roll of paper. "Your business is probably the most important."

Sonny sat down in the chair and pulled up his social node. He had to rest his finger on each key for a couple of seconds before it would register. Once he got a connection he had to answer several authenticating questions to prove he was himself, since there was no retina scanner. He looked through the small, barred window to the shore of the stream, where everyone else was lounging in the grass reading their sections of news. He saw Rufe bolt to his feet and let out a shout.

At long last he reached his entryway portrait, a picture of a well-scrubbed boy who bore a vague resemblance to the scruffy-bearded creature Sonny had seen in the mirror this morning. He pulled up a status update, longing sharply for a camera. "Hi everybody," he typed, regretting his choice of such a long word as "everybody" after he begun typing it. "I'm in Bonterra. Going to Deuce, more updates when I get there."

He checked his messagebox, hissing with impatience as useless things like invitations to long-since-passed parties popped up. There was nothing from his family since Marilyn's last post, a photo of them all grouped together outside the house, just before they got in the car. She had left her deld at home after taking that picture. She had rushed back into the house to leave it on her desk, and she had come back out holding her teddy bear. The one she had left lying on the bed at the Hotel Argalia.

Sonny's eyes filled with tears and he sat back. He could hear Rufe outside threatening to kill someone or other. Blocker and Quicksilver were talking over each other in raised voices. Kai was standing near the door watching them, and when he noticed Sonny staring out the window he politely asked if he could go next. Sonny logged out, stood up and walked outside.

Rufe was assaulting a tree. The tree looked like it had seen a lot worse, although he had managed to leave a gouge in the bark. Jack was heading rapidly back toward the newspaper offices. As Sonny's eyes adjusted to the sunlight Rufe turned toward him. "You were there. You saw who killed him. Premier Lance, the guy who colluded with the Qoros to kill everyone in Manganela. He died on the equinox, by my hand."

"Shoosh," Risha said, glancing back the path toward the office. Somebody was rapidly leaving on horseback.

Sonny sank down in a tuft of grass, refusing to answer Rufe. Kayliss came over and plopped down beside him, handing him a roll of printer paper, and he began to read. About a tragic earthquake that had befallen the city of Argalia as it recovered from destruction caused by sports riots. The good people of Dysz had been on hand to rescue several survivors, and had been commended by the new leader of Vanram, Premier Cello. Who went on to give a speech about the bonds of friendship between the two nations, which was cut off at the bottom. Sonny didn't think he was particularly missing much.

"See?" Kayliss whispered. "They are rescued survivors."

"They haven't sent me any messages. I just sent one to everyone I know, telling them I'm here."

"How many people do you know?" She shot him a condescending expression.

"Hundreds," he snapped back. She blinked.

Horses arrived outside and commotion appeared at the back gate as Jack returned, accompanied by Meggy and an old man with an impressive cascade of curly gray hair, dressed in a grand magenta uniform, who identified himself as Constable Applebaum.

"Good afternoon, Constable!" Risha greeted him warmly. "I was about to stop by and see you!"

"Good afternoon, Mizz Petrichor." Applebaum executed a flourishy respectful gesture in Risha's direction. "Mizz Boggs told me you were back, and she mentioned you had brought some guests."

"Why yes I have. She gave them all kinds of trouble about using the only connect in town --"

"Speaking of which --" Applebaum countered Risha's raised index finger with his own. It was wearing a ring shaped like a dragon biting its tail. "Why don't we conduct this discussion at a ... safe distance."

"Fine." Risha folded her arms. "I was headed over to see my lawyer. I suppose we could have our discussion there. Unless you'd prefer that it occur at your office."

"Holly's office is fine." Applebaum headed back toward the newspaper office. Sonny went to help Dioni get the carriage ready. Kai refused to come out until he was finished, and once he was done he grumbled to them about the suboptimal qualities of this arrangement for persons with seventy-nine letter surnames.

"You could always change it again," Risha suggested as they climbed into the carriage. "I think most people came up with new names after the domes. They encouraged it. A fresh start in a fresh world."

"An ancestor of mine selected the longest possible name he could think of upon registering in the domes, in homage to another ancestor as well as to minimize the potential for identity theft. My family has worn it with pride ever since."

They rode a short distance to the Law Office of Chrysanthemum P. Holly, where they were seated around a table inlaid with different woods that formed a picture of a lake in front of a mountain, and served tea. Mizz Holly made certain they were not under arrest, and the constable made it known he was only taking a report.

First they discussed whether Rufe should be charged with punching a tree, which was not technically illegal. Nobody was terribly impressed by his status as a celebrity athlete, but they both agreed the matter could focus more international attention on Chianina than anybody really wanted, and the matter was dropped, and the constable agreed to have a talk with Mizz Boggs about public access to the terminal.

Kai produced a small waterproof booklet bearing his seventy-nine letter name and embellished with visa stamps from around the world. The Bonterrans bent their heads together to examine this, admiring the various seals before Holly added one featuring a rearing arotar similar to the one on the coins.

After Kai charmed them it was Quicksilver's turn, and he displayed his international medic's credentials by making a symbol glow across the back of his hand. He also looked at a mild rash on the constable's elbow.

Blocker was conversant in legalese, and had a discussion with Holly and Applebaum that mostly flew over Sonny's head. They argued over whether Sonny and Kayliss were wards, or unaccompanied minors, or detainees, or refugees, ultimately concluding it didn't really matter since they were heading to Deuce shortly.

"Kay Ellis," the Constable said aloud as he wrote the name on an official looking document. "And yours, young man?"

"Sonny," he replied. "Also known as Leroy Joseph Knight. From Royal Beach, Braganza."

"Sonny Knight," Quicksilver said, with a snicker. Rufe palmed his face and groaned.

"You may want to read up on these issues, Henry." Mizz Holly was middle-aged and plump, and comforting. She had a fluffy little brown dog named Themis who slept in a padded basket beside her desk.

"International law is complicated. I could loan you some books."

"So I'm free to go if I promise not to punch any more trees?" Rufe flexed his skinned knuckles. Mizz Holly passed him a handkerchief.

"I'm going to administer Mizz Blocker some pain medication," Quicksilver said, clasping her hand. "She probably won't be capable of giving you more information at this time."

"You're welcome to come up to the house and ask more nosy questions." Risha displayed her dimples. "Both of you. Give us some warning and mama will bake a pie."

●

"They hate me," she told them during the trip home. "They've hated my family from way back. It all has to do with how we Petrichors think we're so wonderful because our house is on the hill."

"They also hate us because of our money," Dioni contributed from the driver's seat. "I'm looking forward to never dealing with money again."

The wagon clopped slowly back toward the house. Dioni had no inclination whatsoever to make the horses move faster than a casual saunter, as long as they were headed in the right direction. They sped up on their own when they got near home, eager to shed their harnesses, and Sonny helped them do that. Then he played with Hina for a while, until Arabella rang the dinnerbell and everyone gathered in the dining room.

"We kept it strictly family last night," Dioni explained when Sonny asked about all the extra people at the table. The old man from the stables was there, and he recognized a couple other stable workers. He counted fifteen people in addition to the people he'd arrived with, and Risha's family.

"Do they work for you?" The old man was the only one Sonny had dealt with.

"They live here, but they're either not related at all, or not in the immediate family. If you don't have your own house, or if you're an outrider that's gone soft, you have to go find a household with room for you, and you usually take care of some kind of chore in exchange for your room and board. We've got nearly thirty people living here."

The next morning Sonny went for another trail ride with Dioni, and then he headed back to the house while she showed the new man, DuBois, how to do all her chores. When he got back to the house he learned the outbound train was delayed, and they were stuck until May second. "Unless you want to do it outrider style, on horseback." Risha showed them some apologetic dimples. "You are all certainly welcome to our hospitality for as long as it takes, and now you'll get to see our Mayday celebration."

Rufe didn't like this news. He left the house, announcing his intent to find nightlife. Jerod went out to look for him a few hours later and came back reporting that he'd found it, and Kai and Quicksilver headed out to help him enjoy it.

Sonny settled into a routine where he spent his mornings with Dioni and the animals, and his afternoons lounging around the house. The Petrichors had an actual library, complete with a wheeled ladder on a rail so you could climb up to the top stacks. Kayliss could usually be found there, rapidly scanning her way through ancient novels. When his eyes got tired from reading static text, he headed out to the pool, which was a natural spring, with a hot section in one corner. The house had been built around it, and the town had been built around the house.

They invited Kayliss for a morning trail ride once, and it was a disaster. She was so nervous about riding that she fell off, and that made her more nervous, leading to subsequent falls and ever-increasing anxiety. She was also convinced the woods were full of lurking panthers and bears and sasquatches, all of which were popular themes in outrider novels, even though Dioni assured her that most creatures bigger than wildcats hadn't survived past the dome years.

"Most dangerous thing out here is domestic animals gone feral. Usually dogs, sometimes pigs. There's a spider, the size of your pinkytip, that'll make you sick if you get bitten too often. There's also an invasive vine that gives off flowers that a lot of people are allergic to. There's a venomous snake but you don't see those too often. Plenty of bees. Human beings, but those are another type of hazard altogether."

"I guess I'm a townie," Kayliss said when they cut the ride short after her horse dumped her in the creek.

"Looks like," Dioni smirked.

"She's just not used to trees," Sonny said in Kayliss' defense, friendliness fully engaged. "She's used to sailing around underwater in a tiny little boat surrounded by fish big enough to eat you."

Dioni shuddered. "I couldn't do that."

Kayliss returned to the library, seeming much happier after the attempt at including her. Occasionally Auralee and Arabella cornered her there and tried to make her look closer to what they considered feminine, and they succeeded in giving her cleavage. Sonny noticed it when she approached him a couple of days after the ill-fated trail ride. She was wearing a plum-colored dress with a deep neckline that displayed a distinct cleft, lightly dusted with cookie crumbs.

"I want to go downtown and go online again but I'm not sure if I can get past that newspaper lady. She's a real shit sandwich. If you'll help me, I'll try to find out more news about your family," she whispered conspiratorially.

The little wooden key teetered on the edge of her small canyon. Sonny snatched his eyes away. Pretending to like a terrorist was one thing, helping one talk to the other terrorists was an entirely different question. And getting worked up over terrorist cleavage was a very bad idea. He wondered if Quicksilver had given her secret cosmetic surgery.

"Sounds like something that could get us in trouble."

"I could get in trouble for helping you, but I'm willing to do it anyway."

Maybe her side had won, he reflected as they ambled down the shady sidewalk. They were in charge of Rufe's country, giving their version to the press. If they were capable of conquering a nation full of big aggressive guys like Rufe in one efficient swoop, maybe he should back them. They seemed like they knew what they were doing. The one walking along beside him didn't seem to have much of a clue about anything. But since nobody else had offered him anything concrete as far as making sure his family was okay, he would help her.

"They say you and Dioni are falling in love," she informed him after the first couple of blocks.

Sonny rolled his eyes. "I'll bet they say all kinds of things."

She burst out laughing. "It's true. They think you can catch viruses from sleeping with the window open, and that watching screens makes childrens' brains all soft and mushy, and they're always picking on Risha. I kinda like them. They fuss over me, as long as I watch my mouth and don't talk shit."

"No doubt that's a strain, horseapple brain." Sonny swerved neatly to avoid a stack of horseapples in their path. He wondered how Kayliss would feel about riding behind him on a horse, but ruled it out when he realized he would have to touch her. "I'm too young to fall in love with anyone. And I'm too worried about my family."

They walked along in silence for several more blocks. "They're giving me all kinds of books to read," she said. "Not just outrider stories. Fiction, all kinds. There was this one about a girl who was trying to trick a man with a pissload of money into marrying her. It's kind of weird that someone would write a book about that, but I liked it."

"There are all kinds of stories. About all kinds of people."

"Some of those outrider stories aren't true, did you know that? Like the one about the sasquatch? That never happened."

They stopped a block before the newspaper office and drank tepid water from a pump set up for the public. Music issued from a saloon much grander than the one in Austin. Sonny pointed to it. "I wonder if that's the one where Rufe is staying."

"He's right there." Kayliss pointed toward the newspaper office. Sonny followed her finger. Rufe was standing with his back toward them, talking to Meggy. She was holding a big bouquet of flowers. Sonny watched Rufe lean forward and kiss her on the cheek.

"We have to hide." Kayliss pulled at his arm, dragging him toward a heap of foliage. "He's got that enhanced eye and he'll spot us in a heartbeat. I don't want him to know I'm out here."

Sonny felt the twinge of divided loyalties again as Kayliss dragged him underneath a heap of ivy. Rufe had saved his life a bunch of times. Plus Sonny had a definite impression Rufe was doing something very similar. Just being friendly.

"This is so perfect," Kayliss whispered as Rufe and Meggy exited the newspaper office, promenading down the street toward the large saloon, passing by in a cloud of perfume and cologne. Once they were inside, Sonny and Kayliss hurried in the other direction, toward the newspaper office.

"I want to check my messages," he said to Jack with a sheepish and apologetic expression. Jack nodded and unlocked the room by the mill, retrieving a sheaf of printouts as he left them to the device. Sonny logged in with only a few verifiers, since the network remembered he had connected from this relatively remote spot before. He had a flood of messages, including one from Uncle Duke, but nothing from his immediate family or Lenny or Dan.

He logged out and closed his eyes. He didn't care about their stupid politics. He wanted his family, and he wanted to go back to ignoring parts of the world that didn't directly concern him. "I'm done."

It was his turn to watch the waterwheel turn while Kayliss logged in somewhere. She didn't seem to have to do a lot of typing. He glanced at her display a few times and saw dense fields of text that she was rapidly reading.

"Knight, Steven. Knight, Jodie. Knight, Marilyn. Reyes, Leonard. Kral, Daniel." She read aloud. "They all live at the same address on Dragonfly Court in Chelisary Village."

Sonny's knees liquified and his ass hit the floor. "Can we call them?"

"We can't call anyone on the island. Comm is down since the earthquake. They've got the subs out repairing the lines and have sent word the island is far enough away from the eruption to be out of danger."

Sonny mentally filed that information away for later. He watched her slowly and deliberately enter information. "What are you telling them."

"To have someone meet me in Deuce to get me back home, before they put me in jail." She closed out her connection and the screen went grayish. "I guess there's no point in telling you a big lie."

"I have problems with your country. Not with you."

She closed her fist around the little wooden key. "I made a whole bunch of promises, and I'm going to keep them, and in order to do that I have to be alive."

"Do Qoro promises count? We should get out of here before they come back." He stood up. She logged out of her screen.

"Do anybody's? Let's go."

They skirted the saloon by a couple of blocks and happened to find an ice cream parlor. Sonny bought himself and Kayliss a large chocolate sundae to share, wondering if weight gain from all the crazily rich food in Bonterra had caused her cleavage to appear. The news that his family existed as digital data had made him deliriously happy, and he realized he didn't really care if she got away, or if she ate most of the sundae either. Rufe probably didn't either. Their quarrel was with someone else.

After the ice cream, they took a long, meandering walk back to Risha's house, stopping to hear a string quartet playing in a gazebo, and pausing in a museum full of paintings. They arrived tired and dusty, their feet sore and their throats dry, and headed for the pool.

Blocker was wallowing in the shallow end with Grandma Celeste, and most of the other family members were sitting at the patio tables nearby, drinking iced tea. Risha was actually swimming. They were all wearing local style swimsuits that sheathed them in nubbly fabric from shoulders to mid-thigh. Sonny had seen those before, on tourists, and he had giggled at them.

He found himself putting one on, behind a privacy screen of hedges. And once he dived in, he could see the rationale behind keeping your body insulated. The pond was like recently melted ice. The shallows were a little warmer. The hot spring section was giving off steam, and he stroked over there to thaw out.

Risha splashed over to join him. "I'm going to miss all of you," she said, glancing back to Kayliss, who was sticking close to Blocker.

"Maybe I can come back and visit you." For a year, or two, or several. For his eighteenth birthday, when she'd realize he had a truer heart than any of the other guys that might try to win her heart over the next couple of years. He would be very happy living in her house, in fact. Riding around on the trails, reading his way through the library.

"That would be marvelous. You're always welcome here. Everyone likes you."

She dived back into the cold part, letting out a whoop when she surfaced. Sonny leaned back against the warm rocks, looking at the house, and the round moon rising behind it.

●

Dioni got progressively more anxious with each passing day. On Sunday she gave everyone gifts. The other locals were all preoccupied with their Mayday garb, and the parlor smelled like mothballs and boot polish, with bright fabric piled on every available surface. "Nothing ever really goes out of style," Risha informed them. "Of course, nothing is ever really in style, either."

Sonny was standing with both arms extended, trying on a shirt Grandma Celeste picked out, when Dioni appeared with her boxful of gifts. His was a fancy pocketknife with several attachments, and a handle carved with rearing horses. He thanked her profusely as she gave a curt nod, giving Blocker a wooden box with animals carved on it, and Kayliss a lump of amber with a scorpion in it. Judging by Kayliss' quivering lips she was moved, not only by the gift itself but by the fact she had received one.

"I hope you all have a swell time at Mayday," Dioni said. "I'll be long gone."

"May the stars shine ever on your trail," Kayliss said with much serious intensity.

Dioni turned to face her, sizing her up. "This guy is a buddy of mine. Not a boyfriend and not a lover. He's more than that, he's my friend. And he's a decent guy. You do what you can to help his people. Y'hear me?"

Kayliss had gone bright scarlet. She stammered a little and glanced at Sonny in a side-eyed way. "There's not a lot I can do about anything. But I told him I would help. He's got my promise."

"All right." Her eyes twinkled as she gave them one last wave. "I shall bid you goodnight as I prepare to spend my last night under a ceiling."

●

Dioni's horse wasn't in the stable when Sonny went to feed Hina on Mayday morning. Du Bois was there, and the old man with missing fingers. Sonny helped them clean the stalls and feed the beasts. He fed Raspberry a handful of alfalfa and stroked his nose. Then he helped drag the big carriage out into the driveway and park it on blocks until everyone was ready to go.

There was a massive breakfast featuring just about everything you'd want to eat for breakfast, and then some. After they ate, and packed up the leftovers, and tidied up the kitchen, everyone got dressed. Then the garden was ransacked for fresh flowers, and these were woven into hair and beards. Sonny was fortunate in that neither his hair nor his stubble was long enough to be decorated, and he got away with a single white rose tucked into the lapel of his outrider coat.

Which he insisted upon wearing. It contained most of his worldly goods, tucked away in the pockets. His gold, and his pocketknife, and his crumpled and waterlogged Vanram money. And it looked stylish, with its deep vent up the back for unimpeded riding, the leather white and scuffed around the sturdy seams. In the mall back home, they'd call it distressed, except it would be made of flimsy fabric that wouldn't last long enough to suffer any distress.

As things turned out, the carriage was so stuffed with costumes and flowers and wheelchairs that a couple of men in less voluminous clothes volunteered to ride alongside, and Sonny joined them, riding Raspberry, after first changing back into his comfortable outrider pants and boots. He kept the shirt they'd dressed him in, a tunic that came down to his thighs with flowers embroidered all over it. Whenever the coat tempted him into pretending he was in an old west movie, the shirt brought him back to reality.

The town seemed deserted. Their horses clopped along with the street to themselves until they got near the heart of town, where the festival had engulfed the town square, extending to the creek that powered the mill, while leaving a wide perimeter around the dangerous computer terminal. The streets had been decorated with flowers, and there were vendors selling flowers, and pictures of flowers, and dried flowers, and pictures of dried flowers, and everything else, as long as it was hand-crafted.

DuBois parked the carriage in a street designated for that purpose and began unhooking the horses and assuring the ladies that he'd bring them back at dusk. Sonny almost turned Raspberry over but was intercepted by a girl of about ten, who rapidly informed him that her school club would pasture his horse for only a couple of coins, and for an extra coin they'd braid flowers into his tail. Sonny wasn't particularly interested in the tail-braiding. He did think DuBois looked like he had his hands full, so he took the girl up on her offer and was assigned a claim check in the form of a leather tag bearing number nineteen.

He turned around and saw that the ladies had exited the carriage. Grandma Celeste and Blocker were both riding in flower-adorned wheelchairs, and everyone had floral parasols to shield them from the sun. Including Kayliss, who looked as though she'd been through many hours of combined effort on the part of Risha's entire family in a futile attempt to make her look like a pretty girl, rather than the evil terrorist clone that she was. Sonny saw right through it, but he admired their efforts anyway. Her lack of hair was disguised by a flowing scarf, and there were globs of makeup on top of her pimples. She wore a close-fitting dress, mostly in purple, and he couldn't really find any faults in her figure, although he spent a few minutes trying.

Looking good was reserved for Risha. "I would give anything for a camera," Sonny blurted once her splendor traveled from his eyeballs to his brain.

She laughed at him, and slipped her arm around his, and they all strolled into the festival. Arabella pushed Grandma Celeste's wheelchair, with Kayliss driving Blocker's wheelchair carefully in her wake. Food smells assaulted them from a dozen directions. "You'd probably work up an appetite by the time you got to the end of one of those lines," Risha remarked. The idea of standing in a line made Sonny feel queasy.

A bluegrass band was playing as though their lives depended on it as they established a little camp beneath a tree, with blankets and a thermos jug of sweet tea, which was soon joined by cider and ale as friends dropped over to say hi, and be introduced, and exchange clothing admiration. The crowd seemed to be about two-thirds female, but due to all the hats and hair and flowers, and the fact that skirts were a popular fashion choice with all genders, sometimes it was hard for Sonny to tell.

He could tell that Hina was feeling a little bit constrained. They hadn't gone for their usual trail ride that morning. "You don't know it yet," he told her. "But tomorrow you're going to be cooped up on a train."

She slurped his face. He told everyone in everyone in general he was going to take her down by the creek. Kayliss looked up and he hurried to make his escape before she joined him. Keeping the friendliness up around Kayliss took lots more work than someone like Dioni, who was content to ride along without particularly saying anything at all. Or Hina, who adored him no matter what he did.

But it was Risha who got up and followed him. "Wait. I'll come with you."

He immediately stopped and allowed himself to be caught. She was moving with little mincing steps due to her encumbering skirt. Sonny noticed every eyeball in their vicinity traveling toward her as he extended an arm for her to clasp.

"Could you really be happy here?" She stepped back as a chihuahua riding in a wicker basket let loose a sharp volley of yaps at Hina.

"I dunno." Sonny smiled at her. He would be happy anywhere as long as he could look at Risha every day. "Aren't you happy here? It's your home. It seems pretty nice."

"Nope. Over there." She pointed toward another bandstand, at the other end of the festival. He followed her well-manicured finger toward a group of people who weren't dressed in bright colors. Outriders, he saw as they got close. The book covers hadn't completely lied about the boobs. Several of the women had mighty breastworks, constrained in leather corsets and counterbalanced by sturdy, muscular bodies. There were also some skinny women, and old ones, and ones who kept their chests covered, and they were in the minority here, surrounded by a sea of beards. Natural, bushy beards for the most part, although a few opted for braids. Every last one of them was dressed very much like

Sonny, in a leather duster and riding boots, and pants with seams on the tops of the legs.

Risha laughed once Sonny caught on. He blushed. "I don't want to get beat up. They'll know I'm not real."

"I'll bet I could pass you off as my addleheaded little brother who got kicked in the head by a horse and don't remember much," she drawled. Her accent was particularly thick today. The outriders' section had their own band, one that was far twangier. They launched into *When I Get Home* and Sonny groaned slightly, as the tune had gotten caught in his brain the first time he'd heard it. His mother called them earworms, songs that got stuck in your head and kept piping up at odd times whether you wanted to hear them or not. He believed it had to do with the hiccup in *gonna have a reee heeel good time.*

He looked at Risha's smiling lovely face, and opened his mouth to say something to her when something behind her caught his eye. A clone.

A clone? He squinted into the sun. There. A man with dark hair. Not one of the outriders, he was dressed more like a townie, but in subtle colors, without flowers. Same pointy nose. Same weak chin. He vanished around a cluster of people.

"What are you looking at?" All her dimples were showing.

Sonny blinked. "I thought I saw something."

"Rufe?" She drew a disapproving breath.

"No, actually there's Kai." Sonny pointed him out, relieved. Kai was a man who was easy to spot in a crowd. He was in a small cluster of what Sonny supposed passed for the fashionable set in Chianina. The doctor was with him, wearing an obnoxious yellow suit. Risha squealed and hurried toward them, and cheeks were kissed.

During the cheek-kissing part, Sonny's eyes scoured the crowd, looking for the clone. Blander than the townies, brighter than the outriders. He didn't find him, but he spotted Rufe, walking along dressed to the nines, with Meggy Boggs on his arm. She was dressed to the tens.

Hina whined and headed off to the side, and then she stopped, uncertain. Sonny followed her, wondering if her nose had found the clone. He heard an ear-piercing screech and turned around to see Risha and Meggy exchanging the loudest fake good-to-see-you in history. Hina whined again, but Risha had moved on to calling Rufe some very bad names, and Sonny was transfixed. Until Hina barked.

The clone was headed toward Rufe. And as a matter of fact, he had a twin, approaching from the other side. Also dressed in bland everyday Bonterran streetclothes, and this one actually had Bonterran facial hair; a crisp goatee and lightning-shaped sideburns.

"Rufe!" Sonny yelled as loud as he could. Rufe looked up. Sonny pointed, one hand at each clone. Rufe's eye scanned the area. He gave a barely perceptible nod as Risha and Maggy commenced throwing mighty amounts of shade at each other. Sonny backed away as more of the crowd stepped up to watch the women do battle. He lost sight of the first clone as his eyes fastened onto the one with the goatee.

Rufe suddenly let out a bellow and pounced at goatee, and the crowd around them screamed and collapsed and reconfigured. During the shuffle Sonny saw sunlight flash from a knife. A big survival knife, like the kind Dioni strapped to her boot. The clone was coming at Rufe with a clumsy overhanded stab.

Rufe caught his arm and swept his leg, and the clone went down.

The crowd screamed in horror then, exploding outward like popcorn. Sonny took shelter in a doorway with his arms wrapped around Hina. There was suddenly a gun, and a clone was holding it, and it went off. It was not wrapped in a red bandanna, not at all.

The gun was aimed at Rufe. The bullet didn't hit him. Instead it went wide and shattered the front window of the ice cream parlor, sailing over Rufe's head. Rufe was down on one knee, and that knee was resting on the goatee-wearing clone's back. He had the shiny survival knife in his hand, and he threw it as the gun-wielding clone aimed his second shot. The knife landed very solidly in the side of the clone's neck and his shot went up in the air.

The goateed clone heaved upwards, knocking Rufe back. For a split second, Rufe's shoulders were touching the mud. Then he boiled upwards, directing a considerable amount of force into his left fist, which hit the goatee clone's chin with a sharp crack and sent him flying towards his brother, who had dropped his gun and was struggling to remove the knife from his flesh. The effort was only making him bleed out faster. The punched clone wobbled and lunged forward, and Rufe delivered a kick very much like the one he did at the playoffs back in January, connecting solidly with the clone's throat.

Police officers surged into the area like tide rushing in, decked out with flowers in honor of the holiday and backed up by several burly outriders. They had billy clubs approximately the size of Sonny's thigh, and they brandished them at Rufe who was standing meekly with his hands in the air, two motionless bodies at his feet, the gun shining in the mud. Risha and Meggy were screaming, and they continued doing that as the police surrounded them. Sonny watched Quicksilver and Kai get handcuffed, along with the entire crowd of people they'd been with.

As curious people started filtering in to watch, Sonny edged out of the doorway and started doing a slow backwards fade into the crowd. He watched the police line the handcuffed people up in a row, and he recognized Constable Applebaum, who seemed to be in charge. He headed over to talk to Risha and Meggy, the last two civilians in the area who hadn't been arrested but Applebaum got there first, snapping a pair of handcuffs on Risha while Meggy ran away, sobbing.

Risha was escorted over to the line of prisoners. The locals were jeering at them, slinging insults about people too stupid to enjoy a pleasant holiday. Sonny's stomach felt all sour inside as he backed up. Just another guy in an outrider coat, with a distinctive dog.

His heart skipped a beat. He located the nearest puddle of spilled beer and scooped up a double handful of mud, smearing it across Hina's striped back end while she wagged her tail furiously. When he straightened up, he saw the prisoners being marched to the jailhouse, which was only a block away.

He shuffled along aimlessly, trying to walk like an outrider who spent more time in the saddle than on his feet. His heart was pounding and he wasn't exactly sure where the Petrichor picnic spot was, and he spent a long time trying to find it. He reached the general vicinity just in time to watch from a distance as the police arrested Blocker, and Kayliss, as Risha's family squawked ineffectual protests. He also watched them stop and question a boy near his age in townie clothes, accompanied by a dopey looking setter.

Sonny dived into a booth and hid behind a rack of merchandise, pretending to be inspecting it. The racks happened to contain hats, and he bought a floppy leather one with a big brim that hid his face. He exited through the back and found a booth selling meat pies. He was starting to get hungry again, and when they hit him with a high pressure sales pitch to buy a whole sack of pies for the price of two, he folded right up. The vendor threw in a bag of peaches that were just about to go bad.

Once he got through the meat pie booth he was behind the festival. There were a few people milling around, including a couple of drunks peeing by the roadside, but there were no cops. Sonny headed straight for his horse, telling himself that sneaking past cops who dressed like parade floats and didn't even have phones shouldn't be too difficult. And it wasn't. Even so, his adrenalin was flowing by the time he made it to Raspberry, and that made Raspberry nervous, which annoyed Hina. Eventually he got his animals sorted out and after leaving a nice tip for the horsesitting girls, he headed toward Risha's house.

Once he had gone a little ways he reflected that maybe he should be heading to the train station instead. Probably there were a bunch of police there. He stopped in the middle of the street to think, and eat a meat pie. Hina looked up at him curiously, and he tossed her a meat pie too. The police would probably head to both the train station and Risha's house, and going to Risha's house wasn't worth the effort because Risha wasn't there. And that meant Dioni needed to be there.

She was heading to the middle hill. She had several hours head start, but she'd camp for the night, and if Sonny kept going after dark, he'd run into her. Knowing Dioni, she would be camped at some point along the shortest, most direct path.

He rode out of town, stopping on the outskirts to fill his water bottle at someone's pump, and letting Hina drink from his cupped hands until she was no longer interested.

Sonny aimed himself at the middle hill and rode. It didn't take him long to reach the edge of town. There was a trail, leading into the wide grassy meadow between Sonny and the middle hill. It seemed like a nice easy ride.

He began to question his decision around sundown, but by then it was too late to turn back. Probably they'd let Risha go. And Rufe, since it had been clearly self defense, and everyone else, since they hadn't been involved. Dioni would be mad at him for stirring up unnecessary drama. The prairie was probably full of those venomous spiders. He would miss his train back to the civilized world, where you could have music and cold air at the touch of a button.

There was plenty of moonlight. He rode until his back muscles throbbed, but he didn't spot Dioni. Finally he gave up and stopped, letting Raspberry graze while he and Hina polished off the meat pies and half the peaches. He slept curled up in his coat, with Hina to keep his belly warm. Without a ceiling.

When he woke up he didn't notice any kind of new mystical state brought on by the lack of a ceiling, and when he looked at Raspberry and thought about another day riding, he cried. There was nobody to watch him cry except the animals, and they didn't care, so he cried like a little baby. Like Marilyn still occasionally did when she got tired and cranky. He sobbed and sobbed, depleting precious water. Then

Hina licked his tears away and he lifted the saddle back onto Raspberry's back.

When he resumed his journey, the hill still looked as close as they had yesterday. His train would soon be heading north without him, if it hadn't already left the station. He even thought he could see the smoke, although it might have been a cloud. He had probably gone a distance that would take ten or fifteen minutes to drive in a car, assuming you had a car, and a road to drive it on. The only manufactured objects within sight were the ones he was wearing.

He looked back over his shoulder every once in a while for dust clouds raised by pursuing police, but none appeared. There was nobody at all out here. Not even a trail. Just acres of green grass, and occasional streams where he could refill his water bottle, after first checking for fish and frogs. According to Dioni, you didn't want to drink any water that couldn't support fish or frogs.

He rode along at a slow walk, occasionally letting Hina ride in his lap once it was clear Raspberry didn't mind. Toward afternoon, the trees actually got closer. He reached them about an hour before sundown, and he found the outriders' camp with his nose. They had about fifty arotars corralled behind temporary wooden fences, and all of them bellowed in unison as Sonny and Hina approached. Having read far too many outrider stories, he knew to approach slowly, hands extended to the sides. The outriders still greeted him at gunpoint, but he was expecting it.

Dioni was with them, and she stepped forward. "What are you doing out here, townie boy?"

"There was an emergency. With Risha. May I dismount?"

"Greetings Sonny Knight, we grant you the hospitality of our encampment under the stars," Dioni said in an irritated rush. "Yeah, get off of poor old Raspberry there, he'll want a rubdown."

"He's holding up just fine." Sonny tried to dismount gracefully but his back was sore and he couldn't help wincing a little. Dioni caught him as he sagged while fending off Hina's enthusiastic greeting. She dragged him to the cooktent and made sure he got a large helping of cornbread and chili, which went down well considering he and Hina had eaten nothing all day but peaches. Hina received a bowl of meat scraps after the other dogs checked her out.

While he was eating, he was approached by a big burly man with a flood of curly dark beard, below a nose that looked just like Risha's. He planted himself in front of Sonny and scowled.

"You say there's an emergency involving my daughter?"

"Risha's in jail."

"Jail? Great jumpin' balls of flaming horse shit, on what charges?" He had a bass voice that made Sonny's ears rattle.

"Standing near someone who got shot, and being acquainted with the guy who did the shooting. They were looking for me too. It didn't seem like a big thing but they took her away in cuffs, and all of us people staying with her, so I thought I'd better get Dioni."

"I have to go back to the house," Dioni said in a choked voice as the color left her face.

"You'd best git," her father said. "Hold on, I'm coming with you. This is some serious shit. If she's a periphery to a shooting she's gonna wind up in prison."

The idea of getting back on a horse made Sonny's leg tendons throb. "Should I come with you?"

Risha's dad snorted. "You couldn't keep up with us, townie boy."

"I could just beat the shit out of your right now for bringing me bad news," Dioni added. "You best stay here. Jeremiah!"

She waved over an older outrider with a weathered, craggy face and whispered a few things. Jeremiah gave Sonny a long appraising look, approaching him as as Dioni and her father rode off.

"We're gonna drop the beasts off after we get 'em all scanned. There's a main herd and these fools got isolated and started edging out of their regular habitat. After we do that, we're headed up to the north coast, up near that zeppelin I hear you'd like to catch. About a week, maybe two. Do you have any skills?"

"I can cook. But mostly seafood." Sonny didn't happen to see any of that lying around. "I can tie knots."

"You sound like a sailor," Jeremiah said derisively, and a couple of the outriders laughed.

"I'm too young to be anything in particular," Sonny replied. "I'm still learning. Show me what you want done, and I'll do it."

"The boy's got ya there, Jeremiah," someone called out.

They gave him a blanket and a pillow, and showed him where to sleep under the ceilingless stars, near the fire. In the morning they fed him breakfast and put him to work sticking labels on tiny vials of arotar poop. There was also some tree measuring, and insect capturing, and surveying, and carrying wood from one place to another.

The outriders were slightly friendlier after they saw him working industriously, but they had clearly pegged him as a townie, and one who would be leaving them shortly. Most of their conversation was about areas where Sonny was completely ignorant, like rainfall averages, or nitrogen content in soil. They hadn't seen any movies lately, they didn't follow sports and he didn't understand their jokes. Sometimes they gossiped, but he didn't know any of the people they were talking about. They had their own jargon, and sometimes their twangy accents made it sound like a completely different language.

After three days, they moved the camp, driving the arotars along in a big pack. Sonny and Raspberry and Hina stayed far behind the experienced drovers, breathing their dust and stink. They rode along until afternoon, built a temporary pen and rested, and the next morning they did it again. The ground got more and more uneven until finally they had to take the arotars up a hillside. When they got to the top they could see the larger herd of arotars they were about to join. Sonny stared at it with his mouth hanging open like the townie he was.

"Amazing, innit?" A grizzled old guy named Hodge appeared at his side. "Go back a couple thousand years and you'd see herds of buffalo that big, right on this very ground."

"How many?"

"Eighty-seven thousand, four hundred and ninety-five." Hodge clapped him on the shoulder. Sonny had imagined the outriders being as youthful and glamorous as their book covers, but in reality most of them were more than twice his age. There were indeed some big boobs among them. Jeremiah's wife's were pretty large, and she tended to keep them inside a buttoned up plaid shirt on top of a thermal undershirt, which was what everyone but Sonny was wearing. He still had his fancy townie tunic, which was growing increasingly filthy, plus he'd been stealthily removing bits of embroidery and decoration.

Outriders didn't really bathe. They didn't smell too bad because they smeared herbal lotions all over themselves that did something to neutralize their body odor and stress the arotars less. They tended to wear the same clothes every day, mending the tears around the fire at night as they sat around in their thermals, which they did change frequently, boiling them clean on the other side of the fire from the chili and cornbread, and steeping them in the same aromatic herbs.

They did eat other things besides chili and cornbread. They showed him a particular kind of tree, with spade-shaped leaves and smooth bark, that grew round, reddish fruits. Townies didn't like them because they were bioengineered more than most of the local plants, and some of the outriders didn't like them either and wouldn't eat them, and everybody called them labfruits. Sonny tried them and thought they were delicious, sort of like fresh pears. He was told they all tasted different – some were like apple, or banana, or eggplant, or mushroom, or tomato. That was another reason people avoided them, since you never knew what they'd taste like. They did have plenty of nutrients, and they grew all over the place thanks to a dedicated band of outriders who had gone around planting them until they were too numerous to eradicate.

They laughed when he told them he'd read lots of books about outriders. None of them were readers, and one went so far as to state that books were for townies. They had a few hair-raising stories though, mostly about people who took advantage of the isolation to do rotten things to each other.

"We take a census every couple years," Hodge said. "We get a list of everyone living in the remotes, and we ride out and say hello. Record all the births, investigate suspicious deaths, take everyone aside and make sure they're generally happy with their situation in life."

"Make sure they're not being held prisoner," Sonny said. They were generally familiar with his situation but he hadn't given them any details.

Hodge nodded. "We don't hold with that."

●

When they reached the herd, Sonny gratefully accepted a bandanna to tie around his face. Raspberry was on a lead rope, with Hodge holding the end, a careful distance back. There was so much mooing and bellowing and snorting and general vocalizing from the arotars that it was hard to hear each other, and they were communicating by whistles. Sonny didn't speak whistle. He had Hina resting on his lap, and he could feel an occasional nervous quiver run through her.

The renegade arotars had been successfully reintegrated with the greater herd, and the outriders were just walking past, at the tail end of the massive bovine mob. He reflected that it could quickly become the front end of the mob. All they had to do was turn around.

The outriders were headed for a ravine on the other side. Beyond that were some lush green hills. Sonny was looking forward to terrain that didn't smell like arotars, and air that didn't turn his snot black with dust. He was the last one in line, and he was almost past the arotars when someone up ahead gave three sharp whistles.

Hodge kicked his horse, tugging sharply on Raspberry's lead. Raspberry didn't like that, and tried to fishtail around, and Sonny wrestled to keep him in check while keeping Hina balanced, which was tough.

When he finally got Raspberry oriented the right way he heard the hoofbeats. Raspberry heard them too, and he reared. The lead rope whipped out of Hodge's hand as Sonny struggled to keep himself and Hina from falling off. He was successful, and he didn't even fall off when Raspberry took off running, parallel to the ravine.

Sonny glanced over his shoulder. The arotars were stampeding. Headed directly for him. The fact that Raspberry was trailing a lead rope concerned him. It was tied to his saddle in a quick-release knot and he released it, letting it slither to the ground. Then he leaned forward and hung on, squashing Hina against the horse's neck. She didn't complain.

The arotars overtook them, thundering along on either side of Raspberry as he angled toward the ravine. Sonny was steering him very gradually. The arotars seemed to respect another hooved mammal running among them, and they gave Raspberry exactly as much space as he needed.

An arotar plunged into the ravine beside him with a startled bellow, and he heard it splash. The arotar behind them did an evasive maneuver, bodychecking Raspberry's rear-end as it slid out of the way. Raspberry squealed angrily, and Sonny found himself riding along with the rim of the ravine to his right, and a great many arotars to the left.

Ahead of him was a rabbit. It was perched on the rim of the ravine, watching the oncoming stampede, ducking over the rim at the last possible second. As it vanished, its white tail flashed, and Raspberry spooked. He stumbled. Sonny's weight shifted and Hina fell off. Sonny grabbed for her desperately and succeeded only in pulling out a handful of her short bristly fur as she fell away with a terrified yelp. Sonny felt like his heart had just imploded inside his chest, and he noticed he was also falling. He shifted his weight desperately, grabbing at the reins and Raspberry bucked. All four feet came off the ground. Sonny went flying over his head.

He landed on the arotar in front, which gave a surprised moo as it twitched him off to the side. He landed on a steep slope and he rolled downhill, tumbling over and over.

Several trees broke his fall as he bounced from one to the next, earning himself a few nasty bruises but nothing too serious until he splashed into the stream at the bottom and his knee slammed against a rock. He yelled, and tears came to his eyes.

His coat lining was indeed buoyant, and it carried him along the swift running stream, although it wasn't much help deflecting off the rocks. A dead tree loomed up ahead and he crashed into it, scrabbling for a grip on the wet bark. He found one, and he hauled himself up and lay there shaking.

He yelled again. Just in case. Nobody yelled back.

He dragged himself over to a gravely stretch of ground beside the water and lay there for a while, feeling generally bad. His knee was throbbing but the heartache was actually worse. Terror was waiting in line.

He finally sat up and shrugged out of his coat, followed by his shirt and his undershirt, spreading them on rocks to dry. His pants were tight against his swollen knee, and a little blood had seeped through, and even gently touching it made him want to vomit and pass out. He rummaged through his coat pockets and was relieved to find his gold was still there, and even more relieved to find the knife Dioni had given him. He used it to cut away the leg of his pants, and the thermal pants underneath.

His knee was huge, and there was a gash across it but it wasn't bleeding very heavily. He used his pants legs to make a bandage for it, tying strips together and wrapping it firmly enough to keep it from flexing. He wasn't sure if that's what a doctor like Quicksilver would do, but at least he didn't have to look at it.

Then he sat on the bank, and worried. Occasionally he yelled for help. He had no doubt in the outriders' ability to rescue him but first they had to find him. Between the swift stream and the even swifter galloping of Raspberry, he was a good distance away. He supposed there was a chance they would drop everything and track him, but when he thought about it, he realized that tracker would have to be able to pick out Raspberry's hooves in the stampede, and then account for his long drift downstream. All for some townie boy who wasn't even from this country. With a warrant out for his arrest.

At least he still had his hat. It was lying on the gravel where he had collapsed, dry from the warm afternoon sun. He had enough gold to get out of here as long as he could find a town, and a train. He could even pay someone to haul him to a town, assuming he found someone willing to do that. There didn't seem to be any people nearby at all. Even the stampeding arotars had passed on by.

There were frogs, and some songbirds up in the trees, and a squawking raven too. A dragonfly buzzed along the stream, brilliant blue, and a couple of butterflies observed from a nearby bush. He saw a fish jump in the stream, mocking his lack of a fishing pole. There was also something rustling in the bushes. He could hear it panting. Thoughts of Dioni and her pistol that kept feral dogs away flashed through his mind. He didn't have a pistol. The best he could do was throwing rocks. He felt around for a palm-sized one, just in case.

The bushes parted. Hina stepped out. When she saw him she let out a joyful howl and gathered herself for a mighty leap across the stream. She fell in, and she paddled like mad to reach his side. He dropped his palm-sized rock and ran his hands over her as she licked his face. There was a short gash on her hip and she limped slightly, but other than that she seemed fine.

He fanned out the attachments on his knife to see if one of them could possibly help catch a fish. One of them was a magnifying glass, and he laughed, envisioning a little old man holding it up to his eye to bring an advancing bear into focus. When he accidentally burned a spot on his leg with it, he remembered that magnifying glasses could make fires.

He made a small fire. He used the dry end of the dead tree for fuel. He found a grassy spot with fewer rocks nearby and dragged himself there, and as he sat thinking of different ways to catch fish without a fishing pole, Hina splashed into the stream, caught one in her jaws and threw it at him. Then another, and another, until he had a small pile of them to execute, and clean and filet with his small knife. They feasted on trout and curled up together by the fire, Sonny's coat providing a blanket.

He slept fitfully, waking up every so often to feed the fire, and worry, and wonder if anyone could see his fire. Probably not, since he was still in the ravine. By the time the sun was up he had decided he definitely needed to get out of the ravine, even if he had to crawl. And he didn't really have to crawl if he could float. The stream might take him to people. At the very least, it would take him out of this place where there were no people.

His knee was stiff and immobile, and a sunset of bruises peeked through the edges of the bandage, but it wasn't hurting quite as bad. Putting it in the cool water of the stream soothed it, and he did that as he bundled his boots and shirts together and tied them over his shoulders, like a backpack. He kept the coat on.

The current wasn't as bad as he'd remembered. He was able to bob along on one leg without drifting out of control, or setting too fast a pace for Hina. She was limping along the shore, occasionally stopping to eat frogs and pee on bushes. Sonny found a buoyant branch to lean on, and a long stick to propel himself along.

It took hours before the ravine started to flatten out. As it did Sonny noticed a green, spade-shaped leaf floating on the water. Once he remembered what it was his eyes scanned the banks for labfruit. He found a tree close to the bank, and when he leaned on his long stick and gritted his teeth against the pain, he could stand up to reach plenty of fruit on the lowest branches. That night he and Hina feasted on trout, served with both cooked and raw labfruit, which tasted of broccoli, onion and strawberry, even though they all came from the same tree and had the same mealy flesh.

In the morning he dragged himself up the grassy shore and past more labfruit trees. There was another steep drop, and he lay still for several minutes, stunned by the view. He could see the ocean, far to the west, a slender band of dark blue on the horizon. Below him were rolling meadows, and patches of forest. His stream forked, becoming a good-sized river toward the north and a slightly larger stream toward the south.

Sonny didn't see a single sign that humans ever passed through the land stretching beneath him, which was probably half the size of the entire country of Braganza. No roads, no signs, no buildings. No smoke from outrider cookfires, no dust clouds from their beasts. He would have cried in frustration if it hadn't been so beautiful.

Then he noticed a manufactured structure, in the form of a trestle bridge, running across a lake, far to the west. He peered at it, wishing he had an eye like Rufe's. He wondered what Rufe was doing. Maybe he had paid his fine and was already on the zeppelin.

A puff of white smoke moved toward the trestle bridge. A train. Sonny let out a whoop, and Hina took her attention off the squirrel she was stalking to glance at him. He followed the barely-visible line of train tracks with his eye and spotted a second train bridge, much smaller, across the south fork of the stream. It seemed like an excellent place to hang around waiting for a train.

To get there he had to cross the stream again, without getting swept into the north fork, which descended in a magnificent waterfall. This wasn't too difficult since he had his long stick to stab into the muddy bottom, and assistance from Hina. Once he was on the south bank he did a three-legged crawl to a waterfall that was much less magnificent, where he crawled crablike down the rocks beside it, only jarring his knee a couple of times.

The stream was much deeper after the waterfall. Sonny crawled alongside it for a while, and then he found a big chunk of log wedged in some weeds. It was big enough to straddle like a horse, and he did that after he freed it, steering with a new long pole pole as Hina ran alongside on the bank, with occasional playful leaps into the water.

They stopped for the night near another grove of labtrees. Sonny collected a lot of fruit, which provided their entire dinner. Hina couldn't catch many fish now that the stream was deeper and muddier, although there were plenty of them swimming around. When they reached the bridge the next day, after making camp beside it, he cut off the lower sleeves of his undershirt and carefully unraveled them until he had a fishing line. He found a stick that would serve as a fishing pole, and he used his knife to carve a twig into something vaguely hooklike. He baited it with a chunk of labfruit, and soon afterwards he had a trout the size of his forearm wriggling beside him.

The bridge was a comfortable place to live. He could crawl underneath it for shelter if the wind came up, and he could rest in its shade during the heat of the day. He couldn't resist carving "Sonny was here" on one of the support beams, noticing that quite a few people had inscribed their own names over the years. None of them had remained. He had all the land within sight to himself.

One day there was a rainstorm. Sonny wasn't sure of the date; the moon was a tiny sliver but he couldn't say whether it was waxing or waning. He huddled under the bridge with Hina, watching the trout jump to catch raindrops. He had all the trout he needed for the day, roasted in a leaf with chunks of lemon-flavored labfruit.

Lighting blinded him. The thunder rolled in almost immediately afterward. He crawled up onto the bridge to take a look and saw a puff of smoke to the north, hanging over the trestle bridge, several kilometers ahead. There might have even been a bright tongue of flame or two. It wasn't very clear, and after a few moments everything was drenched in sheets of rain, except for the parts of Sonny that were covered by his coat. It would keep him dry as long as he wasn't actually immersed, and it kept both himself and Hina warm all night.

He accumulated several handmade fishhooks. The trout here seemed a little naïve due to the lack of fishermen, and quickly bit at his lures, as did the catfish, which tasted just fine once you got past their creepy appearance. There was a labfruit grove within crawling distance, as well as a few pear trees that had cross-pollinated a little. Other than the minimal time it took to feed himself, and dig holes to poop in, there was very little to do except wait for the train.

He spelled out "HELP" and "STOP" in white rocks beside the train tracks, just in case a train snuck up on him while he wasn't looking. He was pretty certain he would hear it, and he planned to get up and wave his shirt to flag it down. His outer, townie shirt, which was now thoroughly ragged, although it still had traces of bright green and blue that might hopefully catch someone's eye.

He sang Hina every song he knew, and he made up a few new ones. He laughed and cried and raged. He masturbated from time to time. He rehearsed exactly what he'd say to the guy who gave the order to kidnap his family, in case they happened to meet someday. He practiced informing Risha that he loved her and imagined her falling into his arms and showering him with kisses, and taking off her shirt. He threw rocks into the water, and watched them splash. He craved company more and more with each passing day. The slim crescent moon grew thicker each night until it was halfway full.

One day a train came. First Sonny heard the track vibrating, a low thrum that shook the whole bridge. He put on his undershirt, which was mostly dry, and his coat, and grabbed his outer shirt. He climbed up and stood next to the track, leaning on his walking stick, watching the smoke cloud arrive. Hina sensed his excitement and stood next to him wildly wagging her tail. When the train came into sight Sonny waved his shirt frantically.

As it approached him, he noticed that nobody was driving it. The engine was completely empty. As he stared at it in disbelief as it slowly passed by, he noticed something that looked like a broomstick jammed against some kind of lever. The coal tender was next, and nobody was in there either. Sonny kept waving anyway. The train was going at walking speed and he peered through windows as they passed. He saw a passenger car, and he thought he could see a face looking at him from behind the curtains. In the next passenger car window he saw a bunch of guys in uniform, playing cards. A closed boxcar followed, and behind that was a boxcar with an open door.

Sonny took a deep breath. He jumped.

He landed square on his bad knee. For a brief instant, he was in more pain than he thought he was capable of having. Then he was lying on his back, and Hina thumped down beside him and started licking his face. They were moving, slowly, over tracks.

He still had his walking stick, and he used it to climb to his feet. He was surrounded by crates and pallets, but the car was only about half full. He sat down on a crate for a moment and collected himself.

The door at the end of the boxcar was open and Sonny swayed as he confronted the gap between his car and the next. Hina hopped across just to demonstrate to him that it was no big deal, but all four of her knees worked. This seemed to be the kind of maneuver that required multiple knees.

Sonny backed into the boxcar and rewrapped the bandages around his throbbing knee, tight. He stared at the gap, summoning his strength before he launched forward, vaulting with his walking stick and collapsing onto the floor of the next car. He didn't fall on his bad knee this time, but he jarred it, sending another spike of pain up his leg. He got up and gathered himself for the vault into the car where the uniformed men were playing their card game.

A couple of them drew their guns as he collapsed on the floor of their car. He kept his hands visible while they looked him over. "Some outrider kid," mumbled one of the uniforms, and all the guns went back into their holsters. A flash of pleasure that he'd successfully passed for an outrider cut through Sonny's throbbing knee pain.

"Halp," he said. "Tried flaggin' ya down. Messed up my knee, might need to see a doc. My dog's over there and I'm gonna call her over, so don't shoot."

"Yup, you probably should get that seen by a doctor." The engineer jammed his striped hat onto his head in a desperate bid to gain authority. Hina bounced over and snuggled against Sonny's side.

The man next to the engineer was a proud member of the Railway Police, according to the embroidery on his shirt. He had an impressively-shaped crop of whiskers. "We got one on the train."

"We can't go lettin' ..." his partner started, just before shutting his mouth.

"Seth, if you've got a doctor that can treat this young man's injury, bring him on out here." The engineer folded his arms, making it clear it was his damn train, and he'd drive it with a broomstick tied to the throttle if he felt like it.

The two cops conferred in whispers. "We were running from a stampede and my horse saw a rabbit and spooked," Sonny said in his outrider accent. "Oh hey, you might want to check out that trestle bridge before you go drivin' acrost it."

They asked where the stampede was, and Sonny told them it was a few days away. The cops reached their decision and both of them headed off to the next car Only one returned, escorting Quicksilver. He was dressed in a baggy outfit of a vaguely brownish color, with a bright orange number painted across the chest. His hands were cuffed, and he was complaining that he wouldn't be able to do much unless they were unlocked.

Sonny tried not to show any sign that he recognized the doctor, who was doing likewise. The wooden cuffs were grudgingly removed, and Quicksilver flexed his shoulders. Sonny thought he looked even skinnier. "You didn't miss much," he murmured as he bent down to examine Sonny's knee. Sonny felt a quick stab from his retractable finger needles, followed by a warm and welcome lack of pain as his leg went numb.

Hina chose that moment to stick her nose in Quicksilver's face. Sonny saw Quicksilver stop himself from reaching out to pet her. They stared at each other for a moment. "Mighty friendly dog you've got there," Quicksilver said in a joking way that sounded just a little bit forced.

Sonny glanced back at the uniforms to see whether they had noticed anything suspicious as he grabbed Hina and whispered "down!" She obediently crouched and froze, the tip of her tail quivering. "She's a good dog," Sonny said, his accent broad and thick. "Catches fish."

"Ain't never heard of a dog that could catch fish," said the cop, apparently suspicious about something but not exactly sure what. Sonny was pondering over what to say next when a gunshot rang out from the car up ahead.

Quicksilver sighed. His arm moved with blurry speed as he grabbed the cop by the wrist, and not long after that the man was sliding to the floor, limp. After he finished doing that, Quicksilver took his gun. The railroadmen were standing against the wall with their hands up, as if they'd spent some time rehearsing their train robbery drill procedure.

"Get your ass out here where I can see you, shithead cop!" Kayliss screamed as she appeared in the doorway holding a gun, dressed in the same outfit Quicksilver was wearing.

"He can't see anyone right now, he's taking a nap," Quicksilver said mildly.

Hina barked excitedly as Rufe came in, carrying the other cop, who was wearing his own cuffs and informing them of all the thousands of laws they were violating at that particular moment. Quicksilver reached over and pinched the cop's arm and he joined the first cop in slumber while Rufe removed the first cop's gun. Then he nodded at Kayliss. "Well done."

She nodded back. Rufe fondled Hina's ears. "There's a problem with the bridge," Sonny said. "Up ahead. Hi."

Rufe bent down and lifted Sonny, tossing him over his shoulder, holding the gun in case the railroadmen decided to resist. "I got my hand out of the shackles when he released the doc," Kayliss told Sonny, following behind. "Then I got his gun and shot him in his big fat foot."

They headed to the next car and Sonny's heart sped up at the sight of Risha, who even looked beautiful wearing prisoner clothes, her hair stuffed under a knit cap. Kai was carrying Blocker, who was ranting about the most unprofessional law enforcement she had ever seen. They all looked thinner, and tired.

"Stay in your compartments," Rufe yelled to the rest of the car. "Don't open the door or I'll shoot."

They crossed into the coal car, at which point Quicksilver dashed ahead, then came back to inform them nobody was driving the train. Someone in the passenger car they'd just departed fired a shotgun in their direction and Sonny heard a loud splintering crack as it hit something. From his upside-down position he could see blue water below as the train began rattling over the trestle bridge.

"Ass breath," Kayliss yelled. She returned fire but she aimed down, toward the coupling between the two cars. It shattered, leaving the back half of the train sitting still while the engine chugged on.

Rufe put Sonny down, tenderly, and jumped to the engine. The shotgun went off again and Sonny actually saw the bullet clink down on the track as they passed out of range. It sparked when it landed. His hearing was blunted from all the gunfire but beneath it he heard more loud, splintering cracks, from below. The trestle bridge was collapsing.

"The bridge is falling," he yelled at the top of his lungs, as Rufe and Quicksilver managed to shut the engine off, releasing a huge cloud of steam as the train jerked to a stop. Kai looked at Blocker in his arms and said something inaudible. She replied and he tossed her, right over the side and into the lake. Then he jumped after.

The drop was maybe ten meters, Sonny thought. He watched them splash in. Kai swam to Blocker with powerful strokes, catching up with her and assisting her towards shore. The train jerked downward as though it were in a broken elevator, and Sonny watched Risha dive next, followed by Quicksilver and Kayliss. Even Hina jumped.

"Come on," Rufe said, extending his hand. The train dropped another notch and began to slowly roll toward the gap.

Sonny was paralyzed. Falling. His brain was just not going to allow that to happen again. No.

Rufe grabbed him anyway, by scruff and seat, flinging him into the air. Sonny yelled as he flew. He splashed into the lake, and his mouth filled with cold water. His buoyant coat jerked him to the surface, where he bobbed around, kicking with one leg, his anesthetized one hanging uselessly below him. He spun around to watch the locomotive splash into the water, uncomfortably close, followed by a shower of broken supports. It made a wave that pushed him toward the shore. Kai was already there, arranging Blocker on the grass, and he returned for Sonny, towing him to shore as the rest arrived, waddling to shore with their wet prison garb slapping at their legs.

"I thought I got away from you people," Sonny joked as they gathered just inside the line of trees. They could see the stranded back end of the train sitting at the end of the bridge as people gingerly climbed out of the caboose and gathered in a little crowd.

"I saw you through the window," Kayliss said. "At first I thought it was an outrider."

"He does look similar to one," Risha said, plucking at Sonny's grungy undershirt. He had lost both his outer shirt and his hat, leaving him dressed in outrider clothes from head to toe. She kissed his cheek, making it turn red.

"I went to get Dioni," he told her. "And your dad. The outriders were going to take me where I needed to go, but stuff happened and I messed up my knee."

"It needs surgery," Quicksilver said. "Are we near the zeppelin?"

"The spire's over there." Rufe pointed northwest. "If you can't see it, that means we'll have to do some walking."

"I doubt it," Blocker said.

After Rufe and Kai did some good-natured arguing over whether Sonny weighed more than Blocker, Sonny found himself riding on Rufe's shoulders, keeping an eye out for wild arotar herds and police, while Kai gave Blocker a piggyback ride. None of them were hesitant to try labfruit after Sonny pointed some out. "They feed you in prison," Rufe told Sonny. "Plain oatmeal, a big pile of tasteless greens and a slab of the blandest cheese ever made, three times a day."

"I still don't see why they took me into custody," Blocker said. "Especially after I identified myself. They wouldn't even verify me. They were going to send us up to some maximum security prison to do that, and then maybe in a year or two we'd get a trial."

"And we weren't anywhere near it," Kayliss added.

"Shooting a gun in town is the worst thing you can do," Risha said. "Aside from being friends with me. I'm sorry. First that ship ride, now this."

"Memo to self, avoid rural law enforcement in the future," Quicksilver said.

"You did the right thing," Rufe whispered to Sonny, squeezing his calf. "Once I kick those assholes out of my country I'll give you a barony."

CHAPTER THREE: May 20, 3748

They approached a small farm around nightfall, and Risha pointed to it. "Sonny! Let me borrow your clothes!"

Rufe swung him to the ground, laughing at his reaction. Sonny sat down and hesitantly removed his coat. "Are you cold?"

"I'ma go over yare and buy us a mule or a pan o' biscuits or a bottle o' diddlywobble, whatever they got t'sell." She flashed her dimples at him.

"That's a mighty bright plan, sister." Sonny drawled back at her and stripped off his undershirt. "Gold's in the pocket thar, don't spend it all."

"Yeppers." She turned her back, discarded the prison shirt in one fluid motion and put on Sonny's undershirt. It looked much better on her. She shrugged into the coat and held out her hand for the pants.

"Not the underwear." He leaned over on his side, gingerly removing his cut-off shorts without moving his injured knee more than necessary. He tossed them to Risha, and she marched behind a screen of bushes to change. Finally, she confiscated his boots and set off toward the farm. Kayliss found an apple tree, and Rufe announced he was going to keep an eye on Risha. From a distance. Just in case.

His cautions were unfounded. She returned on a horse, with a big bundle of stuff strapped behind a worn old saddle. She slid down and gave Sonny his coat back, and he took it gratefully, since it was getting cold. The bundle turned out to be clothes the farmer was saving to make scarecrows, bundled around a loaf of bread, a round cheese and a sausage. Kayliss added her apples and they feasted.

In the morning, Sonny rode the horse, with Blocker riding behind him. He wore his coat over a threadbare outfit that made him look like a destitute townie and the others were dressed much the same, their prison clothes buried in a hole beneath a labfruit tree. The horse was old and slow, but at least it didn't seem like the kind of horse that would buck him off into a stampede. Risha explained they were actually returning it to someone who lived closer to the spire. The farmer had refused any kind of reward, and most of Sonny's gold was still in his pocket.

Their first few attempts at conversation all swiftly grew into arguments, so they walked in silence, appreciating the birdsong. They got close enough for everyone to see the spire, and when they had almost reached it, the zeppelin floated in. Everyone broke into ragged cheers and stepped up the pace, until they finally reached the station.

Two slender people wearing bright, unnatural colors not normally found in Bonterra were tightening ropes next to the spire. Beside them was a shack containing a bench and a customer service desk, covered with paper and disposable pens. The door was open to catch the afternoon breeze.

Risha rushed in, with Quicksilver close behind her. The worker at the desk was male but it took Sonny a moment to register that information, as he had been living around males with beards for so long. This male was Jimmy Jellybean, according to the sign on his desk, and he was clean shaven and handsome and slight, with shoulder length hair lasered into an optical illusion pattern. His jacket was bright blue, and he had a tie printed with little yellow zeppelins.

"Darling! You look horrible," he said to Risha, leaning over the counter to clasp her hands.

"Oh, Jimmy, don't I know it. I'll be back to rights as soon as I get on your blimp."

"Jimmy." Quicksilver nodded.

Jimmy blinked repeatedly. "Lucas? Is that you? You look even worse than she does."

"We had a few inconveniences. Party of six for Deuce, if you'd be so kind. Is it leaving soon? Is there a first class?"

"Every luxurious seat aboard the *Celestial Albatross* is first class," Jimmy replied, whipping out a brochure. It was machine-printed in sharp colors, with photographs. "We offer a beverage and snack service, and you'll be spending almost three hours in flight. Now, if I could just see your paperwork. Oh, my goodness."

Kai settled Blocker on the bench and turned around, showing his tattooed face. He gave a friendly feral smile. Rufe plopped down on the bench beside Blocker, looking large and thuggish. Hina collapsed beside them and gave a big yawn, showing off her teeth. "You really don't want to upset them," Risha said sweetly.

"We don't need paperwork," Quicksilver said, pawing absentmindedly at his own scruffy beard. Sonny limped in, leaning on his stick. Kayliss stuck close to the door, keeping an eye on the old horse. It was grazing on the grass outside and seemed very unlikely to go anywhere.

"And why is that?" Jimmy gave him a charming smile.

The room was silent while Quicksilver thought about it. "Medical emergency," he finally said. "That's a therapy dog."

"Six medical emergencies."

"At least two of them require immediate surgery. You're allowed to bypass the regs in the event of a medical emergency."

"We were in a train wreck," Sonny offered.

"From the looks of you, I can believe it." Jimmy frowned at them.

"Want me to step it up?" Blocker's voice was raspy. The pollen had been affecting her on and off, and at the moment her eyes were red and watery.

"Not yet." Quicksilver stuck his hand in Sonny's pocket and pulled out a coin. He turned to Jimmy and made it walk across the back of his knuckles. "First let's resort to bribery."

"Let's head directly to threats." Rufe stood up and stretched his arms. "It's cheaper. I've killed more than one person in your charming country, and I'm going to kill a lot more if anyone tries to arrest me again. I'll kill them in creative and gruesome ways. I will paint the walls of this establishment bright red with their blood. I will place their severed heads on stakes outside."

"And I'll help," Kayliss said, stepping forward in solidarity with Rufe.

"Luke, you're spending your time with some rough folks," Jimmy said as he dealt out six tickets. "Get on. I never saw these people. And you owe me a big favor." He held out his hand and Quicksilver tossed him the coin.

"This horse out there belongs to Mister Felipe Gutierrez," Risha said to Jimmy. "Would you see that it is returned to him?"

Sonny refused Rufe's help with the ladder, which was a narrow spiral with handrails on both sides that he could navigate with one leg. Up at the top was a slender girl with lavender hair, wearing a shirt printed with yellow zeppelins. She ushered them into the gondola, which was set up in compartments like the train, except everything in them was sleek and trim. The seats were light blue, and the surfaces were smooth and flat and had clearly been molded in a factory. No wood, no flowers, no decorative carved wood.

Quicksilver let out a giddy cheer, and danced around the cabin in a burst of hyperactivity as a flute-heavy pop song began playing softly in the background and cool air hissed out of the vents. Risha burst into tears, and Rufe told Bonterra exactly what it could do with itself. A flight attendant in a zeppelin-printed dress came in, her haircut short and blue and asymmetrical, her bare arms shockingly skinny compared to the substantial women of Bonterra, and set out bowls of popcorn and cups of icy cold melon soda.

Sonny leaned his oily, dirty face against the cool glass of the window and watched Jimmy and another attendant do something involving the long cables tethering the zeppelin to the spire. He heard a low thrum as engines powered up, and then the zeppelin jerked and drifted out to sea. When they were a good distance from land, the propellors began to spin, and they sailed off toward the sunset.

Quicksilver soon discovered a cleanbeam in the bathroom, powered by sun and wind, and he made certain everyone else knew. They tidied up to the extent possible.

"Cheese Dragons!" Quicksilver exclaimed as the flight attendant brought in a bright purple bag and tipped the contents into the empty popcorn bowl. These turned out to be airy cheese-flavored crackers, shaped like dragons. They had a funny aftertaste but it was difficult to stop eating them, and the bowl emptied rapidly.

"Restaurant tonight," Risha murmured. "My treat."

"If they don't kick our visa-lacking asses right out," Blocker said.

"Where are they going to kick us?" Kai had lost enough weight to make his cheekbones stand out sharp under the spiraling lines. "Into the water? The *Lono* should be down there, unless some of our terrible luck remained on board."

"I'm replacing the cash the police confiscated," Risha said. "Everything will be fine. I'll throw in a little extra for hazardous duty pay."

The bright lights of Deuce came into view long before the buildings. There was an illuminated sign when you got close. "Dual Towers Self-Sustaining High Rise Community," and beyond that was a brighter sign, a pack of cartoon cool-kids with fabulous mod hair, making various hand gestures to indicate they accepted you as one of their own. This one said "Welcome to Deuce."

The towers were cylindrical, each approximately the diameter of four blocks of downtown Royal Beach and covered with windows. They rose into the sky until their tips vanished in clouds, and their bottom ends descended many meters deep in the ocean floor, according to Quicksilver, who was prattling on with various random facts. "I never quite understood patriotism before but I'm feeling very sentimental at the moment."

A big platform at sea level connected the towers, although there were a few fragile-looking bridges at higher levels. There was a spire for the zeppelin at one end of it, looking comparatively tiny next to the towers. It was windy, which complicated tying the zeppelin to its new mooring but finally they got it lashed down and the extendable ladder was attached. A fierce wind shoved at them for the first few meters. Sonny limped with his stick, holding fast to a makeshift leash he'd rigged for Hina using one of the scarecrow shirts. There was a tunnel on the platform that kept some of the wind off, and they sat for a moment on a bench until a little electric cart came along. It was driverless aside from a display screen showing an animated face, asking their destination.

"Medical emergency," Quicksilver said. "We're bypassing customs. This is Doctor Lucas Quicksilver."

The face looked blank for a moment, as though it were having a minor philosophical crisis. Then it smiled at them. "Affirmative, Doctor Quicksilver. We'll have a crash team waiting."

"Two crash teams," he corrected. He squeezed Sonny's hand that was holding the makeshift leash. "They won't let you have pets in the hospital, and they'll probably keep you a couple of days. I'll take care of her."

"Thank you." Sonny turned over the leash and explained the situation to Hina, not sure whether she understood any of it. He wasn't sure he understood it. He had never spent days in a hospital before.

"I'm staying with her," Kayliss said, snaking her arm protectively around Blocker's shoulders. "You can arrest me or whatever once she's stable."

Rufe leaned forward, making the cart rock, and gave both of them a clumsy hug. "My issue is with your country," he said to Kayliss. "Not you."

"Likewise."

The cart slid to a halt and Sonny found himself in the arms of his very own crash team. They started to trim away his outrider coat but he yelled, insisting on folding it up neatly. He didn't mind them cutting away his scarecrow clothes, which they did.

He and Blocker were separated immediately into different elevators. His elevator went up several floors, then he took a decompression break, which meant he was parked in a room while the crash team conferred and the air composition got shuffled around and everyone checked readouts. There were screens everywhere. People were wearing delds, and laser-styled hair, and their slender bodies were dressed in clothes made of thin fabric. He could hear music oozing out of speakers. He went up even more floors, then he was moving horizontally, into a bright room where everyone was wearing scrubs.

●

Everything was still, and quiet, and clean. Sonny sat up in panic once he realized Hina was gone and he wasn't wearing his coat. Then he remembered the doctor had Hina. And he had saved his coat, and right now he was dressed in a teal hospital gown. His leg was sheathed in a light, comfortable brace, with tiny pinprick scabs where the machines had reached in to rearrange his tissues. A band of numbness extended from the top of his thigh to the middle of his calf.

Movement flashed at the foot of his bed and he leaned forward. It was only a mirror reflecting his own motion, but Kayliss happened to be sitting next to it, holding very still. She had on a form-fitting purple outfit and her hair was styled to show off the white streak. It was probably the anesthesia wearing off, but Sonny thought she looked nice.

"Hi," she said. "Blocker's still not awake. I'm going to check one last time, and then I have to go do something. If I miss her, could you please tell her I said goodbye?"

"Where are you going?" Sonny tried to get out of bed but his leg had other ideas.

"Don't worry about it. And thank you for everything." She suddenly seemed shy and flustered. She picked up a bulky backpack resting by her feet and made a swift exit.

Sonny sank back into his clean linen. He lay there for a moment, troubled by the fact that Kayliss had looked attractive. Her body was slender and graceful, like a swimmer or a dancer. Her waist nipped in and her breasts swelled out, not terribly large but enough to make cleavage if you squished them together in a bodice Bonterra-style. Her new haircut made her weak chin look cute in an elven way.

He punched his pillow. He tried again to stand, this time making it to his feet. They had taken away his walking stick, but there were grab bars everywhere and he explored the room. There was a tiny closet but it was empty. No coat. He punched the wall this time, and thought about Kayliss and her backpack.

He staggered back to his bed, wondering if he should call security. He decided against it, since he was tired of dealing with the police. Besides, he couldn't think any reasons she might want his stuff other than escaping from Deuce altogether, which meant that she would be someone else's problem. Probably he'd never see her again, and he was fine with that. He punched his pillow a few more times.

Then it dawned on him that he was sitting next to a wall of screen. He could just reach over and tap it and open up a portal, so he did, logging into his social node. A retina scanner popped up to save him from the relentless verifying questions, and he tapped out his rhythm code in another panel. Just like that, he was in. His node popped up at the center of a ring of advertising, message box full to bursting.

He posted a picture of himself lying in his hospital bed, pointing at his knee brace and smiling, his hair hanging dark and shaggy around his face. They had combed it while he was under anesthesia, cleaning out the tangles and leaves and twigs, and his face was clean-shaven and smooth. He sent a message to Uncle Duke, and then he relaxed into a comfortable familiar world of high school sports scores and endless prom videos from last week.

Breakfast arrived while he was catching up. There was a stack of pancakes topped with chunks of chocolate, a scrambled egg parfait with layers of sausage and sour cream and vegetables and some kind of frothy breakfast drink that tasted of coffee and raspberries. Beside them on the plate was a dry biscuit wrapped in a shiny silver envelope, and the attendant serving him tapped it to make sure he noticed it was there. It was comparatively bland and tasteless, and he only ate a few bites of it.

After breakfast, he worked up the nerve to check the news, and found all the stories were much the same as the ones he had read in Bonterra. Sports fans had rioted during the championship game, tearing up the city. An earthquake had torn it up more. The heroic nation of Dysz sent relief efforts. Premier Cello was in charge of Vanram, following the tragic sudden death of Premier Lance, and there was a picture of him, showing his weak chin and pointy nose, posed next to a flag in an article about anti-government violence in the wake of the disaster. All the news out of Vanram seemed to come through one particular reporter, Henry Ajian, who accompanied it with photos showing burned out buildings as evidence of the sports rioting.

There were no messages from his parents, or Marilyn, or Lenny or Dan. Lenny's node was untouched since his last post before the trip, a cartoon girl with big blinking eyes doing a jerky little dance. There was a memorial set up on Dan's node. Sonny's stomach convulsed at the sight of that, and he wondered whether Dan was actually dead. Maybe he'd been killed trying to escape.

His family's nodes had no updates since their trip, and Sonny's parents' messageboxes were both full. Marilyn's node full of pictures of kittens and bunnies hadn't been touched either. None of them had official deceased notices that popped up on dead peoples' social nodes, indicating they were about to be archived so that people who felt the urge to go through their ancestors' status updates could check them out in the future. They were just inactive.

He sighed and started to compose his own status update. This turned out to be a more difficult task than he initially realized, and he was distracted by his growling belly despite the immense breakfast. He was just about to buzz the nurses and ask about lunch when it arrived, a fat greasy cheeseburger smothered in fried onions, with orange soda and fries and another foil-wrapped biscuit.

Sonny devoured everything, including the biscuit, and then he lounged back in bed looking at the biscuit wrapper, which indicated it was for adolescent males, size large. He didn't think of himself as particularly large, but he supposed he was a little bigger than the average guy from Deuce.

After lunch a doctor came in to talk with him about his knee, showing him animated graphics on the wall and explaining it had been mostly fixed, and would always be a little bit wobbly compared to his other knee. He was hustled away for physical therapy in an immersion vat, with tiny airstreams guiding his limbs through an abstract workout cartoon full of shapes that lit up when he touched them, backed by encouraging music.

Once he was back in his room he got a visit from an immigration officer, who verified he was Leroy Joseph "Sonny" Knight of Royal Beach, Braganza, and seemed perfectly satisfied with his answer that he didn't remember anything between the clashball game and this morning. She smiled and told him he would be deported, free of charge, as soon as his doctor cleared him to leave, and hoped he'd enjoy the remainder of his stay.

He spent the rest of the afternoon lost in his social node, looking at normal people doing normal things as they traded bright smiles with each other, constantly aware they were surrounded by cameras. He doubted if any of them knew how to tie a knot. Or cook a fish.

He posted another update. "Messed up my knee riding horses in Bonterra and now I'm in the hospital in Deuce, getting my knee fixed." Sixty-seven people liked this news so far, and some of them had posted sympathetic wishes for him to get well soon.

Then he ventured into the local media feed, which he noted with alarm was full of pirated stuff, plus they had lots of movies made by didges, which those were banned in Braganza. Sanctimonious little messages were posted everywhere, advising him that in Deuce, "Words Are Free." There were a lot of free words to sort through, but once he got the hang of searching he started catching up on all his favorite series.

He was halfway through the season finale of *Space Police* when Uncle Duke called. Sonny paused the video and dragged Uncle Duke's portal to the center of the the fifty portals he had live at the moment, which took up most of the wall surface he could reach from his bed.

Uncle Duke was wearing a loud sports shirt. Behind him was a jester juggling torches. His condo complex was themed like a castle, with campy medieval touches in all the common areas, and the juggler was one of them. "Busy day, sorry I didn't call you back sooner. So you're in a hospital?"

"I messed up my knee." Sonny aimed his portal camera at his knee brace for a moment before turning it back to his face. Uncle Duke had the deld in his right palm focused on his face, while his left hand held a drink garnished with a pineapple spear. "It's mostly fixed. I didn't see any messages from mom and dad."

"There haven't been any." Uncle Duke took a long pull from his drink. "At first I was worried. I was sending messages everywhere, and I got various conflicting replies about sports riots and about earthquakes."

"Terrorists," Sonny said in a low voice, in case Kayliss was hiding under the bed. With his stolen coat. Even though he knew she was probably far away by now, and he hoped she was uncomfortable. "I don't remember a whole lot. I even forgot my name for a while. Everybody calls me Sonny now."

Uncle Duke gave him a long, patient look that clashed with both the jester and the tropical drink. "I had just assumed you all were dead and they hadn't found the bodies yet. But then I got your message, and I sent you a reply a couple of weeks ago. How was Bonterra?"

"I was out in the country and I couldn't send messages, but I'm getting deported as soon as the doc says it's okay to travel. I hope it's okay if I stay with you until Mom and Dad get back. They're all alive, but

I don't know any details yet, and I don't really want to talk about it a whole lot unless we're face to face."

"I've got an extra bedroom. I'll clear it out."

"Oh, hey, I have a dog."

"Oh cool! Big one?"

"Pretty big. With stripes. Her name is Hina."

"Probably see you within the next couple weeks, then?"

"Yeah. I'll give you more details once I know them."

Sonny flicked the portal closed and lay back on his clean linen, remembering a cheerful guy who was always ready with a funny line from some TV show. A guy who was usually game for a movie or a pizza or a concert or a few rounds of one-on-one. Someone who always knew the sports scores and the latest hit songs, who would show up and pad attendance numbers. A pleasant-looking guy, who was always dressed in clean, coordinated, relatively fashionable clothes. Mysteriously lacking in talents, despite the fact that talent was his country's biggest export.

The wall chirped to let him know he had an incoming message. He acknowledged it and a cheerful cartoon girl popped up in a portal to let him know he was being deported tomorrow at 14:30, departing from Pier 77. It occurred to him that not having clothes would save him lots of time as far as packing.

He found the smiling face of Lucas Quicksilver, M.D. in the hospital directory and left him a message. The doctor called him back a few minutes later. "I didn't think you'd be leaving so soon. I'll bring her tomorrow when they discharge you. She's doing fine but she misses you very much."

"I need to ask you another huge favor. Do you have a sweatshirt or something I could borrow? And some pants? I can mail them back when I get home."

Quicksilver laughed and agreed to bring him something to wear, and they were saying goodbye as a loud rumbling thunderclap sounded. It silenced after a long decay, and Quicksilver and Sonny stared at each other for a long moment through their portals. The doctor was in a lab somewhere, surrounded by readouts and centrifuges, talking through the deld strapped to his palm. Sonny finally spoke. "Do you have a window? Is there a smoke cloud?"

"You thought so too. I'm facing west so it would be behind me."

"It sounded pretty similar."

"It did. We're perfectly safe in here, you know, these towers have been here for hundreds of years. There's been an odd disaster here and there, from time to time." Quicksilver reached his arm out of his portal and de-opaqued a section of the adjacent screen with a scrubbing motion. Blue sky appeared. Sonny looked out at it.

The doctor suddenly looked distracted. "Incoming, gotta go, I'll see you tomorrow," he said, shutting down the portal. Sonny rubbed at his own wall, making a circle of blue sky appear.

"Am I intruding?"

A voice startled him from the doorway. Blocker, sitting in a lightweight wheelchair. She looked several decades younger now that she wasn't in pain. Her skin was smooth over her austere cheekbones. Her eyes were no longer running and red from the pollen, and had reverted to being kind and wise. Her hair had gone from streaked with gray to full salt and pepper at some point during their journey, and it was just long enough for tiny curving lines of braid across the top of her head. "Did you hear that loud noise?"

"Yes." Sonny nodded. "I was just talking with the doc. He says the towers have been here for hundreds of years and there's nothing to worry about."

She tapped at a shiny new deld in her palm, opening up a portal on his wall, and called up the local news. There were five hundred and three different feeds to choose from, and she went for the most popular. The two of them stared, engrossed, as computer graphics began to play. The western cluster, with its hotspots highlighted. "Glad I'm not floating around out there in a wooden boat with a broken leg," she said.

An announcer appeared and Sonny struggled with his revulsion. It was a didge. An animated woman with sharp features and a squiggle of magenta hair, surrounded by a glowing purple aura.

They had lied to him about Sirens, he knew that now. Presumably they had also lied about didges. Sonny's only experience with them had been indirect, in the form of listening to adults complain that they weren't really people.

Didges were people who had converted themselves into digital beings. Their operating systems were supposedly based on the brains in their physical bodies, and they purportedly had all the same memories they experienced during their lifetimes.

They were hated in Braganza not for philosophical reasons but for cinematic ones. Didges could do amazing things with movies. They could recreate any set, copy any sound, shape themselves into any actor that had ever existed. But they couldn't seem to do it with one hundred percent accuracy.

Sonny had seen documentaries about this which had focused on the failures. Elbows that moved out of arc, scenes where some extras are in slow motion while others zip around frenetically, conflicting shadows that could only be filmed on planets with two suns. The facial fails were the most horrible. Some actor would be delivering a speech and suddenly their chin would grow or their eyes would spin around or their mouth would drift to the side of their face. Sonny still remembered one with an innocent crowd shot of children for some toy commercial, where suddenly all the kids' heads pivoted and their eyes flashed red at the camera.

According to the consensus of nearly all the experts in Braganza, this sort of thing could harm small children by giving them nightmares. It could also damage the handmade motion picture industry, by making people afraid to watch movies. Therefore, video from Aqueduct was banned in Braganza, except for a few novelty bars near the beach where digital people could park their avatars on the wallscreen and interact with flesh and blood tourists.

Blocker tapped at her palm. A ghost rose from the didge's avatar, drifting over to the side and opening up its own portal while her original continued delivering the news. Blocker moved the audio output from the news to the ghost.

"Acknowledging Special Agent Blocker." The ghost curtseyed. "Acknowledging unidentified civilian."

"Hello." He managed a little wave. "I'm Sonny Knight."

"Cute. I like it." She spread her hands as if she were holding something about the shape of a bowling ball and a round display appeared, showing the video footage of Sonny getting kicked in the face. "Also known as Leroy."

"Currently known as Sonny." He watched the image on her round display change to video of an erupting volcano, with bright sparks shooting out of the top along with a familiar ominous dark cloud.

"What are you folks projecting on that thing?" Blocker furrowed her forehead as if willing the eruption to stop. "Is it gonna calm down soon?"

"The planet has been through worse." The didge performed an elaborate shrug of her animated shoulders.

"Do you know if Chelisary is out there? My family's there."

The volcano camera turned and flew like a bird, rising high into the air, revealing plenty of deep blue sea. Scattered over it were patches of thick cloud. "The clouds are islands. Dysz lays claim to several of them, and Chelisary is one of them, and nobody but the Qoros knows exactly which. And you have an unusual amount of knowledge regarding this area for such a young man, particularly one from Braganza."

"You have cameras that can fly all over the planet."

"Drones, the size of your pinkytoe. They only last a few days." As if on cue, the one flying over the cloud-shrouded islands suddenly plummeted, and the display went dark.

"You know my real name, you know I got kicked in the face once. Maybe you also know about how Dysz attacked the clashball game and took everyone hostage, including my family."

"He hasn't been statementized," Blocker said. "Waiting to have a responsible adult present, and an attorney if he wants one."

"I want one," Sonny said.

"We are waiting for the boat to take us to Braganza to do that, but there's a volcano sitting right smack in the way." Blocker sighed.

The didge inclined her head toward Sonny, pointing to a spot at the crown of her head where the purple aura was brightest. "Touch."

He did, almost expecting to feel wiry magenta hair instead of cool flat screen. When his finger contacted the screen, another portal popped up, informing him he was talking with Daisy Spring, award-winning newscaster and active Ambit field operative.

The portal went on to state she had been born ninety-seven years ago in a small town in northern Scose. After winning an olympic gold medal in first person shooters, she had joined Ambit and spent several decades chasing smugglers and carbon thieves. Then she served as an embedded data gatherer in the War, and she'd been burned over 80% of her body surface when a Dysz drone ignited an Ambit shelter instead of the military target ninety meters away. At that point she opted to become a didge, and since then she had written one hundred and forty-seven books, and served on many factfinding committees, and set up her own twenty-four hour news network.

"We deal with time in a slightly different fashion," she explained. "And we're good at multitasking. There's an activity log. You can look at every word I've ever said, and every conversation I've ever had, and everything I've read. We are excruciatingly translucent because we know you don't trust us."

"You seem pretty straightforward," Sonny admitted, even though he didn't feel like scrolling all the way through her various accolades.

"I'll be straightforward with you. Dysz has suddenly inflated its population, claiming the new residents are refugees from the riot who fell in love with the tranquil countryside and decided to emigrate. Stop turning red, quite a few of us agree that's complete applesauce. They have supplied medical data for these citizens and none of them appear to be under physical stress. Therefore, Dysz meets the population requirements imposed on it during last year's International Conference and is allowed to remain a member nation of Ambit. They have presented extensive video evidence of the earthquake and riot, and at the same time, we have more than a few complaints about missing persons, and yours will certainly be added to the pile."

"Show him the bad stuff," Blocker ordered. "He needs to know."

Daisy's portal came to life, showing a grainy photo of a scene Sonny recognized immediately. The War Memorial, over near the Hotel Argalia. A flimsy-looking gallows had been built beside it, and bodies were dangling. The next grainy photo showed a pile of bodies, a big dark stain leaking from them. Finally there was a photo of a man wearing a gaudy military uniform, shooting a bound prisoner in the head. The shooter's face was blurry but the pointy nose and weak chin looked very familiar.

"These photos were purportedly taken last month by a man who claimed to have seen this invasion. He said he took these on a military grade camera he'd been saving for the post-game celebration, and then he left town at night in a small boat. He made it all the way to Braganza, where he posted these while waiting for a ship to Zentaro, along with his account of what happened. He never arrived in Zentaro. Apparently he fell overboard at some point along the way." Daisy repeated her elaborate shrug.

"Sounds like a good excuse to stay in our cabin and get room service," Blocker said. "Thanks, Daisy.

I've a good mind to jump in there and join you. I'm not terribly thrilled with dragging a body around these days."

"You'd love it in here," Daisy said as her image morphed into a chorus line of identical Daisies, extending their arms toward a white stairway with a vacant throne at the top, grinning sweetly.

"Not if you're going to start getting surreal on me. I can't hold with that."

The ghost Daisy waved goodbye as her portal winked shut, leaving only the newscaster Daisy pointing to a graph labeled "World Soup Consumption." Blocker closed that portal herself.

"I used to work with her, before she went digital. She looks a little different and she's got all kinds of bizarre tricks, but she's straightforward, as you said. All her memories of me carried over."

"I've always heard you might go crazy if you watch them for very long. People in Braganza don't like didges very much."

"You know what they don't like where I come from? Bigots." She said this in a thick Scose accent and Sonny couldn't help but laugh.

"Probably because they're always beating me at video games. Them and the vatters, with the yellow auras."

Blocker sighed. "That might be an option for me too. Floating around in a vat in Justice with all the other folks not entirely ready to give up their bodies, sending my cartoon character out to play with all the other cartoons.

"Why did you settle down in Vanram? If you're from Scose originally, I mean. I kinda thought you weren't originally from there."

"Nobody's asked me that question in a long time. I always used to make up silly answers. I like the weather. I get a kick out of buying all my clothes off the extra small rack. Truthfully I was there for one reason only, to keep an eye on Premier Lance. After Manganela I made it my life's mission. He surrounded himself with a crew of people just as dirty as himself, so assassinating him wasn't going to be any kind of answer, but I was kind of hoping he'd have to answer for himself someday. Get hauled before the world, tell them all why he thought killing a third of a million civilians for no apparent reason was a good idea."

"He's dead," Sonny said. "Rufe killed him. I saw it."

"People would kill you for saying that in public, and now you have a little more background as to why." She reached forward and clasped his hand in her bony fingers. "Now that I've disturbed your dreams, I shall leave you to get some sleep."

"If they need people to stay in Ambit, then my family is safe." He said it as a statement, not a question. He wanted her agreement, desperately.

"You heard what she said. They've submitted medical data." Blocker opened up another wall portal. This one wanted her retina scanned and her palm examined before it would let her in. She paged through several long lists of files until she found the one she wanted, and she opened it up on the screen.

A spreadsheet. Sonny could feel his eyes redden as he tracked the various columns. Male, forty-eight. Male, thirty. Male, twenty-seven. Female, thirty-one. Male, nineteen.

"They have a lot of males in their country, don't they? The names are confidential, and the important part is in the red column, here. If a person is under stress, such as from torture, their biochemistry changes and we can track it. An elevated score here would show that a person is undergoing extreme physical pain, or anxiety, or fear. Every last one of these people shows a nice low score."

"None of them are anxious or scared?" Sonny wrinkled his nose.

"Happy drugs would be my first suspicion. It's unnatural to have a population that calm. Ambit tracks those numbers in the census. Even the outriders do it when they're out collecting samples. If your population is in misery we want to know why. None of these people are miserable. They are well fed, they exercise, and they'll probably sleep better tonight than you will."

"Can you sort them by height?" Sonny asked.

"Height?" She frowned and sorted, coming up with someone the approximate size of a refrigerator.

"No, show me the smallest." Blocker reversed the sort, and this time the top entry was female, nine. Apparently there had been only one nine-year-old girl in the whole stadium. Marilyn. Her stress level was a nice even zero. As he stared at the zero, tears began streaming from his eyes. Blocker gently reached out and closed the portal, logging out. She patted his shoulder and wished him goodnight and wheeled herself away.

●

Quicksilver presented him with a couple of sweatshirts from past medical conferences, some slouchy pants with a drawstring waist and a pair of yellow clogs that Sonny eyed with distaste, although they were very comfortable. Hina was overjoyed to see him and spent several ecstatic minutes slurping his face before she began sniffing at his leg brace.

He could walk, clumsily, while using a cane. He ambulated out into the lobby and got his discharge instructions from a smiling nurse, along with a slim envelope of pain med patches. Blocker wheeled out to greet them, dressed in a tasteful black athletic suit with a tiny, discreet Ambit logo embroidered on the chest. Quicksilver gave her a kiss on the cheek, and a box of fancy candy. He escorted them through a few elevator mazes while emitting a constant stream of soothing small talk.

They had apparently been way up in the clouds, as they were still many stories above the ground according to the view from the transfer floor where Quicksilver said his goodbyes and wished them luck, and waved them toward the single elevator that would take them down to sea level. They still had eight more minutes to decompress before they could descend again, and there was a comfortable lounge for that purpose, full of padded benches overlooking the dark cloud east of them.

"Not many people have seen it from as many directions as us," Blocker said softly. Sonny squeezed her hand.

"Hey hey!" Sonny looked up. Rufe was advancing, wearing a red polo shirt and polkadotted pants that flared slightly at the ankles, with red clogs. Sonny almost felt better about his own footwear. Rufe sank down on the bench beside Sonny, making it creak, and ruffled Hina's ears. "Headed out?"

"Are we on the same boat?" Blocker smiled as he kissed her fingers.

"Pier 77." Rufe glanced at his deld. Sonny was mildly jarred, as he'd never seen Rufe with a deld and somehow assumed he was a low tech type of guy, but he tapped his palm like a native user. He caught Sonny looking and grabbed him in a friendly headlock, knuckling his scalp. "I grew up with them. Dysz didn't take out the electronics until what, '38?"

"We had the heavy duty field stuff that worked for a while," Blocker reminisced. Sonny had a feeling he was headed for a voyage full of war stories. And accompanying nightmares. The War was interesting, though, in a way that threatened to suck him into obsessiveness. He felt an urge to learn everything he could about it, because it seemed to be directly related to the reason Marilyn's height had been recorded on that creepy spreadsheet.

"It'll probably fold up and die once we get downwind of Vanram but I'll use it as long as I can." Rufe flexed his hand, clearing the display.

Their decompression timer was up and they headed toward the last elevator. A translucent blister sliding down the east side of the tower, giving them a panoramic view of the smoke cloud rising from the volcano. Sonny's recently acquired fear of heights nudged him. He looked down at Hina for reassurance, grateful the floor wasn't translucent.

About a second after they began to descend, Rufe said, "We're all about to die."

Sonny looked up at him. He was peering ahead, squinting. Thirty or so people were in the elevator with them and they gave Rufe glances that ranged from indulgent to annoyed. Rufe kept staring, straight ahead. Hina pawed at him and whimpered. "It's a tsunami," he explained.

"Another one," said one of their elevator companions, excitedly, and everyone started talking at once. Rufe and Blocker had a brief argument about whether to phone in a warning, which was cut short when an alarm went off. A light, pleasant, beeping sound. The elevator slid to a halt.

Sonny dragged his gaze off the floor, swept it over the boat traffic far beneath them and looked out toward the east horizon. Yes, there was a tsunami out there. Headed directly toward them. He couldn't really tell the scale, but it was probably ten times as high as the surrounding waves.

"Do you get tsunamis a lot?" Rufe's voice was light and conversational but his knuckles were wrapped tight around the railing encircling the elevator.

"We've had a few," one of the locals said. "That's a big one."

They had their delds in camera mode and were posing for pictures of each other as the wave drew closer, throwing a shadow. "I hear it," Sonny said, recognizing the sound. Blocker was muttering something to herself.

The top of the wave reached the floor above them. Sonny felt a mighty concussive thump as it hit. The tower itself thrummed like a guitar string, vibrating until everyones' teeth rattled. The locals screamed, holding up their hands in the back-off gesture people made while filming. The view was occupied by angry green froth, and then that washed away and became air again, and blue sky.

Sonny sat down on the elevator floor, feeling dizzy. An official sounding voice came through the speakers, instructing everyone to remain calm, except for first responders, who were to respond immediately.

"I think our departure just got delayed," Blocker remarked. She was looking down. Sonny followed her gaze to the harbor and saw major wreckage. A container ship was lying on its side atop the platform where he'd entered Deuce. Cranes were scattered around like spare parts from a kid's construction set. Some of the ships were still tucked neatly in their slips, capsized.

The elevator jerked and dipped a few floors and opened onto a crowded lobby. Rufe shoved his way through and volunteered to help. Sonny found a corner for himself and Blocker and Hina, where they waited until people in emergency vests came over to ask questions. When they learned Blocker was with Ambit they summoned an Ambit agent, and he began to wheel Blocker away.

"Wait!" Sonny stooped down to soothe Hina. "Where am I supposed to go?"

Blocker and the agent exchanged whispers for a couple of minutes. Sonny heard the agent call up a couple of hotels on his deld, only to be told they had no vacancies, and the two of them whispered some more while Sonny stroked Hina's neck. The people around them were experiencing a wide palette of emotions, which seemed to be vicariously upsetting her. In addition to that, the lights were flickering and loud recorded voices frequently advised them not to panic.

"Sonny?" Blocker's voice cut through the chaos. "The doc says you can sleep on his couch for a couple of days, until everything gets sorted out."

●

The elevators were running extra slow and it took Sonny and Hina hours to get to Quicksilver's floor, including several altitude adjustment stops. He had to stop at a gatekeeper floor first and get clearance from a didge receptionist to enter a side elevator. He found himself walking down a hallway of identical doors. Since he had no deld he'd been forced to remember the directions, and he'd been chanting Quicksilver's apartment number to himself for the last couple of hours. When he finally reached it he had an urgent need to pee.

The doctor opened at the first knock. Hina bounded inside and settled herself on a small couch, taking up most of it. The room wasn't much bigger than their stateroom aboard the *Lono*. Besides the couch there was a puffy armchair, a kitchen nook and something Sonny thought was a walk-in closet, overflowing with piles of scrubs in various shades of green and teal. When he asked politely about the bathroom, Quicksilver smirked and directed him toward a pair of silver foot-shaped oblongs in the corner.

Sonny planted his feet on them and an opaque cloud sprang up around him. Soft, peppy music began to play. A row of cartoon ducks pranced along a panel at eye level, telling him, "Don't forget to drop your trousers!" Beneath them was a control panel listing various personal grooming options. There was a soft bump on the back of his legs as the throne rose up from the floor and clicked into place and once he sat down, a shield sprouted to direct his pee into the receptacle. The cartoon ducks flew down to give him another panel to look at while he was peeing, summarizing the top news headlines, the first of which was "Eyewitness Videos of Today's Tsunami." Sonny recognized his fellow elevator passengers in the third most popular video. After he finished and endured little puffs of scented air in his nether regions he stood up, and was presented with a reminder to put his pants back on, and a button to click once he achieved that. After he clicked the opaque cloud faded away and he was back in Quicksilver's miniscule living room.

"Animal food is in these packs, people food over here." Quicksilver gestured. "We're in the same approximate range even though I'm nearly twice your age. And I left you some sood."

He gestured toward a half-full bag of Cheese Dragons, a box containing most of a pizza and a sack of jelly donuts. Sonny grabbed one of the jelly donuts. "So sood isn't food?"

"If you try to live on that stuff you'll die. It's only for giving your intestines a workout. You can skip it entirely or eat as much as you want. Just make sure you eat three of these a day." He tossed Sonny one of the foil packets. This one was marked for adult males of normal size. It tasted just as bland and chewy as the one for large teenage males. The jelly donut, however, was delicious, tart and sugary in just the right proportions, although it left a slight chemical aftertaste.

Quicksilver climbed into the walk-in closet and began pawing through the piles of clothes. Sonny noticed there was a bed underneath them, making it a bedroom rather than a closet. The doctor vanished behind the door for a moment and came out dressed in a different set of scrubs, then he stepped onto the silver footpads and vanished behind an opaque pillar. By the time the pillar dissolved Sonny had eaten a second jelly donut and was feeling vaguely sick. He also really wanted a third.

"I'm heading back to work. You'll probably be bored to tears but that whole wall is screen, and there's a dog park nearby where I was taking Hina for exercise. The receptionist can probably tell you how to find it. Stay out of my bedroom, and don't make a mess, but if you do, clean it up." He waggled a switch on the wall and arrays of cleanbeams mounted in the floor and ceiling flashed, sending a static tingle through the carpet.

The doctor opened up portals on the wall so Sonny could scan his handprint and his eyeball and granted him door access. Then he left and Sonny shoved Hina over and sat down on the couch beside her. She thumped her tail while gazing at him adoringly, and he stroked her until he felt terrible for leaving her for nearly two days.

After she fell asleep with her head on his thigh, Sonny tapped experimentally at the wall but couldn't get it to do much other than change patterns. Quicksilver had it set to a theoretically soothing display of amoeba-like shapes in greens and blues, and Sonny briefly made the room look like it was on fire before setting it back. He found the real screen over the window wall, which was currently translucent, even though there wasn't really a view of anything except clouds. Sonny tapped on it and a portal appeared.

He logged into his social node and left a message for Uncle Duke about his delayed departure. He found his elevator-mates' video and shared it on his own node, and a few minutes later all of the elevator people were his friends, along with about a hundred tsunami-loving friends of friends. He spent a very social evening on the couch, talking to people and watching video and playing games.

When he woke up the next morning, there was a carton of tacos and a plate of cinnamon rolls waiting for him, and a scrawled note that he thought read, "lunch at turkey" until he realized it actually said "back to work," and that Quicksilver had terrible handwriting.

He tried watching some local television while he munched his foil wrapped bar. The production values were terrible, and a lot of it was digital and therefore looked artificial. He got sucked into a science fiction show called *Roger Asteroid* that had the worst production values he had ever seen, all greenscreened against a series of silly-looking backdrops, but the dialogue was great, even though probably half the jokes flew right over his head. There were six seasons, and he plunged into Season One. He was halfway through the Season Two finale when a voice announced "You have a visitor at the door."

The door had turned translucent, so Sonny could see three teenagers, one of whom looked quite similar to Quicksilver. They didn't seem to be able to see him. He palmed open the door and said hello, which is what a normal person would have done back home. He had no idea whether it was normal here, but they all returned his greeting.

"I'm Bradley Antelope," said the boy who looked like the doctor. "Cousin Lucas asked us to stop by."

The other two were introduced as Tina Candelabra and Marco Calliope. Bradley was light-skinned like his uncle but his hair was a darker shade of sandy. Tina was also pale, with purple hair she had somehow configured into an artificially windblown state, like she was flying through the air at high speed. Marco was darker, with dark blue hair and a tiny chin beard shaped like a fleur de lys. Sonny envied his ability to grow consistent facial hair. They wore bright clothes that would last about five minutes in the wilderness, and they had bright colored clogs on their feet that were just like Sonny's, except they also had strategically contrasting socks, or tights patterned with optical illusions in Tina's case. Hina pushed forward to inspect the visitors and have her ears petted.

"We're supposed to take you shopping," Marco said. "Because you were in a disaster and have no clothes."

"Yes, that's true." Sonny looked at them doubtfully, unsure whether he could get away with wearing Deuce clothes anywhere but Deuce. He reasoned that since it looked like he was going to be in Deuce a few more days, having something to wear would probably be a good idea.

His leg brace made a pleasant hissing noise as they walked down the hall. It anticipated his knee and ankle movements and was covered with sleek detailing that made him look more like a cyborg assassin from the future than a lame guy limping along. There wasn't too much actual walking to do, since Deuce was mostly vertical. It all had to do with choosing the right elevators.

They emerged into a forest of attention grabbers, with a soundtrack of competing pop songs. Lollipops shaped like animals! Talking pillows! Log cabins made out of french fries! Ankle boots that changed color when you tapped the heels! Sonny gawked like the tourist he was and Tina grabbed his arm, steering him towards a store full of animated mannequins that did exaggerated impersonations of the customers pawing through the racks.

"I'm depending on you guys to not make me look like a derp," Sonny said. "I have no idea what derps wear over here, or even what you call them."

"We call them droobals." Marco snickered and jerked his chin toward a group of four boys sitting at a café across the hall, all wearing colorful and stylized cowboy garb. Sonny laughed out loud.

The body scanners took his measurements and apologetically told him he was too large for anything from the racks, while offering custom tailoring in thirty minutes or less for a small additional charge. Tina conferred with a couple of other fashion experts through her deld while Bradley slapped his deld on the payment counter. Sonny's picture was morphed into the store's spring line and enhanced to show how handsome and dashing he would look wearing it, and the four of them narrowed it down to four outfits, with matching socks and a few cans of spray-on underwear.

When they emerged from the store they noticed the fake cowboys had cleared out of the café. Sonny's new gang took over their table, ordering something called the Super Snack Assortment while Sonny pondered the list of strange soda flavors like cantalope and blackcurrant and banana before settling on pear. They sent him friend invites and posted each others' pictures while they were waiting for the order. Sonny was wildly jealous of their delds but buying one here that wouldn't work at home would be a waste.

"So you actually live in Royal Beach," Marco said, looking up from his hand.

"When I'm home." He had tried to avoid discussing personal details and they all seemed fine with that, nattering away about clothes and the tsunami and *Roger Asteroid* – they were all fans.

"They don't really have much of a music scene," Marco said. "Just a lot of dance pop."

Sonny laughed. Marco was trying to pull music snob one-upmanship without realizing that Sonny's close personal friend Daniel Kral was an expert at that particular sport. He had a sudden pang of concern for Dan that was so sharp it was almost physical. That didn't mean he had to let it show. He delivered a bright, lazy smile that belonged on a surfboard. "You'd be surprised. We have a lot of historical music, for one thing. Operas and symphonies and jazz bands. But yeah, there's plenty of catchy stuff for the tourists to dance to. A lot of people visit us for some reason."

"I like jazz bands," Tina commented as their order arrived. At first Sonny thought it was a toy. It was a three-dimensional model of a forest scene, straight out of a children's book, crowded with colorful cartoony animals and trees, fab printed in minute detail right down to the birds' nests and whiskers. At the middle of it was a blue pond. The locals each grabbed an animal, dipped it in the pond and crunched away, and Sonny followed suit. The dipping sauce in the pond was okay even though he couldn't quite tell what flavor it was supposed to be, but his frog tasted like broccoli and cilantro and he made a face. The tiger was better, cheese and bacon-flavored.

His clothes were ready by the time they finished eating. He changed into one of the new outfits right away, and then they all helped him carry his shopping bags into the barber shop, where another conference was held as to what his hair should look like. He firmly refused to change its color, but he allowed the stylist to lengthen it a little. After it was done they led him to a full-length mirror.

The scraggly-bearded outrider was gone, and in his place there was a sleek spaceship pilot, complete with cyborg leg and chiseled cheekbones. He was a bit chiseled everywhere, with visible ribs even through his shirt. He had visible muscles too, straining against clothes cut to flatter the extremely lean.

A stop at the shoe store was deemed unnecessary, since Sonny's yellow clogs went with everything. They all took more pictures with him, posting the after shots on their nodes next to the befores. Then they walked him back to Quicksilver's apartment, explaining they had places to go, and promising to invite him to places they were going in the future. Hina greeted him like he'd been gone a year. She wasn't fooled by his new look but she was definitely curious about his new smell.

As he was making his own posts thanking them for an awesome afternoon, Quicksilver returned. His latest food offering consisted of spaghetti-pops, olive turnovers and three large bags of Cheese Dragons. He looked frazzled, and he burst into laughter once he saw Sonny's new look. Sonny was offended, and wished the place was big enough for him to go into some other room and slam the door.

"No, no, no, I'm not making fun of you." The doctor plopped down in his armchair, which had become his turf now that Sonny had the couch. "I'm hysterical due to exhaustion. Scruffy outrider to sophisticated citizen of Deuce in less than a week."

"It would be nice if I could be a boat passenger in less than a week." Sonny grabbed a handful of Cheese Dragons, since he was suddenly starving. Then he smacked his forehead and got up to fetch a foil packet, opening one for Hina at the same time. "Eating real food again."

"Tell me about it." Quicksilver said through a mouthful of Cheese Dragons. "The latest news is that it's taking twice as long as they thought and it's going to be ten times as expensive to fix it. Which is normal. We're very close to capacity. Shipping traffic to the Mericas has stopped and we're stuck with a lot of stranded people. Besides you. And I've been thinking of leaving myself. People are always telling me I should take a vacation someday. I tend to sign up for fieldwork instead. Once you've been out there." He waved his hands expansively. "You know what it's like. Suddenly you start thinking, 'This place I'm would be perfect if it wasn't missing something. Something crucial, and yet you don't really know what it is. The only thing you can do is get out there and start looking for it.'"

"I can't say I've ever felt that way," Sonny admitted.

"Hundreds of years ago," Quicksilver said, his chair reclining as he prepared to deliver a rant. "Over a *thousand* years ago, you could just get into an aeroplane or a flying car or a motorcycle or a big nice comfortable ocean liner or a fast efficient train and not some rattletrap antique. And you could go everywhere. Sometimes I wish I had a time machine. I'd go back before the magnets started malfunctioning and the chemistry changed. Back when the air could hold a signal and there were animals everywhere."

"And no cleanbeams," Sonny pointed out. "Or Cheese Dragons."

The doctor let out a long dramatic sigh, massaging at his temples. "I'm seriously thinking about Asia. There's a cross-cultural program for doctors and I'll be able to get my continuing education requirements out of the way for at least the next decade assuming I physically survive crossing the Pacific, and that's actually not too bad, from what I've heard. I'd have to make do with translators because I can't get a language chip. I've got too much onboard already. That's really what's driving my decision. I suppose I'd best show you since you're directly involved."

He dug into the side of his chair and came up with a silver gadget which he slipped over his forehead like a loose tiara, tapping it into place. He cleared his throat and a portal opened up, even though he hadn't cued it from his deld, or physically touched the screen. Inside the portal was a view of the room, through Quicksilver's eyes, with Sonny and Hina sprawled together on the couch. At the periphery of the display were hundreds of tiny icons and graphs and displays, and a little red selector dot that bounced from one to the next.

The doctor stared directly at Sonny. On the screen, the indicator dot selected one of the border icons, and suddenly Sonny's heartbeat was amplified through the speakers, and a ghostly cardiac monitor materialized over his head, displaying his pattern. The red dot moved to another selection and the loud heartbeat was replaced by heavy breathing and information displays about the number of breaths per minute he was currently taking, and the capacity of his lungs.

"That's what the world looks like through your eyes?"

"My heads-up display. Spent hours on it." The red dot floated to a new icon and a new overlay appeared, and Sonny recognized one of the simple little pattern games that he used to play on his deld whenever he found himself sitting around waiting. The doctor's high score hovering in the corner was into the hundreds of billions.

"You've got games built into your eyeballs. I'm jealous. Can you watch movies too?"

"As a physician with full field medic capabilities, I am an isolated system, which means no onboard communications devices that could compromise patient confidentiality. But I can download."

The scene on the wall froze. The doctor hit rewind, with an occasional pause. Pause for the zeppelin flight. Pause for a small brick cell with no furnishings beyond a cot and a bucket, the game overlay indicating this was where Quicksilver got his last high score. "Jail in Chianina," he explained. Pause, eating garlic noodles on the *Lono*, with Sonny visible at the side of the frame.

"You were filming everything."

"I suppose you could say that. My rig piggybacks off the nerves to my eyes and ears, so while I may have one memory of something stored in my brain, I've got a photographic record stored in my implant. Usually the two match. The ones that make it into my brain are more or less permanent even though I can't reproduce them, but the stored memories get overwritten after three months, provided I'm out of the country. It doesn't record anything in Deuce because any procedures I perform are already being filmed by the clinic."

He backed way up, until the date March 20, 3748 appeared beneath Hina's familiar face, split into one of her extremely wide yawns. Hina yipped at the sight of herself onscreen as Quicksilver let the memory play. Sonny stared, feeling heaviness crept into his chest. Quicksilver wandered over to look at the game, pacing back and forth.

Having seen thousands of movies, Sonny noticed an odd quality to Quicksilver's eyeball cameras, since they only focused on whatever he was looking at. In a movie, unless they were doing some kind of specific foreground effect, the extras would stay in focus if you felt like looking at them instead of the leads. In this video he was forced to follow the doctor's gaze as it bounced from object to person to object in a jerky and nonlinear way. Look at that player pouring sweat, run a quick temperature graph. Look at that guy in the band making a serious face as he puffs on his horn. Look at that fan with his face painted red and gold, colors streaming in the heat. Look at the Rams' mascot aimlessly bashing its horns against the side of its cage. Look at Rufe Marshall, leaping in the air and making a ferocious face. Look at that player on the sidelines, shirtless and damp, lifting his chin in an attempt to catch a breeze – look at him again, then on to something else.

Sonny made his entrance with a loud crash. Quicksilver's gaze did a quick and dizzying half-circle as his ears filled with Hina's screams. The live Hina cried along in sympathy. The doctor's mumbled "shit!" came through loud and clear as he bent over Sonny's broken body, which was lying atop Hina's broken body. Sonny's stomach lurched as he noticed the angle of his spine, and his bad knee throbbed now that he knew it had once been much, much worse.

The bodies mercifully dissolved as the doctor applied some kind of imaging overlay that turned them into broken skeletons, and then a heap of quivering muscle. Text flashed rapidly across the top of the screen, too fast for Sonny to read, the doctor mentally answering "affirmative" faster than he could vocalize it. His hands reached out, his claws extruded from his fingertips. He caught Hina at the base of the neck with lightning speed, holding her jaws back as she howled in pain, and he caught Sonny firmly around the bicep.

Then he was dragging their limp bodies out of the wreckage and arranging them on the floor, and people were buzzing around to help as the doctor's gaze bounced between them while occasionally shuffling to Sonny and Hina. He zoomed in for a close-up as Sonny's knee, turning him into a tangle of pulsing red veins. "That's as close as I can magnify it, but all of those dots are tiny factories that hitch a ride to the scene of the crime on your white blood cells, and once they get to the destination they analyze what went wrong and haul everything back into place and cement it down. Miraculous, really. Unkilling people. It's the main reason I became a doctor."

Sonny recognized the look on his face as Quicksilver sat back watching his own memory. It was the one Rufe had when he talked about past games, or the one Kai wore when he was regaling them with maritime lore. Blocker had been wearing it when talking with her didge friend about other countries and their secrets. It was the look of someone who had a talent, that they'd mastered, out of sheer love for doing it. That made Sonny even more jealous than Quicksilver's ability to play videogames on his eyeballs. Not that he wasn't extremely grateful.

His body fluttered and stood, and Sonny watched himself chug down an impossible amount of water while dancing from one foot to the other like a little kid struggling for bladder control. He barely heard the scream when it sounded, but the on-screen Sonny had clearly heard it, and he took off like a shot. The doctor was moving a little slower after dispensing his payload of microscopic factories, and it took him a couple of seconds to realize Sonny was running.

Quicksilver tore after Sonny and burst into the private box. He caught Risha out of the corner of his eye, and there was another audible "shit" on the soundtrack. Then there was Sonny's voice, saying "Hi. I love you. Will you marry me?"

The doctor glanced over at this, capturing Risha's "Sure!" and the nervous laugh that followed it. His eyeball cameras rolled sharply upward, and the speakers delivered his mutter of "oh, please" as he turned to a furious, red-faced old man with a bloody, broken nose who yelled "Get your hands off me!"

The old man punched the doctor in the face, sending him reeling back, clutching his bruised cheekbone. There was a vague hint of chaos beginning outside as Quicksilver's overlay turned the old man into a silhouette. Red flashing text appeared above him, something about "toxicology."

Premier Lance's silhouette was drawing his gun. The doctor switched back to a more photorealistic image of him, confirming the gun. More warning text appeared for him to affirmative his way through as he backed toward the door. Quicksilver became distracted by the artillery fire at that point, and then by Rufe smashing his way into the box. Rufe actually body-checked the doctor as he lunged for the champagne bottle, his face filling the screen as he growled a stern "You stay out of the way, doc. I'm gonna kill this asshole."

Rufe then spun around, delivering serious force to Premier Lance's skull. Quicksilver shifted into skeleton mode, and Sonny was grateful for that. He watched Premier Lance bloodlessly sustain multiple fractures in the region of his eye. And fall. On top of Sonny, who was on the floor with Risha.

The doctor darted in to grab Risha's outstretched hand and pull her toward the corner while several more messages about toxicology flashed. He changed his overlay of Risha into a weird skinless construct that was still somehow extremely beautiful. Graphs appeared around her, showing her heart rate and respiration and blood pressure and many other things.

At that point, two clones arrived and shot the Premier's dead body, throwing it away and revealing Sonny with a gun in his hand. This Sonny was grubby and wild-eyed, clothes ragged and covered with his own mostly-dried blood, clutching a gun. Not just any gun; this was the Premier of Vanram's own beloved special personal private gun, shiny and slick with preservatives. Vanram's climate tolerated metal, as long as you kept it inland and regularly coated it with preservative. It seemed safe to assume someone lovingly coated this weapon with preservative every single day. It was almost a cartoon of a gun, oversized and heavy and unwieldy, and it looked even larger in the hand of a crazed-looking teenage boy.

In Sonny's memory, he cowered in fear when the Qoros demanded he drop his weapon, meekly submitting. On film, he slowly laid his weapon down while holding the clone's attention with his own spooky-eyed stare, his teeth showing in a way that made him look violent and demonic. Then Rufe made his move and Quicksilver was diving out of the way as more violence happened. Once the people on the screen fought their way to the water and jumped in, Quicksilver snatched the tiara from his forehead and threw it across the room.

The doctor pulled up another portal and logged into his social node, which was just as cluttered as his visual field. He dragged his segment of video into it and did something, and a moment later Sonny's own social node was beeping to get his attention, in a discreet wall corner since he didn't have a deld. He opened it up to find a friend request from Quicksilver, which he accepted. It came along with a chunk of video. He closed out the portal, afraid to touch it.

"Some people want that memory," Quicksilver said. His voice was tired and raspy. "Other people would kill me over it. Now you have a copy."

"You should just make it public," Sonny blurted. He stopped to ponder whether he really meant that.

"Words are free?" Quicksilver snickered. "Perhaps I should talk to your agent. Maybe I could get it shown on NBS. After all, it's probably the only video of the game in existence. It does show you in a rather unflattering light, however, looking like you just crawled out of a sewer, waving that ridiculous gun at a world leader.

"I didn't do anything wrong," Sonny protested.

"Do you know what the word 'toxicology' means?" Quicksilver's voice was even raspier.

"Poison," Sonny said.

"Did you give the Premier poison?"

"No."

"Who else was there?"

The Cheese Dragons bag crinkled in Sonny's hands. It couldn't be. There was no reason for it, not in a million years. She would never do that. Risha would absolutely not travel to a weird violent country full of weird violent men to poison the Premier. She just wouldn't. No. Finally a "No" made it to his lips, and Quicksilver gave him a bitter, raspy laugh.

"That smoke was poison."

"That's an excellent point, and many of my tox alarms did indeed involve the smoke that was putting everyone to sleep. You were already high as a kite from being restored, so it wasn't hitting you as hard. But anybody who knows what to look for would be able to tell immediately."

"Well, what about Rufe? He committed murder."

"Probably not by Vanram law. They let you kill people in self-defense, defense of another, defense of your sheep, defense of your right to do stupid things from time to time. Besides, Rufe wanted to kill him. You heard it. He was planning on it."

"But they've got my parents. And if Rufe makes trouble ..." Sonny drew up his knees. Hina whined and licked his ear.

"I could sail off to Asia." Quicksilver hauled himself out of his chair and headed to his sleeping alcove. "By the time I get back, I'll have new memories to replace it."

Sonny watched the video after Quicksilver shut his door, and then he watched it again. After he watched it a third time he locked it up under heavy security, forbidding access to anyone who couldn't pass a retina scan. Then he buried it under several other layers of boring things so he wouldn't have to look at it. As he was doing that, he noticed an incoming message from Marco Calliope, bearing a gift of music.

At first he winced. If someone back home had given him thirty hours of music, they had probably spent serious cash. But here in Deuce all the music was free, so he gathered he was under no social obligation to provide a return gift. Sonny scrolled through a list of verbose titles before finally hitting random shuffle, turning it down in consideration of the doctor's slumber.

The first song was a guy singing over two chords. An hour later, Sonny had come to the conclusion that most Deuce music consisted of a guy singing over two chords. Sometimes it was a girl. Sometimes there were three chords. Their lyrics slid through his brain comfortably, without sticking. His mind was shuffling through its own playlist, unable to hold onto any particular thought longer than a couple of seconds.

He had always seen himself as a nice, normal, likeable, visually pleasant sort of guy. He couldn't get the image of the deranged punk from Quicksilver's video out of his head. If a character like that were to appear in a movie, he'd probably show up to deliver a single snotty, sarcastic line before getting smacked around by some superhero. Some guy like Rufe, who could splinter a man's orbital bones with one mighty swing of champagne.

Having already survived viral fame, he had an idea of what it was like. Strangers saying weird things. A bloated in-box, although his was helped by the fact the Nothing But Sports Network gave him a professional screener who made sure he never saw anything negative. It had peaked for about a week, then the public had become fascinated with a cat in Geelong, Australia that could bark like a dog. Then his fame had dwindled until there was nothing left but a trip to Vanram.

"Our shocking top story tonight: kicked-in-face kid turns evil, tries to assassinate foreign leader," he said to Hina, ruffling her ears. At least he had a bodyguard.

He had an urge to talk to Risha, and he tried looking her up. He had figured she probably didn't spend much time online, being that she was a Bonterran girl. To his surprise she had a well-decorated social node, which was surrounded by many layers of privacy. Sonny couldn't even send her a friend request, since all of his contact attempts were redirected to some law firm in Virginialina.

He only found one picture of Risha online when he had assumed there would be thousands. This picture was hosted in Petrichor Industries' corporate node, right next to the annual report. A smiling and heartbreakingly lovely Risha was posing in front of a fancy doorway, wearing a businesslike blue dress that was tailored to her curves. The photo was dated 3741. Sonny had been eight.

Maybe someone else poisoned Lance. Maybe Risha just happened to be there. His mind replayed the event, and as he did that he noticed his memories were starting to merge with Quicksilver's vision around the edges, although parts of them were crystal clear. The part where Lance had loomed over him, looking sick and sweaty, trying to focus his gun. Maybe he had been poisoned, but that didn't have to mean Risha did it. There had to be a perfectly sensible reason she had been there.

Rufe was also hard to contact, with all his messages diverted to a publicist in Zentaro. Kai was comparatively easy to find, even though Sonny had no idea how to spell his surname. The *Lono* had its own node, complete with a smiling photo of its captain, and when Sonny left him a note hoping the ship had weathered the tsunami, he got a reply call within a few minutes, from a screen set up in Nepenthe's room. Sonny could see her mermaid avatar beyond Kai's shoulder.

He shared his woes about being stranded, and listened to Kai rant at length about the damage to the harbor, and to the *Lono*. "Just got her repaired and now she's down for repairs again. The shipyards here are terrible, and I had to bribe them to expedite their terrible work so I can limp into Carquinez and turn it over to the professionals. One financial detriment after another."

"Can I go with you to Carquinez? If I can't find another ride before you leave? I'll work in the kitchen or wherever you need me."

"I thought you were headed in the opposite direction."

"It's starting to look like I'll have to go around the whole planet to get home."

"I have an incoming call," Kai said abruptly. "I will be in touch."

Sonny researched traveling on the internet. There wasn't much information available. There was a shipping route directly from Carquinez to Shanghai, and another one from Lisbon to Zentaro. Both journeys took two to three weeks, and Sonny wasn't familiar enough with the currency to tell whether they were expensive. Once he got to Shanghai he could take trains all the way to Lisbon, unless he decided to check out Australia or Japan along the way.

There was also a train in Passiter, low on the west coast of Samerica and technically within Vanram's borders. It even linked up with another train that would take him directly to Braganza. This train had a scattering of one- and two-star reviews from previous travelers, and there was a section where you had to wear protective gear and breathe through tanks while the train made its way through an old battlefield that hadn't been remediated yet. Their online presence was primitive and it took him a while to figure out how much the fare was. Then he pulled up a currency calculator and struggled with it.

He had money in his account. Enough to buy five or six outfits, or to pick up the tab at a pizza party, or to attend forty movies, or to purchase a new deld. In Vanram, this was enough to buy a house, but the train cost twice as much. He had enough to get to Lurie, the capital of Carquinez, but not enough to get anywhere beyond it. He had a small trust fund set up to keep him from spending most of the NBS money, but it was locked away until he was eighteen. He supposed he could ask Uncle Duke for a loan, but he didn't really want to do that.

Hina distracted him by whining while jerking her head toward the door. She knew how to use the footprints, which had a special housepet mode, and it took Sonny a few minutes to figure out that she wanted to go to the dog park and run around. Sonny closed down his portals. Worrying about money was like feeding the chickens at Risha's house; you started out with just one, then all the rest figured out it was feeding time and you got mobbed. The more he thought about his impoverished state, the more it led to worrying about his family and his future, right when he'd gotten to a state where he could be content for several hours without being ambushed by any bad emotions.

He looked up directions and carefully memorized them, but Hina knew the way, leading him through four different elevators until they arrived in a big lobby where people accompanied by animals were standing in line. There were cats and dogs and rabbits, miniature horses and elephants and rhinos, along with several fluffballs of indeterminate species. Hina didn't stand out at all, and Sonny was privately very relieved.

In fact, there was something remarkably calming about the entire room. He watched a cat aim a lazy swat at the back end of a miniature pig. A small puff of pink steam arose from the floor, surrounding the cat, which flopped over on its side, purring.

The line moved fast, and soon he was talking to a smiling attendant who directed him into a section of the park for Hina-sized creatures, and they stood in a very brief line behind a golden retriever before being admitted to a cool leafy forest. The illusion was so tight that it made the hair stand up on the back of Sonny's neck. Dirt and pine needles were beneath his feet, almost indistinguishable from the real thing. He awkwardly bent over to touch it. Definitely dirt, although his fingertips met with floor a few centimeters down. The trees around him felt real, although the ones in the background faded to digital.

Something flashed in the bushes and Hina took notice. A squirrel appeared, streaking from tree to tree. As it passed close by Sonny saw it was an animation, sort of cartoony in fact, leading Hina on a circuitous chase. He heard a bark up ahead and saw the golden retriever chasing a squirrel of its own.

There was a forest path lined with perfectly sized throwing sticks, which bounced off the camouflaged hallway walls unless you threw them straight ahead, along an unmarked path which led to a green meadow where prairie dogs popped up at random intervals. There was a round plaza in the center, full of benches for humans to occupy while their pets ran up high scores. Some of them were even placing bets on a sleek gray weimaraner that had pounced over a thousand animated prairie dogs this session, according to a tasteful simulated carved wood signpost. Another signpost bristled with arrows pointing to other mini-environments like "Splashy Beach" and "Stick-Throwing Creek." Screens and backdrops melded seamlessly with rooms full of dirt and plants and water, as long as you stayed on the paths, and Sonny noticed that everyone did.

The air was permeated with happiness, in a low dosage. The dogs romped but didn't fight, the people traded friendly chitchat. Above them was an artificial blue sky projected on the ceiling, complete with a scattering of fluffy white clouds, and a sun in approximately the same place as the real one. No gloomy dark clouds of volcano smoke here. There were flies, but they were actually tiny drones, converging whenever poop happened and attacking it with spray that made it rapidly decompose.

Hina helped him find his way back. Quicksilver was slumped in his chair inhaling the steam from a mug of tea, working his way through a congested in-box. Sonny settled himself on the couch as the doctor retrieved one from Rufe that started out with a jovial "ey-hey buddy!" and worked its way toward a demand that they get together, soon. The doctor deleted it, and two more just like it. There was also one from Risha with an oblique "we should talk," and the doctor deleted that one too. Then he deleted several from Ambit, aside from one acknowledging receipt of his request for assignment to Japan, or any country near it.

He jiggled his wall switch a few times and his array of cleanbeams flashed. "I'm going to expedite my request. You can stay here if I should leave before you find transportation."

"I want to get a job," Sonny said.

The doctor frowned. "You can't. That's the short answer, but you look like you're about to ask why. We're post-cash here, in case you hadn't noticed. We got an emergency credit issued for your fashion makeover, your medical care is free, the government provides your basic rations. When I leave the country I expense everything to Ambit, but once I'm here there's nothing to spend it on except for a few luxuries."

He ripped open a bag of Cheese Dragons and stuffed a handful into his face. Sonny grabbed a few for himself. He was starting to develop a taste for them. "So I can't just, I don't know, go clean boats or something?"

"Oh no, if you were to get injured it would be a bureaucratic nightmare. Citizens work, and if they do a good job they get credits which they can spend on Cheese Dragons and vacations and new hats for their video game characters, assuming they're too useless to figure out where the free downloads are. We have a few people like that here. In return, we all get to enjoy our infrastructure together. We don't get a lot of immigrants, although we get a fair amount of tourists. You, as usual, are somewhere in the overlap."

Life settled into a rhythmic uncertainty. The doctor worked for shifts rarely shorter than twelve hours, then he came home and slept for long stretches. Usually he brought some kind of sood with him. The foil packets were delivered in cartons every week, by a robot. Sonny always ate those, but he had reached a point where he could take or leave sood, which left an oily chemical aftertaste no matter what it resembled. The doctor had noticed his lack of interest and had stopped bringing back the kind of sood that directly resembled food, instead going for the kind locals preferred. Elaborate printing in intricate detail so it felt more like you were eating collectable figurines than food, flavors you couldn't quite place. He was still heavily addicted to Cheese Dragons, and brought back a bag of them at least every other shift, and Sonny usually grabbed several handfuls for himself. The savory artificialness of the cheese went along really well with the chemical aftertaste.

He wasn't quite clear on what sort of life-threatening medical emergencies were keeping the doctor busy. He suspected a lot of it had to do with keeping too busy to think, something he was doing in his own way. He made regular visits to the dog park, and he watched hours and hours of movies, including several he was pretty sure were pirated. He felt guilty about that. He got caught up on *Roger Asteroid* and a few other shows. He reactivated his subscription to HeroLand and got his Ice Viking to max level, and then he optimized its gear. He spent more time staring into space than he planned to.

He made it all the way through Marco's playlist, and only one song caught his attention. It started out like every other song recorded in Deuce, a line of lyric, then the guitar or ukulele or dulcimer or didgeridoo would start churning, changing to the other chord at predictable intervals, while the singer related a dry and wordy tale full of local idiom that sailed right over Sonny's head. This particular song did that, but at the same time there was a good rhythm track. Sonny couldn't help tapping his foot.

After it was over, he wound the song back up and listened to it again. The rhythm track was somehow dragging a melody out of the singer. It confronted him, forced him to answer questions, bounced right over his vague replies. The song was called *Ice Bubble* by Bippy Borp.

Bippy Borp had two members: Milton Dandelion, from Deuce, and Gilbey Park, from the United States of Korea. According to their official bio, they had never met in person and had no languages in common. They did their communicating through translatorbots and their performance through screens. Dandelion played a kinetic synth that was strapped to his body and translated his gestures into sounds, while Park sat down at a grand piano, although any sound at all might emerge from it, depending on the song. They had one album out, *Twin Pears*, and were about to release a new one. Sonny listened to *Twin Pears* three times in a row, while reading the lyrics, which were heavily cross-referenced. Several of the references had to do with movies as both of them were cinema fans, and Sonny caught some of them without even having to travel through the links, which made him feel smart.

He messaged Marco back, telling him *Ice Bubble* had been the only decent thing on his playlist, which must have earned him several music snob points because Marco responded with an invitation to a party commemorating the release of Bippy Borp's next album, which was happening in a couple of weeks. Sonny promised to be there if he was still in Deuce.

He was surprised when Quicksilver congratulated him on the one-week anniversary of his knee surgery. June twenty-eighth. He felt like he'd been incredibly busy, although when he thought about it, he'd mostly been watching movies and chitchatting, with some gaming thrown in. His school had offered him credit if he turned in an essay about what happened, and he'd started it a few times without ever managing to make his way out of the first paragraph.

Quicksilver sentenced him to physical therapy, with the prospect of removing the brace in another week. This happened in the main gym for their section of the tower, which took up three floors and was similar to the dog park, on a bigger scale and without the dirt. You could do weightless freefall yoga in space, or swim along a river with surprise environment changes around every bend, or ride a bicycle through various historical periods, or dance your way through scenes from famous musicals guided by an exoskeleton that would hold your joints in place while keeping you from falling on your butt. Sonny was more familiar with gyms that had more mirrors than screens, but Deuce gyms were not conducive to large crowds, and Deuce people worked out solo, or in pairs.

Sonny's knee-strengthening regime involved a lot of treadmill time, on a miniature treadmill that was just long enough for his stride, inside a pyramid of cubes containing treadmills just like it. There was a helmet you could wear if you wanted to be somewhere else, and everybody wore them. Sonny usually set the visuals to random while tromping along listening to *Twin Pears*, or sometimes music from home that had a good beat for walking. Marco had sent him more music, including Milton Dandelion's previous band, but he just wasn't as good without Park.

Gym every day, dog park twice a day. Mornings were for checking messages, afternoons for responding. At three his Ice Viking met with a pack of his fellow Heroes logging in from various countries and spent an hour fighting arena matches against Saxons and Mongols and Leprechauns. There were slots for reading novels while listening to music, and watching videos, and an hour each day for a thing called Calmitude. This was a program where he put on a helmet and entered a pretty virtual meadow, complete with pond and butterflies, while listening to soft voices reading inspiring things over music.

Calmitude was part of his medical treatment; the helmet gathered his biometrics and occasionally gave him meds administered through a quick buzz at the base of his skull. He suspected some of the meds suppressed his emotions, since he felt far less sad, and he often caught himself enjoying things he didn't normally like, such as gathering video game mushrooms, or reading about celebrity gossip.

Not the news. The news frequently had the power to rip beyond the thin scab of calmitude he was developing and catch hold of his nerves. Volcanoes, earthquakes, money, families and clashball were among the subjects likely to set him off, and start him down a worry spiral.

Blocker occasionally touched base, letting him know that Dysz was refusing to provide personal info on its citizens due to privacy concerns, and blaming the volcano for knocking out communications. The biometric data was still arriving regularly every few days, proof of the citizens' health and good cheer.

Recently it had also provided photos of a village, full of houses made of dark brick. They were attractive in a solemn and discreet way, very different from the bright colors and floral explosions of Royal Beach. They all lacked front windows, and front yards. The next photos showed interiors with sunken firepits, and huge black bathtubs, and kitchens that looked like starship command decks. There were no people in the photos, which was mildly disturbing.

When Sonny asked how exactly they were sending the data without being connected, Blocker had further alarmed him by letting him know there were Qoros living in most countries, and some of them were somehow in contact with Qoros from Chelisary, and they were very secretive regarding their methods. "Those two Rufe killed had been living in Bonterra for over a decade. They're all over the place, blending in. Presumably they don't agree with their homeland's politics, or possibly they're deep agents. If you've got a machine that can tell the difference I'd like to buy one."

"Some of them are in Deuce?"

"Afraid so. There aren't any officially in Bonterra anymore, aside from the ones in what looks like a labor camp according to the satellite photos. Assuming they're still alive. We've requested their biometrics but you know how it is, data keeps getting lost, harvest season and stampedes and such."

"A labor camp." Sonny didn't know what that was but it didn't sound like much fun. "Is the government of Braganza doing anything, do you know? About my family?"

"All the countries involved have agreed to let Ambit handle it." She made a sympathetic expression. "I'm sorry, Sonny. Things can move slow once you start involving rules and committees."

Marco's apartment was much the same as Quicksilver's except it had two sleeping alcoves, one of which belonged to Marco's parents, who had made themselves scarce so that twenty teenagers could pack their bodies into the small space to listen to the new Bippy Borp album. Sonny felt slightly guilty for being the largest one. Even though he was as thin as he'd ever been. Especially his bad leg, which was finally free from the brace and visibly smaller than his good leg, but you couldn't really see it while he was sitting cross-legged on the floor, which many people were doing given the lack of seating.

His turquoise and purple outfit and front-spiked hair would have earned him merciless teasing back home, but here it put him somewhere in the comfortable middle of the flashiness spectrum. Even better, his look appealed to at least two pretty girls, Jillianne and Katiana, who were sitting on either side of him. Jillianne lived here, but her cousin Katiana was a tourist, from Scose, who had been visiting for spring break and was now trapped. "They're repairing a train line in Bonterra, and once that's done we can just take a train. It takes a couple weeks until you get to Virginialina, then everything speeds up. So I'm thinking it won't be as boring as the ship that got us here."

"Yeah, I heard there was a train bridge that collapsed or fell apart or something like that." Sonny sipped at his frothy super-carbonated soda. There was a hint of ginger in it, which reminded him of eating ginger noodles on board the *Lono*. "You'll probably see some outriders."

They listened in rapt attention as he explained what outriders were, and shared a few highlights from outrider books he had read, since they were far more interesting than his actual interactions with outriders had been. None of them had involved the kind of constantly-flowing conversation that went on here, filling the tiny apartment with words. If you asked an outrider what color the sky was, they'd tell you it was blue. If you asked someone from Deuce, they'd describe the shade, and tell you how they personally felt about it, and cross-reference fifty or sixty things that were blue in a similar way. While carrying on a couple of side conversations on their delds via text, or maybe they were leaving their deld mics open so that other people could overhear.

Sonny still didn't have a deld. Or any indication of when he'd be able to go home and buy one.

Bradley was at the other end of the party, doing a jerky little dance to some band that wasn't Bippy Borp, and therefore sounded like every other band in Deuce. Marco was near him, nibbling on a cellist from an edible orchestra that had been set up in the middle of the room as a party snack. Sonny's back was against the screen-coated window separating him from a countless-meter fall into the turbulent Pacific ocean, and occasionally that fact popped into his conscious mind.

The people in the middle of the room were colorful and articulate and curious. Their skin and hair colors came in a wider range than they did back home, where everyone sort of centered on a golden tan, with hair that was brown, or blond, or brownish-blond. Some of the people here were as pale as Quicksilver while others were as dark as Blocker, and a couple had opted for exotic shades of purple and green. Sonny supposed that was only really possible if you completely avoided direct sunlight, and he realized that aside from himself and Katiana, most of the people in the room had never been outside. And Katiana had probably traveled from a tower to a ship to a tower, as she was a little bit puzzled by concepts like uneven terrain.

A portal binged on the wall and all the chatter suddenly ceased. Sonny reversed himself and reclined back on his elbows, glad to have a more solid portion of tower against his back. The food was covered, and people settled into comfortable listening positions as the words *"Some Bricks Are Yellow"* flashed on the screen, followed by Bippy Borp's stylized logo. A moment after that, Katiana decided he would make a good pillow, and squirmed beside him with her head resting on his ribs.

His brain sizzled momentarily with the knowledge that a girl was touching him in a friendly and slightly intimate way. He carefully rested his hand on her shoulder, and she didn't shrug it away or scream so he left it there, cuddling her as the music began to play. Portals opened up on the windowscreen showing Dandelion and Park, bouncing and spinning in matching jumpsuits that changed color under the lights. The room was absolutely still as the music played. Sonny kept his hand steady on Katiana's shoulder, never actually stroking it but occasionally splaying his fingers.

Bippy Borp played eight songs with no visuals beyond themselves. Then they took a simultaneous bow and faded into the video for the ninth song, which featured a curvy woman with short blonde hair, always filmed from a distance, far above or behind. The lyrics had to do with wizards, and the beat was aggressively catchy. Sonny's fingers tapped on Katiana's shoulder, and her fingers tapped lightly on his belly. Dandelion's voice rose to an impassioned scream as Park's rhythm built, until finally the camera caught up to the woman and zoomed way in, as she turned to look over her shoulder.

Sonny half-sat up in startlement and Katiana's head rose from his chest. "Are you okay?"

"No, I ... she reminded me of someone." Sonny watched Risha's face fade as the music ground to a halt. Marco brought the lights up as the last hour's pent-up conversation spilled out of everyone's throats.

"Someone I know? Someone bad? That was really a brilliant album."

"Yes, it was. Someone I used to know, except she never had blonde hair." He sighed. Katiana had curly brownish hair, and she was touching it self-consciously.

"Sonny!" Marco hollered from across the room. Sonny gave Katiana's shoulder a quick pat that he hoped was reassuring and slithered his way through the bodies to a small subsection of the party where music snobbery was occurring. Bradley was playing, as well as Marco and a few other guys, dissecting the lyrics they had been frantically transcribing. "What did you think of our provincial western music?"

The crowd around him snickered and Sonny grinned back at them. "I liked that a lot."

A guy wearing a little droobal-type hat that was cocked to the side spoke up. "The reference to the bricks of yellow in the title means gold, because gold used to be stored in bricks. So it's all about money."

"It's about *The Wizard of Oz*," Sonny said. "The yellow brick road, and all the stuff about wizards at the end. Old movie, from when they first started making them in color."

The music snobs fell silent except for the faint sound of fingers scratching on delds as they all simultaneously researched *The Wizard of Oz*. Marco was the first to verify that it had been a real movie, featuring both yellow bricks and wizards. And munchkins, which had been referenced in track seven. And the winged monkeys from track three.

"Wow," Katiana said as she caught up to Sonny and squeezed his shoulder. "He's right. I've seen that movie."

The guy in the droobal hat gave Sonny a sour glare as his comrades enthusiastically exchanged research notes and composed their reviews. "There were also quite a few references to money."

"Posted!" Marco threw up his arms gleefully. "I'm officially the first one to mention the *Wizard of Oz* reference."

Several of the music snobs around him growled in frustration, and a couple of them abruptly left the party. To be fair, the party was starting to break up, having accomplished its purpose of listening to the album. Jillyanne was tugging on Katiana's elbow, and Sonny accepted their invitation to accompany Katiana back to her hotel.

He had never been in the tourist area before, even though he was one. When the elevator doors opened he staggered at the overwhelming smell of food. Some of it was pleasant, sizzling steaks and hot vanilla, but most of it ran together and reminded him Deuce food didn't smell at all. It didn't taste like much, but it didn't even smell that bad when you pooped it out. Consequently, Deuce people didn't go around smelling like whatever they'd been eating.

Jillyanne wrinkled her nose. "They have foreign food up here. Stinky!"

"It's better than that paper food you like," Katiana teased her back.

Katiana was staying at the Perfect Plaza Inn, and she kissed Sonny's ear as they said goodbye, inviting him to a Bippy Borp concert on Friday night if they were both still around. He accepted with as much enthusiasm as he thought it might be cool to display, and asked hesitantly whether the tickets were expensive. Katiana told him the tickets were comped, and that he shouldn't worry about it. Then she kissed the very tip of his nose before vanishing into her hotel. Jillyanne seemed mildly upset by that, and she melted off into the crowd.

Sonny explored. There were fountains and neon and restaurants and gift shops, and plenty of flashing displays. Arcades and cafes, piles of whisper-thin shirts in all colors bearing pictures of the sun setting behind the two towers, so they looked like a big II.

He was examining a glittery snowglobe when he heard Rufe bellow his name. It was unmistakeably Rufe, he had heard Rufe bellow on many prior occasions. Sonny left the shop and looked around, trying to identify the direction of the bellow. He spotted a sports bar bristling with screens showing people competing in many different games. Rufe was the biggest guy at a full table, and he waved madly when Sonny looked in his direction. He was wearing a red and yellow polo shirt that looked vaguely like a Rams jersey, and his hair and beard were freshly lasered, but at the same time he exuded profound disappointment.

Sonny wasn't really sure he wanted to talk to Rufe, but he responded anyway. A chair was found for him and inserted beside Rufe. Someone started to pour him a beer but Rufe interfered, and Sonny found himself faced with a coffee-flavored soda instead. "I saw you earlier, with two girls," Rufe said, sounding impressed.

The guys at his table elbowed each other and giggled. Stuck travelers from all over, even including a few from Vanram. From Sonny's current perspective they were all huge and rangy and sloppy, pores reeking with meaty sweat and stale farts. He must have looked like that himself a couple weeks ago. He overheard a couple of them whispering to each other that Sonny looked like a girl himself given the way he was dressed.

"We were listening to this local band." Sonny smiled and sipped his drink. He could see several people holding their palms in camera mode, aimed toward him and Rufe. Rufe saw them too, leaning in to get their heads level and offering his snarly smile.

"You still staying with doctor whatshisface?"

An invisible wall of defensiveness went up behind Sonny's smile. "Yep. He's always working hard. Saving lives."

Rufe snorted. "He could save a few more if I could get him to return my calls." His voice got louder as he addressed the table. "Sonny was there! He saw it all."

Cameras chirped like crickets. Sonny felt blood draining from his face. He could hear muttering about the kid who got kicked in the face, that one time. "I don't remember much."

A steak appeared in front of him, perfectly seared, paired with a baked potato oozing with rivulets of butter. It had been hours since his last foil-wrapped biscuit. His stomach growled. He forked a bite of steak into his mouth as Rufe blathered on about the game. His tastebuds notified him that this was the most delicious steak he had ever eaten in his life, and he attacked it as Rufe spoke of the invasion, and the conspiracy to keep it out of the news, and how he was actually the rightful ruler of Vanram.

The steak and potato vanished and a slice of cheesecake appeared in the void. Sonny's stomach was round and drumlike but he ate it anyway, and then he sat there in a trance as his body marveled at the introduction of actual food. "They've still got his family," Rufe concluded, and the crowd cooed with sympathy.

"I think some kind of government thing is handling it," Sonny said. "I wouldn't want to mess that up. I probably shouldn't talk about it."

"Once I'm the Premier, it'll happen. We'll force them to turn everyone loose." Several of the men at the table cheered at this. Sonny glanced around at them. Stranded travelers, mostly from Scose and Virginialina. Sports fans, whooping it up like they were headed to a rematch. Rams versus clones.

Sonny's belly convulsed and for a moment he thought he was going to puke, right there at the table. He fought with his stomach muscles for a moment as the cheering died down. "Rufe, they've still got my family and all those other people. They're at least providing medical reports so we can tell they're not being tortured."

"And you'll continue receiving them," Rufe said, in a booming stage voice. "Until they die of old age, or of something else. Until someone does something affirmative to get them out of there. Maybe they'll grab more people. Grow themselves a whole country. They might even have enough players to put together their own pro clashball team."

This drew a laugh, as Sonny focused his entire strength of will on not puking. Rufe leaned over the table at him, delivering his speech right into Sonny's face. "I am the person who will take that action. I will stop them, from harming you, or your family, or anyone else. Ever again. I swear that to you, upon the blood of my father. Who was betrayed by the man calling himself Premier Lance. Who is dead. Tell these people who killed him."

"You did," Sonny croaked, without puking. "Smashed him in the eye with a champagne bottle. I was there. I saw it. I have to go."

Palm cameras flashed and cheers sounded as Sonny lurched to his feet and mumbled goodbye, his words swallowed up in the sound as men crowded around Rufe, offering their funds and their contacts and their warm, enthusiastic support. Sonny dashed for the exit, heading directly for the public restroom, a little corner with a grid of discreetly spaced footpads. "You look like you're about to throw up," commented the cheery animated ducks, just before Sonny threw up on them.

The toilet went into vomit mode, applying suction to his face until his stomach ceased heaving, then sponging his cheeks and chin with something damp and warm, followed by a minty fresh mouth rinse. Cleanbeams pulled at his clothes, and a little video lecture about responsible use of mind-altering substances commenced, delivered by the animated ducks.

Both his good and bad knees were wobbly as he made his way back home. Once he got there he spent a solid hour on the couch, curled around Hina, worrying. After that he spent another hour raging. It wasn't fair. He'd been having fun. He had impressed the music snobs, and met a girl, and they were going to a concert together, and his heart had been light. Rufe had stolen that, and now he had those images in his mind again. People dying. People being stolen.

He paced, and swore, and yelled. Hina encouraged him with her own noise. He was in the middle of an angry roar when Quicksilver opened the door. Sonny's yell trailed off and Hina got a few more barks in before rushing to greet the doctor. He bent down to give her an affectionate hug, and when he stood up and looked at Sonny, the affection was gone.

He tapped his palm and the wallscreen erupted in a portal, in which a flushed and sweating Sonny sat amongst tourists, saying the words "Smashed him in the eye with a champagne bottle."

"It's all over the news."

Sonny flopped down on the couch. "I ran into Rufe. He wants you to call him."

"He's declaring war." Quicksilver flung himself into his own chair. Hina ran around the room a few times in case all of the forcefully-flung bodies were being playful. Once she realized they weren't she curled up in a corner.

"Did they edit out the part where I told him not to put my family in danger?"

"Was it with the part where you politely asked him to stop using you to make political points? I mean, you've demonstrated you have enough onboard intelligence to live under a bridge for several days. One would think you would be able to figure out when you're getting played."

Sonny took a moment to do battle with his temper, reminding himself that Quicksilver had saved his life, and he had absolutely nowhere else to stay. "They were wound up when I got there. I met someone, at a party, and I was taking her back to her hotel. And Rufe was there. The tourist district is kind of small, and crowded."

"And tacky," Quicksilver added, clicking his cleanbeam array on and off. "Smells terrible. *You* smell terrible, in fact."

"I wish I had grabbed a to-go bag and brought it back for Hina," he said. Hina thumped her tail in agreement. "How did you ever handle real food the first time you went outside?"

"It was rugged. And stop trying to distract me. This conversation is concerned with your idiotic behavior, and your directly endangering others, all because you failed to keep your mouth shut."

"I didn't say that much!" It came out much louder than he intended, and he repeated himself in a loud whisper.

Quicksilver played it back. *Smashed-him-in-the-eye-with-a-champagne-bottle.* He played it over and over, a few times. Sonny stared at his image, not quite sure what Quicksilver wanted him to see, noting how different he looked as a skinny, anxious Deuce teen with mod hair. Quicksilver emitted an exasperated sigh. "Is that from your memory? Or is it from mine?"

Sonny blinked. He had figured out that it was a champagne bottle. Later, after the fact. Quicksilver had actually seen the impact, and in fact at that part of the video, Sonny was on the floor, rolling out of the way. "It's your memory, and my knowledge."

"And your knowledge of my memory. Which means you just confirmed to Rufe that my memory exists, and you've seen it." Quicksilver rubbed his eyes. "I was prepared to say that you were never in the room. You had nothing to do with it, you were uninvolved. It's the truth. You were a bystander, who literally fell from the sky, on the unluckiest day of your life."

"I saw his face," Sonny said. "After Rufe smashed him. Close up. I still have nightmares about it."

"I could give you a referral for cognitive therapy, but you'd probably scare them. Happy drugs are always an option, especially if you're in the habit of blundering your way into unfortunate media situations. Perhaps something that keeps you nice and lethargic and just smart enough to play amoeba pinball." He pulled up a portal with an especially colorful game of amoeba pinball, by way of demonstration. Sonny made a face.

"I could do another interview and tell everyone I didn't actually see it, I just sort of made an assumption that Rufe killed that guy. Maybe I could ask for some donations so I could pay you back for staying on your couch."

"No, no, no." Quicksilver made an exasperated noise. "No media. Promise me. Keep your promise and the intense anger and disgust I'm currently experiencing will dissipate over time, no doubt. Swear it on whatever you find holy, if anything. Let Ambit handle it, through peaceful negotiation, and science, and respect, and fairness, and people not getting killed, and all that sort of thing."

"I promise I will not talk to the media," Sonny said.

●

When Friday morning arrived, he was still around. So was Katiana. She answered his call right away, and they arranged to meet at seven. Which gave him the whole day to spend going to the dog park and gym, as well as getting his hair trimmed and his face shaved by the toilet console's grooming mode, and using up his daily attempt at getting the dragon in Wurm Canyon to give his Ice Viking a rare drop sleipnir steed.

He had spent the week not talking to the media, at all. No updates. No text conversations, or voice ones either, aside from occasional groupchats where he said things like "Yeah" and "Awesome" and

"Agree." He was also filtering his incoming messages, blocking anyone he didn't already know. He did know a few people at the Nothing But Sports Network, and a few of their messages got in, but he refused to open them. Rufe sent him a steady flow of friend requests, which he also refused to acknowledge. He almost ignored Blocker, but when he listened to her message expressing surprise, since he had never spoken about it, he sent her a brief reply that he was going to resume being silent, and asked whether she had heard anything about any ships. She responded that she hadn't.

He was a little bit perturbed over losing his ability to socialize when he had finally made some friends. Sometimes he would leave a portal open to an audio channel used by Marco and a bunch of his friends to share music and friendly insults and pointless discussions, and often he had some kind of text groupchat going, maybe three or four of them. He didn't really have any deep-conversation friends at the moment, but he had lots of friends who would distract him with anecdotes from their nice, normal lives, or toss him an inspiring picture every now and then, and they meant a lot to him.

He knew the drill. He had been through it after becoming virally famous. Your words are probably being intercepted, so use as few of them as possible. Don't advertise your activities, unless you want crazy ranting sports fans showing up in the pizza parlor blaming you for last season. Report all threats, verify all transactions, record all interactions with strangers. He couldn't really record on his own without a deld, but he was never very far from wallscreen that could open up a camera portal in a pinch. He didn't think his latest bout of fame would last very long, since it wasn't nearly as funny as getting kicked in the face.

Instead of talking, he'd been reading. He went through all the news reports about the game, figuring there wasn't much nightmare exposure potential since he was already having them. Hina frequently stopped them by sitting on his chest and licking his face.

The very first news reports, from March, strongly implied that the clashball championship had broken out in a serious sports fan rioting, resulting in the destruction of millions of dollars worth of property until the city of Argalia was under martial law, at which point it was wrecked by a tsunami, and the heroic people of Dysz had swooped in to rescue many people. By April, the heroic people of Dysz were asking for relief money on behalf of their pals in Vanram, devastated by catastrophes.

Last month, when Sonny had been curled up in his coat to survive the nightly ice-cold winds, conspiracy theories had arisen. The heroic government of Dysz refused to comment on them, and Sonny got his first glance of President Effarren, the guy who had helped Premier Lance kill all those people in Manganela. He looked just like Kayliss would look if she were an old man. He also had something Sonny interpreted as a gleam of craziness emanating from his eyes, although it might have just been the retouching.

Premier Cello, the new leader of Vanram, looked much the same. Weak chin, scary intense dark eyes, pointy nose, dark hair, widow's peak. They were maybe two decades apart. Cello was just starting to go gray around the temples and Effarren was all the way gray. Sonny wondered if clones knew in advance which week their hair would turn change color, and why they didn't just step into a salon for fifteen minutes and recolor it, and maybe do something about the nose pointiness while they were in there.

A couple days after his encounter with Rufe, a smug-looking Daisy Spring gave a snarky report about a pro athlete who had drunkenly challenged his own country to a duel. She didn't have any video, but several other news sources did. Through those, Sonny found Rufe's fundraising node.

It was a full virtual worldette, a place where the sky was always red and the white Romanesque entry point was always lit at a dramatic angle. It was staffed by a purple-auraed didge and two vatters with yellow auras. All three of them were dressed in fantasy armor that revealed lots of muscular flesh, and when Sonny accessed the portal they greeted him enthusiastically, directing him toward various floating displays with labels floating over them. "Cause" and "History" and "Facts."

Sonny enlarged the portal until it took up the whole wall. Stirring orchestral music played in the background as he wandered through the exhibits. One door led into a simulation of the city of Argalia, much cooler and cleaner than the real thing but still realistic enough to accelerate Sonny's heartrate, and he hurriedly backed out of that room, and found himself in an exhibit featuring his picture.

Kicked-in-face-kid was getting his face kicked in an endless loop. Each time, he looked up at the camera directly afterward, displaying the imprint of a muddy shoe edge across his eye, which wasn't sleepy-looking at the moment. Both his eyes were wide open as he made his reaction face, and Sonny had to admit it was a great reaction face, well deserving of its brief international fame. The first time he had seen it he had refused to leave the house for two days. His parents had finally sat down with him on the couch, showing him endless clips from comedy films, where people got smacked in the face with pies, cakes, fish, boxing gloves and various other objects. He was finally forced to admit that getting smacked in the face could be entertaining, and funny.

Plus you could get paid for it. His dad had then shown him a message from NBS discussing terms.

He tore his eyes away from the spectacle of his abused face and found a picture that was even worse. This was a shot of him with the crash team upon his arrival in Deuce. The boy in the picture was skin and bones, with shaggy matted hair and a scruffy beard, covered with dirt smudges. His leg was wrapped in a dirty bandage. His eyes looked sorrowful in their sleepiness. To someone unfamiliar with outriders, he probably looked more like an extra from a historical movie, or maybe a zombie.

There was text and sound surrounding the two photos, explaining exactly how the dastardly fiends of Dysz had turned a fine, athletic boy into a grubby refugee, and that your donations could help make it right. As Sonny's eyes traveled further, they fell upon pictures of his family. Someone had mined them from his social node. Right next to that was the video from the sports bar.

"Take this out of here! Right now!" He was yelling, and he didn't care who heard him. "Right now! Tell Rufe I'm going to call a lawyer. No, tell Rufe he can kiss my butt! I'll tell him! Get in touch with him, right now!"

He found himself suddenly evicted from the temple, facing a blank wall. He continued yelling at the wall for several seconds, even though he knew nobody could hear him except Hina, who was hiding under the couch.

He stopped yelling, and took a few deep breaths. He checked the time. He had enough time to listen to most of *Some Bricks Are Yellow* one more time before seeing them perform it live, while he changed his clothes, and coaxed Hina out from beneath the couch. He apologized to her as they both ate their foil packeted meals, stroking her ears.

Katiana was waiting, and she lit up with a bright smile when she spotted him, and greeted him with a hug once he got close. They joined a brief line that curved around velvet ropes and stanchions. Sonny didn't particularly feel like talking about his day so he asked about hers, listening sympathetically to her tale of trying to buy a particular brand of shoes, and encountering nothing but knock-offs. "That's all they seem to have here is counterfeits. If you get the real kind in Manhattan they're good quality, but the ones here just fall apart."

"You don't really have to walk that much," Sonny pointed out.

"Still."

The line snaked its way into a concert hall that took up three floor levels, with steeply sloping rows of seats and a big floor dotted with delicate bistro tables. The stage was mounted on the wall about halfway up, with lever arms that could extend it into the middle of the room. Katiana was agreeable when Sonny suggested sitting at floor level, and they found themselves a table with a reasonably good view.

Katiana was feeling talky, and Sonny had gotten in the habit of keeping his mouth shut, so he let her go on about the awesomeness of Manhattan, and her friends, and her school. He could tell she missed them, and he certainly knew what that was like. He made occasional sympathetic statements while he checked out the crowd. It was relatively small despite the large venue, and he and Katiana seemed to be the only tourists. He noted with some amusement that he was one of the biggest guys there as far as height, and shoulder width. Aside from that he didn't stand out much, and neither did Katiana, with her brown hair hanging in two tails, one over either shoulder, secured with sparkly clips, and her lean body wrapped in a skintight dress printed with black-on-black latticework.

There was an opening band called Glib Job that sounded exactly like every other Deuce band to Sonny. To his surprise, about a quarter of the audience got up to dance. Their dancing was a simple two-step, side to side, and they all did it in unison. Certain words set them off; when the singer uttered the word "moon," the crowd sang "moon" back at him, circling their arms over their heads. When he mentioned "love" the crowd loved him right back, fingertips pressed to hearts.

"I've never seen this before," Katiana said, taking pictures from her palm. "This is the first time I've been to a live show here."

After each song, the crowd circled their right arms above their heads, twirling invisible lassos, rather than applauding. There didn't seem to be any particular reason behind words that invoked a response, "separate" and "perpetual" and "gray" all did. Sonny was forced to revise his opinion about Deuce music, in that it wasn't necessarily boring. In Royal Beach you listened respectfully to performers, clapping when it was appropriate, and Deuce music was only boring when you listened to it that way.

Glib Job finished up and took their bows. The house lights came up and Katiana started chatting up a girl nearby, asking if the response-dance thing had a name, and how they learned which words to use. While Sonny sat there, feeling drained, glad to be a cool guy in a cool place with a cool girl. Surrounded by people his age. Being entertained.

The lights dimmed and suddenly Bippy Borp was there, floating out over the crowd on their stage, giving Sonny and Katiana a view of the soles of Dandelion's dancing feet. Park was present as a screen, flat and two-dimensional and slightly taller and wider than he actually was. When the stage rotated Sonny noted the back of the screen showed Park's back, as if he were only a couple millimeters thick. Other screens showed the view from Park's end, a different concert hall with an Asian audience and a flat, two-sided screen containing Dandelion.

Bippy Borp's lyrics were full of words that cued the crowd, energizing them enough to break them out of their two-step rhythm. On the Asian side, the crowd did something a little different, singing brief sections of Park's musical riffs back at him, like an echo. Lights whirled around the concert halls and visuals projected on the walls and ceilings and furniture and floors, turning them into gardens, and spaceships, and rows of bright candy. The last song ended with a giant image of Dorothy skipping down her yellow brick road. The Asian audience bowed to the audience in Deuce, who bowed back, then the Deuce crowd did their lasso gesture, which was reciprocated.

"That was probably the best concert I've ever seen," he said to Katiana as the lights came up.

"It was different," she agreed, reaching over to squeeze his hand. "Let's sit here while the crowd leaves."

Sonny started to tell her it wasn't that crowded. Then he noticed her lips were parted in a kissable way as her face moved toward him. He kissed her. It lasted for a long time. Her breath smelled of real food in a way that was not unpleasant, chocolate and apples. Their tongues became acquainted. One of Katiana's hands moved up to Sonny's cheek.

They parted to catch their breath, smiling shyly at each other, and then they kissed again. And then, out of the corner of his eye, Sonny saw a curvy woman with short blonde hair. His face must have changed, because Katiana stopped kissing him. "Is something wrong?"

"I just ... saw someone I know."

"Oh?" Her eyes scanned the room, immediately falling on Risha. Deuce women just weren't that curvy next to Risha. They were lean, slender, svelte, coltish, elven. Katiana was a little taller than most of them, and built in a similar streamlined way. None of them had Risha's hourglass curves. Tonight she was displaying them in a pink dress that was little more than body paint, and several people besides Sonny and Katiana were staring at her.

"She's an old friend," Sonny explained. Katiana withdrew her hand from his face. He told her he'd be right back.

When Risha saw him she screamed his name and greeted him with a hug. "Did you like the show? I didn't know you were into Bippy Borp! One of my old friends sent me their album and said they were looking for a girl to be in their video, and I won the audition. Did your knee get fixed? You look so handsome, all dressed up."

He had assumed Katiana had followed him and he turned to introduce her, but she was actually still sitting at the table. Scowling. He turned back to Risha, who was smiling happily, as beautiful as ever. "I had surgery and they fixed it up. I've been waiting for a ship."

"You and me both. I'm thinking it might be faster to just head east."

"I tried to call you up and say hi, but I got redirected."

"Oh, that." She made a face. "Venusian Designs. That's my company. Try that one."

"Venusian?"

"From Venus." She pointed to a section of wall that had been de-opaqued so they could see the stars, indicating a bright spot. The moon was completely dark. "Ever wish you could just hop into a spaceship and leave this planet in your dust? Anyway. I should let you get back to your girlfriend."

"She's not my --" Sonny looked over his shoulder. Katiana's chair was empty.

"It was good seeing you!" Risha twinkled her fingers at him and made a quick escape through a door bearing an Authorized Personnel Only sign.

Sonny trudged back to the elevator, wondering if he should call and apologize. On the other hand, a girl who was too jealous to even let him say hello to an old friend probably wasn't worth pursuing. However, it had been his first kiss, and he didn't want to be on bad terms with Katiana. He wondered if she was still in his network of friends, or if she had blocked him.

He palmed open the door to Quicksilver's apartment. He got an immediate sense that something was wrong, but he couldn't single out any evidence until Hina whined. A sad, small, hurt whine.

"Hina?" He turned in her direction. He heard Quicksilver yell something, just before pain seized through his body and sent him flying.

He was sprawled on the floor. Dazed. His ears were ringing, and that might have been from the concert and it might have been from the stunrod the Qoro was holding in his hand.

He was a typical-looking Qoro, dressed in a shirt with a black and red geometric print, his hair sleek and perfect. There was another Qoro behind him, holding a knife to Quicksilver's throat. The doctor looked extremely angry but he was holding himself still.

"Enjoy the concert, assmunch?" The Qoro with the stunrod reached down to give him a hand.

Sonny ignored it. His eyes swept the room for Hina, and found a limp furry form lying in the corner, in a puddle of blood. "Hina!"

He tried to move toward her. The Qoro with the stunrod dealt a vicious kick to his solar plexus, leaving him gasping on the floor.

"Torturing animals and teenagers," Quicksilver commented, disapprovingly.

"Shut your face," said the Qoro holding him at knifepoint. Then he opened Quicksilver's face, giving him a diagonal shallow slice across his nose that bled profusely.

"I only want to know one thing from you," said the stunrod Qoro. "Have you ever seen this guy's onboard recordings? Of anything?"

Sonny blinked, fighting to get his lungs back into their normal routine. Quicksilver's eyeballs were slowly moving from side to side, making a "no" gesture.

"Oh yeah, we downloaded a bunch of them. I've got them saved. Would you like to see them?"

Quicksilver looked very unhappy with this response, but he didn't say anything. Sonny made a big dramatic deal out of picking himself off the floor, trying to give himself time to think. The Qoro hurried him along with a kick to his lower back. "Move your ass."

Sonny made his way to the wallscreen and opened up his social node, fumbling through his files. He could hear Quicksilver moaning in the background. He scrolled through a series of scenes from his eleventh birthday party. "No, that's not it, it's here somewhere."

He dropped his left hand. He opened a very small portal beneath it, a camera portal. His right hand moved to the real video, opening it up on a freeze frame of Sonny looking his most thuggish, wild-eyed and covered in blood.

"That's it," said the Qoro holding the doctor as he sunk the knife deep into his throat.

Sonny's heart was beating so fast he thought his own blood would come surging out of the top of his skull, like a fountain. He hit record, and then he hit broadcast, and then he wound the video back to the beginning. Quicksilver slumped to the floor as the Qoros focused their attention on the video, transfixed, and Sonny enlarged the camera portal to get a view of the entire room.

Then he sent the video stream to his social node. So that every single one of his friends had their own copy of it.

"After this video finishes playing, you're going to watch two members of the Qoro family murder a teenager," he said, softly. "They've already killed an innocent doctor because he recorded this, and they also killed my dog."

The Qoros took a moment to drag their attention away from Sonny's video. Both drew weapons as if to prove his point.

He kept talking, a little louder. "They've already stolen my family and locked them away on their island, and they won't let me talk to them. They attacked the whole stadium. You're watching a video of it. I wasn't taking a video myself, but I was there, and that's exactly what happened. Now you all know the truth. Pass it along."

"Turn that recording off," screamed the knife-wielding Qoro, lunging for Sonny.

"It's locked." He slumped against the wall, grinning a hysterical grin. "I can't. Wave to the audience, you're live. Look, I'm calling emergency now."

He opened up yet another portal as the stunrod-clone opened up a portal of his own and tried to override Sonny's. The knife-wielding clone landed on him as he began yelling about emergency, police, murder, now, right now, right now.

The knife landed dangerously close to Sonny's face but he managed to catch the Qoro's wrist with both hands. The Qoro tried to punch him in the face with his knifeless hand, and that put him off balance. Sonny shoved the wrist up at an angle, making the Qoro howl with pain.

The stunrod Qoro turned away from his portal. "You're going to die, dickrot, and I don't care who sees it. Get off him."

"Just a second." The knife Qoro recovered his equilibrium and went ahead with his plan to punch Sonny in the face, all the while straining to bring the knife down. He was extremely strong. Sonny might have been one of the biggest guys at the concert but the Qoros were bigger. It was taking both his arms to keep the knife hand away, and the punch had seriously hurt.

"Just let me zap him and let's get out of here." The stunrod loomed closer. Sonny was having a little trouble seeing it through his recently-punched eye.

"Don't zap him while he's got hold of my arm, idiot." Another punch rained down, this one landing on Sonny's forehead. Sonny took one hand off the knife, letting it drift closer, and punched the clone back, in the mouth, before grabbing the knife hand again.

"You're both idiots," Quicksilver said, standing behind the Qoros, drenched in blood and steaming with anger. His hand landed on the first Qoro's arm and squeezed, then the second. Both of them went limp, and Sonny rolled to the side to avoid being trapped underneath them.

The doctor was already attending to Hina, and Sonny heard her tail thump as he opened the door for the police. He collapsed on his couch and sat there, staring straight ahead, as the bodies were hauled away. Quicksilver's voice was a little raspy as he drank glass after glass of water, explaining to the police he was under Ambit jurisdiction, and then an Ambit team arrived and the police left. Sonny kept the camera running the whole time. At some point Hina crawled up on the couch beside him, trembling and covered with dried blood, and he wrapped his arms around her. He could feel stickiness in her fur that seemed to be a stab wound, but she seemed intact, although she shared Quicksilver's extreme thirst.

Finally a softspoken Ambit officer loomed over him and asked him if he was finished recording. Sonny said yes, and hit stop. And unlocked everything, and logged out. The police left, and Ambit had a quiet discussion with Quicksilver over in the corner, and then finally Ambit left too.

Quicksilver opened a little closet and took out a spiderlike cleanbot, and set it to scrubbing up the bloodstains. Then he flashed his array of cleanbeams until all loose particles vanished from their hair and clothes and skin.

"It was a pretty good concert," Sonny said, after the doctor finished up and collapsed into his chair. "I ran into Risha."

"Did you." Quicksilver got up to get himself a fresh bottle of water, and refill Hina's bowl, and then he paced around in circles. "I'm high as a kite. I did an auto-restore. I am the king of my apartment! Do not meddle with me!"

"They killed you." Sonny shook his head. "I can't believe they killed you. Are we going to be in trouble, like Bonterra?"

Quicksilver did a precise cartwheel, and then a backflip. "Nope. Not here. Besides, I didn't kill them. Unless they had weak livers to begin with, of course, and there's a good chance they'll exhibit a few glaring neurological deficits once they recover, assuming they do. Doctors are allowed to incapacitate persons who are insane to the extent they're endangering persons and property, and committing a crime is evidence one is not altogether rational. Murdering me is not rational. Did you get that on camera? I think one might also make a good case that cloning oneself hundreds of times is not rational at all. I should probably tranquilize myself."

He sat down in his chair, grasping the arms and taking deep breaths until his body began to wilt. All but his right leg, which was bopping and grooving as if it were participating in a jitterbug contest all by itself. Sonny cautiously opened his social node, just enough to notice his messagebox was getting slammed and he had several hundred new friends demanding acknowledgment. He checked the hit counter on the video and noticed it was already in the thousands. People in Nairobi and Adelaide and Constantinople had seen it. It was trending in Aqueduct. Sonny shut down the portal.

"You have a visitor at the door," sang the cheery voice. Sonny looked over his shoulder and saw Blocker through the translucent door. She was standing up, with a brace on her leg that was a little bulkier than his. She was wearing a gray sweatsuit, with her hair stuffed into a knit cap, looking like she had just gotten out of bed.

The doctor turned his head around in slow motion as Sonny went to the door and let Blocker in. Hina greeted her, sniffing curiously at her brace as she made her way to the couch.

"Good evening, Dee," Quicksilver slurred. "Always a pleasure. I hope you are well."

"You boys are nothing but trouble," she said.

"We have had considerable amounts of expert assistance," Quicksilver replied.

They pulled up the video on the wall and watched it again, discussing it in detail. Sonny ceded Blocker the entire couch, stretching out on the floor beside Hina. He felt both hyped and exhausted, victorious and despondent. He was elated that Hina was alive and well, and terrified by her near-death. His lips still tingled from Katiana's kisses and his ears were still ringing with music.

"I'm pleased the record notes I died attempting to keep that particular footage away from public consumption," Quicksilver finally said, with a pointed glance at Sonny.

Sonny sat up. "It's the truth. It's what happened. They stole my family, they tried to kill me and a bunch of other people, and now the world knows about it."

Blocker threw a grid onto the wallscreen. Qoro faces, wearing a variety of hairstyles and facial hair. The older ones all had the same midtone skin that was a little lighter than Sonny's, but the young and middle-aged ones ranged from Blocker's darkness to Quicksilver's paleness, and included a few women. Kayliss was last, wearing a scarecrow's blouse and floppy hat at the bottom right corner, fresh off the zeppelin.

"They live all over the Mericas," Blocker said. "They are doctors and scientists and engineers, academics and merchants."

Sonny's eyes were drawn to one of them toward the middle, who seemed to have had some very subtle plastic surgery that tipped him toward handsome, with a shaggy mane of hair that flattered his features. "How many of them live here?"

Blocker outlined a handful of headshots, letting the rest fade away. She circled two of them, young men who looked very familiar. "These two are tonight's visitors. They were on a ship with these individuals which left shortly after we arrived."

She corraled more of the headshots in her circle, including Kayliss. Then she excluded Kayliss off to the side. "The ship had to turn around, and they all came back to Deuce. All but one."

"Do you think they killed her?"

"I do." Blocker pursed her lips. Sonny was surprised to feel the old familiar heavy chest sensation setting in for Kayliss. He noticed each Qoro had three letters beneath their headshot. The two visitors were JXN and JBL, and Kayliss was KLS. "The rest are being detained for questioning."

She enlarged her loop to include some of the old men, and a woman named JLN with bright two-tone hair, and plenty of makeup. Sonny didn't think he could pick her out of a crowd of random Deuce women.

"Fabulous. I'm trampling innocent peoples' civil rights by defending myself in a non-lethal fashion." Quicksilver hauled himself out of his chair in slow motion. "I need to sleep for several hours."

"Is there any word on a ship?" Sonny couldn't stop moving his eyes between Kayliss and JLN. He could feel his opinion revising with regard to Kayliss' ugliness, and it was uncomfortable. Especially since he was inexplicably sad about her death. If Kayliss had lived long enough to get a haircut and some eyeliner, she could have been attractive.

"None at all." Blocker sighed, rising to a standing position with a quiet whirr from her brace's motors. "I imagine we shall be in contact, and therefore I will bid you goodnight."

●

Venusian Designs had an elaborate entry portal bordered by thousands of species of flowers, each rendered in fine detail. It was a worldette like Rufe's, but the similarity ended there. When Sonny opened the portal, he found himself on a terrace, overlooking a city full of waterfalls and cathedrals and geometric gardens. Spinning carousels and children with balloons.

He navigated through the city, stopping outside a shop that sold eggs containing tiny dioramas. He entered the shop, which was far bigger than it had looked, with a domed ceiling studded with geometric tile. There was a back door leading to a courtyard with a bubbling fountain. Sonny went through the door and found another city. This one was in a pine forest scattered with snow, overlooking a blue lake, with buildings made of wood and dark gray stone.

He noticed people as he navigated his way through the new city. The stylized avatars of vatters and didges with their glowing auras, and meatspace dwellers like himself with their generic paperdolls that sometimes bore their own faces. They all seemed to be tourists like himself, taking in the sights, occasionally clumping up in crowds for a busker or puppet show.

A windowbox exploding with geraniums caught his eye. It looked vaguely familiar, and when he went inside the shop beneath it, which sold flower arrangements, he found himself in a virtual rendition of Bonterra. Chianina, in fact. He recognized the bank, and a grin broke across his face when he noticed the newspaper office had been replaced by a pig sty, containing a muddy sow that vaguely resembled Meggy Boggs.

There was the Petrichor house, up the street, on its hill, faithfully rendered. Sonny marched his avatar toward it, noticing an ambient loop of "When I Get Home" was playing in the backround, a tinkly piano version. The front gate was open but none of the people who normally would be bustling around were in attendance, and the front door was locked.

Sonny knocked. A yellow-auraed woman opened the door and showed him into an exact copy of Risha's parlor, where he stood examining an embroidered wallhanging showing outriders silhouetted against a mountain at sunset.

"I'm so glad you're all right!" Risha was suddenly beaming at him from a painting on the wall, which showed her in an apartment two or three times the size of Quicksilver's. Big enough for two couches, and a chaise longue, upon which Risha was sitting, wearing a frothy green thing that displayed tempting swaths of shoulder and belly and leg. Sonny tapped his own camera and his face appeared atop his paperdoll avatar. Risha gasped sympathetically. Sonny hadn't looked at himself in the mirror but he knew his lip was split and puffy, and he was pretty sure he had a black eye.

"They almost killed Hina. And the doctor." Sonny touched his eye gently. It was definitely swollen. A popup appeared announcing that Venusian Design was now his friend, and he patted it in acknowledgment.

"I hope everyone's okay." Her voice trembled with concern.

"We are. Aside from waiting forever for a ship."

"I've got the same problem. Nobody wants to risk it. Sonny, can you meet with me? In person? I've got something I want to tell you. In private."

The word "sure!" leaped out of his mouth before he consciously thought about saying it. He watched Risha's assistant whip out a long elegant quill pen and scribble some exquisite calligraphy on a slice of rough, homemade paper that had flower petals pressed into it. She folded it into an aeroplane and threw it at his inbox, which lit up.

"Give me two hours," she said. "And please don't tell the doctor, it'll only make him worry. Go ahead and look around. Here, I'll give you a universal transportation buff. Just say go. Or stop, if that's what you prefer."

She pressed a button somewhere and a gold box lit up at the bottom of his screen. Then she turned to go, but Sonny stopped her. "Wait! What is this place?"

She thought about it for a moment. "I'm a person from a place full of natural beauty who recreates it for people who live indoors. I paste images together from various places in history, and make up some of it myself. People can buy sections for their worldettes or games, and in fact there's a dance hall in Bern, Switzerland that's based on my original design. Maybe we can go there someday, if we can't get a ship willing to sail in the other direction."

She twinkled her fingers at him and dematerialized like a ghost as her portal faded.

He left the parlor and said "go," and an array of options appeared before him: horse, unicycle, penny-farthing bicycle, roller skates, being carried in the arms of a strapping rider. He opted for shoes with wings that popped out of the heels. These moved a lot like ice skates. Sonny had gone ice skating a couple of times in real life at skating rinks, and several times in simulation. He set the wallscreen to communicate with his physical movements rather than his feeble commands tapped into the wall, in lieu of a deld, and he stood up. His knee ached a little when he did that, and he worried he might have twisted it in the fight.

A little meter-square patch opened up beneath his feet, a few cameras swiveled out to watch his back and hips. The room dimmed, the screen resolution sharpened. Sonny skated down the street in virtual Chianina, reaching freeway speeds. Kicking sent him up, soaring over the rooftops, and he buzzed the muddy sow, who grunted and waved a trotter. Inside the bandstand was a portal to another world, and Sonny took it. This world was a perpetual musical, full of synchronized crowds in wild sets, bop-she-bopping their way through various songs, just waiting for someone to come along and take over the lead. Sonny was not that someone, not today, and he darted into a gazebo that led into a lonely little cabin beside a moonlit pond, beside a forest where fairies sang in a circle, surrounding a portal that led to a goofy space battle full of odd-looking space ships shooting gelatinous goo at each other.

He stepped back, off the footpad. The scene froze and the room lighting returned to normal. Sonny tapped the wall and shrank Venusian Designs out of the way. Had it been two hours? He opened Risha's message and read it several times, committing it to memory. He was wearing the same sloppy sweats he wore to the gym and dogpark and everywhere else. He rapidly flashed the cleanbeams to freshen them and headed out the door.

He had to stop for a decompression break halfway there, in a swank lounge where you sat on silky pillows and sipped complimentary tea while listening to light jazz. After decompressing, he had to stop for three different password checks and a retina scan before reaching her floor, which had lush deep carpeting that didn't appear to be heavily used. The idea that Risha might be a poisoner popped into his mind just before he knocked, but he dismissed it. From what he knew of Premier Lance, just about everybody wanted to kill him, for excellent reasons, and if Risha had been among them, he wouldn't hold it against her.

The door opened and there she was. Still dressed in green, and smelling faintly of flowers. Her mouth dropped open in shock at the sight of him and the next thing Sonny knew, she was stroking his bruised face with her immaculately manicured fingertips, and kissing him, while exclaiming "Oh! My poor baby!"

Her apartment was five times as big as Quicksilver's, he decided, as she settled him on a blue leather couch, tucking an unnecessary crocheted throw around him. She had a section of her wallscreen deopaqued, showing a much closer view of stars than Sonny had ever seen. The rest of it was decorated to simulate a view looking out over a lush garden, rioting with colorful flowers. She returned with a mug of hot soup, rich with meat and beans and spiciness, and Sonny savored it as Risha sponged delicately at his split lip and black eye.

"I'm surprised the doctor didn't fix this for you."

"He was pretty busy. They actually killed him. He restored himself, so he's fine."

She winced. "It's all over the news. Your video. I was watching it over and over. I couldn't believe I was watching myself. It seemed so long ago, but it hasn't even been three months."

Three months since he had seen his mother. Risha's comforting had reminded him sharply of Mom, distracting him momentarily from his crush. He had hoped the crush would dissipate now that they were apart, but it was every bit as strong, if not stronger. He was almost afraid to say anything, in case a set of absolutely wrong words jumped out of his lips, the kind that would lead to eternal banishment from her friendlist.

She plopped down next to him on the couch and fiddled with her deld – a light, elegant one trimmed in something shimmery. A portal opened up between the flowers and the video appeared, Sonny's thuggish face floating among the tulips, advancing on Risha as Quicksilver ran up the hall. Proposing marriage.

Risha stopped the video right there. "Sonny, I've got a horrible problem and I need your help."

Her hand was on his shoulder, a small soft starfish. The flowery smell intensified, and beneath it was the smell of Risha's armpits. He knew it well. On the ship, among the general stench of ocean and fish and everyone else's armpits, Risha had stood out in the nasal cacophony as being the only person who never smelled bad, even when sweaty and unshowered. Possibly she had smelled as strongly as everyone else, only he didn't dislike it. Either way, he was hypnotized. Maybe she had already poisoned him, with her soup, although it was really good soup, the kind she might conceivably make for herself when she got tired of sood and foil-wrapped biscuits. Expensive imported ingredients, to go along with the expensive imported furniture.

Poisoned or not, Sonny was euphoric. "Sure, I'll help. You can always count on me."

She played back his offer of marriage, and her acceptance. "That's a legal proposal in Vanram. You're an adult at fourteen there, and my father isn't on the premises to challenge you to a duel, although I daresay he'd kick your ass."

"Yes, he would," Sonny agreed. "Probably Dioni could kick my ass too. I might have a chance against your grandma."

"Never." Risha shook her head. "And I would never get married in Vanram, where all the wife's property goes to the husband. The stockholders would be very upset. But you're not from Vanram, you're from Braganza, where husbands and wives can keep their assets separate, and you can get a divorce for any reason you want, and most importantly, both the husband and wife have the right to reorganize any of their business contacts from before their marriage. So for example, if I married a man from Braganza, I could rearrange the trust so that mother can occupy the house, instead of Dioni or myself."

"It sounds like you know a lot of lawyers," Sonny said carefully.

"The short version: since we're already legally engaged, let's get married! I fix my house situation, then we get divorced. I'll give you a chunk of cash in exchange. It will be swift and painless."

Sonny shivered beneath the crocheted throw. He was suddenly glad it was there, and he bunched it up in his lap to prevent further embarassment. "But in Braganza I'm not an adult yet."

"That's the beauty of it. We can officially be engaged for the next three years, while I get all the paperwork drawn up and talk everyone into signing it. Then we'll have a great big party of a wedding and break up a week later."

Sonny closed his eyes. He had to know. "In the video, Quicksilver said there's evidence Lance was poisoned. Before I even got there."

Risha sat back. Her posture stiffened and she looked at Sonny through a narrowed eye, over the cliff of her cheekbone. "It's true. He was."

"I ... didn't mean to ... he was a bad person." Sonny spluttered.

"A terrible person. I didn't poison him, but I was there when he took it. My ex-boyfriend gave it to him." She shot Sonny a twisted smile. "Shortly before we broke up. Lance had a feeling it was going to happen. I could tell you more, but it would drag you in deeper."

"How much deeper ... never mind." Sonny picked up his soup and finished it, demonstrating that he trusted her.

"If his plot had succeeded, we would have gotten married long enough for him to amend the Vanram constitution to make an exception, just for me. Possibly longer. Long enough to get me out of the house, anyway."

"And you trusted him."

She nodded. Her lower lip quivered and a tear bulged from the lower rim of her eye. Sonny had an irresistible urge to wrap his arms around her, so he did. She leaned into him and sobbed, gently. Her boobs were pressed against his chest, and Sonny squirmed, readjusting the crocheted throw as he cradled her head against his shoulder. Her blonde hair was showing dark roots, and her natural curl was starting to reassert itself around the edges. "They can't prove I gave it to him," she whispered. "It's not my fault."

"I will help you," Sonny murmured into the fragrant-smelling crown of her head. "Don't worry."

She sniffled and sat up. "Thank you, Sonny. I always had the feeling you were a nice boy. You scared me at first, you know. You looked so wild. That's why I was so agreeable, I didn't want to make you angry."

"I look terrible in that video," Sonny complained, and Risha chuckled.

"You look much better now." She stroked his ear. The skin of his ear tingled in her fingertip's wake. "Kayliss called it. She said there was a diamond lurking somewhere underneath all that rough."

Sonny tore his focus away from the part of his brain that was mentally replaying the ear-stroke. "What?"

"Kayliss and her mad crush on you. I suppose I can talk about it now, our agreement has been null and void since she ran away."

Sonny felt as though he had plunged into an ice-filled swimming pool. "Kayliss? Had a mad crush? On me?"

Risha nodded. "Oh, yes. They give them meds to offset the harsh effects of puberty, and since she abruptly stopped taking hers, she blossomed before our eyes. Grew a set of boobs, developed a waist, was bound to crush on someone and picked you."

"She didn't say anything about it to me. Just stole my stuff and left."

"She wanted something to remember you with. Something that smelled like you. You'd been living in that coat a couple weeks, I daresay it smelled like you. Wet sheep as well."

"I honestly had no idea." His stomach gurgled loudly, responding to the soup. Risha took it as a sign he wanted more. She padded over to her full kitchen and uncovered a shiny copper pot simmering on the stove, ladling out cups of soup for each of them. Then she reached into the oven and took out a small pan of cornbread, serving Sonny a thickly buttered wedge.

They ate in blissful silence, watching the artificial garden grow. "I love it here," Risha suddenly said. "I came here for college when I was sixteen. That's when I started the design company. They're strange about money here, they don't really believe in it, so I don't get paid for any of my artwork, but they did give me a free studio so I can keep making it. This is the one in progress."

She tapped her deld and the garden transformed into waves, gently lapping at a private beach. It looked very similar to the one where they'd camped while the *Lono* was being repaired, except Risha had made everything just a little bit prettier than Sonny remembered it. She turned the camera inland to reveal cliffs and jungles and waterfalls and mysterious caves and misty valleys, alongside wide blank areas where she hadn't filled in the terrain yet. "I'm thinking of putting a massive banyan tree here," she said, calling up a side bar with photographs of various banyan trees, including the one in Royal Beach Marketplace that was always being decorated for one holiday or another. "With a zipline so you can glide right through it."

Her eyes were sparkling, and she was sitting with her spine straight and her legs crossed, drawing designs on her palm. She was so deeply focused she didn't care about Sonny's greedy eyes. Her face was blissful and serene. He watched her install her banyan tree, scaling it and angling it, adding a few creepers here and deleting a few there. Aligning the way the sunlight fell upon it as compared to the neighboring vegetation, which was something Sonny's mom would have appreciated. Matching the color scheme, and inserting it in a thick stack of layers of vegetation, the way they used to make cartoons in the very earliest days, stacks and stacks of glass slides with a camera suspended above.

"Ta da!" She grinned and hugged her knees, extremely pleased with herself.

"The most awesome banyan tree ever! When we make it to Royal Beach I'll show you the one in the marketplace. I used to climb on it when I was little."

"You've seen one?" Risha was impressed. "I've only seen pictures. They don't grow in Chianina."

"I'll probably be eighteen by the time I make it back there, at the rate things are going."

"I could happily sit here for the rest of my life drawing pictures and going to parties and listening to new bands." She stretched, her spine flexing in a catlike way. "But we need to deal with the lawyer stuff. I'm headed out on Thursday. I'll do my best to sneak you on board."

She stood up and removed the crocheted throw, arranging it on the back of the couch. "Don't mention this to anyone. If I get thrown in jail for corrupting a minor, the deal's off."

Sonny turned bright red. He stood up, clumsily. "Let me know what time on Thursday." He paused for a moment. "If I can't take Hina, the deal's off."

She giggled. "I wouldn't dream of leaving Hina here to a life of foil-wrapped protein sludge grown in anonymous vats by people who have slept under ceilings every single night of their lives."

"A lot of them probably never go outside at all."

"I'll be in touch." She blew him a kiss.

He made his way to the decompression lounge in a daze. It was mostly empty. According to the wall clock, it was 1:14 in the morning on Saturday, June tenth, meaning he had three days. Fresh air. Wind. Temperatures that varied – he had almost forgotten what it was like to be hot, or cold. Food that would probably send his belly into agony for a couple of days, but it would taste like food. Besides, Risha's soup hadn't incited any agony yet. Three days, and then he'd be traveling with Risha. Plus he had three whole years to get her to fall in love with him.

Quicksilver had a portal up containing a handsome Asian guy, surrounded by little subscreens. The Asian guy nodded at Sonny and spoke a clearly enunciated sentence at him which he didn't understand. Bright lines of dialogue appeared on the subscreen reading, "Greetings, it's good to meet you," with the accompanying translation in two alphabets. Quicksilver read his line of dialogue and the Asian guy corrected his pronunciation, then he headed into the reply. "I would like to introduce my."

There was a dropdown and he scrolled through brother, father, son, nephew, cousin, husband, before settling on "friend." The Asian guy gave him the phrase and the translation, and this time Quicksilver got it the first try.

He settled on the couch and Hina instantly wriggled onto his lap, and he stroked her as they watched the language lesson continue for another hour. Then the Asian guy nodded goodbye and logged out, and Quicksilver bounced up to make some tea. "I'm headed out. My assignment's still in progress, but I'm tired of waiting for it to clear."

"Congratulations. I think I might have a lead on a ride as well."

"Excellent. I suppose whomever leaves last should lock the door, and do something about the plant." Quicksilver pointed toward his forlorn spider plant, which was dying a protracted death in a pot suspended from the ceiling. "It's supposed to water itself but it's never quite worked right."

●

The doctor's focus shifted from obsessive work to obsessively learning Asian languages. Sonny privately couldn't see the point in learning anything beyond "where can I charge up my deld so I can call up a translation bot?" He didn't really understand why the other continents hadn't gone the same way as the Mericas, with everyone speaking more or less the same language once they came out of the domes. Then again, the other continents hadn't been geographically reconfigured to the same extent as the Mericas.

Even further, he didn't know very much about the other continents, other than that they disgorged tourists much less frequently than other countries in the Mericas. These tourists usually travelled in big packs, wearing matching shirts, extending their palms in unison to record everything on throwaway delds.

Sometimes Sonny wondered if Risha was planning on traveling through Asia. He checked his messages frequently, in brief bursts. Lately he had lots of messages from random strangers, and the last one he'd opened had said, "You're a crappy little punk and I'm going to kick your face in, so be afraid." But there had been nothing from Risha, nor Blocker, nor Kai. He was already packed, so he could leave at a moment's notice if someone came through, although he wasn't sure he wanted to wear Deuce clothes anywhere but Deuce.

On Monday, he ran into Rufe in the lobby of the gym, which had rows of cleanbeams to make sure nobody left in a stinky condition, and a little kiosk that sold sood versions of crisp fresh vegetables. Sonny was leaving, after a promising workout in which the readout had informed him his bad knee was only .17% worse than his good knee. It felt completely normal, and he was glad for that, since he wasn't sure how well the brace would travel, and he was getting very tired of wearing it.

"Sonnaay! We need to talk, bro." Rufe bolted out of the weight room and parked himself beneath the cleanbeams, blocking the door.

"I don't want to talk. And take my picture off your node."

"It's bringing in tons of donations, my friend, and that is why we need to talk." Rufe wrapped an arm around Sonny in either a gesture of goodwill or a wrestling hold. He towed Sonny toward a door marked "Do Not Enter" and barged into a room full of people who looked up and did a doubletake as Rufe's largeness registered.

He gave them all a carnivorous smile. "Could you guys ask Tommy if I could borrow his office?"

They headed into it without waiting for a reply. Sonny found himself facing Rufe over the gym director's desk. Pictures of athletes were everywhere, including one of Rufe, with his arm around the shoulders of a smiling guy doing a martial arts kick straight overhead, whom Sonny gathered was Tommy. "Rufe, I don't want to inspire anyone to go get killed."

"You're inspiring a lot more than that. Have you seen the news lately?" Rufe sank into Tommy's seat. It was a little narrow for him.

"I've been avoiding the news."

"Kids these days, so ill-informed." He sighed dramatically and folded his hands behind his head as Tommy's chair groaned in protest. "Promise me you'll go home and watch the news. You may have a strong urge to talk to me after you do. And before you do that, I'm offering you a full lieutenancy, with promotions if and when I see fit. That would grant you citizenship in Vanram, with honors. You'd get your own parcel of land, and then you'd have no problem getting yourself a wife or two or three. Go to school, farm sheep, build a replica of the great pyramid. Drive around in jeeps in the desert, shooting off your gun collection. Sit around in your underwear watching cartoons all day while your bots tend the crops. Whatever you want."

"I want to get on a boat and sail out of here, and I'm planning to do it soon. And I don't want my family getting killed because of what you're doing."

"What I'm doing is trying to get them back. Do you see anyone else actually standing up and saying, 'Hey! These people are prisoners! Turn them loose!' Ambit's in there negotiating, and believe me, those clones can keep that going for years. Have you actually been in contact with them yet? If you haven't, then they're prisoners, and I'm demanding their release. My entire country is being held prisoner! This is bigger than just you, Sonny."

Rufe was yelling, and Sonny's heart was thumping. He wanted to burst into tears like a little kid, and run away. Rufe watched him squirm, the corner of his mouth twisting.

"I'm leaving soon myself. There's a railway running way down south, to a little town called Passiter. I'm using it as a staging location for people from around the world who wouldn't mind earning good pay kicking some Qoro ass. If I'm not mistaken, you can catch a train directly to Royal Beach. There is room on my ship for Lieutenant Knight, but there is no room at all for a cowardly kid who can't make up his mind. You have five hours to give me your answer. And tell the doctor I said hi."

Rufe turned and marched out of the room. Sonny held still, taking deep breaths until he was calm enough to slip through the lobby and head to the elevators.

"Konnichi wa," said Quicksilver when Sonny burst through the door. His latest language instructor, a Japanese guy apparently dressed for a musical number in a space opera, typed a row of kanji at the bottom of the screen, with a translation flashing beneath, inquiring if it was time to take a break.

Sonny flung himself on the couch. Hina snuffled at his face, concerned. "Yeah," Quicksilver said. "I mean, hai."

"I saw Rufe," Sonny gasped, after the portal closed. "He told me to watch the news."

Quicksilver opened up a portal and Daisy Spring appeared in the middle of it, displaying footage of the erupting volcano. Sonny watched carefully to see if Quicksilver could get her into a conversation, but so far it appeared only Blocker had that power. They watched silently together as Daisy spewed geological jargon. Quicksilver paged through her list of top stories. He selected one and a video replaced the livestream. A picture of Sonny's face appeared. Beneath it was a caption reading "Lance's Assassin?"

The photo had been retouched quite a bit. Sonny's skin was darker, and grimier. His eyeballs had been subtlely readjusted, making his expression feverish and demented. The gun in his hand had been retouched too, glinting with light from some fictitious source. They had even sharpened his incisors slightly.

"I died to keep that from getting released," Quicksilver said quietly. "Just noting."

Daisy nattered on about how the government of Dysz had analyzed the video, frame by frame, and had concluded that Lance had actually been shot by a teenage thug just before Rufe clocked him with the bottle, thus making the teenage thug eligible for the position of Premier of Vanram. She slanted her digital mouth sarcastically as she added that a group of separatists were in disagreement, with an action shot of Rufe playing clashball.

Sonny scrabbled for his messages. A red indicator light was flashing, indicating he had a critical backlog. He scrolled frantically through threats and encouragement from strangers, looking for the one giving travel information, which didn't appear to be there.

Quicksilver was doing likewise on the other side of the wall. At the top was a message from someone whose name was so long it ran off the side of the page. He opened it, and a few moments later Kai's face appeared. "Tomorrow at oh-five thirty?"

"Yeah." Kai rubbed his forehead. He looked distinctly unhappy.

"On the *Lono*?" Sonny couldn't help butting in. "You're sailing tomorrow? Can I go?"

Quicksilver and Kai exchanged a long glance through the portal. "Go ahead and tell him," the doctor said. "He's already undergoing some anxiety, a little more won't hurt."

Kai's tattooed face turned balefully toward Sonny. "I have been faced with a deluge of lawsuits and claims blaming me for the destruction of the Argalia Harbor, kidnapping a minor, and so forth. My insurance company is denying they ever knew me. Until I am victorious in my numerous court battles, I will not be violating the laws of any nation in any respect. You have managed to enrage a nation full of people I've never personally gotten along with, demanding your blood. Sonny, I like you on a strictly personal basis, but the last thing I want is trouble."

"I won't be any trouble at all," Sonny said. "I'll sit in my bunk twenty-four seven, unless you want me to clean things, and work in the kitchen."

"The kitchen assistant has made a full recovery." Kai rubbed at his forehead. "It's incredibly dangerous out there, Sonny. That Caribbean storm was nothing compared to what the Pacific can do. I'm packing on as many paying customers as I can, and you're more of a liability than an asset. I am not in a position to assume further liability at this time."

Sonny stared imploringly at Quicksilver. "You guys are abandoning me."

Hina snuggled into his shoulder, letting him know that she would never abandon him, as Quicksilver sighed. "You're safe here for the moment."

"So I guess my only choice is to join Rufe's army."

Kai and Quicksilver exchanged another long glance.

"Lurie," Kai finally growled. "I'll drop you off there. And your dog. Presuming we survive."

"I'll keep them sedated for the voyage if needed," Quicksilver said.

●

Sonny was freezing. He was wearing most of his clothes but Deuce clothes were made on the assumption nobody would ever wear them outside, where the wind was fierce. The rest of his earthly possessions were in a shopping bag wrapped around his wrist, along with a makeshift leash that was attached to Hina. She was plastered against his side, shivering.

The sun hadn't gotten around to rising yet. Sonny hadn't slept. He had a sudden burning desire to study history, even though he kept running into disturbing facts that prodded his anxiety to record levels. The rage plague, for example. If you caught it, a few days later your brain would get inflamed, right in the region where your fury lived. Dysz used it against Vanram soldiers in the hopes the afflictees would kill their fellow troops.

The rage plague had been a plot element in *Scorpion Sand*, a war movie with action star Max Machin, who spent a couple of enjoyable hours running around looking tough while shooting various kinds of weapons at various menacing creations, such as scorpion tanks and camouflaged drones that crawled silently along the ground. It had plenty of excitement without delving too deep or showing much blood. At the same time, it had introduced the possibility into Sonny's mind that his people were being subjected to gruesome medical experiments.

After *Scorpion Sand* there had been hours of documentaries. Dysz had gone so far overboard with their creative use of biological weapons that Ambit had stepped in, forcing them to limit themselves to short bursts of lethality under pain of pissing off the international community, who mostly treated it as an irrelevant skirmish between the two weakest players at the poker table, until it bled over the borders and affected them in the form of tiny airborne creatures that fed upon circuitry, and sentient sea monsters bred to destroy ships.

Archived propaganda from both sides was available. He watched a sad documentary about a small Vanram town that had been sacked by remote controlled drones, and right after that, he watched a touching animated feature about a silent, big-eyed girl innocently filming with a camera drone who was pursued by big, loud barbarians who all looked a lot like Rufe. He visited a virtual memorial to Manganela, with a towering display of photos of people who had died there. Sonny found General Marshall, along with several of his sons, all of them closely resembling Rufe.

Rufe was on the ferryboat with him. Surrounded by a small pack of men, all dressed in matching dark red jackets. He had refused to acknowledge Sonny, but he had nodded curtly at Quicksilver, who had replied with a minimalistic jerk of his chin.

Risha and Blocker had acknowledged them. They were also on the ferryboat, Risha pushing Blocker in a compact wheelchair. They had expressed happiness that Sonny had talked the captain into letting him on board, and Hina had been glad to see them both.

There were a lot of other desperate people on the ferryboat. Sonny peered at each one of them in the dim light from the wheelhouse, looking for pointy noses and tapering jaws and intense eyes. He was relieved when he didn't spot a single Qoro.

The ferryboat pulled up alongside the *Lono*, anchored on a shallow spot a good distance from the city, along with a few other deepwater ships. Sonny could smell recent carpentry, underneath the freezing salty breeze. A longboat descended to lift the first batch of passengers and Kai leaned over the gunwale, delivering an orientation speech.

"You will be confined to your quarters at all times. Anyone causing disruption will be traveling in chains. You will endeavor to keep your bodily wastes confined to the buckets provided for that purpose. We shall arrive at our destination at some point in the future and anyone caught making repeated inquiries of my crew shall be given half rations. Maybe a week. Maybe a month."

Sonny watched Risha and Blocker go up in the first longboat. He got into the second, along with Rufe's entourage, and found himself seated next to one of them. A lean, muscular guy with a bladelike face. As the longboat started to rise he leaned closer.

"You need to figure out which side you're on."

Sonny blinked sleepily. "What?"

"If you're going to be the enemy's weepy-eyed little toy, you need to just come out and say, 'I am the enemy's weepy-eyed little toy.'"

"I have no idea what you're talking about," Sonny replied. The longboat reached the gunwale and stopped, and bladeface stomped on his toe disembarking, possibly deliberately. Nguyen stepped forward to help Sonny and Hina out. Sonny noticed that both Blocker and Risha were staying in the captain's quarters.

Sonny was staying in a hastily-constructed stateroom half the size of the last one. There was no window, and the furniture consisted of three hammocks. Even Quicksilver seemed to think it was cramped, especially given that their third bunkmate was Rufe. "I'd have expected you to be staying with your new friends," Quicksilver had said.

"Pardon me for disrupting your fantasy," Rufe had snarled back, and that was the last attempt at conversation for many hours.

Sonny crawled into the bunk on the bottom, and Hina crawled in beside him. He took off her makeshift leash and stuffed it in his shopping bag, which he stuffed under his pillow. "Stuck here for a while. You know the drill," he whispered to her, and she licked his face.

Once the humans had been unloaded onto the *Lono*, the ferryboat chugged back toward the city. Sonny pulled his blanket over his shoulders, wondering if it was the same one he'd used before. He heard feet running around all over the top deck, and the creaking of the anchor chain, then the loud whump of the sails unfurling, and they were off.

The literal chill in the air wore off by mid-morning, as the air grew hot and muggy. The figurative chill persisted. Rufe lay on his back above Sonny, arms crossed atop his chest, apparently lost in deep thought. Quicksilver had the top hammock, where he was lying with his forearm across his upper face. Sonny wondered jealously if he was playing video games inside his eyeballs. He longed for a book.

Around noon one of the sailors came downstairs to pass out neck floats and ginger soup. The sea had been calm so far but Sonny knew what ginger noodles meant, and he fastened floats securely around his neck, and Hina's.

They found the rough sea that afternoon. Lurching up, crashing down. The hold began to reek as passengers fumbled with their buckets and water invaded the floor, dampening Sonny's butt and shoulderblades. There was no special bed for Hina this time but she was accustomed to sleeping with him on the couch, and the two of them together probably took up less mass than Rufe.

Quicksilver became very popular, dispensing seasickness cures left and right. Rufe left the cabin to visit his men, and Sonny could hear their voices through the thin partition, but he couldn't make out what they were saying. He could hear the other passengers babbling, sobbing, whimpering as the ship groaned around them. An amusement park ride, the kind with a height restriction, and you couldn't get off for a week, or maybe a month.

Sonny was fairly certain his own seasickness cure had included the promised sedative. All he wanted to do was nap, on and off, in between devoting most of his energy to anticipating waves. If he anticipated them just right he could take the shock on the soles of his feet, or on the side of his butt. Anticipating them wrong could result in a banged head, or elbow, or knee. It was almost like dancing. Hina seemed a little bit lethargic too, stretching out beside him most of the time, occasionally swiping at his ear with her tongue.

Rufe came back after night fell, folding himself silently into his bunk. In the morning he gulped down his ginger noodles and headed back to his friends. "Sonny," Quicksilver said after he left, in a raspy voice. "Hand me that blue bag."

Sonny got up, his muscles creaking. After he handed the bag to Quicksilver he did a few stretches. Hina copied him. Quicksilver unwrapped a carton of foil-wrapped biscuits and tore one open, sinking his teeth into it. "Want some?"

"Sure." His belly was just a bit uncomfortable from his reintroduction to solid food, and he supposed he should have been eating more sood all along, even if he didn't see the point in it. He stuffed a handful of biscuits into the pocket of his innermost shirt. "Thanks."

"You're welcome. I'm beat. Constantly having to replenish." He yawned dramatically. "How are you doing?"

"Sedated." Sonny stood on his tiptoes, pressing his palms against the ceiling.

"I'll give you less. Let me know if you're going to explode in hysterical shrieking, my ears couldn't possibly handle it."

"I'm not really a shrieker." He braced himself against the ceiling as the floor slanted sharply. Hina slid into his leg.

"You have nightmares. Sometimes."

Sonny nodded in agreement but Quicksilver was already asleep, a foil wrapper crumpled in his hand. He took advantage of the relative privacy to empty the bucket, which Hina had already used, and use it himself, and dump it out again, and rinse it, which was a challenging operation given the tilting floor. This took much longer than it should have, since he was fiercely determined not to spill. Then he crawled back in his bunk and resumed his intermittent napping, while playing Bippy Borp songs over and over in his head.

●

Rufe's entrance coincided with a wave that had a little flourish on the end, and as a result he cracked his head on the doorframe, which prompted a couple minutes of very bad language. When he was finished, Quicksilver responded with a weary "Shut up, you asshole, I'm trying to sleep."

"Bite me." He kicked the luggage pile. Quicksilver had two bags and Rufe had a large one, and together they took up about a third of the space that wasn't occupied by their beds.

The doctor rolled over and glared down at him, his shoulder scraping the ceiling. "Are you fellows planning your invasion? Going to rush in dual wielding machine guns, or perhaps go retro and use swords?"

"We're planning the most expedient way of murdering Cello and his boys without doing any harm to anyone else. Think of it as prepping for surgery." Rufe folded his arms, balancing on the tilting floor. "Are you feeling left out?"

"My life is one big social whirl."

Hina sensed the animosity crackling through the room and whimpered. Rufe squatted down and ruffled her ears. He glanced at Sonny, who was trying to make his expression as neutral as possible. "You'd be welcome to join us. I know it's a little late in the game."

"He is not interested in joining your war!" Quicksilver shouted. "Learn to respect a negative response."

"Your face is a negative response," Rufe yelled back. Hina whined more emphatically.

"Stop it," Sonny said. Quietly. "We're all miserable and you're making it worse."

"They are *using* you," Rufe said, his index finger jutting out. "As a pawn. If they claim you're the one who put a bullet in Lance, and your parents are both listed on their citizenship roles, then you're their property, and so is my country. They can walk all over a free independent country, that kicked their ass seven years ago, and get away with it. There are eleven Ambit countries and now they've got two. No doubt they'll bankrupt our treasuries trying to bribe someone to be the third, assuming the Qoros aren't planning any more assassinations. My response to that is simple. No. Every one of those men in there agrees with me. And while we'd appreciate it if Sonny made some kind of public gesture indicating that he supported us, in light of the fact that people are in fact going to die over this, it's not necessary. Not at all. He's a traumatized little boy, and he needs some time to heal."

Sonny's eyes narrowed to slits. They were level with Rufe's hairy calves, now that he was standing up and pacing in his limited space.

"I suppose where you come from, the most recommended therapeutic intervention for a traumatized adolescent is to put a weapon in his hand and march behind him waving flags. Right in the face of people who are holding his family at gunpoint." Quicksilver argued from above.

"You were going to surrender him to them," Rufe countered. Sonny's eyes opened wide.

"I was not surrendering anybody, there is no war declared. You are not a nation, and you can't declare war all by yourself. I declined to state a position regarding the issue." Quicksilver dramatically turned his back on everyone, with slight difficulty given the small space.

"Surrender?" Sonny stared at Rufe's bobbing calves.

"The illustrious nation of Dysz demanded you be released into their custody," Rufe told him. "To your parents' custody, actually. The government of Deuce was waffling, but they didn't really have any legal authority to refuse. It was all over the news. This guy didn't tell you about it?"

"No." Sonny looked up at Quicksilver, who was turning slightly red in the dim afternoon light. "No, he didn't."

"That's why the captain didn't want you on this ship," Rufe said. "He's in a pile of legal trouble right now and doesn't want to throw any more fuel on the fire."

"That's true," Quicksilver said. "I did ask him."

"So you were all going to sail off and abandon me."

"You'd be with your family," Quicksilver said. "Which is what you want. People are working day and night to negotiate a civilized resolution to this, I can assure you. And given two options, I reliably choose the one involving less death. Having recently died myself, I found it very unpleasant."

It wasn't cold at all but Sonny found himself shivering uncontrollably. Hina did her best to comfort him.

"I leaned on him a little." Rufe crouched down, resting his hand on Sonny's shoulder. "I told him the least he could do was drop you off in a place where you're less likely to get extradited. We can always claim you stowed away. I could hold it over your head and tell you that you owe me one, but I was just being generous."

Sonny had a vision of himself sitting in Quicksilver's apartment, playing some stupid game and stuffing his face with Cheese Dragons, when suddenly the door informed him there was a visitor, and the visitor was a pack of Qoros, along with a Deuce cop to let them in. Then he'd find himself alone with them, surrounded by them, with their wiry strength and their pointy noses and their intense eyes, and one of them would turn to him and say, "you caused us a lot of trouble."

"You'd be welcome to seek asylum in Vanram, provided the government changes, and I think it will." Rufe patted his shoulder affectionately.

"Assholes killing each other. Nothing changes," Quicksilver growled over his shoulder. "The rest of the

Mericas manage to get along quite nicely without declaring war on each other. Most people gave up on the entire concept of war centuries ago."

The silence returned.

It lasted for a couple more days, Sonny thought. He had lost track of them again. The sunlight was gray and murky, with occasional scatters of volcanic ash. Fresh air came down the stairwell occasionally, and when it got there it swiftly turned into a miasma of pee and puke and sweat. Passengers wailed and sobbed and prayed. Sometimes they argued, and one morning there was a stabbing, according to whoever was beating on the door.

Quicksilver threw himself out of his bunk in a liquid sort of post-exhausted motion, catching Sonny's eye on the way out. "Go upstairs and tell the captain."

Sonny asked if the stabbing victim was dead but nobody was sure. He wobbled out of the compartment and saw a crowd of people jammed into the narrow hall, yelling at each other over the heavy, coppery smell of blood. Sonny's stomach quivered and he made his way to the stairs, climbing carefully and holding onto the rail.

When he got out on deck he was blinded by the bright sunlight, and he blinked until the world came back into focus, clinging white-knuckled to a rail. He was drenched in salty spray within seconds. Once he could see he noticed a huge funnel cloud, far behind them, extending high into the sky. There was another one off to the other side, slightly closer. As he was looking at it, he heard someone come thumping up the stairs.

A forearm suddenly met with his throat. Bladeface. Looking grimier and thinner and angrier than the day they left. "You little puke. You need to throw in with us the minute we land. Do you understand me?"

Sonny made an inarticulate sound to indicate his lower back was being jammed into the rail and it hurt, a lot. He heard a snarl, as someone else came charging up the stairs.

"Hina! No! Down!"

Her paws scrabbled on the slick deck, and she checked herself mid-charge at Sonny's yell. Bladeface spun away, confused, and Hina did an awkward slide toward the opposite gunwale. She would have bounced away if it hadn't been for the flourished wave, launching her upward and over the side.

"Hina!!" Sonny leaned back and used both his feet to kick Bladefast in the chest, hard, making his knee twinge and sending Bladeface into the stairwell. He charged toward the gunwale and vaulted over. It was a long fall, and it reminded him uncomfortably of the stadium, but there was no time for that, he needed to find Hina.

There. Splashing awkwardly through the waves, toward him. He yelled and stroked toward her, colliding with her. He inflated her neck float, then his own. He extended their lanyards and tied them in a secure knot, so they wouldn't drift apart.

He turned to wave at the ship. It was much farther away than he had expected.

He yelled and waved, bobbing on top of the surf, until it was out of sight.

CHAPTER FOUR: June 20, 3748

No land in sight. Just sea spouts. And waves.

Sonny and Hina drifted, their bodies dangling into the water. It was comfortably warm. The neck floats kept their noses pointed upwards while turning them in random directions. Sonny was no longer disturbed about the fact he was going to die, and he was glad it would happen in a comfortable, warm place, beside a loyal friend, with no cameras anywhere near. He still had a few foil-wrapped biscuits in his shirt pocket that would prolong it somewhat.

According to Kai's globe, his parents were nearby. He could see the sense in using submarines, living out here where the waves were taller than people and the horizon was littered with sea spouts. Behind the erupting volcano, its smoke covering half the sky. It was an ironic place to die, and he wondered if anyone would ever find him.

He spent some serious time plotting ways to kill Bladeface if he happened to survive. That was ironic too, because Bladeface was supposedly fighting for his cause. He finally got tired of hating after a while, since it drained energy. Not that he'd need much. There was no point in swimming when you didn't know where the closest land was. Eventually he'd run into land if he went southeast. He couldn't see the sun well enough to tell which way south was, but eventually the Southern Cross would come out and assist, assuming it wasn't too cloudy to see it.

Something cold and slimy wrapped itself around his right ankle.

He yelled, and reached toward it. Something goopy and slippery was enveloping his foot, and he couldn't seem to peel it off. At the same time, he heard someone calling his name, over and over.

He relaxed, and let his enslimed foot dangle. He could hear something, similar to the way a deld transmitted audio up through your arm bones into your eardrums without bothering people sitting next to you. A voice spoke in chords, three octaves at once, calling his name.

"Nepenthe!"

"Yes! I can hear you very faintly. I am sending up an amplifier. It will be green in color."

There was nothing green in his visual field at all. Just blues and grays. He held one hand up in the air until the wind dried it, then brushed the salt droplets from his eyelashes. Then he saw it, surfacing in front of him, a deep green. It looked more like a blob of seaweed than an amplifier. He spoke to it. "Hello?"

A triumphant orchestral hit swelled up through his ankle. It didn't actually interact with his eardrums, but it was loud. "Too loud, turn it down," he told the amplifier, and the next orchestral hit was softer. "Perfect."

"Loud and clear." Nepenthe's voice sounded like it was coming from right over his shoulder. "Consider yourself located."

Sonny burst into hysterical happy laughter, and Hina joined in with a few barks. "Thank you, Nepenthe! Is the ship coming back?"

She laughed, and his heart sank. "I'm afraid not. But don't worry, I'll get you to safety. There's a few shipwrecks in this area and I'm scanning for supplies. I'll have to get back to the ship soon to tell them you're alive. Everyone was quite upset. When I left they were discussing flogging."

Sonny emitted a small, bitter laugh in celebration of his enemy's suffering before returning to thinking about his own. "We don't have any water, but I have some food."

"It'll rain in two or three hours, so that will take care of your water."

"I don't have anything to catch it in."

Several minutes passed without reply. Then something large floated up to the surface, startling both Sonny and Hina. It was bright orange, and compacted into a cube. Several of the jellyfish blobs surrounded it, and they appeared to be lifting it.

Sonny swam up to it and felt along the edge. His fingers found a tab to pull, so he pulled it. Then he backpaddled as the emergency life raft inflated itself. "They had it locked up in a cupboard," Nepenthe explained, her tone descending to indicate sadness.

Once it was inflated Sonny boosted Hina into the raft, then he clambered into it beside her, which took all his strength. He rested for a moment, then he fumbled his way through untying the lanyards and deflating the neck floats. The jellyfish thing had slid from his leg once he emerged from the water, and it took him several minutes before he realized he could no longer hear Nepenthe. The green amplifier was still floating nearby, and he faced it and yelled to her that he was trailing his hand in the water. A few moments later, a pinkish blob rose from the ocean depths and swallowed it up to the wrist.

"I'm sorry, I wasn't thinking. Thanks for the cool boat."

"You're quite welcome. Make sure you catch plenty of rainwater. You're a couple of days from shore."

"What shore? And how do I get there?"

"I will send a bright orange to serve as a beacon. I believe that model raft is equipped with a sail. Can you operate a sail?"

"I guess we'll find out." Exploring with his free hand, Sonny found a side compartment with a collapsible mast that fit into a bracket near the bow, along with a pair of oars, a neatly folded sail and several coils of rope. There were also some survival rations that had expired ninety-seven years ago, and a fishing line with a set of hooks. According to the labels this raft could hold ten people, and would last thirty to ninety days depending on local oceanic composition. It smelled of old chemicals.

"The orange beacon will lead you to an island that doesn't have a name," Nepenthe informed him. "But it has a shelter. There are thousands of these outer islands that have shelters set up, with everything a human needs. People come along and live on them for a while, then move on. There was a philanthropic group that went around building them, hundreds of years ago, and other people come out and maintain them. I'll send out a message once we get closer to Lurie. Someone will come along and get you eventually."

"Hopefully someone friendly," Sonny said, ruffling Hina's drying fur. She was stretched out with her eyes closed and a blissful expression on her face.

"You're just on the edge of the rough water. The waves will get smaller and you'll start to see fish. When you do, it's probably safe to put the sail up. For now, just try not to capsize. I'm heading back to the ship. I'll check on you later. Good luck." He waited several minutes to see if she'd say anything else before withdrawing his hand from the water. The pink slime slid away and vanished into the depths.

Riding the waves on an air mattress was far easier than in a wooden box full of sharp corners. Sonny had a chance to focus on his growing thirst. He opened all the packages of expired food and dumped the contents into the sea, which gave him a set of empty containers that could be used for storing water, plus one he spontaneously decided to use as Hina's pee collector, whipping it beneath her as she began her squat.

Nepenthe's predictions came true. The waves decreased to maybe a meter in height, and then warm fat raindrops came pattering down. Sonny spread the sail out to catch it, and didn't begrude Hina when she thirstily lapped up the first serving. There was a lot of volcanic ash in the water, and he filled containers and strained them into other containers using his middle shirt as a filter.

By sunset the waves were gentle and smooth, illuminated by a colorful sky. A glowing orange blob had surfaced and was floating alongide, just ahead of the bow. Sonny took the collapsible mast out of its compartment and snapped it together, and seated it in its socket. He carefully raised the sail, squinting at the faded diagrams etched inside the compartment. Soon the little craft was speeding along the tops of the waves, headed toward the orange beacon and the Southern Cross. Hina arranged herself in the bow like a figurehead, smiling a doggy smile at the wind on her face.

Sonny experimented with the controls, getting a feel for the way they worked and gaining respect for Kai's ability to sail on a large scale. After spending far too many days holding still and not doing anything, he was thrilled to actually be doing something important. The moon was nearly full and he had plenty of light. The orange beacon glowed in the dark, occasionally attracting the fish Nepenthe had also predicted, and Sonny stayed right on its path.

He sailed all night and was rewarded with a brilliant sunrise. He celebrated by breaking out more foil-wrapped biscuits and shirt-filtered water, and patiently holding the pee collector underneath Hina. He could see a cloud far ahead, in the direction the orange beacon was indicating.

He kept up a babble of running commentary generally directed at Hina, letting out all the backlogged words he had kept to himself. "Back home, on the last Thursday of every monthy, they have two-for-one night on the Raging Dragon. That's a roller coaster. It takes fourteen point seven minutes to ride all the way through the track. It goes along the beach, and when the sun hits it just right, it glows like fire. Maybe you'll see it someday. You don't have to ride it, but there are plenty of dogs out on the beach near it, with their humans."

He sang to her, just like he had done when they lived beneath the bridge. First a couple of Bippy Borp numbers, then he switched to *When I Get Home*, which made it lodge in his brain for longer than he liked. Experimenting with his man voice. He had always been privately sort of embarrassed by his singing voice because it was high-pitched, and the only popular songs in his range were ballads by pouty-sounding girls who complained in quavery voices about their boyfriends over slow chords and fake strings.

His man voice, on the other hand, was good and loud. It was still high pitched, especially compared to Kai's bass rumble or Rufe's tough-guy bark. It had all the promise of turning into a fine adult singing voice, if he practiced enough. And memorized the lyrics better, so he wouldn't find himself singing "blah blah blah" when he forgot. And maybe it would help if he learned to play an instrument, although he would never be as good as someone like Dan, who had been playing since he was in diapers. It was good enough for serenading Hina, making up his own lyrics that proclaimed her Queen of the Pacific Ocean.

The ocean gradually changed from surly gray to an inviting cerulean blue, with friendly little waves and water clear enough to see coral fortresses and schools of colorful fish below. His island destination came into focus. It was a tiny speck of island, barely bigger than a cruise ship. It was slightly elevated in the middle, with a patch of trees and an elevated water tank. Once he got closer Sonny could see an unobtrusive building blending in with the foliage.

It was close to sunset when his boat crunched into the sand. Hina bounced out and did a frenzied sprint down the sand. Sonny dragged his boat out of the water and tore down the mast. He had three foil-wrapped biscuits left, and he stowed them in the compartment. While he was doing that he noticed faint music coming from the building. A guitar, and a singing girl.

He heard a bark, and at first he thought it was Hina, but it was actually a big yellow dog with a homely face. It bounded over to Sonny and emitted another officious woof as Hina dashed over. Once she arrived the two animals went through a formal greeting. Sonny stood perfectly still as they reached their terms and the yellow dog led them uphill toward the building. It was actually more of a compound, Sonny thought, with several buildings grouped around a courtyard with a pool. He thought it was a swimming pool at first, then he noticed it contained live fish. There was a garden that had a mango tree alongside a couple of trees that looked related to the labfruit trees in Bonterra.

The yellow dog barked once they got to the courtyard, and the music stopped. Sonny pawed at his hair in a futile attempt to make himself more presentable. His Deuce clothes were not made to withstand the rigors of being outside and were falling apart. Both of his shoes had loose, flapping soles. He decided that he fell far short of presentable, and should probably aim for harmless. He held his hands out to his sides, fingers spread wide.

A door opened in the largest building and a woman brandishing a machete appeared. Behind her was a white-haired woman wielding a steaming teakettle.

"Hello," he said. "My name is Sonny, and I fell off a ship."

"You *fell* off a *ship*." The machete-holding woman was somewhere in her twenties, with a topknot of frizzy, sun-damaged hair that would have sent any respectable Braganzan screaming into the nearest stylist's shop. She had a family resemblance to the teakettle-holding woman, and they stepped back and whispered to each other without taking their eyes off Sonny.

With the older woman still covering him with the teakettle, the younger one put her machete down and looked at Hina, making a clucking noise with her teeth. Hina responded with a playful crouch and a waving tail. "This your dog?"

"Yes. Her name is Hina."

The women exchanged looks, then the younger one clucked again and Hina dashed forward to lick her face while the yellow dog looked on approvingly. "If this is your dog, you're okay. I'm Cindy, and this is my mama, Marisa."

"She fell off the ship too," Sonny explained. "Actually she fell off and I jumped in to save her."

"Ohhh!" said the women said in unison, ushering him into a huge, comfortable room. It had ceiling fans and a big wide lanai overlooking the water. There was a serious kitchen with a built-in barbecue pit at one end, and there was a bubbling pool of water at the other end. Inside the pool of water was a third woman, who was introduced as Lily. She was round and fat, plus she was topless, her huge boobs floating atop the water. There was a fourth woman that Sonny noticed once he got over the initial shock of the floating boobs; her name was Shashi and she was also topless, although one of her boobs was covered by an extremely small baby. There were also a four year old and a two year old, both lolling sleepily on a pile of cushions.

Cindy rummaged around and found him some cargo shorts and a towel, directing him to the building that contained showers. He noticed Marisa was doing something involving food and his belly growled at the very idea.

Soon afterwards he found himself sprawled on his own pile of cushions, wearing nothing but his new cargo shorts. His Deuce clothes had all disintegrated the moment he tried to wash them. He didn't particularly care because he had a big bowl of the best noodle soup he had ever tasted in his life in his lap, and floating in it were shrimp and chunks of fish and vegetables. There was a skewer of grilled shrimp on the side, painted with tangy sauce, and some little steamed dumplings full of crabmeat, and big orange smiles of perfectly ripe mango.

He told an abbreviated version of his tale between bites. They watched the sunset together, then Cindy noodled on her guitar while Marisa applied cooling lotion to Sonny's sunburns. He was nearly asleep when he suddenly remembered his friendliness, and asked if he could help clean up the kitchen or anything. She laughed, and told him no, and aimed him toward one of the adjacent buildings, which had rack of bunks, with the same kind of permanently soft and fresh bedding he'd enjoyed on the *Lono*. Even better, the bunks were man-sized, Carquinez version, with plenty of room for him to lie with his legs straight, and plenty of room for Hina, her belly round and full, to lie snoring beside him.

●

He woke up feeling happy. That hadn't happened for a while.

The air smelled sweet, thanks to a flowery tree growing right outside the doorway. He went outside and had a closer look at the garden. Some of the plants were strictly ornamental, like the torch ginger and the traveler's tree, but most of them seemed to bear some type of food.

His belly was feeling overwhelmed by food at the moment. He ducked into the bathroom, a large building divided into stalls, each containing a compost toilet that cycled back to the garden, where he forced the air filter to work overtime. Then he hiked around the entire island. It took about an hour. He went slow, since he lacked shoes and his feet were pink and tender. He found the women's canoe, a big solid wooden one with an outrigger. He wandered into the extremely gentle surf and watched crabs skitter across the sand.

When the children quieted down he headed into the main building and helped Marisa cook breakfast. She was very pleased to witness Sonny's skill at murdering delicious sea creatures and grating ginger root, and immediately after breakfast she taught him how to make ceviche out of finely sliced raw fish and veggies and oil and spices.

Then he took a break, and had another shower, and chased Hina around the beach, and went for a swim. He romped with the little kids, spinning them gently through the air and tickling them to hear them giggle. Then he collapsed on his cushion pile and stared aimlessly at the ocean. The women spoke of people he didn't know and places he'd never visited, and he basked in the ambient melody of their voices, happy they had judged him harmless and worthy of overfeeding.

Lily stretched her arms out of her head and leaned back, groaning and stretching. She reminded Sonny that her boobs were exposed and he felt his cheeks redden under his sunburn as he quickly looked in a different direction. The danger of being caught staring at boobs was just too great with Lily, as they made up a considerable percentage of her mass. "Sonny Knight of Royal Beach," she said.

He flinched. "That's me."

"There's pages of stuff on you." She yawned. Sonny could feel his relaxation dwindling and his anxiety begin bubbling to the surface.

"Have you got a deld or something?" Sonny looked back at the pool, aiming for an area adjacent to Lily's boobs. There was a blob floating in the water, very similar to his orange beacon and green amplifier, except it was purple. He watched Lily towel and lotion her hands, flexing her fingers.

"It's like an underwater deld," Marisa said. "Lately seems like all the kids got 'em. Me, if I wanted to run around connected all the time I'd just live in the city, but I guess that's me."

"You can't have delds out here," Cindy picked up her guitar and played an arpeggio. "Harsh climate, don't you know. Plus where you gonna pick up a signal from? Need those heavy duty kind. Expensive."

"We're all alive because our ancestors modified their genes when they were inside the dome to be able to deal with a chemically reconfigured world," Lily said. "Nobody shared this game plan with the inert objects."

"Plus we got blowback from the war," Marisa added.

"I've seen something like that before," Sonny said, approaching the pool in what he hoped was a harmless way. "Something to do with Sirens, right?"

Lily gave him a long, appraising look. "I got extras if you want to learn. You gotta climb into the water. Can't let them touch air, they don't like it. Make yourself comfy, I gotta water the flowers."

She exited the pool, giving Sonny a close up view of her butt in the process. Once out of the water, she demurely wrapped herself in a bolt of purple fabric. She grabbed a walker made of bamboo and hobbled off toward the toilets. One of her legs seemed to be crooked. Sonny rubbed his knee, thinking that's probably what would happen if you got injured out here, far away from a hospital.

He slid into the pool, keeping his shorts on. It was a comfortable temperature, and had a cushioned seating ledge. There was an underwater net bag holding several colorful blobs. "Plobs," Lily corrected him upon her return. "P as in perpetually pianissimo. As in blob of protoplasm. That's what we call 'em, anyway. You want to get a firm grasp."

It was a little like pinching a raw oyster. The plob was slimy, and the hairs on Sonny's arms stood up when he first touched it. Once he got it settled in his hands it made a round little weight between his palms, soft and yielding.

Something flashed across his eye. He rubbed his face against his shoulder, and Lily laughed. "No, no. Hold still. Just kinda stare at the water."

He did. The letter "a" was repeating across his visual field, over and over. He could only really see it if he looked at a background without a lot of contrast, such as the pool of water, or the blue ocean outside, or the wall. "I see the letter a, over and over."

"Move your fingers."

He did. More letters appeared, a string of random keyboard gibberish. "Okay, now I see lots of letters."

"Let me know when you figure out how to type. Then we'll start lesson two."

It took Sonny a couple of days to figure out how to type. It wasn't like popping up a keyboard interface on your deld, with glowing letters that showed you where to put your fingers, and an autobot that secondguessed your words and finished typing them for you. There was no visual cue at all, and you had to rely on muscle memory, with half the alphabet on each hand, plus a series of alternate keyboards for punctuation and emojis.

His fingertips had all turned into prunes before he could even type his name. Lily showed him a special kind of hand lotion she used, which dried into a thin film, turning into the equivalent of whisper-thin waterproof gloves. That didn't solve the fierce cramp he got between his shoulderblades, but Marisa's massages helped those.

"Can you send video on this thing?" He let his plob sink as he stretched his arms out to the sides, flexing his muscles. Thanks to all that gym time in

Deuce, he had a nice muscular chest, which made him feel better about not owning a shirt.

"You can, but it'll mess you up." Lily winced at the memory. "Most people just type."

"What does it do to you?" Sonny was intrigued.

"Imagine if you're wearing glasses, with a screen on each eye, and they're connected to cameras attached to some other guy's sunglasses, yeah? And this guy, he's got a great big head. His eyes are a few centimeters farther apart than yours, plus he's colorblind in one eye. Your own eyes are watching this movie and they're trying to compensate for being in the wrong size head, with the wrong color adjustment. Your optic muscles get strained, and then you have a big ass headache. If you keep doing it, for some people it just snaps into place, and they figure out a way to translate it without doing a number on their eyeballs. Not many people are that dedicated."

"I'm not that dedicated," Cindy said. "You can keep your headaches."

"Headaches are bad," Sonny agreed, and he resigned himself to teaching memories to his finger muscles.

"They'll figure out how to fix it," Lily said. "This stuff is brand new."

Once he progressed to the point where he could spell his own name nine times out of ten, Lily showed him how to get into a talk channel. The first one he entered was for new users, and had seventeen other people fumbling around. From there he progressed into a channel for kids sitting around talking about nothing, which was exactly as described. Finally he was allowed to enter North Carq General Chat, one of the main places where Lily hung out, which had a couple of hundred users exchanging polite and civilized conversation about things like the weather, and the volcano. You talked by leaving messages, which might get answered right away, or later, or never, and everyone could see the conversations.

Lily's messages were fast and smart and grammatically correct. Once she saw he had a handle on using the plob she sent him a verbose private message, explaining that she had looked up the news, and read all about him, and discussed him, and had come to an independent conclusion that he was okay. Also, she had never liked Premier Lance. Sonny was beginning to wonder if anybody had.

One morning Cindy demand that he help her catch fish. This consisted of getting in a rowboat, rowing twenty meters out, throwing a weighted net over the side and hauling it back to the surface. The hardest part was transporting the live fish to the fishpond in a barrel after Cindy sorted out the ones that didn't meet with her approval and threw them back into the sea. Sonny helped her clean out the fishpond and fill it with fresh seawater before transferring the prisoners, and together they fed them a last meal of whatever veggies were nearly past ripeness, grated fine.

Shashi finally announced she was ready to travel. Sonny was tempted to stay by himself on the nameless island, thinking he could probably come up with a good name for it eventually. Instead he helped the women load their stuff into the canoe. He didn't really own anything at the moment except his life raft, and it was scheduled to fall apart soon.

He sat toward the back. Lily was in the very back, and in the middle was what amounted to a large cage containing the dogs and children, all of whom were wearing float vests. They were also shielded from the sun by a canopy, and they smelled like coconuts, thanks to Marisa's coconut oil based sunblock.

It took Sonny a little while to get the rhythm of rowing. At first the only relief from the heat was speed, which meant rowing faster, which made them hotter from the exertion. Then they reached a current, which sped them along as fast as if they'd been sailing, with no effort on their part. They kept going through the night, under an amazing field of stars, heading straight into the Southern Cross. Passing the water bottles back and forth, changing and feeding babies without slowing down, chewing on fish jerky and mango.

They reached their destination in the middle of the next day, tying up at a boathouse which had five or six other canoes, as well as a few kayaks and dinghys. Sonny could hear music playing from up the hill, where the buildings were. This was a much bigger island, with a larger cluster of buildings and a small orchard. The breeze shifted and he caught a whiff of grilled seafood.

The women were enthusiastically greeted, especially Shashi and her baby, while Sonny stood patiently awaiting his turn at the attention. Once it arrived, he gave everyone big friendly smiles. They were more interested in Hina, and one of them, who happened to be wearing a weathered Sharks t-shirt, recognized her.

Sonny nodded. "She was the Sharks' mascot. She got injured when the terrorists took over the stadium, but we got away, and she bonded to me, so we've been together ever since. I love her."

Somewhere between twenty and thirty people were clustered around, and several of them clasped their fists over their hearts. Sonny wasn't quite sure what the gesture meant but he had seen Marisa and Cindy do it a few times. Apparently it meant acceptance, since he found himself sitting down to lunch. Hina had a place beside him, or possibly he was beside her, since she was served first, with a thick steak of lightly seared tuna.

There were four other dogs and two cats living on the island, along with somewhere between thirty and forty people in a wide range of ages. They all had deeply tanned skin and weathered hair tied up in ponytails or topknots, and the older ones had deeply etched wrinkles. Most of them wore cargo shorts with drawstring waists exactly like the ones Sonny was wearing, although some were draped in fabric, like Serena.

Dyes didn't last long out here. The sun and salt water bleached away most of the color, and the people were drab compared to the flowers and fish. They didn't have many possessions, which Sonny supposed made sense if you spent your life moving around between islands. He could see a lot more islands from this one.

The people were warm and welcoming, and Sonny found it easy to talk to them about cooking, and fishing, and sailing. They were bigoted and dismissive whenever he mentioned other places he'd visited, so he learned to stop bringing it up, although they seemed to like Royal Beach, and a couple of the elders had been there on their honeymoon. It took him a little while to notice, but nobody asked him a single prying question about his age, or his nationality, or how he had managed to get into their country. The Carqs valued privacy, and they assumed that since he was already there, he wasn't out of place.

Lunch was followed by music. They had some nice analog instruments made of wood; guitars and flutes and drums, and they played a lazy hypnotic jam that didn't seem to be broken up into songs. Lily beckoned Sonny to a big tree overhanging the water, and when he got there he found several people lounging on the partially submerged branches, their fingers plunged into plobs, flickers of light flashing across their eyes as they gazed down into the water.

There was an underwater net bag full of plobs. Sonny grabbed a nice big greenish-yellow one and found an unoccupied forked branch in the shade that was shaped just like a springy lounge chair.

Once his plob was active, Lily invited him to a chat group that turned out to consist of all the people sitting around him in the tree. Eight in total, including a graybeard and a kid who looked like she was about his sister's age. They answered a few questions that had been on his mind. Plobs were extremely basic animals that didn't eat, breathe or poop. The only thing that harmed them was clumsy people exposing them to air. If you fed them a special solution, they would divide, and then you'd have two. Color and size made no difference. There was a guy on some other island who could receive video through plobs, but he drank a lot and was probably crazy.

They answered his questions about people, too. No, not all of them lived here full time. Carquinez people didn't mind being called Carqs, and they were constantly splitting off and regrouping, and making frequent moves to other islands, to avoid overstressing their foodbearing potential. The islands outnumbered the people, and most of them contained shelters.

There were city Carqs too, and they lived in Lurie. Sonny's new companions knew plenty of jokes about them. There were a few bigger islands that had actual towns located on them, and the closest one was named Horseshoe. His companions all agreed that Horseshoe was Sonny's best bet for catching a boat to somewhere else. They linked up with another chat room that was crowded with handles, forcing Sonny to scroll and pause to keep up with the conversation.

Eventually Sonny was connected to a guy named Paolo, who said his dad was heading to Horseshoe and needed another crew member, and could pick Sonny up in three to eight days depending on the wind. Sonny replied that he wasn't sure if he was experienced enough to count as crew, and Paolo laughed and assured him everything would be fine. The people hanging out in the tree seemed to vouch for Paolo, and his dad, and Sonny supposed that would have to be good enough.

The idea of work made him think of money, and reminded him that he didn't have any. He asked Paolo if he would have to pay anything, and Paolo laughed again, reminding him he was crew, and they'd be paying him.

He brought it up later with Marisa, asking delicately if there was any kind of labor he could do to pay for his upkeep. "Look around you," she said indicating the musicians and the plobheads and a few people playing boardgames or idly staring into space. "How much labor do you see? If we wanted to labor we'd move to the city. If you wanted to help me make ceviche, however, that would be fine."

While waiting for Paolo and his dad, Sonny learned seven new ceviche recipes, as well as a few for poke, and he traded the sashimi techniques he had learned from Watanabe. As a result, he ate a lot. Besides fish there was also vatgrown meat, heavily armored in packaging to keep it safe from the tropical sun, and a clay oven that constantly produced steaming circles of delicious bread, and fragrant fruit pies.

He spent the rest of the time sitting in the water texting. Reading, mostly. He tried to get into his social node and discovered the internet and the plob network did not interconnect. There were plenty of shady sounding people advertising that they could make it happen, for money. Sonny ignored them. He could send himself a message though, and he did, updating his status as "having a relaxing tropical vacation."

It struck him that he was having exactly the experience Royal Beach advertised to tourists: relaxation, good food, uncrowded beaches, friendly people and music, no work. He had to admit it was an effective setting for relieving stress. His own had subsided to a dull throb that only flared occasionally. He attributed part of this to being far away from all the backstabbers on board the *Lono*, and therefore he flinched when Nepenthe found him.

"Sonny Knight! Is that really you, talking on the networks? It is I, Nepenthe!"

This was followed by an intricate, shaded drawing of a mermaid made of letters and numbers, with a slight animation that made her tail flick as it scrolled by. Sonny smiled over his flinch. "I survived. Headed to Horseshoe. Have become addicted to plobs."

"You're welcome for the plobs," she typed back. "Are you still stuck in text mode?"

"I've heard bad things about video mode."

"Not entirely founded. Tell me if it starts to hurt."

His vision suddenly dimmed. That was because there was a mermaid image swimming on the inner surface of his eyes, and it was out of focus. He felt his pupils dilate as the light shifted. "I'm not sure I want to do this, Nepenthe," he typed.

"Audio check," she whispered in his ear.

"Audio works," he typed back, and the mermaid slipped into dazzling focus, almost too sharp. Then she softened around the edges and went half-opaque, a colorful ghost superimposed on the water before him. "Wow," he typed, as she waved and smiled.

"They're stuck in Lurie. I've taken my leave and I'm visiting with friends. We have a nice colony established out here. Sculpting coral, making plobs."

"All the Sirens who left the south coast of Samerica," Sonny guessed, and the mermaid nodded.

"Kai brought a lot of us through, then we figured out a way to circumvent the dangers, and now we're all over the world. Some of us prefer a fixed address, and this is one of the safer ones." She flashed a demure smile. "We're in the process of getting the human governments to recognize us as a sentient species, but it's a struggle. The kinder ones consider us an endangered species of marine mammal."

"Well, you are." Sonny typed back. After a moment he added "that was intended to be a humorous wisecrack, just in case it failed."

After another moment, Nepenthe's melodic laughter flooded into his ear. "By the way, Bippy Borp lifts most of their good riffs from a band called Baap de Borp that was popular three hundred years ago in Northern Europe. Pretentious hipsters probably aren't aware of that."

"Ouch," he said. "Look, I'm not endangering you. You're more sentient than lots of people."

"Thank you." The mermaid vanished into the waves, leaving a nice calm field of text behind. "I'm sorry," she typed. "I didn't mean to get political."

"You've got my vote, if I ever have to vote on it." He wanted to rub his temples but his hands were occupied. "I could tell everybody on the internet, if I could connect. I can't, because I'm broke."

"I can connect you once you get physically close to a transmitter. I believe there's one in Horseshoe. Call me when you get there. And go lie down, rest your eyes."

●

Paolo was a wiry little guy who was slightly younger than Sonny. His dad Lester was also small and wiry, and he wasn't too much older than Sonny. They had two crewmembers who were in their twenties, Jonah and Sebastian, and a boat called *Moondance,* which might have been called a yacht in Royal Beach. It was a hard-working fishing boat in Carquinez, with a hold full of coldboxes containing frozen fish and a set of industrial-sized nets amidships.

The crew of the *Moondance* spent the night, and when they sailed out at dawn, Sonny was with them. He followed their orders, cleaning and stowing things as needed. Paolo spent most of his time in a special seat attached to a bucket of seawater, with a syphon arrangement to keep the circulation flowing, his immersed hands sunk deep into a turquoise plob.

"There's a channel where the didges hang out," Paolo explained after dinner, which included ceviche made by Sonny. "They ping images off of boats with their insect drones, trade us back info on what's going on underwater. You can get 3D topography if you're one of those video guys. Me, I just type."

"You kids are gonna mess up your brains with that stuff," Lester said. "Where you headed after Horseshoe, Sonny?"

"Royal Beach, Braganza," he said, and the men whooped and pumped their fists, with Sebastian adding a little gyrating dance. Sonny grinned. "No, really, that's where I live. I understand there's a train in Passiter, on the mainland."

"Train got wrecked long ago, in the war, but they'll drive you to the train in old military transport trucks." He laughed. "That's the talk, anyway."

"Probably costs a lot of money, right?"

"There's a bunch of guys heading out there to go fight some kind of war." Jonah laughed derisively. He was a bulky guy with a hammerhead shark tattooed on his bicep.

"Ugh." Sonny made a face. "Yeah, I heard about them too. Maybe I'll just go to Japan. Or stay out here."

"Plenty of room," Lester said. "Lots of empty islands. Nobody really knows how many people. We don't believe in taking census. Goes against privacy."

Jonah gave Sonny an appraising look. "It can be dangerous."

Sonny gave it right back. "What's the most dangerous thing out here."

"Lester's farts," Sebastian answered, and Paolo giggled.

"Lack of common sense," Lester offered. "Your neighbors, if you piss them off. Megs."

"Ever see a meg?" Jonah raised an eyebrow.

"Nope. What's a meg?" Sonny kept his own eyebrows at their original level so as not to escalate things.

"Megalodon. It's like a shark." He pointed to his tattoo. "A regular shark can get as long as this boat. Bad news if you fall in, but usually you don't unless you lack common sense. A meg could eat both that shark and this boat in one gulp."

"Kind of like a pliosaur, then?"

"Back when I was your age there used to be pliosaurs out here," Lester said. "The megs ate them."

Sonny sat down on the nearest flat surface. "What's the best way to make sure I never see one?"

"The Sirens got 'em mostly penned in, with coral." Paolo piped up. "That's what everyone's saying anyway."

●

Horseshoe was shaped like one. An apathetic crater that gave up, resulting in a curved, skinny island with plenty of coast. The boats were all clustered on the lee side. Mostly wooden, a couple of composite. Nothing made of metal, although some had various kinds of engines powered by sea and sun if the wind should fail. The *Moondance* joined them, and Sonny spent a backbreaking few hours transferring boxes of frozen fish from the *Moondance* to one of the composite boats. After that was done, Lester handed Sonny a wad of colorful Carquinez money, small flat fabbed tokens decorated with flowers and fish and made out of some indescribably tough substance, with holes drilled in the corner so you could string them around your neck. Sonny preferred keeping them securely buttoned up in his cargo shorts.

The *Moondance* crew said their goodbyes, and Captain Lester said he would happily provide a reference as to Sonny's capable grasp of basic seamanship. Then they sailed away, leaving Sonny and Hina in Horseshoe. It took him about an hour to walk from one end of Horseshoe to the other, walking slow. The windward side was cluttered with buildings extending on piers out into the ocean. Music throbbed from some of them.

The building in the exact center of the crescent was made of blocks of some kind of smooth building material that had a subtle shine like abalone. Inside it were small, grainy patches of wallscreen available for rent at exorbitant rates. There was also a bulletin board covered with slips of paper, notices about people looking for boats, crew, fish, cash, each other. He read through the crew wanted listings, but didn't see anything current.

Hina was warmly welcomed in the Horseshoe saloon, and Sonny was grudgingly admitted since he was with her. They wouldn't serve him anything from the intoxicant menu, but they were glad to serve him a cold soda and a fish sandwich, and they threw in a free bowl of scraps for Hina.

As he ate, he studied the people around him. He had a hard time reading them. Everybody was wearing faded-out thigh-length shorts, accessorized with shirts and hats and wraparound sunglasses and flipflops. The crowd was mostly male, although not exclusively.

He saw an obvious group of prospective soldiers, about six of them, with short hair and bulging muscles. They were drinking beer and getting loud. Sonny watched them from the corner of his eye as he ate. He didn't see Bladeface among them, but they all reminded him of Bladeface as they sat discussing men less masculine than them and women too ugly to be worthy of them. Most of the other patrons ignored them.

Sonny leaned toward the bartender and asked about the cheapest hotel in town, and he was referred to a place seven doors down, where the cheapest lodging available was a hammock in a room containing several of them. Sonny paid for a week up front. Then he romped with Hina on the tiny stretch of beach for a while before looking for a place to hang out that wasn't the saloon.

His eye fell on a small grungy café. It was tucked behind the other buildings and was hard to see unless you noticed the faded sign with a picture of a cup of coffee on it. Inside were a dozen small tables wobbling on an uneven plank floor, while a crabby-looking woman served tea to a handful of patrons. Most importantly, she had a big open back porch, perfect for staring at the water. Sonny found a seat and commenced doing that, and when she finally crabbed her way over to his table, he asked her for the cheapest thing on the menu. She gave him an appraising look, a mug of tea and a broom, and told him she'd keep his mug full as long as he kept the floor swept. Sonny agreed to these terms.

The café drew a constant trickle of business. Sonny chatted with a local tattoo artist, and a guy named Gil who delivered interisland mail, and a couple of women who specialized in fishing for squid. None of them knew anything about plobs. Sonny renegotiated his pay to include food for himself and Hina, and agreed to expand his duties to include bussing tables and mopping. When things were slow he took breaks to run around on the beach with Hina, and swim.

When the café closed he retreated to his hammock and tried to fall asleep as the room gradually filled with men, some in various stages of drunkenness. Hina growled softly whenever they got too close.

In the morning he reported to the café and the crabby woman, whose name was Annie Lu, gave him a bowl of rice and eggs to share with Hina before ordering him to clean out the bathrooms. Horseshoe had modern toilets that sanitized and deodorized whatever entered them, but several of the patrons seemed to have difficulty aiming. When he was done with his task Sonny needed a shower and a swim, and another shower, before he was ready to deal with the lunch crowd.

Two of Rufe's mercenaries came to the café for lunch. They were well-behaved and respectful, calling Annie Lu "ma'am" whenever they spoke to her. Sonny thought about asking them about transport to Passiter. He also thought about being trapped on a boat with someone like Bladeface, or possibly several of them. Hina got along fine with toddlers, cats, horses and most people. She was safe in a crowd as long as none of them were bullies.

Another café table was occupied by a family passing through. The daughter had a supply of plobs and she agreed to give one to Sonny in exchange for an extra slice of Annie Lu's famous coffee cake, which Annie Lu immediately deducted from his wages. The daughter brought him the plob in a bucket of seawater, and Sonny stayed at work until the coffee cake issue was settled.

Then he bought a net bag from a cluttered little store, along with a floppy fisherman's hat that had a brim. He waded out to sea with his bucket, carefully transferring the plob into the net bag once he was in the water. On the leeward side the bottom was meter-deep for a long stretch before dropping off, and he settled himself halfway between the beach and the drop. He plunged his fingers into the familiar slimy sponginess and connected.

A comforting barrage of text scrolled over his visual field moments after he advised everyone on his list of friends he had arrived safely in Horseshoe. Nepenthe, being one of his friends, popped up within a few minutes. Not long after that, he had a shadow profile under the name of Sonny Knight. It copied posts to Leroy Knight's social node, and it broadcast whatever Sonny felt like posting to both Leroy's extensive friendlist on the internet as well as Sonny's new pals on the plob network. It also had a flashing red border around his portrait announcing that he was a minor, younger than sixteen, and Nepenthe had apologetically informed him this was a rule that couldn't be broken.

He paused before looking at his inbox, collecting his thoughts. It was a beautiful warm day, and the sun wasn't beating mercilessly on the top of his head thanks to his stylish new hat, and he was floating in tropical perfection. Nobody was shooting at him, or stabbing him in the back. There was a strong possibility Annie Lu would let him have the last piece of coffee cake for half price at closing time.

Thousands of messages awaited him. The entire first page of them were urgents, and his eyes danced rapidly through the text, scanning their headings. He had legal notices from several countries ordering him to stop whatever he was doing and pay attention, and he breezed past them all. Quicksilver had dumped a ridiculous amount of news in his feed, and his eyes caught the words "massacre" and "Lurie" as he swept them aside. He made a special pile devoted to things to look at later and began tossing in all the messages that leaned heavily on audio or pictures, and while he was doing that, one message caught his eye. It was from "Mom."

It looked like it had come from her regular social node. He couldn't see the profile picture, of course, but he could see her name, Jodie Louise Knight, and her location was given as Chelisary Village, Dysz. Goosebumps broke out on his skin despite the tropical sunshine.

There was a video clip that he couldn't see, and a text message. "Hello Leroy! We finally got our connection fixed. There was an earthquake, and everything was down for a while. I don't want to interrupt your tropical vacation, so let me know when you plan to be around. Everyone's fine and says hello. Love, Mom."

His fingers opened up a reply while his head was still thinking of what to say. He sent a quick "Hi Mom!" and then he bobbed in the water with a blank space before his eyes, unable to fill it with words. It occurred to him that he should just go rent some screentime and have a proper video exchange. He could earn more money later to pay any excess charges, now that he knew how to earn money.

While he was staring the letters flashed at him and scrolled, indicating he had an incoming call. From Mom.

He toggled over to the window where he had been talking to Nepenthe and typed "help!!??!" and when she asked him if he was really sure, he said yes. Headaches could be survived. He would stay connected long enough to say hi, and that he would call her later on a rented screen. Nepenthe set up the interface as he kept his vision static on the blueness of the water before him. The images encroached across his eyeballs, slowly solidifying into his mother's face.

It was similar to his face, with smooth and agreeable lines. Mom's hair was in her usual short neat bob, with bangs, like a little helmet protecting her face. She was wearing a blouse with sleeves and a collar, very businesslike, sitting on a plain dark couch in a sparsely furnished room. She opened her mouth and her voice rumbled through his fingers, all the way up to his ears. "Leroy? The channel's open but I can't see you, and I can't hear you."

Something deep and red surfaced just in front of him. For a moment he thought it was blood. Maybe a shark had come along and bitten his foot off while he was distracted. Maybe a meg. It turned out to be another plob, one with photographic capabilities. His face appeared on a small inset screen, bobbing with the gentle waves. His scattering of fuzzy beard had returned. His hair had swiftly degenerated from its pristine Deuce styling into a hank of sun-bleached straw, but fortunately the hat concealed it. He was facing Horseshoe, so his background was nothing but blue sky and sea. "Hi, Mom," he said out loud.

Mom's gasp traveled up through his wrists. He could feel the headache starting. He noticed a control box in the corner where he could turn the volume down and he did that as words rushed from her mouth. "Leroy, we were so worried about you! We thought you were dead, and that volcano took out all our connectivity, and then once we got it back we started hearing bizarre things."

"Most of them aren't true," he assured her. "I'm in Carquinez now. I'm heading back to Royal Beach, but I don't know when I'll get there. I had some experiences but I'm in good shape. I have a job, and a house, and a dog."

"Your voice is so deep! And you have a dog?"

"Her name is Hina. She's a good dog, you'll like her."

"Leroy, you know we don't live in Royal Beach anymore. We sold the house. We heard you were going to be coming to join us from Deuce."

"Are you happy there, mom?"

He stared into her projected eyes, looking for emotions. They seemed slightly dilated, similar to they way they looked when she'd had a cup or two of intoxicant after a harsh day at work, but there was also a defiant sparkle that had been lying dormant, waiting for his question. "Some days I feel like the whole world wants to know the answer to that question. We've been on the news, we've been interviewed by Ambit. They've asked us plenty of questions about you. I tell everyone the same thing, that I don't really remember the earthquake and the volcano, and that I am very pleased with my new country, and hope that someday everyone can learn to live in peace, and I look forward to being reunited with my son."

Her eyes darted to the side. Sonny could hear some kind of commotion going on in the background. It made his temples throb. Doors slammed open and shut, and then Kayliss appeared in the frame, and Sonny blinked.

She looked good. She was dressed in something formfitting and black, with her dark hair in a spiky shag, the blonde streak standing out prominently. Something dark was smeared around her eyes, diminishing from the pointiness of her nose. She was wearing Sonny's coat. Its natural brown wooly color was now decorated with bright splotches of orange.

"Is he still connected?" She demanded, and Mom nodded, at which point Kayliss swiveled toward the screen. "Tropical vacation? You fartlicker."

"Your face is a fartlicker," Sonny replied, unable to think of anything more clever due to the shock. To compound his shock, Mom laughed out loud. Kayliss sank down on the couch beside her and they hugged, pressing their cheeks together. Then Kayliss wormed out of the tasteless coat and folded it neatly, placing it on Mom's lap. She dug her hand into the pocket and found the pouch of gold coins, which she dangled briefly before plopping it on top of the folded coat.

"I didn't steal it. I was just borrowing," she explained.

"Orange?" The color stood out against the blue water in a way that was almost painful.

"I needed a surfactant to keep the peppermint oil and baking soda from dispersing too fast and all I could find was paint. It'll probably come out after you run it through the cleanbeams a few times."

"The peppermint smells nice," Mom added. "Very fresh."

"Peppermint and baking soda and paint?" Sonny wrinkled his nose.

"I had it packed up in balloons so I could pop one every couple of hours, but some of them broke open when I bailed. The megs react to it, it's a design feature. Water smells a little alkaline, uh oh, peppermint oil, I'm heading into bad water, I'll starve, better turn around. It only takes a whiff. They're not exactly smart, you know. Not like the Sirens, setting up clandestine underwater communications networks."

"It works pretty good," Sonny said. "You jumped over the side?"

"They were going to send the ship back to Deuce and I didn't want to go there. I didn't like the people I was traveling with. The sub found me after a couple of days. That's a very buoyant coat. It saved my life."

A crush. She had a crush on him, according to Risha. He knew what that was like. She was still essentially Effarren in eye makeup, and she was his enemy, and she had helped kidnap his mom, even though it appeared the two of them had become best buddies. And she was still nowhere near attractive, even though she now looked passable enough to get into a grade B nightclub, or be cast in a crowd scene. A sharp pain developed behind his eyeballs as he struggled to maintain his grip on friendliness.

"I'm glad you're alive. I heard a rumor you died and I felt terrible."

She bounced. She actually rose several centimeters on the couch. When she bounced, Sonny caught motion at her neck. Focusing in was physically painful, but he did it and confirmed she was still wearing her little wooden key. From her dream date, with her first crush. Mom gave her an encouraging little shoulder hug following the bounce, as if to reassure her that yes, Leroy liked her enough to mourn her untimely death.

"Is Dad there? Or Marilyn?"

"Marilyn's in school, and so are Lenny and Dan. They've become part of our family. So has Kayliss, in a lot of ways." Mom and Kayliss were holding hands now, their fingers interlaced. "Your dad's at work. I've been working from home today, storyboarding." She waved her hand toward some other portal on the wallscreen that he couldn't see.

"You sound busy."

"Oh, yes. We have a lovely big house, in a brand new development. I'm directing a film, and your father is designing a park. They went around asking all the people in the Village what we could do, and then they gave us everything we need to do a good job." Her eyes misted over slightly. "It's not a beach party, but it ain't bad."

It was a movie reference. From a full-length animated movie that had played on the Knight family wallscreen hundreds of times, since it was released at a time perfectly overlapping Sonny's and Marilyn's demographics. *Seconds Ticking* was a beach party musical about a school full of mean teachers who made their students start their summer a week late.

Migg Idgie was a comic actor who played a kid who sucked up to the teachers, in his first and breakout role, and his big punchline was "It's not a beach party, but it ain't bad," while trying to convince his fellow students that extra studying was no great hardship. Right after delivering the line, Idgie's character was subjected to a hail of projectiles including beach towels, water bottles and flipflops. Mom gave Kayliss an extra shoulder squeeze for emphasis.

"I'm just walking down the yellow bricks, trying to stay away from the flying monkeys," Sonny replied, and Mom's eye twinkled back.

"A parade every day, and two on Sundays." That was from another musical, *Welcome to Happyville*, about a town where a town of cute little elves elected a troll as mayor after he built a magical fountain in the town square that spewed pure happiness. Sonny took this to mean they were all heavily medicated.

"The same side of an airlock," Sonny replied. On one of his favorite episodes of *Space Police*, the main squad had been split up into separate spaceships, and during an emotional teleconference had agreed they wouldn't drop the struggle until they were on the same side of an airlock. Or until the evil green frog men killed them with blasts from their laser tongues. He meant this to symbolize his determined wish for a reunion, and Mom nodded.

"Is that science fiction?" Kayliss blurted. "I like science fiction."

"That's another thing you have in common with Leroy." Mom squeezed her hand. Sonny felt as though one of the evil green frog men was doing gymnastics behind his eyeballs. His distress must have showed on his face because suddenly they both looked concerned. He blinked and rubbed his eyes.

"Video gives me a headache. Text is easier. I'm going to have to disconnect soon. I love you."

He meant it for Mom but from Kayliss' tiny squeal he could tell she had included herself in the splash. Fine. I love you too, Kayliss. Thanks for ruining my cool coat. Thanks for … for giving Mom a stash of gold in case of emergency. And telling me how to make meg repellant.

And for looking after them. Something shifted in his field of vision and suddenly the faces were crystal clear, floating ghostly before him on the waves, hopeful and concerned. "I don't want you to get a headache," Mom was saying. "We'll talk again soon. Let me know when you've got a regular screen."

"I will," he promised. "Take care."

His hands spasmed and the plob slipped out of his hands. He had to dive for it, increasing the pressure behind his eyeballs to nausea-inducing levels, but he got it safely stuffed in its net bag, and he anchored the net bag to the bottom with a sturdy rock. He lost his hat while doing this but the waves slapped it back against his leg once he was halfway to shore, nearly blind with the pain. He bent over to grab it and nausea struck, and his puke slick washed back at him a couple of times before dissolving into the surf, but he held onto his hat. He slapped it on his head and pulled it over his eyes. Once he got to shore he dragged himself to a puddle of shade formed by two adjacent buildings and collapsed, wrapping his forearm around his eyes to block out the light.

Annie Lu found him there, hours later, with Hina's help. She helped him into her storage room, which was tiny but dark, and fed him sips of lukewarm water interspersed with whiffs of sweet-scented steam. Finally the headache broke with a brittle pop, leaving him blinking and euphoric over its absence.

He staggered out of the pantry on wobbly legs and collapsed at a table. Annie Lu placed a big bowl of chicken noodle soup before him and massaged his shoulders while he ate it, slowly savoring each exquisite bite. She scolded him for getting what she had thought was sunstroke, and he didn't bother correcting her.

●

He worked extra hard for Annie Lu the next day, cleaning everything cleanable and keeping the customers well-supplied with condiments and water. He avoided his plob until midafternoon. He was almost afraid to touch it, since the headache had been one of the most painful things that had ever happened to him. He fought with urges to just go back and take a nap on his hammock as he waded out to the rock, and when he initially couldn't find his net bag he was tempted to surrender.

But no, there it was, right where he'd left it. He freed it from its bag and positioned his fingers. Text appeared, and he braced himself for the onset of a killer headache, but that didn't happen. Text was fine. Looking at the water was fine, even if there was sun on the water. All fine. He said hello to his local friends and found Lily had invited him to several chatrooms concerning the volcano and other local events. He accepted and said his hellos in there.

He found lots of dense verbiage containing scientific terms. As he was coursing through it he found a highlighted section which he brushed in an effort to scroll past it.

And suddenly he was underwater. He was a floating eyeball that could see for hundreds of kilometers, in all directions. He saw schools of fish and spots of coral, a shipwreck over here, a rock formation over there which might once have been a building. He could pan, he could zoom, he could adjust the lighting, and only after he'd been doing that for several minutes did it occur to him that he was operating in plob video.

And not only that, he didn't have a headache.

He logged into his social node and resumed shoveling out his message box, deleting the least interesting messages. He noticed a new one at the top that had an official government seal, this one from Carquinez, with an attached video. He expanded it and read a notice that under Carquinez law, all internet video conversations between adults and minors were recorded and posted for public viewing. And there was a link to the conversation with his mom, with a split screen between her smiling face and Sonny's watery one.

He still didn't have a headache, but he was starting to worry that one might develop. He replaced his plob in its bag and anchored it underwater. He headed back to Annie Lu's, where he worked an energetic dinner shift, earning himself and Hina an elegant supper of leftovers.

There was still no headache the next day, despite a drunk who had awakened Sonny several times during the night with his renditions of classic show tunes. He was feeling optimistic as he waited for the early lunch crowd to descend. He had broken the barrier. He was among the select few that could watch video through a plob, and that meant he could talk to his family every day if he felt like it.

Hina let out a chorus of yips, startling him out of his reverie, and charged toward a man entering the café. Sonny was halfway committed toward rolling underneath his table when he caught himself, realizing that Hina was being enthusiastically friendly as opposed to aggressive. The object of her affections was laughing and fondling her ears. He was a solid, bulky man with his dark hair in a tight braid, swaying slightly as though he'd just gotten off a boat. His face was broad and homely but pleasant. It wasn't until Sonny mentally superimposed facial tattoos that it clicked.

"I think she's mistaking you for Kai, although maybe she knows you from working for the Tigers."

"Go Tigers." The man, who was obviously blood kin to Kai, clasped his fist over his chest. The two men behind him, sun-leathered sailors, did likewise. "I'm Kimo. This is Gary and Little Phil."

"I'm Sonny." He nodded in turn at each of the men and set up a table for them. "Go sit down, Hina. I recommend the chicken noodle soup."

"Sounds good. You've been around my nephew," Kimo said. It wasn't a question.

"Yeah, Kai," Sonny agreed. "Lots of tattoos."

The three men laughed and elbowed each other. "He said something about rescuing the Tigers' mascot. Like he was some kind of big hero or something."

"A lot of rescuing happened," Sonny said. "I lost track of it all."

Annie Lu bustled out with a tureen of chicken noodle soup, and Sonny turned around to deal with a party of happy fishermen. Usually the happy fishermen showed up early for lunch, while the grumpy fisherman didn't get there until dinnertime. After Sonny got them seated he cruised past Kimo's table, noting that all three of them seemed pleased with the soup.

"Hey kid. We're delivering his boat, out to Acanella. Could use an extra man in our crew, if you know any starving sailors."

Sonny thought about it for a moment. So far he hadn't heard of any offers. The idea of sailing Kai's new boat before he even got a chance to look at it was tempting. "I'm looking for a boat. Where's Acanella? Are there a lot of people?"

"Mostly in-laws. Supposed to be couple hundred showing up for the party." He made a face and extended his arm. "Out that way a few days. I was kinda hoping for someone with some experience, but it's a pretty easy stretch."

"I've got a little experience," Sonny said, as he began to have misgivings about crashing an enemy's party. "There's a guy named Lester that'll vouch for me. I can receive video on plobs."

He smiled sheepishly, figuring they'd laugh, but instead they held a whispered conference. Kimo gave him an appraising look. "You can run a nav station?"

"I've never even seen a nav station," Sonny replied.

The men conferred again and this time Little Phil spoke up. "Go out there and have a look at the boat. See if it interests you."

Sonny rapidly finished bussing his table and headed out the front door. You could see everything from everywhere in Horseshoe since it was so small, and he saw the usual ragged assortment of fishing boats tied up at the pier. At the very end was a tall-masted catamaran flying a blue and orange sail.

Sonny was drawn to it. Once he got closer he peered into the salon and saw seats with deep blue cushions that matched the ones on the operator's seat, sitting high at the back of the right-hand hull, beside a dinghy suspended on davits.

He was still gawking when the crew of the nameless catamaran came strolling up the pier, and the only word he could manage to emit was "Yes."

They gave him a bucket and sent him to fetch his plob. Once he hauled it on board, he was directed to a seat inside the salon, just forward of the captain's perch. He thought it looked like a toilet at first, then he realized it was like Paolo's blob station, except much fancier. He found the siphon line and turned a tiny spigot, making seawater flow into the well. Once it was full he carefully transferred the plob and settled himself on the seat just behind it, with the well between his knees. He found a tube of the same lotion Lily used in a nearby hatch, and he smoothed it onto his hands and arms. He sat back for a moment waiting for it to dry, admiring his surroundings as Hina curled up beside him.

On either side of the salon were stairs leading down into the twin hulls. The salon itself was nice and roomy, dominated by a table with a bench wrapped around it. The galley had fittings made of composite finished to look like well worn copper, and an intricate setup of cupboards and utensils that made Sonny long to cook something. There was no harpsichord, but there were speakers mounted in the ceiling. Unlike the *Lono*, this boat had electricity, although the light fixtures were fake candles in deference to Kai's retro sensibilities. There was also a panel of wallscreen that was currently offline.

"Go ahead, call it up. Tell me where the shipwrecks are, on the bottom." Kimo tapped his toe on the window separating the pilot's seat from Sonny's nav station. Sonny dipped his hands into the water and clutched his plob. Once he was connected it occurred to him that he had no idea how to find the data for his location. He did know a bunch of people he could ask, and they asked a few other people, and finally Paolo himself supplied a link, with directions on how to calibrate it to his location. The plob network seemed to struggle with the very concept of location, showing him a wide approximate slice of sea floor that he had to narrow based on his estimate of the sun's position. The text version floated in the corner of his visual field, showing all the arcane codes he would have had to memorize if he had been a text-based nav.

Then he was gliding under the waves, his underwater view superimposed on reality, a light green grid pattern helping him gauge distance, a floating compass rose giving him direction. Sea anemones waved at him from the ocean floor, ten meters down. "There's a big one off to port. If you come around ten degrees you'll pass right over it."

Sonny figured out how to relocate on the fly, with directions passed along from his assorted chatroom friends. It was sort of like a video game he'd played once, themed around space exploration. He figured out how to call up weather maps, and sonar, and realtime video of the ocean floor. He guided them to a school of tuna, and shortly after that he was sitting at the table peeling rubbery film away from his fingers while Little Phil brushed marinade on thick tuna steaks and Hina gobbled down a large hunk of sashimi.

"You say you just learned how to do that?" Gary nodded his head toward the nav station, where the well was safely closed with a watertight lid.

"It's a lot like using a deld, just with a slimier interface." Sonny collected his rubbery strips of goop and rolled them up in a ball.

"We didn't grow up using delds. Got screens in the house, but." Kimo laughed and held out his hand alongside Sonny's. His fingers were callused and scarred. "Thirty years of hardcore woodworking. Those things require a much softer touch."

"Don't you get headaches?" Little Phil slid plates of seared fish before them, accompanied by soft mounds of rice and some kind of spicy salad.

"Yeah, at first. Then you get to a point where it works and the headache goes away."

"The fewer headaches I have, the happier I am." Gary fiddled with the sound system until it spit out island-style jam music.

"O2 gets rid of headaches," Little Phil reported. "Most of 'em. Let me know if you start getting one while you're working the nav and I'll give you a whiff from the tank, Sonny."

"What's ohtu?"

"Oxygen." Little Phil laughed. "There's a tank down below. Kimo, make sure your nephew's smart enough to keep it away from the cannon."

"This thing's got a cannon?" Sonny bounced out of his seat, interested. In the glow of a tropical sunset, Kimo showed him the cannon, mounted beneath the salon and retractable into a nondescript housing at the touch of a switch. It had heavy shock absorbers to cushion its kick, and you reloaded it through a hatch in the floor.

Little Phil showed him another hatch that contained spare ammo. "Needless to say, you gotta shoot something with a cannon, you don't want to have to worry about it a second time. These are explosive rounds, kinda special. No good against ships. Not bad against living things. Terrible if you accidentally shoot your O2 tanks, they'll explode."

"Megs," Sonny guessed. All three men nodded solemnly. Hina whined.

"The explosion melts the casing off a capsule on the inside that's full of concentrated neurotoxin," Phil informed him. "These are a new kind. Based on some kind of jellyfish the Chinese sampled before the domes. Supposed to be ten times as effective as what we were using before."

"Does it work?" Sonny looked at the cannon doubtfully. It was tiny compared to the ones on the *Lono*.

"Not sure. We were going to test it along the way. Good thing we found a nav operator, hey?"

●

The catamaran cruised parallel to the reef. Up top it looked like the same old expanse of blue, but there was a lot going on underneath the surface. The reef itself was tall as a skyscraper, and Sonny's image didn't expand enough to encompass the entire thing. On the other side of it were numerous large moving things. Some were schools of fish, and Sonny was usually able to distinguish them by their ragged irregular shapes. Others might have been whales.

"Are there any whales around here?"

"Some are starting to come back, way south of here, and not usually until the winter. They won't come up here near the megs, even now that they're under control. Mostly." Little Phil was cleaning the gears. These were made of heavy-duty composite, and they were swapped out weekly and carefully inspected for stress fractures and chips. There weren't many of them but they made tasks like raising the sails and anchor much easier. The boat also had a small engine made of composite, and the windows were polymer with various exotic treatments. Everything else was solid wood.

Sonny let the plob sink to the bottom of the well as he stretched his arms out behind his head. "Phil --"

"Little Phil. Phil's my dad."

"Little Phil, you seem like you know a lot about chemistry and stuff."

"Don't they teach you that in school?"

"I went for a different science elective. Statistics and audience demographics."

Little Phil made a derisive sound. "I know a little."

"I was talking to someone who was tight with the guys who created all these megs."

"They've only been around for a couple of decades at the most. Trying to discourage all the smugglers and traffickers during the war."

"Well, what I heard is that this person was in water near a bunch of them. And used baking soda and paint and peppermint oil to chase them away. I don't know if it's true but it might be."

Little Phil looked thoughtful. "Baking soda would change the acidity of the water in a very small area. No idea why you'd want paint and peppermint."

"The paint was a ... facton."

"Surfactant. That would keep it from dispersing as fast. But peppermint?"

"They probably have terrible breath," Kimo said from above. "Let's try it."

Little Phil located a large package of OwMyTummy and a bottle of Minty Fresh mouthwash and dumped them in a mixing bowl. Instead of paint he added a generous dollop of cooking oil. He stirred it into a sludgey batter and poured it into a rubber glove, making a fat five-fingered balloon. Then he fumbled around in another hatch and came up with a pinky-sized firecracker, with a waterproof fuse. "Find me a meg," he ordered as he tied the explosive to the glove's wrist.

Sonny reengaged with his plob and studied the ominous shapes on the other side of the reef. "There's a big school of fish that are acting kind of agitated, like something's attacking them."

"How high is the reef?"

"It's within a meter or so of the surface." They had all assured him that the coral had some kind of treatment that discouraged megs from crossing it. It made sense, he knew for a fact there was coral back home designed to keep Sirens from crossing it, along with other large sea creatures that might interfere with tourism. He was also pretty certain the catamaran could go at least twice as fast as a meg, assuming nothing stupid occurred. "Here comes one. It's gonna break the surface at about seven o'clock."

The boat listed gently as everyone looked toward seven o'clock. Sonny heard sounds that seemed to indicate the fin was visible. He watched the silhouette of the underwater portion of the shark, merged with the dissolving outline of the school of fish. Little Phil climbed up to the roof with his glove bomb and a few moments later Sonny watched the silhouette of it landing, not too far from the shark, and exploding in a little bright puff.

A moment or two later, the shark's outline came out of the fish school, separating from it as it departed rapidly into the depths. "It went away!" Sonny blinked, trying to see the salon beneath his sonar overlay. "I think it worked."

His fingers drifted his vantage point forward, toward one o'clock. There was a big smudgy silhouette there, right next to them. Sonny put his eyes back on the dark surface of his well, registering it.

"Shit! Hard to port!" His voice cut through the men's cheering, and they responded. The boat went hard to port, and the meg parallelling the reef cruised closer to the surface. It was easily longer than the catamaran. Sonny's hands spasmed and he lost his connection.

"Bring it around and test the cannon," Kimo ordered.

"No," Sonny disagreed. "You don't want to do that, it's really big."

"So's my cannon," Kimo replied, and Gary adjusted the mainsail while Little Phil popped open the cannon hatch and turned on the little aiming screen.

Sonny fumbled with his plob, trying to get his readout back. The catamaran shivered as the cannon went off, and the plob slipped out of his hands. He saw the meg surface off to starboard, its ugly head breaching, showing a mouth wide enough to walk right in.

The shark launched out of the water, spinning sideways, corkscrewing, its entire body visible as it flew through the air, spasming. Kimo and Gary fought successfully with the sails and avoided crashing into it. It landed portside, making a geyser of a splash that dampened the back of Sonny's neck through the pilot's window. The men were all whooping triumphantly, yet at the same time Sonny noticed they were headed away from the reef at high speed. He was in full agreement with that decision.

"Should've hacked off a chunk of it while it was flying past," Kimo said as they dined on fast little fish with delicious white flesh that had jumped right into their net as they put space between themselves and the reef.

"Jellyfish venom got him," Little Phil said gleefully. "It's sealed up in a coating that melts when the shot connects. Floods their bloodstream. The moment it hits their brain, bam! Massive seizure."

"Or you could just chuck a glove full of repellent at them," Sonny said. The men all nodded at him with silent respect.

Kimo finally made it verbal respect. "You're a good nav."

●

The next day they reached Acanella. It was much bigger than Horseshoe and approximately round, and it had an entire town's worth of buildings. The crowd of people that came to greet the nameless catamaran seemed overwhelming to Sonny, but when he thought about it he realized they would all fit inside the auditorium in his school, with plenty of seats to spare.

Everyone admired the boat extensively but nobody touched it. There seemed to be an unwritten rule out here concerning messing with other peoples' boats. There were plenty of other nice boats tied up to the pier, cabin cruisers and canoes and kayaks and sailboats, more catamarans, a couple of trimarans. Most of them were wooden, and one of the canoes had a Viking-style dragon head carved on the prow.

"I believe we are the only guests from Kai's side of the family," Kimo said to Sonny, *sotto voce*. "These are his wife's people."

"Kai has a wife?" Sonny had never really seen Kai expressing romantic interest in anything other than the *Lono*.

"Luceen." Kimo pointed his big callused finger at the middle of the island. "She'll be in the house. And Kai should be here in a few days. Chill, enjoy the party. It's Luceen's birthday."

They had brought several crates of food and drink to contribute to the party, and Sonny helped lug them uphill to a cluster of buildings nestled around a massive banyan tree, made of composite blocks so weathered they looked like stone. The largest building was a kitchen that smelled enticingly of baked bread and grilled meat. A couple of dozen people of various assorted ages were lingering outside, including a small pack of teenagers who seemed interested in Sonny, making his wobbly-legged way up the path carrying boxes of Squirrelson's Premium Olive Tapenade and Mizz Gorgonzola's Ginger Mango Biscuits.

Hina was even more wobbly-legged, given that she had spent several days cooped up on the boat, secured with knots Sonny could quickly untie in an emergency. She was immediately recognized as the Tigers' mascot, and enveloped in a cloud of people and dogs. Sonny set his cartons down and answered questions. Yes, she was saved from the game, no, none of the Sharks were here with her. Her mouth is supposed to open that wide, and no, she won't bite the babies or the puppies or the cats. Sure, you can feed her a crabcake. No, I didn't paint the stripes on, they're natural. Yes, I'm her handler. Hina's celebrity experience was apparent as she greeted her crowd of admirers. Once they seemed satisfied she went streaking downhill to splash in the surf, accompanied by an exuberant pack of island dogs.

The people turned their attention to Sonny, asking his age, and whether he was married, and whether he liked boys or girls, and whether he had any kids. He was a little embarassed by all the personal questions but he disclosed that he was engaged, then wished he could take it back. They nodded as though being fifteen and engaged was no big deal.

"Looks like it's you and me, then. My name is Caleb." He had a scruffy fringe of beard and his hair was tied up in a knot, and his cargo shorts had a faded dolphin print that was barely visible. The other people lost interest and wandered back toward what they were doing as Caleb grabbed one of Sonny's boxes. "I'll show you where to set 'em down."

Sonny grabbed the other box and followed Caleb into a big storage building. It was stacked high with coldboxes on one side, and the other side had sacks of noodles, and rice, and spices, and flour. There were also plenty of canned foods piled up on pallets, and a rack containing bottles of everything from cooking oil to raspberry flavored drink mix. "You guys eat a lot," Sonny said, and Caleb thought that was funny.

"Eating is our national sport. Even more popular than surfing. You surf?"

"I was really bad at it before I had my knee surgery and I'm probably worse now." Sonny followed Caleb back to the pier, where they collected more boxes. "I like to sail, and catch fish, and cook them."

"Those are more of our national sports. I'm more of a surfer myself. Bummer that you don't surf."

"I appreciate you showing me around, but why are we a 'you and me' if we're into different things?"

"Have a seat, and I'll give you a crash course in how to not be an asshole." Caleb directed Sonny toward a bench sheltered by banyan tendrils.

"I've been living here in Carq a little while, you know." Sonny could feel himself getting moderately offended. "I lived in Horseshoe, had a job and everything."

"I'm divorced. Plus I have a kid, but he's not really mine, and that's why I'm divorced."

"How old are you?"

"Seventeen. It's different on smaller islands where you've only got a few people, but when you get a big crowd like this, they start separating out everybody who's looking for someone and they stay separate until they find someone. Saves on drama, although apparently some guys have no problem secretly hanging out with married women. Everyone who's looking will be wearing a shell necklace, and so will you, except yours will be red to let everyone know you're off limits." Caleb extracted a red shell choker from his pocket, similar to the one he was wearing, and passed it to Sonny.

"How long has it been since you broke up with your wife?" Sonny fastened the shell string around his neck, trying to look sympathetic while making a mental note to avoid all romantic entanglements in Carq. Which was ironic, because there were more exposed boobs in Carq than anywhere he'd ever been. He had almost stopped noticing at least three-quarters of them, and he supposed he'd have to stop noticing the rest too.

"Four months." Caleb sighed. "I'm sorry, I don't mean to keep complaining."

"It's all right." Friendly, friendly, friendly. Sonny focused on the musicians while Caleb told his tale of woe. Apparently no island was complete without a crowd of people jamming away on songs that never seemed to end, and the musicians on this island were pretty good. Sonny couldn't help tapping his fingers as Caleb told him of the lovely black-haired goddess, Lisa, who had seduced and betrayed him, moving in with her lover three hours before she went into labor.

"The kid had his exact same nose," Caleb said, sadly shaking his head. "She'd been with him the whole time."

"That's really rough."

"So yeah, we're the two miscellaneous misfits that aren't eligible to flirt with anyone on this island. I've got two more months of social probation before I can start looking for a new ex-wife to break my heart into a million pieces. And your fiancee ain't here."

"We're probably going to break up." Sonny thought about Risha's dimply smile. Maybe he could spend three years out here in Carq, working as a nav and learning to surf, and then she'd come out to find him and discover a lean, brown, muscular guy with a kickass sailboat, escorting her to her own private island, where she'd dress like a Carq girl, omitting her shirt.

He bent forward at that thought, wishing his shorts were a looser fit. Caleb was droning on about each and every one of Lisa's cold heartless lies. Sonny found himself looking at a foreboding house, shaded by one end of the banyan tree. It had narrow slits for windows, and Sonny could see they were heavily curtained on the inside. The door was thick and solid. "Is that where Luceen lives?"

"Luceen. Yeah, that's her house." Caleb blinked as his mind changed tracks. "She's my third cousin-in-law. I've been to her birthday bash a few times. It's a pretty good party. This one's just getting started. She married this guy who's really rich and travels around the world, and he brings her presents on her birthday, so there's a big get-together with all the relatives. Sometimes he doesn't make it and it's just a freight shipment but this year he's gonna attend in person and pick up his new boat."

"That is one sweet boat," Sonny said, hoping Caleb would ask him to elaborate, but he didn't.

"So you're one of his relatives?"

"It's complicated. I'm from Royal Beach."

"I figured you weren't from around here. Something about you. You look normal, so maybe it's the accent. You gonna catch a ride home on that boat? Everyone says he's gonna try to sail up the south coast, and that he's crazy. If he dies, this might be the last party unless Luceen gets a new husband."

"What's she like?" Sonny studied the thin windows.

"She's all right." Caleb glanced sideways at Sonny. "Here comes non-asshole lesson two. She's got agoraphobia. She panics whenever she goes outside. Especially if she sees the ocean. That's why she lives on this big ass island, so she can always have plenty of family around to bring her food and visit her. She probably won't come outside, but if she does, don't stare at her, or get in her way, or talk to her, stuff like that. You don't want her to freak out and start screaming."

"No, I definitely don't want that," Sonny agreed. He took his eyes off the windows, hoping she hadn't seen him staring and taken it personally. "Do people here use plobs?"

"Oh, you're one of those?" Caleb laughed sarcastically. "We keep the nerd soup over this way."

They got up and walked along a path that wound toward a cliff overlooking the pier and the white blanket of beach snuggled alongside it. Shady trees grew strategically over a swimming pool on the cliff, meter deep and containing a handful of plob fans. There was a net bag of plobs stored at one end, and near it was a handwashing station with large jugs of hand lotion, and a couple of toilet stalls.

"No food allowed, no drinks allowed, no peeing in the pool allowed, no loud allowed," Caleb whispered under his breath as they approached.

"I like it," Sonny said. "I can come back, when you're surfing."

Caleb brightened with the realization Sonny wouldn't die of loneliness if he went off and did something else. He showed Sonny around the compound without mentioning his ex-wife more than a couple of times, including the room where they'd be spending their nights together.

Sonny lingered around the kitchen. It had several griddles and a firepit, and a big clay oven. Most of the people working in it were elderly, and they turned down Sonny's offer of assistance with smiles. Caleb nudged his elbow. "Lesson three, old people are better at cooking, because they've survived more dinners than you."

"I'm not a bad cook," he told Caleb as they walked toward the jamming musicians.

"Lisa was a terrible cook," Caleb confided as they found a shady place to sit, and he proceeded to tell Sonny about everything Lisa had cooked, rating each dish on a scale of one to five. Most of them scored no higher than two.

Caleb was grating, but Sonny listened patiently. Part of him wanted to spill his own tale to Caleb, as the winning entry in some kind of tragic competition, but friendliness won out. He spent the afternoon lying peacefully beneath the leaves listening to musicians that knew their way around the octaves, occasionally saying things like, "that's really harsh" or "you can do so much better."

Dinner was formal and ceremonious. The old people arranged platters on a long table, then served themselves first and retreated to their own separate area. Then several of the middle aged people prepared a tray consisting of a little bit of everything and carried it to Luceen's house and knocked on the door. Sonny craned his neck trying to get a glimpse of Luceen, whom his imagination was insisting was some kind of vampire sorceress with glowing red eyes, but all he saw was the tray being handed inside, to someone.

Other diners stepped forward with their little demographic groups; a cluster of pregnant women, a row of couples, the musicians, the cliques of persons seeking partners wearing colorful shell necklaces in colors that weren't red, then the children ranked by age. Kimo and his crew had fallen in with a group of guys who were seriously concerned with boat specs. Sonny and Caleb went last, but there was still plenty of food, and after they ate it Caleb announced he was going for a sunset surf, while Sonny excused himself to the plob pool.

The pool's inhabitants gave him friendly nods without actually speaking to him as he slathered lotion over his hands, gloving up. He selected a fat purple plob and found a spot on one of the submerged benches. Even though he had been headache-free all through the voyage, he decided to limit himself to text, so he could see the sunset.

Nepenthe pounced on him the moment he logged in. "I was going to ask you where you've been but now that I see where you are I'm dying to ask why."

Sonny blinked at the text floating on the calm surface before him. "I'm here for a birthday party."

"You've been online for the past several days but you're ignoring everything except locational data."

"I was doing nav. On a boat. Kinda like you do, but not as good."

After a long pause, she replied with "Are you familiar with the term 'serendipity'?"

"You go looking for something, and you accidentally find something else that's what you actually wanted."

"Exactly. I've parted company with Kai. I won't do the crossing into the Caribbean again, and it's moot now that we can move through the Atlantic. I miss him terribly, but I must devote my attention to politics and business. The *Lono* is going to Asia and another Siren will be accompanying it."

"Is Kai okay?"

"He is full of anxiety. It's hard to deal with you folks when you're wound that tight." She flashed him an animated dancing mermaid. "But I have known Kai for quite some time, and anxiety tends to inspire him."

Sonny glanced at Luceen's house. "Seems about right. Did you know about the peppermint oil, by the way? And the megs?"

"Peppermint, yes. They use it to contain the megs as well as the pliosaurs. There are a series of bots synthesizing it that demarcate their territory. We lack that particular technology. They tried a similar thing with us involving a heightened sensitivity to eucalyptus but we developed a vaccine."

"If you mix it with baking soda it makes them go away. We tested it. It makes them think they're heading into fresh water."

"Between you and me, we're planning to re-extinct them just as soon as we achieve a few political goals. Baking soda? Interesting. I'll pass it along. We already know they have a much narrower tolerance for pH fluctuation. Chemistry is difficult down here. We're working on restoring oxygenation to see if we can negate a little of the acidification, and that should take care of all the prehistoric beasts. Can't say I'll miss them, but I hope it happens within my lifetime."

●

Days passed. Sonny and Caleb's red-shell necklace clique swelled to four as new boatloads of partygoers arrived. Harley was on probation for committing some unspoken crime, and Morgan had been castrated in an unfortunate diving accident featuring a moray eel, and walked with a heavy limp.

The mateable people seemed to be having a much better time. The pool of singles gradually diminished as people paired off, and swelled as new ones arrived. Sometimes the misfits and the elders sat together speculating on which ones would end up together. Sonny reflected it was probably just as well that he was excluded, since he was leaving soon, and the last thing he needed was a sudden infatuated marriage to some Lisa. Back home people waited until they were at least twenty to get married, and some of them waited until they were as old as thirty, and some never bothered. Uncle Duke was in his late twenties and hadn't paired off with anyone yet.

Then again, he could make a good living here as a nav, and he could definitely feed a family, and give them a beautiful house besides. Nobody here would ever ask for his real name, or look up his history on the internet, and they'd probably get his back if a submarine full of clones showed up. Which wouldn't happen, because he could see them sneaking around underwater on his nav display.

Being unmateable didn't prevent people from socializing with Sonny. Nobody questioned his presence, or asked him nosy questions. At the same time, they didn't volunteer information they assumed he already knew, such as their names. For the most part everyone was peaceful, although there were a few hotheads who got in shoving matches with each other and had to be towed in separate directions by their buddies and talked down until everyone mellowed out again.

The birthday gifts overflowed the warehouse. Some people brought gifts for everybody on the island, and Sonny wound up with a new pair of cargo shorts, some flipflops and a cool pair of sunglasses. He still had his floppy fishing hat, giving him a total of five garments if you counted each flipflop separately. He checked himself out in the mirrory sheen of the plob pool, wondering if he looked native. He had been mindful of his accent since Caleb mentioned it, putting a little more music into his lazy vowels. His skin was just as brown as theirs, and his hair just as distressed as theirs, and he had started gathering it up in a kind of samurai knot, like many of them did.

He was unique in his lack of tattoos. Most Carqs wore a little ink, usually dark black patterns like Kai's, since the tropical sun apparently turned anything detailed or colorful into a featureless blob, from the looks of some of the tattoos on the older people who'd experimented. Caleb confided that it made him look a little shifty and untrustworthy, like he didn't want to be identified. After thinking about it, Sonny agreed that he didn't want to be identified, and passed on numerous offers of free tattoos.

One day he remembered he hadn't bothered with his real world messagebox in quite some time, and logged in to check it. The flood of new messages had calmed a little, and most of the latest ones were from Quicksilver, who felt the need to broadcast his status frequently, usually with accompanying pictures and video. Mom hadn't called lately, and he hadn't called her because he didn't want to get all emotional in front of a bunch of strangers. There would be time for that later. He knew that he could call her, and she could call him, and that was the important thing.

While he was accepting a bunch of friend requests from people who were also in the Bippy Borp International Fan Club, he saw the mast of the *Lono* sail into view. It was too big for the pier and instead it dropped anchor off the shore. Sonny tucked his plob back in its net and stepped out of the pool, watching the *Lono* lower boats. The first one was all crates and pallets, with four men to row, and it rode heavy in the water. The second one was colorful. Sonny identified Kai's peacock blue jacket, and Risha's tropical rainbow dress, and brightly colored shirts on Quicksilver and Rufe. Blocker was slightly more inconspicuous in dress, but she did have a big straw hat which constantly threatened to blow away.

Sonny slipped into his flipflops and headed down to the beach, where he stood in a huge crowd to meet the boats. Kimo pushed through to greet Kai, and they embraced, just before everyone else converged on him to welcome him home.

Rufe hopped out of the boat, wearing neatly pressed khaki cargo shorts with his bright shirt. He helped Risha and Quicksilver out, then he lifted Blocker and set her gently on the sand where she stood, wobbling slightly and leaning on a walking stick. Sonny looked around for Hina, hoping she wouldn't give him away, and noted she was doing her usual afternoon thing, napping in the shade in a pile of puppies.

He helped carry the goods Kai had brought into the warehouse, and while he was in there he noticed a crate of OwMyTummy and a crate of Misty Sea's Peppermint Taffy, and he slid them to one side.

He found himself carrying one end of a crate destined for Luceen's house, and his forehead dribbled sweat at the thought of finally seeing the demon vampire goddess, who was probably hanging from a curtain rod by her toenails eating live frogs. He pulled his hat down low, glad he had sunglasses.

It was cool and peaceful inside Luceen's house. Everything was lit softly by lamps. A soft fragrant smell of incense and sounds of conversation came from the front room. There was a woman there, sitting on a velvet couch, having an extremely subdued argument with an older woman, and Sonny was careful to avoid eye contact as he helped stuff the crate into what looked like a storeroom, crowded with miscellaneous art. There was a heavy duty humidifier humming away in the corner but it hadn't really stopped the paintings from deteriorating, although the woodcarvings were fine.

As they were leaving, Sonny looked at Luceen from the corner of his eye. She was a nice looking woman, somewhere between young and middle aged, with long black hair. He couldn't see her eyes but he was pretty sure they weren't blazing purple. She had a fancy seagreen dress with lots of poofs and flounces, and it seemed to be the subject of the argument.

When Sonny stepped outside the ambient noise level rose considerably, and he realized Luceen had soundproofing that was hardcore enough to override the sound of the surf. He returned to the beach to discover all the boxes had been carried away. He spotted Kai's peacock blue back heading toward the pier and he scurried to follow at a discreet distance.

He watched from the beach as Kai hopped in and explored the deck, and headed below, and popped back out to tug on the rigging. The four of them gathered on the deck to watch the *Lono* head off toward the horizon. Kai's shoulders sagged, and Kimo wrapped an arm around him. Sonny backed away toward the banyan tree.

Risha and Rufe and Blocker and Quicksilver had been absorbed into the general party. Sonny found Caleb sitting with his Auntie Rhonda, who was was telling him all about her grandchildren.

"My fiancee finally got here," he said, jerking his head at Risha.

"Good one." Caleb smiled. "Have you figured out where you're going after the party?"

"I think so." Sonny glanced back at Kai's group, headed up the path, walking slowly and talking intensely. Kai made a dramatic gesture and turned on his heel, stalking toward Luceen's house. He entered, pulling the door shut. "I'm just waiting to catch him in a better mood. Maybe tomorrow, when he wakes up."

"Eeeeeyyy, SonnnAYYYY!" Rufe's cyborg eye had spotted him.

"You know that guy? I heard he's some kind of famous clashball player."

Sonny headed toward them. When he was halfway there Hina raced over, fresh from her nap, and licked Risha's face, making her squeal.

"Hey island boy! I thought you were an outrider!" Blocker laughed and clasped his hand in hers as the doc threw him a sheepish little wave.

Sonny introduced Caleb, and when he reached Risha he winked. "I told him you were my fiancee."

"Well, it's true!" Risha stood up and kissed him on the nose. He hugged her tight, his brain happily awash in her pheromones. Her hair had lost its straightness in the humidity and was curling in all different directions, and lovely dark roots framed her sweet dimpled face. She looked more amazing than ever.

"I hope I'm not going to have to challenge you to a duel, Sonny," Rufe said, laughing, just before he laid a passionate kiss on Risha's mouth. All of the locals sucked in their breath sharply at this rude display of public affection.

Sonny thought of the time he'd been hit with a stunrod, or possibly the time he'd sailed over the tsunami. Caleb's steady arm caught him as Risha kissed back. Then she seemed to notice the disapproval and hastily broke away, cuddling her head against Rufe's chest in parting.

Nausea gripped Sonny's belly. He excused himself and headed for the toilets, where he dry heaved for several minutes. When he came out they weren't kissing, but they were sitting right next to each other. Fondling Hina's ears together. While Caleb offered a pitcher of something to Quicksilver and Blocker.

Sonny stood there clenching his fists, reminding himself that his arrangement with Risha was strictly business, and there were three more years, and anything could happen in three years. For instance, Rufe might die in his stupid war. Maybe his own stupid troops would shoot him in the back for being such a colossal asshole. He watched with slitted eyes as Rufe and Risha headed off to the complex of little temporary private huts that had been set up at the north end of the island specifically for displays of affection. Sonny had watched it from a distance, but he hadn't seen any public displays of affection at all, even though it was clear plenty was going on in private. Islanders didn't mind wandering around half-naked in public but they kept their intimate dealings behind closed doors.

A loud screech broke all the way through the soundproofing, followed by a barrage of argument, in the same voice. Something heavy crashed against a wall. Sonny heard a few interjections from Kai, but most of it was Luceen, sounding extremely angry. Sonny wandered back toward the party, where Caleb was having an animated discussion with Blocker about surfing, which left the doctor unoccupied, drinking from a mug of something and stroking Hina's back. Sonny had a brief urge to head to the pool and talk to people who weren't backstabbers on his plob instead, but instead he sat down, and accepted a cup of whatever was going around.

"You're difficult to kill," Quicksilver said. "Not that I'd want to."

"I washed up on an island of beautiful topless women. It's been one long party ever since." Sonny downed whatever was in the cup as Quicksilver rolled his eyes.

"You haven't been checking your messages."

"Yes I have. My messagebox says blah blah blah Dr. Quicksilver is eating lunch blah blah blah Dr. Quicksilver is trimming his toenails blah blah blah. Dr. Quicksilver has sent you three hundred videos to watch. I was busy working and supporting myself, and learning things." Someone had refilled his cup while he wasn't looking. He downed that too. "And I had other messages to answer. Like the one from my mom."

The birds in the trees were squawking to signal twilight, blocking out the sound of the ongoing domestic dispute in Luceen's house. Sonny took his sunglasses off and put them on the outside of his hat.

The world was starting to look a little fuzzy around the edges.

"How is she?" Quicksilver asked.

"She's good. She says lots of people are in contact, from Ambit and everywhere, making sure everyone's okay. She says they're voluntarily staying there in Dysz, and she thinks she was rescued from an earthquake. Kayliss is with them."

Quicksilver chuckled. "I think she's the chosen one who will bring common sense to them all. Let's take a walk. Show me the island of Acanella."

"You're acting like we're good friends." Sonny said, once they were clear of the banyan tree and reasonably far away from everyone else. "When actually you left me to get picked up by the clones without even warning me."

For once, Quicksilver didn't have a reply ready. He stared at the waves pounding the beach, and the clouds getting into their sunset colors. "I thought you wanted to be with your family."

"I want my family to be with me." They climbed to the summit of Acanella, a hill about a meter and a half tall. "There's the north coast, the east coast, the south coast. There's a sunset about to happen off the west coast."

"Smartass." Quicksilver pivoted slowly, taking in the entire island. "I thought it would be this huge fortress with gargoyles all over it, from what he described."

"The demon queen with blazing purple eyes lives in there." Just as he pointed to Luceen's house, the door crashed open and Kai stormed out, slamming the door behind him.

"I take it they have no children?"

A laugh burst out of Sonny's mouth, and after a moment Quicksilver laughed too. They sat down side by side, taking up most of the hilltop, and watched the sunset. "She has a phobia about leaving her house. I'm not sure if you can do anything about that."

"Brain chemistry is outside of my expertise, but I can tell you from personal experience that we're intoxicated at the moment."

"We are," Sonny agreed, noticing the sunset was especially colorful. Plus there was a general lack of worry seeping through him that just had to be artificial.

"Since you neglected to read my updates, I suppose I'll have to tell you the whole tale." Quicksilver sighed dramatically. "Of what we were doing while you were lounging on your island of bare breasted women. We nearly died in the sea after you fell overboard. The boat was floating on its side for a good while and everything got soaked, and I had to treat multiple fractures and sprains and lacerations from people falling onto the walls and the ceilings. Once we got out of the rough part that fellow who annoyed you was flogged, in the tradition of the British Navy, and everyone seemed to enjoy that."

"Good."

"Once we limped into Lurie we discovered we were under quarantine, and we weren't allowed off the ship for several days despite my emphatic protests. It seems that an anonymous informant reported the Lono had contagion aboard, so we all had to clear a health inspection, and at the same time they appeared to be looking for you in particular. Dee pulled some strings, and we got through the quarantine process without turning over a bit of data more than they were entitled to, thank the Carquinez privacy laws, and they finally let us off the ship, and we had some distinctly grumpy passengers aboard, I'll tell you. Now, you've never been to Lurie, but they've got the city proper, in a tower, like a small version of Deuce, and out in front of that is the harbor, and it's got shops and saloons and marketplaces and music everywhere, and right now it's full of all the people who got turned away from Deuce because it was too full, and there's all kinds of new construction going on. It's a madhouse."

He stood up and started pacing in the limited area of the hilltop. Sonny watched the rippling moonlight on the waves. He was definitely dizzy but it was not unpleasant. "Go ahead. I'm listening."

"We went directly to the Pacific Pearl, which is a big fancy hotel, along with the crew and a bunch of the passengers, and they're packed but they can squeeze us in if we pay an exorbitant amount. We all head to the hotel bar while they're preparing our rooms and we discover a good number of brave men and women headed to fight the good fight in Vanram, and they recognize their conquering hero, and we all wind up tipping back a few. Suddenly the police arrive."

"I didn't even know they even had police out here."

"They do in the city. Big fellows. You know, these locals can get quite massive, not quite in the same way as they do in Bonterra or Vanram, but they all had guns and stunrods and riot gear, and they were paying particular attention to us, even though we'd just arrived and hadn't gotten around to committing any crimes yet. Rufe was demanding to know the identity of the complainant, and they were demanding to know the purpose of Rufe's visit. And at that point a bunch of Qoros walk in. They're on good terms with the Carquinez government, if you can believe that. They're whispering with the police officers, and naturally Rufe sees them. At the top of his lungs, he suddenly shouts 'Those men are the reason the Carquinez Tigers no longer exist.'"

Sonny flashed to a memory. "Those messages you sent me about some kind of massacre. I should have read them."

"It was a free-for-all. The police, the locals, the Qoros, Rufe's people. I spent much of the fight hiding underneath a table with Dee and Risha, and then afterwards I had my work cut out for me. Later on I woke up in a suite, and learned we were all under house arrest until the authorities sorted out exactly what happened. The five of us spent an interminable amount of time locked up in our suite with nothing to do but watch video and argue, and at some point Rufe and Risha decided they were in love. Finally, they let us out. Three days ago. And here we are."

"And you're all going to try to sail back to the Caribbean with Kai."

"They're trying to suspend my license," Quicksilver said in a scratchy voice. "Once I made it to Asia I'd just get my medical modifications deactivated and sent back over here to face up to the disciplinary process. I'll make it out there eventually. For now, I haven't got any choice."

Just a few paces away, people were laughing and singing, sipping on drinks and nibbling slices of the huge pink guava-flavored birthday cake. Sonny and the doctor sat side by side, watching them.

"I want to go back to Royal Beach," he said. "If Kai won't take me I'll figure something out."

"We've been watching instructional videos on sailing, in the hotel room," Quicksilver said brightly, and Sonny snickered. "It's extremely dangerous. There's a good chance we'll all die."

"I've been living on Kai's boat for the past week. We were hunting megs, making sure the cannon works. I was running the nav station. Megs are sharks, but they're about as big as a train car."

"Yes, I saw a picture of one." The doctor clasped his arms around himself, even though it wasn't cold. "I apologize, by the way, for not telling you. At some point between March and the present you grew into a competent adult, and I was too preoccupied with my own concerns to notice. Back when I was young I thought the adults had everything figured out, but once I got older I realized we're all just making it up as we go."

"I apologize for getting you killed," Sonny said. "And for the thing in Bonterra."

"Friends?" Quicksilver extended a hand, and Sonny clasped it.

"Friends. Let's get some cake."

●

Sonny woke up on the floor of the misfits' house, with Hina curled around him. Caleb was missing but the other misfits were snoring away, both reeking heavily of alcohol. He stumbled outside to find pre-sunrise graylight, and he watched a glorious pink and orange sunrise as he showered.

Hina trotted over to investigate all the dropped food that hadn't been cleaned up yet and Sonny headed directly to the pier, staking it out. He was sure Kai would want to sail his new boat today, and he was equally sure he would be in a far better mood once that happened. Several of the guests were already departing, dragging luggage into their boats and collecting children and pets. Sonny stood by being helpful, tossing ropes and passing parcels as needed.

Just as he predicted, Kai came up the path before the sun was far past the horizon, his kinfolk close behind. Sonny removed his hat and sunglasses, feeling rich now that he finally had cargo to stow in his pockets. Kai walked right past him, but Kimo stopped and said good morning.

"I thought you guys might want a nav," he said softly.

Kai peered at him. He had a fresh set of four bloody scratches extending down a cheek, making his tattoos into a tic tac toe grid. He had left his peacock blue jacket behind and was dressed local style, trading one form of conspicuousness for another. "Sonny? How did you get here?"

"He's a good nav," Kimo vouched. "One of the best ones I've worked with."

Kai growled dismissively. "We'll talk later. Gary, go find us a real nav. There's got to be a few around here."

"This nav is for real," Gary said, nodding at Sonny.

After glaring at Sonny for several seconds, Kai jerked his head, and turned around and stalked toward his boat. Little Phil exaggeratedly mouthed some words behind Kai's back that made Gary and Kimo snicker as they followed. Sonny found his plob right where he'd left it, and he settled his butt on the familiar seat. He missed having familiar Hina beside him, but that could wait until Kai was in a better mood.

Kai was a far more aggressive pilot than his uncle, and they whooshed out into the sea, sail square to the wind. Sonny called up information on their location and the tides and the winds and the temperature, feeding it back in response to Kai's barked requests. They made swooping turns, riding on one hull with the other clear of the water, and Sonny was fairly sure they would capsize before Kai got used to the handling, but they didn't. For his final exam, they had him locate a slick of seaweed lying close to the surface, where they caught a good sized mahimahi for lunch.

They brought in the sail while Sonny capped his plob well, and he had chunks of mahi arranged on the tiny grill when the men came into the salon rubbing the windchill from their arms, and arguing about the lack of hydrofoils.

"It's not gonna make any difference," Kimo said. "This boat don't draw hardly nothing, as it is. Fish can spot a fly landing on the water, and they're gonna spot you, but you'll be too fast to catch, unless you dump it in the water 'cause you didn't balance your foils. Then you're a sitting target."

"You could always use repellant," Sonny said casually as he sprinkled oil and spices and lemon juice over the mahi.

"I've got a comparatively short infested stretch to cross," Kai said. "I've got the cannon. I'm more concerned about sailing past Manganela, but I've got a doctor to check exposure levels."

"It would probably be a lot faster if you had a nav," Sonny said. "And some repellant."

"It would go even faster if I didn't have to worry about federal charges for kidnapping a child added to my long list of legal difficulties," Kai said, with an air of finality that temporarily killed the conversation.

"How old is adulthood in Carquinez?" Sonny slid plates of perfectly grilled mahi steak in front of them.

"Sixteen," Gary said. "Good job on the mahi."

Sonny checked the longitudometer hanging on the wall. "July tenth. I'll be sixteen on August second. Less than a month."

Kai forked a bite of mahi into his mouth. He briefly closed his eyes in bliss. Then they popped open again. "I was boarded in Lurie by people looking for you. The subject came up again later, in the bar."

"Good thing I wasn't there."

"You weren't there because you were inexperienced and stupid. You got in a fight. You left your cargo unsecured, and then you jumped in after it. What's my guarantee you won't do something even stupider once our lives are all at risk?" He rose to his feet and raised his volume. Sonny trembled, wanting to yell back, or burst into tears, or slam a door.

"Take it easy —" Kimo lifted an interceding hand but Kai had found a focus for his anger. For a moment Sonny was afraid he would throw a punch.

And if he was going to get punched anyway, he might as well say something. "You wouldn't let me on the ship in Deuce. You let everybody else on but me, even though Rufe's starting some war, and Blocker and Quicksilver both work for Ambit."

"You are a child, and you've undergone considerable recent trauma," Kai returned. His fingers unclenched and his breathing slowed somewhat. "What are you going to do if I suddenly order you to climb up the mast and tie something down? Go hide in your bunk? Argue with me?"

"I'll climb up the mast."

"Climb up the mast. That's an order." Kai pointed upwards.

Sonny looked him in the eye and nodded. He climbed out of the salon and onto its roof. He had never actually climbed the mast before. He had seen Gary and Little Phil and Kimo doing it. He had dealt with the ropes at the bottom. He could see where the handholds were. He kicked off his flipflops and started up.

The first couple of meters were easy. Then he realized he was a tiny dot clinging to a stick in a vast ocean of blue. He was high in the air, and that was very dangerous, he knew it for a fact. You could fall and seriously injure yourself, maybe even die. If he died, his family would be sad. They'd have that crushing sensation in their chests, all of them, and they'd think random sad thoughts about him from time to time, and that would be bad. Dying was bad.

He hauled himself up another meter. He glanced down at the deck, impossibly far below. The men had come out to watch him. He gained another torturous handhold, feeling the mast flex as he clung to it. His hands gripped tight. He had a mental picture of himself freezing right there, forcing one of the other men to climb up and rescue him, and that drove him further, until he was at the very top, up above the point of the jib. He hugged the mast tight with one hand and both knees, and he waved.

"Now jump," Kai bellowed. Sonny looked down, hugging the mast until the vertigo passed. He saw four brown oval faces looking up at him, each about the size of his thumb print, one covered with stripes and holding his hands to his mouth. "That's an order. Jump. Over to starboard."

"No," Sonny said to himself. "I'm not going to be doing that."

He knew for a fact the bottom was far below, and the water was nice and clear, with no floating kelp or circling megs or any of the millions of other terrifying things lurking underwater. It was a warm day. The water would feel cold, and good. Maybe he'd live and maybe he'd die, but either way he would stop being afraid.

"I'm giving you an order, sailor," Kai yelled, his tone sounding vaguely threatening. "Don't make me come up there and throw you."

Sonny relaxed his grip, just a little, feeling the boat gently bobbing beneath him. He aimed for the deepest and bluest section of water, and he counted to three under his breath, and he kicked hard, launching himself into the blue sky, flying.

Landing, with a splash. Respect the water. Don't fight the water, she'll kick you to the ground and laugh in your face. Break through the surface. Not hurt. Alive. Swimming to the boat. Strong hands hauling him to the deck.

"Will that be all, captain?" He said with as much dignity as he could find. His heartbeat was slowing down. He had a crazy desire to climb back up the mast and do it again.

"It was for your own safety," Kai said gruffly. "Mine as well, but primarily yours. If I had a son your age ... well, I don't. And you can probably imagine why."

"She seems like a nice lady," Sonny said cautiously. "The two of you don't seem happy together."

They exchanged private glances and Little Phil snickered. Kai sighed and touched his fingertips to his lacerated cheek. "She would be happier if I stayed at home, and I disagree."

"He tried staying home for a while," Little Phil said to Sonny. "Drove him crazy. That's when he started getting tattoos."

"These tattoos are a proud expression of my heritage," Kai objected.

"Luceen used to leave the house." Gary said. "Before she got married, she did interisland rowing competitions. Can't get much more outside than that.

Anyway, our family comes from off thataway, where we grow the witchwood. Best kind of wood for boats."

"Only kind of wood for boats," Little Phil corrected. "Witchwood was engineered for resistance to this one particular parasite. Then it got out that the same company had bioengineered the parasite, to wipe out the competition, and that's why you don't see a lot of wooden ships these days, other than ours. Witchwood holds up no matter what the acidity level of the water is, and it's extremely buoyant."

"That's why they call it witchwood," said Gary. "Because it floats."

"They had a grand old wedding." Kimo smiled nostalgically. "Party lasted for days. Great music. They were happy for a couple weeks. Then they started to argue all the time. The more he wanted to get out of the house, the more she wanted to stay in it. So he starts collecting tattoos, until he runs out of skin. Finally, one day his family shows up with an old fashioned sailing ship, custom built. He needed it. He was starting to dry up and wither. Luceen didn't like it much, but if she's got something to say to us, she needs to leave the house. She won't do it."

"Home is important to some people." Kai climbed back into the pilot's seat. "Run my nav, follow my orders, try not to get me in more trouble than I'm already in, and I'll take you home. We'll sail at dawn."

●

The catamaran chugged toward the pier with its weak little engine until they were close enough for Gary to lasso the cleat and tie off. Sonny capped his plob well and peeled goo from his fingers. Then he tidied up the galley so it wouldn't reek of old fish and when he got done with that he had an enthusiastic reunion with Hina on the beach.

After that, he wrestled his crates of OhMyTummy and Misty Sea's Peppermint Taffy onto the catamaran, along with an extra barrel of cooking oil. He grabbed plenty of regular provisions too, rice and flour and sugar and salt, coffee and tea, spices and fresh-sealed packages of fruit and vegetables, a big sack of dog food. He filled the tanks for drinking water and shower water, and cleaned out both of the heads. He packed a couple of spare plobs in a bucket with a lid. He straightened the bedding on all the bunks, and straightened the curtains in the extra large captain's cabin in the right hull, which Kimo had been occupying. The left hull had six single beds attached to the wall, with curtains to divide them into sets of two, and Sonny left his hat and sunglasses to mark the ones he was claiming for himself and Hina.

It was late afternoon when he finished. He spotted Rufe playing soccer on the beach and shook his head in response to his invitation to join in. His reconstructed knee felt exactly like a normal knee most of the time, and now that he was employed as an able-bodied sailor, he wanted to keep it that way.

He headed for the banyan tree, noticing that the band had been augmented by the addition of a harpsichord, the one from the *Lono*, and Risha was playing it. A small crowd of men were sitting near her, enjoying her performance. Sonny was shocked to realize that Blocker and Caleb were sitting among them, and that Blocker's head was resting on Caleb's shoulder while his arm encircled her waist.

He made a sharp turn toward the plob pool, not exactly sure why he was shocked. Risha's harpsichord trills interfered with his concentration as he pulled up a connection.

It was hard to access his ghost account from a moving location, since there was a little bit of lag involved as data pingponged through various territories. He had tried it a few times while working the nav, unsuccessfully. Local data concerning the ocean floor and what was happening there came through fast and clear, but anything originating outside Carquinez was flickery at best. Tonight was his last chance to check his messages in video mode before he sailed. Last chance to say goodbye to his family.

And yet at the same time, he didn't want to say anything in public that might lead whoever commanded the submarines to believe something worth shooting would be sailing through their territory. He was pretty sure they'd be watching.

He scrolled through his backlog of messages, watching Quicksilver's videos of the riot in Lurie, and the new Bippy Borp video, and responding to an invitation to a party at Royal Beach Boardwalk on July 27th with "hope to be there."

As he reached the top he saw a message that was marked "extremely urgent." It was seven hours old, and it came from the government of Dysz, and was emblazoned with fluttering red and black flags. Sonny scrolled past it, irritated, until he got to the top. There was another message, this one only two hours old. It was from his dad.

It took several minutes for the connection to come up. During that time, Rufe scored a goal, and Risha played two songs, and Quicksilver fell off the surfboard he was trying to learn to ride, twice. Hina dug a hole in the sand.

The images gradually solidified. All of them, clustered around a table. They all had half-eaten plates of something that looked fancy, with garnishes and artistic dribbles of sauce. They were dressed in clothes with sleeves and collars and jackets, far away from the bright colors and exposed limbs of Royal Beach, and at first they seemed very sad. Then they saw his waterlogged, scruffily-bearded face through their own camera, and they all burst into smiles.

"Weewo!" Marilyn sang out, looking dignified in a burgundy velvet dress, her hair braided with ribbons.

"Hi Larramen." Their baby names for each other. "Hi everyone else. What's for dinner?"

"I'm not sure what it's called." Dad wrinkled his nose. "It tastes good, though. They bring us catering three times a day, but never mind about that, how are you doing? Did you injure your knee?"

"It's mostly healed, and I'm good," Sonny said. "Just hanging out on the beach. Can you hear the music?"

"Is that a harpsichord?" Dan looked much older in his serious clothes. He was growing himself a set of serious cheekbones to go with them, and his hair was combed back, showing his widow's peak.

"It is indeed a harpsichord," Sonny said. "They're very popular in the islands. Do you still play music?"

"I run a recording studio." Dan shot him a snobby look before his face relaxed into a grin. "I'm the only musician that records in it, but eventually there will be more, and until then, I've got the monopoly. And Lenny's got an art gallery."

"Yeah, we're the cultural scene in these parts." Formal clothes didn't suit Lenny at all. He looked like a vaguely uncomfortable gangster, with his curly hair plotting escape from a tight ponytail.

"The movies will happen eventually." Mom's smile twinkled. "There are so many opportunities here."

"Is he still there?" Sonny heard a door slam off camera. Kayliss appeared, dressed in something utilitarian and black that suited her. Marilyn scooted her chair aside to make room.

"Hi Kayliss. Monitoring their incoming calls?" Sonny asked in what he hoped would be interpreted as a friendly, teasing tone.

"We were talking to Kayliss when you called," Mom chimed in. "She heard it was you and her portal went blank."

"I drove fast," she explained.

Lying to Kayliss was not going to hurt nearly as much as lying to the people who actually loved him and weren't just infatuated. He was going to have to ease into it. "I miss you."

He watched her cheeks color and realized he hated himself just a little bit. "I miss you too. I wish you would come here, and live with us."

"I'm actually thinking of heading to Japan," he said. "I was going to go fishing for a few days with some guys I met on the island and discuss it. I figure once I get to Japan I can take the train to Europe, and then I can get back to Royal Beach across the Atlantic."

"We're going to clear a path," Kayliss said sharply. "So ships can get through without having to get too close to the volcano. It's part of being good citizens with Ambit and all that stuff. You'll be able to get through soon. Or we could send you a submarine."

Sonny kept iron control of his facial muscles, forcing them into a pondering expression. "That might work. Let me see what happens with this fishing trip. They're telling me I can get from Japan to Royal Beach in a month. Although I was talking to someone else about Australia."

Kayliss didn't like this answer, and she tapped her palm with her hand, and Sonny's perspective whirled with dizzying speed. He lifted his eyes and focused on the ocean, where Quicksilver was riding a wave, crouched on a longboard in front of a lanky tattooed surfer. When he relaxed back into the plob overlay, he found himself facing a severe office, full of dark furniture and red and black flags. Behind a tall black desk sat a clone.

Sonny recognized him. He had seen him before, among many photos of clones. The handsome one, with the styled hair. His dark suit jacket was flatteringly tailored. His long hands, neatly folded on the desk before him, had recently been manicured. He had an office window overlooking a brief slice of desolate black land bordered by foreboding black mountains, backed by white overcast sky lit by the same pre-sunset glare Sonny was facing, the position suggesting the two views weren't that far apart. On the clone's desk was a plate reading INS, which Sonny gathered was his name. His mind automatically added vowels, translating it into "Iannis."

"Mister Leroy Knight," he said in modulated tones as carefully cultivated as his appearance. "I am very pleased to finally make your acquaintance. I am the vice president of Dysz. I trust you have found your loved ones to be happy and healthy."

"Hi. Yeah, they seem all right."

"You are welcome to reunite with them at any time."

"Actually I was thinking of heading out to Australia, or possibly up to Japan. Haven't quite decided."

"I'm showing your current location as somewhere out in the South Pacific." Iannis grimaced, fiddling with his palm, and Sonny was sure there were dozens of portals lined up on the wall besides his, out of view. "You're using that protoplasm network, and it's sloppy with regard to location."

"I don't even know if this island has a name. We're having a big party. That's what people do in Carq, sail from one party to the next. I'm getting pretty good at sailing."

"Bottom line." Iannis aimed his pointy nose in Sonny's direction. "I want you here. In Dysz. Tell me the most expedient way to make that happen."

It's just Kayliss, Sonny told himself, in a suit, a few years older. He's trying to look scary but he's just an antisocial derp like the rest, plus he's vain. "You're probably the most reasonable Qoro I've ever met," Sonny said. "Most of them just aim weapons at me and try to kill me. My family seems to have a very different experience, but frankly I'm scared of you guys. I want to ask you the most expedient way to get you to let my family leave, just for a visit, but I don't want to see them get tortured or executed because I asked you that."

Iannis drew his lips together until he looked reptilian. "We haven't tortured anyone. Or executed anyone. Did your family complain they were tortured? No, they did not, because it didn't happen."

"Possibly I'm insane," Sonny offered. "I've been through a lot. You seem like a very compassionate and intelligent guy, and maybe I'm just seeing you through my own prejudices. Would you let them out for money? Or what if I found more people who would willingly take their place?"

"Nobody's leaving," Iannis snapped, and Sonny's heart fluttered as he worried if might have pushed too far. "It might be different after this fall, once the new minimum population guidelines are established and the shipping lanes reopen."

"That's why you want them," Sonny said. "Why do you want me? Do you think I killed Premier Lance?"

"No." Iannis smiled and shook his head. "I think you're a teenager who is neither particularly bright nor sophisticated. I will grant you stubborn. I will also concede that you're quite effective at generating donations for Rufus Marshall's campaign of illicit terrorism."

Sonny couldn't help but roll his eyes in disgust. Iannis laughed. "I had nothing to do with that. I told him to stop. He didn't have my permission."

"There are Qoros in Japan, as well as many other places. Did you factor that into your plans?"

"They don't want to live in Chelisary either, so I'm sure we'll have a lot in common. What if I make some kind of public statement. Hey everyone, this is Sonny, don't fight in Rufe's war, okay, and don't send him money. You can broadcast that if you want."

"He'll just claim that you only said it because I'm holding your family at gunpoint." Iannis sighed, and Sonny worked hard on controlling his expression. "That's not literal, Leroy."

"Sonny."

"Mister Knight. We were discussing your parents' desire for your safe return."

"And you were saying you wouldn't let them leave Chelisary until the fall."

"I said ..." Iannis gritted his teeth, looking exactly like an angry Kayliss. "That potentially people will be able to travel to and from Chelisary in the fall, once the shipping routes are clear."

"And after the Ambit election regarding whether you're going to be thrown out for not having enough people. I want you to promise that you will let my parents, my sister, and my friends Lenny and Dan visit me, wherever I happen to be at the time, after the fall election, and that you won't harm any of them."

"We do not harm our citizens." He was struggling hard with his rage, and watching him made Sonny just a little bit calmer.

"And in return I will speak out against the war, and tell everyone not to send money to Rufe. I don't mind doing that. I don't want there to be a war. I think people all over the world should follow your wise example in choosing negotiations over war. I wish Rufe would calm down, and if he could do me a huge favor and not kick any ass until these guys do their politics thing, I would be incredibly happy."

"Wise." Iannis was breathing deeply as he froze into his most statesmanlike pose. "Yes."

"But I don't really have any control over what Rufe does. And I still don't have your promise. Maybe we should make it a wager. If I can make my way home without any of your people catching me, then you'll stop harassing me."

"We are facing a civil war in Vanram and I have no time to play games with a minor child whose parents want him back home. Now."

Minor child. Sonny held onto his words as Iannis' face registered joy over discovering a button to push. He took a deep breath and watched Quicksilver and his buddy glide into a tubular wave and spin. Iannis was speaking frankly, and that seemed to indicate he thought the conversation was private.

"I just want to graduate from high school," Sonny said in his best plaintive voice, thinking of Mizz Lorch, his acting teacher at school. He looked directly into the camera like it was his best friend, even though it was a blob of protoplasm floating just below the surface, just like she'd taught him. "I want to ride my skateboard down the street, looking at the trees and the flowers. I want to grow up around the friends I've known since I was small. I want to take a date to Royal Beach Boardwalk, and I want to have my first kiss under the Raging Dragon."

He studied Iannis' impatient reaction, reflecting he was a clone who probably knew nothing whatsoever about dates, kisses, roller coasters, skateboards and high school. On the bright side, he also knew nothing about acting, or audiences.

"Under the Raging Dragon," Iannis said in a snide voice that indicated perhaps he did know a thing or two about dates, and kissing.

"It's a roller coaster. At night, when the lights are lit up and the fireworks are going off, it's my favorite place in the world to be." He aimed for dreamy and wistful, and then he remembered he had yet another Qoro to charm. "I have a special girl in mind, so this will probably have to happen in the fall. Maybe she could come for a visit, along with my family and my friends. She's very brave, and beautiful, and she has very intense eyes."

Iannis was staring at him with a copy of those eyes. "Would you choose her over Royal Beach?"

"That's a tough call." Sonny smiled, hoping it was a handsome smile. "I'm indecisive. I'm not a natural leader, like you. Given the choice, I'd rather eat pizza at the Boardwalk with a beautiful woman than make difficult decisions."

A reluctant laugh worked its way out of Iannis and Sonny refrained from pumping his fist, since that would have broken the connection. His elbows were stiff and he needed to stretch but he held onto his smile. Iannis leaned forward, amused enough to display crows feet and forehead wrinkles. "Why are you going to Japan?"

"Half of my favorite band comes from Japan. I've always wanted to see Bippy Borp live. Plus I learned to make sashimi from this guy who came from Osakabyoto, and he said they have great food in Japan. And I know how to say konnichi wa, which means 'how's it going.' I'll take a shorter route if I can find one, but I'd love to do some sightseeing."

"Very well. From one adventurous fellow to another." He smiled. Sonny expected it to come out all crocodilian and evil, but to his astonishment Iannis had a smile that would have won him any leading role he wanted. It took over his face, balancing out the pointy nose and the small chin. He even had a dimple that showed up, and he managed to get his eyes to twinkle. "We have a bet. You will attempt to get to Royal Beach, and and my people will attempt to intercept you in a location where international law applies, which would include Japan. If you make it past them, I'll accept your deal, provided I don't find myself fighting a war."

Sonny lacked a powerful politician's smile so he produced a sweet one. The sun was setting in glorious splendor both before him and in Iannis' window and he moved sideways to include it in the shot. "I'm glad we had this talk, Mister Vice President. Thank you for keeping my family safe. I'm going to head off on my fishing trip, and I'll post an update as soon as I reach a continent! Sayonara!"

He flashed the smile again and pulled his hands away from the plob, losing the connection. He had a minor pang of headache as his eyes readjusted to the real world just in time to catch the green flash as the sun sank below the horizon. A cheer arose from the surfers gathered on the beach, and Sonny caught a glimpse of Quicksilver and his surfing instructor locked in an intense kiss.

He fumbled around underwater for the plob and reconnected. There, at the very top, was a fresh blinking message from the protective government of Carquinez, notifying him that his conversation with a grownup had been posted and was now available for viewing.

He copied it a few times, and pasted it on his wall, and then he reposted it to all his friends, and their friends, and the Bippy Borp International Fan Society. He posted it five more times, just to make sure. By the time he got to the fifth he noticed his message box was full again, plus he had sixty-five new friend requests, and he smiled as he accepted them all.

He replaced his plobs in their net bags and showered away the saltiness. He made his way to the kitchen, where the elders fed him until his belly bulged. He had the misfits' house all to himself, and he sat there feeling like a lonely unlovable liar for several minutes. Until Hina came over and nudged him with her nose. He wrapped his arms around her warm and loyal body and fell fast asleep.

●

He woke up just before dawn. The musicians were finally silent, and Acanella was quiet and still. A light was burning in Luceen's house, behind the curtains. The kitchen smelled temptingly of fresh bread, and Sonny headed there, even though he was still full from last night.

He was surprised to find Risha assembling a picnic basket. She offered him a freshly baked cookie and a mug of spicy cocoa, which he graciously accepted. "Is Rufe still asleep?"

"I have no idea. We broke up."

Sonny nearly spilled cocoa on his hand. "You did?"

"We ran up against the boundary of fling, and I decided to get up early and do some baking. Is it time to go yet?"

"Are you two going to be arguing on the boat?"

"Oh, sweetie, you know I don't argue." She sat down beside him and hugged him, and he actually did spill cocoa on his hand, but it had cooled to the point where it wasn't painful. "I'm glad you worked things out with Kai."

"Eyyy, Sonny." Rufe greeted him, pointedly ignoring Risha, before proceeding to the coffee.

"Rufe, I need to talk to you." He glanced at Risha, making sure it was okay to abandon her company. She shrugged and stood up, returning to her picnic basket and Sonny followed Rufe outside, where he was sitting on a loop of banyan, tapping his foot anxiously and drinking coffee as the sun rose.

"You actually got to her first." Rufe took a long slug of his coffee, squinting.

"It's just business. She never touched me."

Rufe laughed a harsh and cynical laugh, with an undertone of heartbreak. "I don't like waiting around."

"Then this is probably the worst day in the world to ask you for a personal favor."

"I've had a few worse days, and this one is barely even started. And you're going to ask me to stand down, and let Dysz walk all over me and occupy my country, while I go off and join some other clashball team, or maybe dedicate my life to peace. And I'll probably say no."

"Go for it. Kick their ass. But give it a few months. I talked to one of their head guys, and we made a deal. He said there's going to be a democratic election in the fall, and he'll let my family visit me in Royal Beach then. After that happens, I don't care what you do."

"In the fall." Rufe scowled. "Who have you been talking to?"

"I got it on video and I broadcast it. You'll see it when you get back. I kinda forced him into a corner, and he thinks I'm headed to Japan. But anyway, if there's a democratic election, you can just get elected without having to kill anyone. Unless they all vote for someone else."

"They wouldn't vote for anyone else," Rufe said, insulted.

"Ambit's watching them." Sonny closed his eyes. "Please work with me, Rufe. I'll make you the best propaganda film in the world, as soon as my family is safe."

"Says the guy who got me locked up for murder because he couldn't resist making a phone call. Also the guy who stole my girlfriend before she was even my girlfriend."

"We could fight, but you'd win."

"You told him you were going to Japan?"

"I could go to Japan if I wanted. Or Australia, or China, or the United States of Korea. I don't speak the languages but I know how to wait tables, and cook fish, and sail a boat, and call up a translator. I can run a nav station, which means the boat might as well have a camera underneath it showing everything that's down there, and I know how to make meg repellant."

"You've got some skills." Rufe drained his coffee cup and shaded his eyes against the bright glittering waves.

"I'm sorry about getting you locked up. That was mostly Kayliss, but I helped. And I'm sorry about Risha."

"You had to bring it up. Asshole." Rufe stood up. "Sonny Knight, I accept your deal. I will expect you to stand good on your word, otherwise I shall call you out in a duel to the death."

He swung his big palm into a handshake, bending Sonny's hand into several intricate handshake variations before concluding it with a light shoulder punch.

Skills. Sonny thought about them as he headed to the boat. Skills were better than talents. Once you had them, you couldn't lose them, and you could always learn more. Talents bossed you around, and sent you on dangerous quests, while skills could help you get where you needed to go.

Kai was naming his boat, painting the last "S" in *Reckless* carefully in red. Sonny didn't dare board until he was finished. "Permission to come aboard, sir?"

"Get your ass to work," Kai said, sealing the lid on his paint can.

"Aye aye." Sonny set about stringing fluorescent orange rope from his bunk to the salon, taping it along the ceiling. He connected the end to Hina's harness with a knot that he could quickly release, giving her enough lead to wander around the salon or visit the bathroom. He fastened a neck float around her neck, and he fastened another one around his own neck.

He passed another to Rufe as he arrived, and to Risha, helping them stow their minimal luggage and reassigning their bunks so they were at opposite ends of the hull.

Blocker arrived in Caleb's arms. He gently placed her in a seat at the salon table and kissed her goodbye. Then he said goodbye to Sonny, promising to send his friendship to Sonny's social node once he got near a screen, so they could keep track of each other. He seemed sad, but he was several levels less sad than he'd been when Sonny had first met him.

Gary and Little Phil, along with a few other guys, packed into a sizable sailboat called the *Tipsytoes* while Kimo headed over to the *Reckless* to help with the sail.

"Hey, Sonny. I'm gonna give a few sailing lessons over here while those guys follow us."

"They've all been watching videos," Sonny said. "About how to sail."

Kimo's eyes twinkled. "Watching ain't doing."

Sonny gloved up and uncapped his well as the *Reckless* chugged away from the pier, followed by the *Tipsytoes*. After he gave Kai his initial readings there wasn't much work to do, so he sat back enjoying the ride. He also enjoyed listening to Kai and Kimo verbally abuse their nervous students. They pitched Rufe over the side when he argued, forcing him to take out his aggression treading water while they leisurely circled back. Then they tossed Risha and the doctor in for good measure, making sure they all knew how to rescue each other.

Blocker was exempt from the physical abuse, but she caught her share of yelling as she sat beside Kai in the pilot's seat, learning to steer. By the end of the day they were all nervous wrecks. Except for Sonny, who serenely guided them to a tiny island where the *Tipsytoes* was waiting with a freshly slain mahi and a smoking grill. Risha added the perishables from her picnic basket and Kai contributed a round of beer, a bottle of hashish liqueur and some ominous brooding music from his fine sound system. The trainees fell into their bunks, exhausted.

They parted company with the *Tipsytoes* the next morning, Kimo throwing in a few last jabs at Rufe over his inept jib-handling as well as the '47 clashball playoffs before they exchanged a complicated manly handshake and said goodbye.

They spent the day sailing through the calm blue waters of Carquinez. The trainees applied themselves with grim intensity, and Kai let up on berating them, although he didn't hesitate to sing out whenever anybody did anything even slightly wrong. In the late afternoon Sonny led them to anchorage on a rocky shoal where there had once been a big city, according to Kai. Hundreds of years ago, when all of this was land.

He pointed it out on a flat map for them after dinner. "We head over here, where we wait for a trough. There's no point taking bigger waves unless we need to. Once we are proceeding eastwards we will have some infestation with which to contend. Kimo informs me Sonny knows how to chase them away, and in the event he doesn't, we have a cannon."

Rufe was very interested in the cannon. He spent a long time looking at its targeting screen and admiring the slender, tapering shells. Sonny pointed out his meg repellent ingredients. Quicksilver volunteered for the task of mixing them and pouring them over the side. "Seems far too dilute but if you're right about their hypersensitivity it should only take a whiff," Quicksilver said.

"I've seen it work." Exasperation found its way into Sonny's tone.

"If we've got a good wind behind us, we'll skate through so fast that it won't be an issue," Kai said.

"What if we have to tack?" Blocker's concern was well placed. They had been tacking against the wind during part of the afternoon, and the captain hadn't been particularly pleased with their progress.

"I'm most worried about the stretch past Manganela," said Quicksilver.

"I brought the suits," Kai said.

"I'm dying of something I caught in Manganela," Blocker abruptly said. "It's been working on me gradually for years but now it's speeding up, and I've got bone growth in my hip and my pelvis that's out of control. Its working on my spine. My legs are both needles and pins from the knees down and pretty soon I won't feel them at all, and at some point after I become completely paralyzed I'll die. I'm on this crazy expedition with you all instead of sailing on a nice comfortable ship to Japan because I want to die a peaceful, orderly death at home. That's how my family does things. They'll appreciate it, since my life has been anything but peaceful and orderly. I don't want any of you to go through anything like this. Especially someone as young as you."

She looked at Sonny and burst into tears. Risha moved swiftly to provide comfort but Rufe beat her to Blocker's side, wrapping her in a bear hug as he turned to face them. "Other than our world renowned cuisine, that's why she stayed in Vanram. We fail at plenty of things, but our medics know how to treat weird combat residuals. That's why smart guys like the doc are always coming to visit us."

"You bought me a few extra months," she said, hugging him back. "Cello would have had me swinging from a rope with all the rest." Then she turned to Sonny. "I told the captain to leave you behind. Thought you were more of a liability than an asset."

"And I thought Ambit was supposed to look out for me instead of handing me over to the enemy."

"Watch it," Rufe said, cradling Blocker protectively.

"Sonny may have became a competent adult very recently," Kai said. "But he is a member of this crew who outranks you in seniority, and you will grant him your respect."

"Don't make me flog you," Rufe said, knuckling the top of her head before releasing her.

Blocker snapped him a smart salute. "If you want to risk dying a gruesome death before you've ever had the chance to do the horizontal shimmy with a naked person who likes you, I will respect your decision, while reserving the right to denounce it as foolhardy and imprudent."

"It probably is," Sonny agreed.

●

The next day they headed into rougher waters, for the advanced class. They sailed up and down parallel to the rough surf for most of the day, waiting for the promised trough and practicing tacking. They took a few scary turns where it felt like they'd tip but they never actually did. Everyone strapped themselves into harnesses and tethered them near the areas where they'd be working as Kai took them into increasingly bigger waves, zigzagging east. They didn't anchor for the night, relying on Rufe's and Quicksilver's enhanced vision as well as Sonny's readings.

Risha spent most of her time near the top of the mast, occasionally flying down on her harness for moisturizing lotion and food. Blocker steered when Kai slept, and simmered pots of beans and rice and noodles in the galley. All Sonny did was stare at the view beneath the waves, and the incoming data. He got to take occasional naps, which were likely to be interrupted at any time. Quicksilver dealt swiftly and efficiently with his headaches, and they all took turns massaging the cramps out of his shoulders.

Rufe spotted the trough far in advance. He climbed up the mast to confirm it. Kai sliced over at an angle and headed in, diagonally across the waves, until they were headed due east.

They entered a dense cloud of humid, steamy fog that made them sweaty and thirsty and sailed through it most of the night, orienting by the Southern Cross and the waxing moon. Toward morning the air cleared to reveal the volcano, spewing a bright flow of lava, with a few companion lava spouts bursting from the water beside it. The air smelled overwhelmingly of sulphur.

"I wish I hadn't deactivated my visual recorder," Quicksilver said as he took a break from chopping up taffy and bellyache tablets and stuffing them into balloons. "Traded it for language modules."

"I'll make a picture of it," Risha said quietly. "After we survive this."

The waves grew gentler on the eastern side of the volcano but the wind was against them, and they tacked in jagged lines. Sonny filled his visual field with plob transmission, looking for megs. The area closest to the volcano had been noticeably lacking in fish, and now they were appearing in large schools.

He checked the chat hives to see if there was anybody within talking range, and found a few scattered Carqs in undetermined locations. One named Bobo was typing rude limericks while waiting for fish to bite his lines, and one named GeeDaddy was listing boats for sale, and one named B3ar was talking in North Central General Chat. Selena's hangout.

Sonny sent B3ar a ping and asked if he could piggyback into the conversation. A moment later he was logged in as SunnyNight, saying hello to Selena and a few other handles he recognized. As he was bantering a shape loomed up to the right. His breath caught before he realized it was over a hundred meters away. He changed his resolution and verified it was one contiguous creature rather than a group of smaller ones.

"Four o'clock off starboard," he yelled at Quicksilver.

Quicksilver had been dozing and he startled. "Four o'clock?"

"Yes." It was moving toward them. "Affirmative."

The doctor added oil to a balloon, sighted and lobbed it precisely as Sonny watched the shape advance. He called for two more and Quicksilver threw them. The creature paused, then wheeled slowly around, retreating back into the depths. "It worked!" he yelled.

"I didn't see anything." Quicksilver peered over the side.

"Where exactly are you?" Sonny's text box flashed with a message from B3ar.

"Sorry, that's secret," he replied, with an animated winking face.

"I saw your video," B3ar replied. "It's pretty popular. Good on you. I hate Qoros."

"I'd say I hate them but maybe you're one of them spying on me. Can't be too careful."

"More like me spying on them. You can do video, yeah?"

"I'm running nav," Sonny typed, peering at what he thought might be a faraway meg.

"Do you see anything?" Quicksilver slouched back in his chair. They were all groggy from insufficient sleep. The doctor had offered a shot of stimulant to anyone who couldn't stay awake but so far nobody had volunteered.

"I'll let you know," Sonny said as he watched a small inset video appear in his nav display, translucent enough to reveal moving objects behind it. A little cartoon bear appeared, dancing.

"I have no camera," Sonny typed. "But I see a bear."

"See this?" The bear made a goofy little farting animation. A bubble reading "access granted" floated out of its butt, drifting to the side to form a new inset video. This one was split horizontally into "com" and "loc". The bear turned a cartwheel. "Loc shows you if any submarines get within range. Com is for talking."

"Thank you."

"Plenty of bored people in Carq passing your video around and placing bets. Should I bet on you?"

"Bet all you've got," Sonny said. The bear laughed, then made a deep bow, its inset video vanishing from his display. Just in time to notice a suspicious large shape. "Three o'clock starboard," he yelled. Quicksilver woke up and pitched.

This time the meg at least granted them a brief view of its fin as it wheeled around, eliciting gasps from everyone but Kai.

"It worked," Quicksilver reported. "I saw it work! I did it!"

"Now you've seen one," Kai said. "Pray you never see another."

They repelled four more megs. None of them came near the surface. Risha climbed into the salon to make a pot of strong tea. Sonny gazed into his well, occasionally noticing his own vacant expression beyond the graphic display covering his retinas. There was a city down here, ancient and covered with sediment but still recognizable as streets and buildings. There were strange sudden concentrations of fish. Sonny gathered that they were food for the megs, and that Dysz plugged them into the ecosystem specifically for that purpose. They must be close to Chelisary.

He kept an eye on his loc screen and shortly after they repelled the fifth meg, it lit up. Sonny watched the sub approach, a little to the port side. Heading straight for them.

His view of the ocean, meanwhile, shifted. He couldn't quite describe it, aside from something irregular down at the bottom that might have been plants or coral. The *Reckless* tacked away, heading away from the submarine. Sonny peered at his readout, struggling to see. There, a big shape straight ahead, surfacing toward them from the depths.

Kai made a remark about the overwhelming scent of peppermint. Sonny caught it too. It grew very strong for a moment, as though they were passing through a curtain of mouthwash. The moment they passed through it a red glowing ball suddenly materialized in the salon and a pre-recorded sounding voice blared out of it. "Attention! Attention! You have crossed an international border. Please cease forward motion and stand by for inspection."

"My ass," Rufe roared.

Sonny caught sight of the submarine, farther to port. It was comparatively small next to the large, surfacing shape.

"Sonny!" Kai bellowed. "Tell me what you're seeing."

He moved over to the com window. "*Hi fartsuckers.*"

Text blazed back at him. "*Shitmonkey.*" Followed by "*Who is this?*"

The gigantic shape loomed closer and Sonny's stomach clenched. He could see the outline and it was a pliosaur. A great big pliosaur, with no dorsal fin, and a gaping mouth. The submarine was controlling it somehow. They were much too close for coincidence.

"What do you see?" Kai barked.

Sonny shut his eyes, blocking out the display. "Can I be the captain for thirty seconds? It's easier than explaining. We need to go hard to starboard, right after Rufe shoots. You work the sails. Blocker steers."

"Rufe!" Kai yelled, climbing out of the pilot's seat. Blocker wrapped her hands around the wheel, sitting up straight.

"What are we doing?" Quicksilver dropped into the salon, followed by Risha.

"Risha, climb up the mast and when you see the water changing color, like something's surfacing, signal Rufe. Straight ahead, not the one to port. Something big."

"Don't shoot your balls off," she said over her shoulder as she headed for the mast.

Rufe loaded the cannon. Sonny opened his eyes. "Thirteen degrees off the bow, Rufe, and angled down."

"*You're not cleared, snotburglar. I'll tell ya later when I see ya,*" he typed into the com box. He had no idea if it was Kayliss, but it sounded like something he'd say to Kayliss.

"Is something out there?" Quicksilver looked through the window anxiously.

The text in his window lit up, bright and angry. *"If this is a drill, assface, I'm not getting in trouble because of some pissknocker who won't even ID."*

The pliosaur was close enough for Sonny to make out its front fins against its body, thick and stubby.

"Give com ID. Now."

Sonny stared at the flashing letters. The red ball lit up and repeated its announcement. The tip of the submarine popped above the surface. Risha let out an ear-piercing yell. The cannon went off, the shot slicing down into the water.

The submarine's cannons slid out of the iridescent bladder like snail antennae, taking aim. One went off. Sonny heard the shot whiz through the air, over their heads. The boat canted sharp to starboard, just as he'd ordered, leaning precariously on one hull.

The pliosaur burst out of the water, trembling and seizing. Much of Sonny's view was obstructed but he saw its dinnerplate-sized eyes roll crazily at them as it flew past. Sunlight glittered from its damp pebbly flesh, deep bluish gray in color.

The doctor launched himself at the portside doorway, clinging to it. He reached down and grabbed the line attached to Hina, dragging her toward him, desperately trying to shift the boat's weight. Water spilled out of Sonny's well and his plob went with it, sizzling as the air hit it.

His shoulder banged into the wall and he closed his eyes. It was over. They were going to spill, and then the submarine would have them, assuming it hadn't been directly beneath the pliosaur. He had failed everyone. Maybe he'd drown.

The catamaran wobbled and righted, slithering gracefully into an eastward orientation. Sonny glanced behind him and saw nothing but calm blue ocean. His ears were ringing, and he could barely hear his shipmates gabbling to each other in excited tones.

He scrabbled for his bucket of spare plobs and pried it open. He was horrified to discover that they had dissolved into a layer of foam. wasn't exactly sure why and he felt vaguely sad as he tipped the bucket over the side. There could be fifty more submarines down there, and now he had no way to spot them. Each one of those fifty might be towing an enslaved pliosaur around. Iannis himself was probably leading them, his cannons loaded with weird biological weapons that would melt their skin off or turn them into sentient frogs.

Sonny collapsed into his seat, feeling useless. He supposed he should just go to sleep but he couldn't seem to summon the energy to crawl into his bunk. He watched Quicksilver haul out a carton of folded white jumpsuits and distribute them. Putting one on took all his strength, and then he was boiling hot, watching listlessly as the doctor showed everyone how to work their ventilator mask.

Clouds appeared to the south, and eventually the land came into view. High reddish cliffs, bright against the blueness of sea and sky. There was something perched atop the cliffs, like the hive of some malevolent insect. "Behold Manganela," Rufe said in a sonorous voice from above.

Sonny recalled the pictures he had seen, before its destruction. A shining city with fanciful spires and gleaming domes, built of smart coral that could repair its own leaks while trapping sun and wind and rain. Much smaller than Deuce, only big enough for about a million people, but still sizable enough to house them and all of their life support. Their vats for growing food, their air purifiers, their energy collectors and condensors and sewage treatment system. It had collapsed inward and melted into a misshapen mausoleum. The ground around it was scorched black.

They headed further out to sea to avoid a concentration of something only Quicksilver could see, and Sonny dozed in his chair. Nightmares chased him out of sleep whenever he fell too deep. The one where a submarine shot a hole through their hull was popular, as was the one where he awoke in time to see the backside of some leviathan's teeth.

"Right back where we started," Kai said in a gravely voice. The stars were out, twinkling over the relatively calm ocean. They were tacking against the wind but the sailing was far easier than the beginning of their trip, which was a good thing, because everyone was exhausted.

"We can probably dispense with these," Quicksilver said, peeling his mask away. They all followed suit. Sonny felt faint from the sudden drop in temperature.

"How far is Argalia?" Rufe shambled into the salon and grabbed a waterpod from the coldbox.

"Not very." Kai rubbed his forehead. "I'm not going near it. Don't ask."

"There could be submarines underneath us," Sonny blurted. "I can't see them anymore."

"We should be in range." Quicksilver slapped the wallscreen. It flashed to life, opening up a blank portal at his fingertips.

"Braganza surf conditions," Kai ordered. Quicksilver obliged, navigating there, and a few moments later they were rewarded with a realtime panoramic showing the entire northern coast of Braganza, with tiny 3D waves. Quicksilver zoomed in on the western border, near the mountains separating

Braganza from Vanram. Through the window adjacent to the wallscreen Sonny could see the same mountains, looming ahead and blocking out the stars.

The screen showed an undersea wall, and for a moment Sonny thought he was looking at another submerged city. It scooped toward the mountains, extending a few kilometers out to sea. An undersea fence, protecting the coast. "Is that the coral Nepenthe doesn't like?"

"Yes." Kai yawned, climbing down from his seat and boosting Blocker into it. "I'm not sure if it keeps the submarines out, but I do know that you folks broadcast everything underwater in realtime, for cargo ships. Like that one."

He pointed on his way toward the captain's cabin. A big slow composite ship was trundling along the coast toward Braganza. Not a cruise ship like the *Principesse Larisse*, a plain old workaday freighter. He watched the doctor locate it on the screen, and then he watched the *Reckless* slide over the undersea wall, putting them officially in Braganza waters. "I've got this," Quicksilver said. "I'll take over the nav for the easy part. You get some sleep."

Sonny didn't argue. He slid down the stairs and fell into his bunk.

●

He awoke to the smell of food prepared by someone who cared what it tasted like. His belly growled, urging him out of bed. His stiff muscles protested as he limped to the head to pee. The boat was hardly moving, and the sail was down, and he sleepily wondered whether that meant trouble.

Hina was already gulping down dinner by the time he hauled himself to the salon, and he blinked to find a formal table had been set. Not only that, but everyone had cleaned themselves up. Risha and Blocker were wearing colorful dresses. Both Rufe and Quicksilver had changed into their khakis and trimmed their beards, and Kai was in a bottle green jacket, a ruffled silk shirt and baggy, paisley-print pants.

When Sonny collapsed into his seat they began to applaud. Kai started it, and Risha quickly joined in. They clapped for him for a good long time as his face split open in a dazed smile.

Sonny couldn't seem to find any words so instead he pressed his fist to his heart. Kai got it first; it was a Carq gesture after all. He returned it, solemnly, and the others figured it out.

"Thank you for ensuring that we survived the most difficult part of the journey," Kai said, loud and clear. "My uncle's estimation of your navigational skills was accurate, and I commend you."

"We're about an hour out of Royal Beach," Rufe announced after another brief round of applause, this time with cheering. "We can head in at any time, but Risha thought you might want to be well fed and camera ready."

He did, and he thanked her as he wolfed down a magnificent meal they'd prepared from the last of the Carquinez perishables that probably wouldn't clear the agricultural inspection. The screen showed colorful fish swimming beneath them.

After he was fed, and showered, and dressed in a pair of khaki shorts donated by Quicksilver, and a shirt decorated with elephants raising tropical drinks in their trunks donated by Rufe, they raised the colorful spinnaker sail and tacked south.

Soon Sonny could see the coastline grinning at him. The surrounding waters were full of other boats, and swimmers, and surfers, and people floating around on colorful inflatables, and an aqua stage where a band was playing a pop song, and a float-up snowcone bar complete with pink neon flamingoes.

Everything looked so much smaller.

The big clocktower on the tallest of the waterslides informed him it was July twenty-first, , and that it was eleven forty three in the morning. A smiling girl in a dinghy motored out to intercept them, and they dropped the sail and let her tow them into a slip.

More tears escaped Sonny's eyes as his battered flipflops shuffled down the pier. The walkway funneled them toward the customs office, which had a giant version of the city seal flapping on a flag outside. A gold crown, with "Royal Beach, Democratic Monarchy of Braganza" floating on a banner beneath it and stylized gold lions on either side of it.

Sonny felt a warm wave of patriotism swell up in his chest. He was home, and safe. The grownups would take care of everything, and his government would set everything right.

The End

About the Author

Charon Dunn wasted several decades of her life trying to think of great novels to write before finally settling down to write this one. She has a day job doing law stuff, she prefers Star Wars to Star Trek, and she lives in San Francisco with an unusually large cat. Keep track of her (and read free short stories) at CharonDunnTheBlog@Blogspot.com.

About the Cover

Cover by Brian Allen, FlylandDesigns.com.